ROTTEN BOROUGH

ROTTEN BOROUGH

Oliver Anderson

FOURTH ESTATE · LONDON

First published in Great Britain in 1937
First paperback edition published in Great Britain in 1989 by
Fourth Estate Ltd
Classic House
113 Westbourne Grove
London W2 4UP

Copyright © 1989 by Oliver Anderson

British Library Cataloguing in Publication Data

Anderson, Oliver, *1912*–
  Rotten borough
  I. Title
  823′.912[F]
  ISBN 0-947795-83-9

Printed and bound in Great Britain by
Richard Clay Ltd, Bungay, Suffolk

FOR THE
INCOMPARABLE DAVID
DEEP DRINKER, DEEP THINKER
PRODIGIOUS LOVER, NOTORIOUS
CONFOUNDER OF THE BURGESS

Contents

" The life of a wild animal has a certain dignity and beauty; it is only the life of a domesticated animal that can be called degraded. The burgess is the perfectly domesticated human animal."

ALDOUS HUXLEY in *Those Barren Leaves*.

1

Mr. Twyte writes a note

MR. CUTHBERT TWYTE, EDITOR of the *Chronicle and Gazetteer*, sat in his office penning his weekly column of chatty little notes under the title " Spotlights From Many Angles ; Quips, Cranks and Quiddities by An Idle Jester."

Although, as he often explained, somewhat unnecessarily be it admitted, his education had never carried him beyond the board-school, Mr. Twyte piqued himself, nevertheless, on his literary taste. Undoubtedly, he flattered himself, he had the knack of the rotund phrase, of the Parnassian period. And if, perhaps, the *mot* was not always precisely *juste*, if the construction at times tottered a little, if the meaning was not always entirely pellucid, he was supported by the knowledge that not even the fires of genius can burn without at least a little smoke.

In spite, furthermore, of the fact that his immediate post-school years had been passed as a barber's lather-boy, Mr. Twyte prided himself that he knew something of news value, and particularly of the beneficial effect upon circulation of a weekly column of nice chatty little notes. This column was, indeed, Mr. Cuthbert Twyte's obsession. Topical he felt it to be, witty and scintillating, light and delicate in touch and relieved occasionally by a more sombre and scholarly note. Caviare, perhaps, to the general but of undoubted appeal to the more educated and socially inclined in the borough. He would have been deeply cut had he known that the " Idle Jester " was more popularly known as the idle something else.

This week Mr. Twyte was letting himself go, for of all the chatty little notes he had written for a very long time this was, he felt beyond doubt, the chattiest.

" I learn," wrote Mr. Twyte, " on the most reliable authority, that this ancient borough of ours is shortly to be honoured by the company of no less a personage than Mr. Julian Ansell, the clever young playwright, whose first work ' Worm I'The Root,' is having such a successful run in the West End in Town. Mr. Ansell is, I understand, on the verge of a nervous breakdown occasioned by the tremendous pressure of his innumerable social engagements, and has been ordered by his medical advisers to take a complete rest in the country in order that he may, so to speak, nip the worm of ill-health in the root. It is interesting to note that he will be staying with his uncle, Mr. Ulric Phont, who, as my readers will doubtless be aware, has comparatively recently taken up residence at the Priory House where he so lavishly entertains. I am sure that all my readers will join with me in welcoming Mr. Ansell to the town and in wishing him a speedy return to health. And, perhaps, who knows, under the influence of his witty tongue, the dinner-tables of local society leaders may out-sparkle even those of the society queens of Mayfair."

Mr. Twyte sat back with a satisfied air. This, he felt, was beyond doubt in his best style. He liked particularly the neat metaphorical reference to the worm of ill-health. And then the nicely sophisticated use of the word "Town" instead of London. A well-bred touch, that. He dwelt with pleasure on the whimsical, the delicately flattering note about the Mayfair dinner-tables, conveying, as it did, the subtle inference that he, personally, was only all too much at home amongst the epigrams and tail-coats. True, he had a momentary qualm about the sense, but to anyone of taste and education his drift, he felt, would immediately be obvious.

That night the two machines at the offices of the *Chronicle and Gazetteer* whirled frantically, if a little uncertainly, to bear like a thunder-bolt the news of the arrival of Mr. Julian Ansell to the all unconscious burgesses.

2

Of Life and Love

Before going into the dining-room Julian paused in the hall and considered his reflected image in the tall gilt-framed mirror. He pondered the sleek black hair brushed back thickly over the ears, the undoubtedly languorous eye, the aristocratically aquiline, if slightly too long nose, the thin line of black moustache. He dwelt upon the yellow shantung tie (a little Bloomsbury, perhaps), the severely cut coat, the flowing trousers. "Dark and dashing" was, he felt, a description not unjustified, and a pleasing mixture withal of the arty and the swash-buckling. A little, even, in a mild way, Edenish.

But lord, this prinking and preening ; how damnably it smacked of the Zoo. How too Whip-snadian. How much, when done for the benefit of the female (as it usually was), how much the ridiculous peacock fanning before the slightly supercilious yet none-the-less expectant peahen.

In the white and gold dining-room he was greeted by a small bird-like man of middle-age, Mr. Ulric Phont, that dark and elegant bachelor, that arbiter of the elegances, that guide and confidant of all young men with the slightest pretensions to being about town.

With the coffee Mr. Phont permitted his conver-sation to descend from those philosophic and artistic peaks upon which it had been so dazzlingly lodged throughout the meal. He took a more personal note.

"And so, my dear Julian, you have come to rusticate, to cast your lot amongst the slab-sided sows and the heifers on the hoof. Charming, utterly charming." Joining the tips of his long white fingers in a slightly sacerdotal attitude, Mr. Phont closed his eyes and rapturously inhaled the fumes of the Mocha.

"I cannot tell you," he proceeded, "how delighted I am to have you with me. To be able to converse once more with a really civilised type is most agreeable. And I am glad to note that for a young man on the verge of a nervous breakdown you are looking quite remarkably fit." Mr. Phont delicately knocked the ash off his scented cigarette and regarded Julian with a perky bird-like glance across the table. "Quite astonishingly fit," he repeated.

"I may as well confess at once that I am," said Julian. "As a matter of fact I have never felt better in my life. To tell you the truth, this nervous breakdown business is merely a useful excuse, an advertising stunt for press purposes, if you like. My publicity man insisted that if I did run away I must at least have a reasonable pretext and, if possible, a profitable one."

"Dear me," said Mr. Phont, delicately lifting an eyebrow, "you have run away? And from what, may I ask, if that isn't too personal a question?"

"To put it dramatically, from success. I was completely bored and utterly exasperated. In fact I got to the point where I began being downright rude to people, and to people that mattered as well.

So I thought it best to retreat strategically before I imperilled my position."

"Strange," mused Mr. Phont. "I must confess I cannot understand your attitude. Here you are only a year down from Merton, with an extremely witty play to your credit, with the world, if I may be permitted a vulgarism, at your feet, and yet you are virtually going into retirement. Good gracious me, you have scarcely given yourself time to sow your oats, never mind reap them and hold the harvest festival."

"I know," said Julian, "but you have no idea how appallingly boring, how excruciatingly tedious it all becomes. The ceaseless cocktail parties, the eternal literary luncheons, the never-ending classy dinner-parties where one is expected to pay for one's entertainment by being smart and witty. And then the people one has to mix with ; the lionising hostesses, the people who write and the people who paint and the people who act, and worst of all, the people who write about the writers and painters and actors. I tell you I have been astounded by the number of people who seem to exist, and exist pretty comfortably, too, by messing about in one way or another with the arts. Half the population of London seems to be connected with the stage or the cinema or literature or painting or music or the ballet. And then the appalling self-satisfaction of these people, their over-whelming complacency with their futile little talents, the petty jealousies, the insidious back-bitings, the nicely calculated log-rollings, and above all the abominable arty atmosphere of it all. Why it's nothing short of demoralising."

"Dear me," said Mr. Phont, "you seem to feel pretty deeply over these matters. Quite fervent in fact ; oratorical even ; but tell me, surely your success must pique you just a little, at any rate? Surely you are not totally without a certain inward glow, a certain warmth about the vitals at the acclamations of the mob?"

"I do, of course, get a certain kick out of it," said Julian. "I shouldn't be human if I didn't. But I have enough sense to realise that it all means precisely nothing at all. I don't flatter myself that my talent is anything more than a superficial flashiness. I am perfectly aware that I shall sink back into my native obscurity as soon as my little vogue is played out, as soon as some other smart young man comes along to flash a little more vulgarly and brightly than I."

"Good gracious me," said Mr. Phont, "I must confess you make me feel terribly jejeune, alarmingly credulous and unsophisticated. In the nineties we fancied we were pretty well disillusioned, pretty completely blasé, pretty adequately fin-de-siècle, but you, my dear Julian, seem to begin where we left off."

"It is merely," said Julian, "that I see through things a bit, I suppose. After all, if you dig down a little, if you get under the surface, however slightly, these things become overwhelmingly apparent. The general fatuity of everything fairly stares at one. I fail to see how, if one thinks seriously occasionally, one can arrive at any other attitude."

"That," said Mr. Phont, sitting up suddenly and wagging a long white forefinger at Julian, "is precisely the trouble with you modern young men.

You think too much, you are too earnest. You probe, you are always digging below the surface. You are too convoluted. In a word, you lack the light touch. Ah," breathed Mr. Phont, tracing intricate arabesques with his cigarette smoke, " the light touch. That is the solution to the whole problem of life. If you would live elegantly, if you would live comfortably, cultivate the light touch. Be content in everything to play the dilettante. Skim the surface, glide lightly and gracefully over the veneer. The young man to-day lacks the flair for living. Life is no longer for him a gracious art. It is a strenuous and often sordid exercise. I must say I strongly deprecate the state of affairs. In my day a young man in your happy position would have, in the vernacular, mucked in. He would have skipped about gaily here, there and everywhere, showing the flag and raising the wind in no uncertain manner. He would have been seen about with all the best people, would have eaten in all the smartest places, drunk of all the best cellars, and would have slept, if I may say so, in all the most exclusive beds. And," breathed Mr. Phont rapturously, " he would have loved. How he would have loved ! Copiously, profoundly, perversely, and, above all, romantically. He would have loved in the grand, the Eighteenth Century manner, in the authentic Crébillon style."

" Oh, I've tried love," said Julian. " In that particular at any rate I come up to your requirements."

" Ah," said Mr. Phont with quickening interest, " you have cultivated the Cytherean, you have been amorously active ? "

" I can never remember having been out of love since I was twelve. It began with a stock-breeder's daughter, significant, perhaps, and ended just before I came away with Jenny Flower. In fact she was one of the principal reasons for my coming down here."

" Good gracious me," said Mr. Phont, " I cannot compliment you on your originality. Why the number of young men whose . . . how shall I put it? . . . whose views have been broadened by Jenny Flower is something at which the imagination fairly boggles. Fairly boggles, I repeat."

" And how much did your amorous education cost you? if I may ask," continued Mr. Phont, after a slight pause. " From what I remember of her methods, Jenny was thorough but expensive."

" I may as well confess," said Julian, " that she made a complete fool of me. It cost me a thousand pounds to get some letters back. You see, I wasn't aware of the presence of a husband."

" Good heavens," cried Mr. Phont, " my dear boy, accept my profound sympathies. A thousand pounds. But what were you doing to write to her at all? Surely you know by now that discretion is the better part of correspondence."

" Well, you see, I happened to be very much in love with her. I still am, for that matter," said Julian, gloomily stabbing at his sugar.

" But a thousand pounds," mused Mr. Phont. " Too much in my opinion, far too much. I think if I had been in your position I should have kept the cash and told her to do her worst. After all, she couldn't have done any real harm. In fact, if she had created trouble it would probably have been a splendid thing for you. Adultery the best advertisement ; scandal fills the stalls and so on."

" I could never have faced the scandal," said Julian. " Too horribly sordid. Life is vulgar enough without that sort of thing."

" I can see," said Mr. Phont, " that in love, as in everything else, you lack the light touch. You are too thorough. Personally I am all for the amorous pleasantries, but I have always taken care to shun the grande passion. ' Love the best parlour game ' has always been my motto, and I have never had cause to regret it."

" Yes, I suppose you're right," said Julian. " It's all very well if you can keep it casual, if you can keep it on the level of a parlour game, but I am afraid I can't. Love, for me, all too inevitably takes on the nature of an art, accompanied by all the pangs and rigours of an art conscientiously pursued. I cannot dabble. I have to work an affair out in its every detail, and carry it through to its logical, or usually illogical, conclusion. However, I do congratulate myself that my affairs, with few exceptions, have been gracefully begun, elaborately developed, and gracefully ended."

" And you have broken many hearts ? " enquired Mr. Phont. " You have made many victims ? "

" I," said Julian, " am all too inevitably the victim."

" And I am not surprised," said Mr. Phont with energy. " I am all for the graceful approach and the elaborate manner in their place, but their place, I fear, is not love. No wonder you make a mess of things. Gracefulness and elaboration may be all

right up to a point, up to the point I might almost say.
But sooner or later there arrives a stage when the
woman wants the brocade removed and the brass
tacks exposed. Never forget, a woman of spirit needs
treating like an intelligent animal, not like a Greek
vase. She doesn't want to sit round indefinitely
playing a game of gentlemanly amorous chess."

"And that is where I fail," said Julian gloomily.
"I never could and never shall be able to face the
brass tack."

"Or, perhaps, more accurately, the brass bedstead,"
suggested Mr. Phont. "But to proceed. The
trouble with the grande passion, with the too thorough
love affair is, as you have doubtless already discovered,
that it always goes on too long. It becomes a tragedy
in six acts, than which there is nothing more terrible,
for the last scene is always one of pure bathos. No,
the older I grow the more I am convinced that the
whole secret of successful love making consists in
knowing when to stop. For, let's face it, love affairs
are like Mr. Coward's plays, amusing up to the end
of the second act, but after that liable of surfeit. And
now, let us take a turn in the garden."

"And how do you like living in retirement," asked
Julian as they examined the July roses. "A little
dull I should imagine. I should hardly have thought
that the country was quite in your line."

"Ah, the country," mused Mr. Phont. "I find it
charming but strenuous. Unleashed passions and
clotted beavers, prodigious copulations and inadequate
closets. Novel but unnerving."

"Many people spoke to me about you in town,"
said Julian. "You are not forgotten I can assure

you. Your sudden disappearance caused quite a
stir."

"That, at any rate, is gratifying," said Mr. Phont,
"but I must say, not undeserved. Without conceit
I say there has only been one Ulric Phont and there
will never be another. I made all life my art, and in
that art I was undeniably a supreme virtuoso. But
now all that I stand for is, alas, passing, if not already
gone. For these days elegance, wit, fastidiousness and
all the other attributes of a man of taste and cultivation
have no significance. We live in an age remarkable
for its grimness, its vulgarity, its earnestness, and above
all, for its lack of wit and intelligence. In such a world
I have no place ; therefore I have chosen to retire
in good order and live out my days in my own private
haven."

"But it was all very sudden."

"Ah, the immediate cause," said Mr. Phont, "was
a matter of waist-line."

"Of the waist-line," inquired Julian.

"Yes. Many years ago I made a vow that the
day I found my trousers would stay up without the
support of braces I would retire. That day occurred
precisely one year ago. It is a remarkable fact, when
one comes to ponder upon it, that the whole of a man's
life can be altered by the question of to brace or not to
brace. It is a point full of interesting moral implications. But there it is. The step is taken. There
is no retreat. Such vulgar measures as the rubber
belt and dieting are not for the man of taste. I
acknowledge nature," concluded Mr. Phont magnificently.

"And you don't find it dull ? " inquired Julian.

" Well, I must confess," said Mr. Phont, " that at times I do find things a little tedious. I do occasionally regret the high old times. Those jauntings in perambulators, those pneumatic drillings in Piccadilly, those junketings on kippers and that igniting of the bishop's long white beard. A notable feat that, and one that stirred the episcopal côteries from end to end. And then, of course, it would be idle to deny that I miss the company of my intellectual peers, and the classy chats on art and the cosmos with which we used to murder the time. But there are undoubted compensations for the man of a speculative turn of mind.

" Down here one encounters incredible and unsuspected types that amply repay investigation. We have, for instance, the local aristocracy, a very interesting and primitive type. Entirely lacking in intelligence, they are gifted, nevertheless, with a certain native cunning for killing off in various ways the birds and beasts of the field and for messing about with one another's wives. An interesting type, I repeat, a fascinating survival from another age, and one that I am thankful of having had the opportunity of studying before its rapidly approaching extinction.

" The borough professional classes have also the fascination of horror. Dear me, I must confess I have had some happy moments watching them in their native haunts, aping the aristocracy, assiduously dining late, if only off a kipper, and twisting one another like corkscrews behind the scenes. And, my dear Julian, the culture ! Really you have no idea. The best subscription at the local library, arty photography on the summer holiday, assiduous attendance at 'good' films, and the dullest of dull conversation. You really must meet these people. You will laugh heartily.

"Further, of course, we have the bourgeoisie, the successful shopkeepers, the brewers, the auctioneers and what not. At these, I own, I cannot laugh. Base money-grubbing, founded on every variety of treachery and double-dealing does not amuse, nor does a social scale founded upon the number of motor-cars one owns. A very low job of work, I assure you, the tradespeople and their confederates, and one I should very much like to rouse."

"But have you no congenial companions at all," asked Julian. "You must feel terribly isolated."

"I have two excellent friends," said Mr. Phont, "the vicar, the Rev. Jasper Skillington, an incredible priest, and Mrs. Meredith. You will like them immensely, particularly Mrs. Meredith. A very lovely lady, no better, I am thankful to say, than she ought to be, and equipped with a most convenient husband who spends most of his days nipping about Europe indulging in big-business and wagging a cavalry moustache at the natives. Ah, Mrs. Meredith," breathed Mr. Phont. "She is the very epitome of what my old friend, Mr. George Moore, so exquisitely termed 'the woman of thirty'. Fantastic febrile, and delicately frenzied. The realisation of the amorous dreams of all artistic young men."

"And then, of course," resumed Mr. Phont, "last but not least, there is my protégé, young Gilbert Bellairs. A most remarkable young man. I congratulate myself on having discovered him, though perhaps it

might be more true to say that he forced himself upon
my attention. To be quite accurate I found him one
morning in the summer-house sleeping off a most
passionate drunk."

"Your protégé?" asked Julian. "What does he
do?"

Mr. Phont lifted a rose delicately to his nostrils
and smirked complacently : "He is going to edit my
newspaper."

Julian gasped. "Your newspaper? Don't tell me
that you of all people are going to start a newspaper?"

"Indeed I am," replied Mr. Phont, a little testily,
"and why not? Really, my dear Julian. There's
no need to behave as if I were a half-wit. Why
shouldn't I start a newspaper?"

"If it comes to that, why should you?" answered
Julian. "Of course if you want to lose a lot of
money in the shortest possible time by all means
start a newspaper. Personally I could suggest no
better way of running through one's patrimony."

Mr. Phont waved Julian's objections away with a
pontifical gesture : "The trouble with you is, Julian,
you are too mundane, too much of this world. It is
plain to me, painfully apparent I may say, that you
tend to view everything from the crass modern angle
of profit and loss. Unlike the hymn-writer, you count
the cost. You fail to realise that a single splendid
gesture, even if it involves one in the loss of one's
whole fortune, is worth a thousand fiddling acts of
successful money-grubbing."

"Wait until you've lost your whole fortune in a
single splendid gesture," answered Julian lugubriously,
"and then you may think differently."

Mr. Phont ignored the remark and proceeded. "My reasons for founding a newspaper are threefold. In the first place I feel it a moral obligation upon me to rouse this Rotten Borough. Although I have only dwelt within its boundaries for a comparatively short time I have come to recognize a state of affairs that throws me into a state of exasperation, anger, and even dudgeon. Upon every side I see graft, complacency, hypocrisy and petty provincialism. I see the poor left to wallow in their poverty. I see the *oourgeoisie* blossoming in vulgarity. I see the professional classes stewing in snobbery and the aristocracy static in stupidity."

Mr. Phont paused for breath and then proceeded :

"In view of all this I have felt it morally incumbent upon me to make some gesture on behalf of the decencies. I am resolved through the medium of my newspaper to shake this Rotten Borough to the core. I am resolved to purge it of civic evils, root out graft and double-dealing and above all, to shake it out of its abominable middle-class complacency."

"Just sentiments," said Julian, catching some of Mr. Phont's moral fervour. "And your other reasons ?"

"They, I fear, are less ethical, but equally cogent," said Mr. Phont. "Firstly I need something to occupy my time, and secondly I must confess I have always had a sneaking desire to enter the sphere of action. Living, as I always have done, the cloistered and elegant life of the dilettante, untouched by the world, I have, nevertheless, at times had an irresistible urge to try my hand in the hurly-burly of life, in the realms of sordid gain. I have long entertained the ambition to become a press baron. And now the moment is at hand. Though I may not be destined to control the affairs of a nation, I have a very definite notion that I am going to play havoc with the affairs of this contemptible borough."

" And when do you launch this organ of salvation ? " enquired Julian. " Tell me more about it. More facts and fewer figures if I may say so."

Mr. Phont rubbed his hands complacently. " The exact date of publication is not yet decided upon, but things are in train, well in train. They march. You arrive, my dear Julian, at a most propitious moment. You will be in the privileged position of being in at the start. Bellairs is dining with us to-night at Mrs. Meredith's to discuss the final points of policy, and to him I will leave the pleasant task of describing our project in detail. Meanwhile, we will take a stroll round the borough."

3

Mr. Phont's Conducted Tour

IT WAS MARKET DAY IN the Rotten Borough, and Mr. Phont and Julian directed their steps towards the Market Place. Standing on the pavement outside Woolworths they surveyed the throng. It was an exceedingly hot day.

Dejected women, sweating in thick woollen garments and sticking out in the most improbable places, dragged howling and reluctant children from stall to stall. Vacant looking youths, guffawing in mobs, shouldered about with the straddling, lurching step of the farm labourer. Upon their heads they wore very flat cloth caps, and the remainder of their wardrobe consisted of hairy, light grey flannel trousers, even hairier sports jackets, and excessively pointed brown shoes, with crocodile insertions in the uppers. They were followed at a discreet, yet provocative distance, by groups of bulbous young country girls whose complexions, rendered more than usually vermilion by the excessive heat, glowed with a purplish tinge through the liberally applied white powder.

They wore loudly-coloured berets at various angles and were given to sleeveless blouses of white, pale blue or pale pink artificial silk. Their powerful looking arms were done to the consistency of a half-cooked beef-steak by the July sun. Periodically, when one of the yobs in front threw back some casual pleasantry, the girls would glance at one another and promptly collapse into scarcely suppressed laughter interspersed with provocative shrieks.

"What I believe are described by the whimsical country novelists as pictures of rude health," said Mr. Phont.

"More like *natures-mortes*," said Julian grimly.

On every hand trade was going forward. Two rival fruit vendors with a remarkable gift for oratory extolled the virtues of their goods and made hay of one another for the benefit of a crowd of listless and sceptical listeners.

The rivalry was intense, and whilst one excelled the other in general vituperation and the liberality with which he gave away samples and dissected specimens for inspection, his rival scored by reason of the intimacy and confidentiality of his style which had an irresistible medical turn : "This is fruit what I'm offering you. You don't want to be running up and down stairs all night with the bellyache. I don't sell rubbish like 'im next door. What I sells is equal to what you can get at the best fruit stores in the country. And 'ow, you asks, can we do it at the price. And rightly you asks, and I replies because we buys in the mass. 'Undreds, no, I'm telling you a lie, thousands of cases we buys at a time. Now this is fruit."

"I pin my faith to the confidential fellow every time," said Mr. Phont. "It's no use bullying your customer to-day. More subtle methods are the vogue, you've got to be persuasive, insinuating, frank, intimate. Above all you've got to get at the snobbism of the masses. Sell them the worst at a stiff price and if you know your job they'll go away convinced they've got the best at a bargain. And of course the medical note ; that's essential. In these disease-conscious days when the medical dictionary has replaced the Bible in every home, one simply must have the medical touch. You can sell a man a wart-hog or a pink elephant to-day if only you muscle in on the germs, nerves and ganglia. For that reason I prophesy that our friend here, who has touched so poignantly on the laxative qualities of inferior fruit, will sell two crates to his opponent's one."

Further on a cross-eyed little man with an incipient beard was trying to dispose of some stringy boiling fowls, to shrewd bourgeois housewives, on the ground that they were asparagus chickens.

" He'll never do it," said Mr. Phont, " but he would if he told them that Lady Wycherley had bought half-a-dozen or that they had come out of disinfected eggs."

Next door was the shrine of Apollo where a raucous gramophone dispensed the latest emetic caterwaulings from across the Atlantic. There was much about love, the moon, the month of June, and other mass aphrodisiacs.

Close by, an amateur apothecary attired, somewhat incongruously, in a cowboy hat, did a roaring trade in potions and powders calculated to correct everything from gall-stones and cirrhosis of the liver to psittacosis.

" I wonder if he has anything for spots before the eyes," hazarded Mr. Phont. " I had a distinct spot before the eye yesterday."

" . . . an infallible remedy for stone, gravel,

internal congestion and spots before the eyes . . ."
roared the man of medicine.

" I shall certainly buy some of that yellow powder,"
said Mr. Phont.   " If it doesn't remove the spot from
my eye I'll give it to my housekeeper.   She has ten
children all with septic tonsils."

" You have only to look at a crowd such as this,"
said Mr. Phont, moving on, " to realise the deplorable
fact that fully ninety per cent. of our rural population
is mentally deficient."

" And appallingly niffy," said Julian, decisively,
lighting a scented cigarette.

" Niffy, yes," agreed Mr. Phont.   " But it is a good
thing occasionally to mingle with the *hoi polloi*.   It
hardens the fibres of the soul."

They stepped into the throng and began a tour of
the stalls.   Presently they arrived at a stall devoted
entirely to the sale of feminine underwear and
administered by a rather stale looking young Jew in an
oily, grey flannel suit.

Mr. Phont called a halt and, entirely regardless of
the curious glances of the passers-by, began with
florid gestures to philosophise :

" Alas, my dear Julian, how typical of the modern
age.   To-day there are no mysteries left ; not even
that most intriguing mystery of all, the underclothing
of the female.   I don't agree with it.   It spells the
death of romance and conversation.   What are we to
talk about in our clubs nowadays ?   In my young days
we murdered many a tedious hour by reflecting and
conjecturing upon what lay beneath those voluminous
Edwardian skirts.   But now the subject is denied us.
We are altogether far too much at home in Zion.   There

is no fascination where there is no mystery. And besides, how can one carry on a dignified conversation in such terms as 'briefies', 'panties', 'step-ins', and 'slip-ons'?"

"Yes," agreed Julian earnestly, " and what staggers me is the amazing scientific approach to it all. Female underclothing to-day lies not so much in the province of the costumier as in the realm of the structural engineer. Think of those bewitching illustrations in the daily press showing saucy and nubile young women in advanced acrobatic poses. The letterpress reads like a treatise on dynamics. Lateral and perpendicular stresses and strains, cross pressures and diagonal torsions, not to mention the latest inventions for imparting angled uplift to the feminine bosom."

"True," said Mr. Phont. " Divided we stand, united we fall, as I once saw it so wittily stated. Of course it must be immensely amusing for the women. For us men dressing is much what it always was. Our clothes are laid out for us and we get into them. At best we never have to do more than adjust the braces a fraction or manipulate a white tie. But consider the women. For them the art of dressing, as you so justly infer, partakes of the nature of an involved experiment with blocks and pullies."

Mr. Phont meditated for a moment and then resumed : " However, I must say modern under- clothing has advanced in the matter of colour. In my young days women were restricted, alas how tediously, to a shockingly small range of pastel shades ; pale blues, greens and pinks with an occasional demi- mondaine excursion into black. But now, I observe, the strong primary colours are pressed into service. Most pleasantly stimulating I call it."

Mr. Phont gestured towards one end of the stall. " Now, for instance, I think that pair in cobalt blue is most uncommonly fetching."

" Possibly," agreed Julian, " but damnably ticklish, I feel."

Followed by a gaping group of the populace, Mr. Phont led the way to another stall. Around it there brooded a singularly furtive atmosphere.

Passers-by either looked the other way with elevated noses, or directed smirking side-glances at the goods exposed for sale.   Customers avoided looking at one another, assumed curious crouching attitudes, and hastily handed their purchases to the blasé and myopic proprietor who deftly shrouded the goods in brown paper.

Mr. Phont, however, was not so bashful, and taking Julian by the arm, he led him to the front of the stall :

" Dear me, we mustn't forget the Halls of Parnassus. Literature for every taste. Everything from the *Apocrypha* to *La Vie Parisienne*."

Julian observed that the stall was devoted to the sale of second-hand literature.   On every hand were piles of American film magazines depicting on the covers bouncing blondes in alluring attitudes. Cheek by jowl with a battered copy of the Nichomachean Ethics might be seen a publication garnished with a stupendously proportioned female nude sheepishly languishing over a lily pond.   *The Female Form Divine* ran the title.   ' Glorious Studies of Radiant Womanhood.   Of great interest to artists and others.'

Mr. Phont picked up the magazine and flipped over the pages. Julian, looking over his companion's shoulders, caught tantalising glimpses of mounds of rosy flesh ; ponderous bosoms, billowy buttocks, thewy thighs, all giving the impression of nothing so much as a pork butcher's shop.

" It is strange," mused Mr. Phont, " the fascination of pornography for the adult mind. Even quite well-educated and reasonable men seem to derive the greatest pleasure imaginable from looking at an inadequate pictorial representation of vices with which they are perfectly familiar in actual fact. Personally, I must confess that the older I grow the more inexpressibly tedious do I find vice, whether it be in fact or fancy."

Julian was looking through a pile of cheap novels in gaudily coloured wrappers.

" Dope for the masses," he remarked bitterly. " That's what ninety-nine per cent. of literature is to-day. Nothing but mental dope. They talk of the dangers of the cocaine habit, but it's nothing like the danger of the lending-library habit. We can't, we won't face life to-day. We escape deliberately and cravenly to a fictionised arcanum. The steps to Hell are paved with best sellers."

Mr. Phont was deeply immersed in *Her First Night*.

" Don't interrupt me, I beg of you, Julian. I've just got to where the husband, passionately drunk on sweet champagne, is hounding his terrified and virginal bride to the nuptial chamber."

" A shameful exhibition of unconscionable lewdity," boomed a portentous voice behind them.

Mr. Phont and Julian swung round to find them-

selves confronted by the Rev. Bath-Oliver, President
of the borough Nonconformist Council.

He was a short, rotund man with a pugnacious
expression, imperfectly shaven, and besmirched as
to the waistcoat with egg and snuff.

Mr. Phont fixed him with a stern eye : " I am
surprised, Bath-Oliver, that you Nonconformists don't
do something about this stall.   I regard it as a serious
menace to the morals of the youth of the town."

" We have done all we can," replied the Rev.
Bath-Oliver, " but what are we against the Watch
Committee ?   I have made representation upon
representation about it, but simply because I'm not
a member of the Rotary Club, the Chief Constable
and the Chairman of the Watch Committee refuse to
lift a finger."

The Rev. Bath-Oliver plunged his hand into his
pocket and offered Mr. Phont a grimy handbill :

" Of course, Mr. Phont, you'll be coming to the
Kiddy Koons Koncert on Friday night in the Yeoman's
Hall.   We're making a great effort on behalf of the
Fenton Street Chapel recreational club.   A real lively
do, I can assure you.   The Tiny Tots Old Testament
Tableaux are little gems.   And don't forget there's
a free ham and tongue supper afterwards for all
those who buy five shilling tickets."

Mr. Phont studied the bill.   " I see that you,
Bath-Oliver, are down to recite the ' Schooner
Hesperus '.   In that event I shall most certainly
attend.   I am a profound student of the elocutory art."

" Capital, capital," said the Rev. Bath-Oliver.
" And now I must be off to labour in the vineyard of
the Lord.   I'm running a new feature every Saturday

afternoon ; you may have heard of it, ' Cheery Chats
for Weary Wives '. They tell me they derive great
benefit and solace from my ministrations."

" An earnest man," said Mr. Phont when the Rev.
Bath-Oliver had padded off, " but it's a pity he spits
so much when he talks. Quite drenching."

Mr. Phont and Julian left the Market Place, and
made their way to the High Street. Here a very
different prospect was disclosed. A continuous stream
of traffic pounded along the road, only to pull up
with a prodigious squeaking of brakes, in an inextric-
able and blaspheming mass at the traffic lights outside
the Granby Hotel, where the main road narrowed
into a bottleneck. The vituperations of irascible
drivers mingled with the hoarse remonstrances of a
venerable looking constable with a falsetto voice,
who was trying to sort out the muddle.

Mr. Phont contemplated the mêlée with grim
satisfaction and then led on, but not before he had
addressed a few words of encouragement to the
bewildered policeman.

As they proceeded along the High Street Julian
noticed the amazing architectural hotch-potch resulting
from the juxtaposition of the old shops with the branches
of the modern chain stores. Portland stone, neon
lights and chromium plating reared themselves cheek
by jowl with timbered fronts and red tile roofs.

The pavements were crowded with the young men
and women of the town, harassed young mothers
uncertainly navigating perambulators, and groups of
farmers glowing with their luncheon beer and whisky.

Two young men, Julian noticed, affected coats

with exaggeratedly padded shoulders, flowing, pale grey flannel trousers and long, pointed, black patent-leather shoes. The young women wore trim little hats at improbable angles, rather too red lipstick and stylish silk stockings.

" It is a regrettable fact," announced Mr. Phont, " that to be distinguished in one's dress to-day, one must attire oneself like a tramp. It's all due to these American films supported by the mass-production clothing firms. Between them, they turn out a race of gigolos and cocottes. But still there is something to be said for it all. We shall never have a revolution so long as we enable the masses to dress themselves up as passable imitations of the idle rich. However, I often wonder where these young women get the money for their silk stockings. Shameful and debilitating practices I shouldn't wonder."

They arrived outside a dilapidated building bearing the legend in very much faded gold lettering : *Chronicle and Gazetteer.* In the window were some tired looking photographs.

" Our rivals, God damn them," said Mr. Phont pleasantly. " May their bones rot in Hell."

As they passed on, the plethoric countenance of Mr. Cuthbert Twyte eyed them suspiciously from an upper window inscribed " Editorial."

At this point Julian perceived a young man approaching them. He was a singularly pretty young man with pallid blue eyes, a full, babyish mouth, horn-rimmed spectacles, and yellow, wavy hair worn in the flowing style and thick over the ears. He had a distinctly benign expression and seemed to be bestowing a slightly supercilious, yet none the less genial, benediction upon the world at large. He was dressed in a suit of very good tweeds of a delicate greeny-blue shade. The most notable thing about him, however, was his walk. He progressed with small mincing steps, his feet crossing over one another's tracks as if he were negotiating a perpetual tight-rope.

"Sink me," said Mr. Phont genially, "if it isn't Esmond Duncan. A most charming youth ; modern languages master at the boys' school. We'll ask him to drink with us."

Esmond raised a languid hand and greeted them : "Impossible day, revolting weather, unspeakable people," he remarked. His voice was slightly adenoidal and maintained itself on a bored monotone.

"My sweet boy," remonstrated Mr. Phont, "really you are too fin-de-siècle for words. Won't you come and quaff with us ? "

"Too charming of you, but I suggest you come along to my rooms. I've just got in some divine absinthe, most exquisitely depraved. I made the captain of the eleven drunk on it last night and the Head gave me the sack this morning. He's always doing it. Really it's getting a most tedious habit with him. Of course he's no gentleman, that's his trouble. He's an impostor. I've told him so often but it seems to make little or no impression."

"I agree," said Mr. Phont. "Mickelthwaite is an exceedingly objectionable little man. I dislike him intensely. He plays cricket."

"I," said Esmond loftily, "choose to scorn. And of course he's no scholar. I discovered the other night that he'd never read Proust."

"My dear boy," said Mr. Phont, "you must

realise that to be a successful head of a modern public school one must not be a scholar and a gentleman but an advertising expert and a master-builder. This mania for building is pernicious and bewildering. In the old days one could judge a school by the number of open scholarships it won and the number of blues it turned out. Now it is a question of how many new buildings it is erecting. A new set of superprivies does more to recommend a school than a Poet Laureate."

"I should suggest the privies are the more useful," put in Julian, "though perhaps the two are most happy when combined."

"I had a most fearful row with Mickelthwaite last night at supper," said Esmond plaintively. "He tried to disgrace me in front of all my little boys. I happened to mention quite casually that I was at Eton, and he said an Eton education was the casting of sham pearls before real swine."

"And what did you do?" asked Mr. Phont.

"My dear, I gathered up my garments and positively floated out of the room."

When they reached his rooms Esmond made himself busy with the glasses and handed round the absinthe. Mr. Phont held his glass up to the light: "Ah! the green sorceress. I must say absinthe is one of my weaknesses. It gives me a delightful *frisson* when I recollect that I am drinking the life blood of the best poetry of modern times."

Mr. Phont turned to Esmond: "I trust you also gave the captain of the eleven Baudelaire to read. So stimulating for athletes, those rhapsodies on depraved negresses and fat Jewesses."

Esmond, who tended to suffer from a one-track mind,

ignored the remark and sighed : " Really I've had a most appallingly strenuous day. I've been weighing and measuring the upper school boys all the morning. Mickelthwaite has a motto, ' vitamins before Virgil, muscles before mathematics,' you know. The result is that the boys' reports read like an article in the *Lancet*. However, it was quite amusing. I'm really quite attached to some of the rugger hearties. Such muscles : you've no idea. No intelligence, of course, just enormous chunks of flesh."

Esmond broke off and wandered across the room to a Japanese cabinet. He returned with a bunch of large, signed photographs.

" I've just been looking over some of my mementoes. Charming lads one and all. The blond with the dark eyes is my fairy prince. Terribly rich ; owns all the railways in South America."

Esmond leant over Mr. Phont and Julian, expatiating on the charms of the young men :

" The Earl of Sporran, marvellous violet-coloured eyes . . . Lord Bagman, skin like white rose petals . . . Viscount Sockett, most amusing man. Scandalised Chester Square by having a whole revue chorus dance naked on the balconies outside his house."

The proceedings were interrupted by a banging on the door. Esmond clasped his hands and swayed slightly :

" Upon my soul ! I had completely forgotten. This will be my young footballer. I met him in the Red Lion this morning. Will you forgive me. . . ."

As Mr. Phont and Julian departed they met on the threshold an enormous young giant with a mop of flaming red hair. They had a parting glimpse of

Esmond pressing a glass of absinthe into the huge paw of the gaping youth, and asking of him in intense tones if he cared for the music of Debussy.

Mr. Phont and Julian had scarcely reached the High Street again before they observed a tall, dark man with a heavy jowl and a grim expression approaching them.

" Heaven help us," said Mr. Phont. " Here's Colonel Barley, the local brewery. You will be able to note, my dear Julian, the lamentable effects of a Harrow education on the son of a village publican."

" Ah ! Phont," cried Colonel Barley, grinding his ash-plant into the pavement, " you're the very man I wanted to see. I'm having trouble with that young gardener of yours. He refuses to join the Territorials. I wish you'd bring a little healthy pressure to bear."

Mr. Phont twinkled genially : " So the boy shows some intelligence, does he, Colonel ? I'm most gratified to hear it. Really I don't blame him in the least for refusing to fill up his leisure time with violent military exercises, and generally to make himself available for slaughter at the earliest possible moment. And what's more," continued Mr. Phont sternly, " I shall certainly not bring pressure to bear on any of my employees. Such methods smack to me suspiciously of the Swastika."

Colonel Barley snorted : " Come, come, Phont. I'm sorry to hear a man in your position speaking like that. It is plain you have never considered the advantages a young man may derive from joining the Territorial Army. Manly exercise, healthy open air life, clean company, monetary allowances. He develops a sense of duty to himself, his King and the Empire. He has unrivalled opportunities for every form of sport. In short he is given a chance to develop into a clean, manly Britisher instead of wasting his time with cinemas, books and thinking."

"An enchanting prospect," murmured Mr. Phont, "but I can't say it appeals to me any more than it seems to appeal to my under-gardener. Of course, I may be biassed. I remember the only time I ever handled a gun was at a week-end shooting party when I was so unfortunate as to direct a charge of small shot into my hostess' rear. I never shot again," concluded Mr. Phont dramatically.

But Colonel Barley was not interested in the major social catastrophe of Mr. Phont's career.

"The Territorial Army," he rumbled on, "should be close to the heart of every loyal Englishman. It stands for all that is characteristic of our island race —courage, tenacity, manliness, the ability to take hard knocks and come up smiling."

"Not to mention," put in Mr. Phont helpfully, "that somewhat revolting process known as ' grinning and bearing it ' and that mysterious practice known as ' muddling through '."

Colonel Barley flushed : " I must say, Phont, I don't like your tone. I think your attitude is at once cynical and irresponsible. What is to happen to our Empire in its hour of need if people in your position go about fostering communistic doctrines ? Why, that boy of yours told me himself that you had advised him to devote his spare time to beer or women."

"Quite," agreed Mr. Phont, "but not, you will note, to both."

"This is not the spirit that prevailed at Omdurman," protested Colonel Barley.

"No," said Mr. Phont, "but it is very much like the spirit that prevailed at Plymouth Hoe."

As they bore away from Colonel Barley, Mr. Phont joyfully rubbed his hands : "Well, we progress. We make enemies all along the line. But these earnest Empire Builders, these all too gentlemanly English Gentlemen exasperate me."

Julian and Mr. Phont had just reached the end of the High Street and were preparing to direct their steps homewards when they saw two large and formidable females with equine faces and flapping feet approaching on the opposite side of the road.

Mr. Phont dragged Julian into a shop doorway where they tried to conceal themselves behind a crate of bananas.

"God !" said Mr. Phont. "Salome and Gertrude Warbler. The vestry virgins. They own the local ironstone quarries. Fairly reek of money and tangled knots of inhibitions. They work it off in religion and an interest in the Boy Scout movement. I call them the horse and the sheep by way of identification. Heaven forbid that they should see us."

But Heaven did not forbid.

Miss Salome Warbler's glazed eye discovered them at once :

"Phont," she cried in hoarse tones, "Phont." And she waved a knobbly walking stick threateningly in their direction.

Mr. Phont and Julian emerged sheepishly from behind the bananas. Once discovered, however, Mr. Phont assumed a stern attitude. He remained resolutely upon his own side of the street and closed his ears to the exhortations of the Misses Warbler that came brokenly and raspingly across the roar of the traffic.

"Damned if I'm going over," said Mr. Phont irritably, "if they want me they can come over here. Let the mountains come to Mahomet, I say. A little dodging about in the traffic will get a bit of that flesh off them."

"Looks mostly like bone to me," said Julian.

Eventually the Misses Warbler arrived panting and militant on the pavement, but not before Salome had had her shin skinned by a passing perambulator.

"Ha! Phont," cried Salome, fixing him with a basilisk eye, "you know what I want with you?"

Mr. Phont smiled coyly: "I could hazard a shrewd guess, but I am too much of a gentleman to say it."

Salome ignored the quip: "It's this matter of the Church Schools. We are organising a fund for the new buildings. Our church schools must be saved. They cannot be allowed to fall completely into the hands of the secular authority. Things are bad enough as it is with half the teachers steeped in communist doctrines. These training colleges for elementary school teachers are nothing but hot-beds of Socialism."

"Hot-beds," mused Mr. Phont, "that sounds very comfortable, not to say matey. However, how can I help you?"

Gertrude came in with a shrill and penetrating falsetto: "We are organising a concert in aid of the fund and we want you to get someone to open it. Someone of position who will lend weight to the affair."

"You put me in a difficult posture," said Mr. Phont.

" You know I disapprove of education altogether. The tree of knowledge is a weeping willow in my fixed opinion. And really, since leaving London I seem to have lost touch with all my grand friends."

" I agree with you about education," fog-horned Salome, " the children are most disrespectful nowadays, not to mention the teachers. The head-mistress of the Church of England Girls' School was quite impudent yesterday when I said I should like to see the girls curtsy when I entered the classrooms. After all I think I deserve some little consideration. I shall certainly take steps to have the woman removed. And what's more I hear she is starting to take riding lessons now. Not at all fitting for one in her position. The fact of the matter is these teachers are all too well-paid for doing next to nothing. I shall certainly make representations to the education officer. However, be that as it may. We have been sufficiently idiotic to educate the masses and now we shall have to make the best of it. What can you do for us ? Surely you know a Member of Parliament or something ? "

Mr. Phont rubbed his chin : " I might get a brace of communist comrades. Failing which, of course, I could open the thing myself. I used to be rather good at making a few choice remarks."

Gertrude bridled : " I fear you are hardly the type of man, Phont. I hear you made some perfectly scandalous remarks about the divorce laws at the Licensed Victuallers' dinner last week. This is a serious matter and not one to be treated with doubtful levity."

" Then I fear," said Mr. Phont, " I can do little for

you. But surely in any event this is Skillington's province. As parish priest. . . ."

" Skillington," snorted Salome, " an odious man. Absolutely intolerable. He had the impudence to interfere in my church last Sunday to the extent of changing the flowers I had put on the altar. And when I had a crib put in last Christmas he became positively obscene. He said it was his job to preach Heaven and Hell and not to spend his time playing at dolls houses."

" He certainly is rather low, I suppose," ventured Mr. Phont.

" Low," bellowed Gertrude, grinding her hob-nails into the pavement, " I should say so. He might as well call himself a Nonconformist and be done with it. Why, he's still at the North-end. We're bringing all the pressure to bear we can, but it'll take him ten years to get round the corner at his present rate."

" And what's more," said Salome, " he's had the impertinence to forbid our attendance at the Boy Scout meetings."

Mr. Phont winked vulgarly at Julian.

" Dear me ! How unkind. I know how fond you are of the little boys."

" Quite, quite," said Gertrude hurriedly, " we always have the cause of youth close to our hearts. And he was terribly rude too about the Girls' Welfare Club. Really the loose behaviour of some of the girls, young girls, in the parish is shocking. We proposed we should give some little heart to heart talks to the girls on the dangers of immorality, and he told us—told us to our faces—that all women were the same at heart, and we could safely leave the girls to the Chief Constable and himself."

" Tut," said Mr. Phont feelingly, " tut."

" Well," said Salome, beating the air dangerously with her ash plant, " since you won't or can't help us, we'll be getting on."

Mr. Phont and Julian had scarcely turned away before Salome Warbler's voice came trumpeting after them : " Phont ! Phont ! Come here."

Obediently Mr. Phont turned.

" By the way, Phont," cried Salome, loping back towards them, " what did you mean by recommending that play to me last week for the Scouts' annual concert ? Sordid and libidinous to a degree. I can only deduce that you had not read it yourself."

" On the contrary," said Mr. Phont, " I have seen it six times."

"And yet you have the cold licentiousness of spirit to commend it for performance by clean, innocent boys ? "

" It is a very fine work of art," said Mr. Phont sternly. " And remember, evil, like beauty, lies in the eye of the beholder."

" You deserve to be damned," said Miss Salome Warbler conclusively, and turned upon her all too manly heel.

" What play was it ? " asked Julian faintly.

" Your own, my dear boy," said Mr. Phont. " ' Worm i'the Root '. None other."

Julian, who was now feeling definitely weak, suggested going home for tea, but they had yet one more encounter to make.

On arriving upon St. John's Green in the middle of the town they were faced by a large, straggling brick building looking like a cross between a Wesleyan Chapel and a lunatic asylum.

" Our Town Hall," said Mr. Phont. " The finest architectural abortion of the last century. But the burgesses simply love it. By the way you should read Twyte on it in his official guidebook to the town. The whole book is a magnificent work of emetic drivel, but the passage on the Town Hall is quite the juiciest part. He refers to it as that ' elegant pile executed in the neo-Byzantine style with Spanish baroque embellishments.' But what have we here? Something scandalous afoot, I'll be bound . . . "

Mr. Phont broke off and indicated two figures standing on the Town Hall steps.

A wicked twinkle came into Mr. Phont's eye : " Bless me if it isn't Alderman Deacon, the Mayor, and Councillor Sam Nurture, chairman of the Town Advertisement Committee. Some back-stairs business going forward, I swear. I'll just rouse them with a few well-chosen remarks."

Twinkling genially, Mr. Phont hove to in front of the two men who eyed him with ill-disguised distaste.

Julian observed Alderman Deacon closely. He was a short, thick-set man with a luxuriant grey moustache and a pompous expression. Councillor Sam Nurture was taller, and stout, with an opaque eye and an air of comfortable smugness.

Mr. Phont disposed himself to do the honours : " Meet the Mayor, Julian. The strong man of the Council. An estimable person who will, I feel sure, be the first to agree with me, that he has risen from nothing. A self-made man and proud of it. Once, the story goes, a Socialist, but now a staunch Unionist. However, it is wonderful what lunching

with Lord Wycherley will do ; and after all it is
only a fool who never changes his mind."

Alderman Deacon was somewhat taken aback by
this lightning biography, but he rose nobly to the
occasion.

" Good afternoon, Mr. Phont. It is a long time
since we had the pleasure of seeing you at one of
our council meetings. We are always pleased for
burgesses to attend, and show a proper interest in
the government of this borough of ours."

Mr. Phont shook his head waggishly : " Well
really, Mr. Mayor, that's uncommonly kind of you,
but there are some things which I feel innocent ears
should not hear. One must draw the line somewhere. However, I promise you I shall attend
more regularly in future. My interest in the affairs
of the town becomes a more personal matter daily."

" I am glad to hear it," said Alderman Deacon
unctuously. " It is up to all of us to shoulder our
fair share of the municipal responsibility. As a
self-made man, and one of the people, I have always
realised that."

Mr. Phont turned to Julian : " By the way, I
forgot to tell you that our Mayor is a foreman in the
local ironstone quarries. You will notice that though
he now holds the highest position the borough can
bestow, he is not ashamed to labour honestly with
his hands. He is an example to us all, and a proof
that in these enlightened and democratic days
humble birth is no bar to the greatest municipal
honours."

Alderman Deacon glowed : " You are too kind,
Mr. Phont, too kind. Lord Wycherley was only

saying to me at luncheon last week that he couldn't understand how I managed to hold down two jobs at one time. But I told him I was a plain man, and we plain men don't jib at a bit of extra work. Plain Tom Deacon, that's me, I said."

" All too plain," murmured Julian sotto voce.

Mr. Phont now moved to Councillor Sam Nurture :

" Meet the chairman of the Town Advertisement Committee," he urged Julian, " though precisely what the committee advertises it would be difficult to say, unless it's their own bank balances."

Mr. Phont smiled coyly at Councillor Nurture, and prodded him playfully in the upper ribs.

Councillor Nurture's dignity was plainly wounded :

" Come, come, Mr. Phont. Surely you realise the great work my committee is doing in putting the borough on the map for the first time. We're telling the world. We're opening the eyes of the country to the industrial, agricultural, cultural and social amenities of the borough. We are forging ahead in every direction. Why our unemployment figures are down by half a century on last year, and the new car-park is creating a veritable ' fewroar '. Why, someone wrote to us from Nishni Novgorod about it last week. Unfortunately the letter wasn't signed, so we couldn't reply."

" By the way," interrupted Mr. Phont sternly, " I hear some scandalous rumours about those new floodlights you're putting up on High Street. Gas instead of electricity, isn't it ? You'd better go carefully, Nurture. They do say you've got a lot of money invested in the Gas Company. Not, of course, that I believe such rumours for a moment, but a word of kindly warning is never amiss. Feeling is running high I can tell you. Very high."

Councillor Nurture coughed : " Rubbish. We've had extensive tests made, and we find . . . "

Alderman Deacon came in neatly : " By the way, Mr. Phont, Nurture and I were just discussing plans for the kiddies' soup-kitchen bazaar. We thought perhaps you might see your way . . . "

Mr. Phont eyed the two burgesses sternly : " I do not, I fear, see my way. I would suggest that before throwing good money after bad into the kiddies' soup, you should get busy over a spot of slum clearance. If some of your councillors were to clear the appalling warrens they fatten on, it would be far more profitable to the public than wasting time over soup-kitchens. And what's more, Nurture," concluded Mr. Phont, turning away, " don't forget what I said about those floodlights. It's a very curious thing that the larger one should have been erected precisely outside your own shop."

Happily Mr. Phont led the way home : " That's the spirit, my dear Julian, that's the mode. Go for them neck and crop. Have at them in the short ribs."

4

The Rottenness of the Borough

MRS. MEREDITH LIVED IN a low, square, white house at the crest of the hill at the southern extremity of the borough.

When Julian and Mr. Phont roared up in ' Bloody Mary '—Julian's formidable, if somewhat battered, Bugatti—Mrs. Meredith was on the verandah awaiting them. She smoked an Egyptian cigarette in a lengthy ivory holder.

Julian saw at once that Mrs. Meredith was indeed all that Mr. Phont had claimed for her ; tall, fragile, dusky-haired, with eyes like pools of liquid shadow. Against the dead ivory-white of her skin her mouth and finger-nails smouldered a dull peony-red. The ghosts of gardenias hung in the air when she moved and she wore a closely-fitting white dress supported by a single slender golden thread about the neck.

When she greeted them Julian noticed that her voice was low, husky, a little hoarse even.

Mr. Phont, kissing his hostess' hand, surveyed her appreciatively with his perky glance :

" Permit me to congratulate you upon the dress, my dear Barbara. I always maintain that in dress-designing, as indeed in all the arts, the success of the effort depends not so much upon knowing what to put in as upon what to omit."

Mrs. Meredith smiled her agonised expiring smile and rang for the cocktails.

The introductions and initial pleasantries over, Mrs. Meredith remarked : " Bellairs is late. He rang me up this morning to say he would come if he could, but he was feeling unwell. He puts it down to too much beer last night and to eating fish and chips out of the *News of the World*. He is a young man of coarse habits."

" Alas ! yes," agreed Mr. Phont. " I fear it is always so. Look at the Elizabethans. Genius and grossness, the Parnassian twins."

At this point they became aware of an uproar at the main gates. Looking down the drive they perceived the bizarre figure of a young man mounted upon an ancient push-bicycle surmounting the crest of the hill from the town.

The general effect was distinctly Maxtonian, a flowing lock of hair, an erratic glint in the eye, a red tie and a bright yellow waistcoat that lent a pleasing Eighteenth Century note to the whole outfit. Even as they watched, the young man descended violently from his machine and, facing the direction from which he had come, began to apostrophise the town :

" Woe ! I say woe unto thee, thou Rotten Borough. Verily, verily I say unto thee it shall be more tolerable for Sodom and Gomorrah, yea for the cities of the plain, than for thee in thy latter days."

Then spitting with deliberation over his handlebars several times, he remounted and advanced precariously up the drive. Arriving before the group on the verandah, Bellairs flourished a battered grey felt hat and bowed :

" Incredibly sweaty work this Solomon Eagle stuff ;
you like the waistcoat ? Neat but not gaudy, I fancy.
Forgive my not dressing but my garments are in the
hands of my uncle."

At this point his remarks were brought to an abrupt
conclusion by a resonant hiccough.

" That," remarked Bellairs dispassionately, " will
be the prawns or possibly the spring onions."

Across Mrs. Meredith's elegant little dinner table in
the pale green dining room Bellairs was declaiming—
chiefly to Julian :

" Before you can fully realise the idea behind our
proposed newspaper, before you can fully appreciate
our moral purpose, you must first clearly understand the
anatomy, the precise structure of this Rotten Borough
which—I may add—is typical of hundreds of other
small towns up and down the land.

" At the one extreme you have the local aristocracy ;
at the other the working-class, the mob, the *hoi polloi*,
given—as the Bard so justly remarks—to tossing its
sweaty night-caps in the air. Against these two classes
we have no particular animus. It is in between these
two extremes that the trouble starts. Here you have
the professional class and the bourgeoisie. The chief
characteristics of the former are complacency, various
forms of snobbery, mild treachery and a spurious
veneer of culture."

" And the bourgeoisie," suggested Mr. Phont.

Mrs. Meredith's voice expired : " Spare us the
bourgeoisie. At least spare us Bellairs on the
bourgeoisie."

But they were not to be spared.

A fanatical gleam became apparent in Bellairs' eye :

" Aha ! The unspeakable bourgeoisie ! As a class they exhibit many of the characteristics of their professional brethren, particularly complacency and various degrees of snobbery. They ignore, however, the culture, for which we may be thankful. But their chief characteristic, their all absorbing mania indeed, is the making of money, and to attain that ambition they will stop at nothing. Nothing. Casting upon one side not only moral scruples of every kind, but also the dictates of common humanity, they resort to graft, treachery, double-dealing, bootlicking and every other conceivable base practice. Their whole standard of judgment is based upon money. A man is only to be valued in proportion to his bank balance."

Bellairs paused for breath.

" Don't," murmured Mr. Phont delicately dismembering a peach, don't, I beg of you, forget the Town Council."

" Ah ! " breathed Bellairs, " the Town Council ! The very root of all the evil. The cancer in the body politic ! "

Turning to Julian, he stabbed at him with an accusatory forefinger : " There you have it. The Town Council ; the Worm i' the Root, the festering plague spot at the heart of the whole putrescent corpse."

" Proceed," begged Julian.

" You must understand,'" explained Bellairs, " that the Town Council consists almost entirely of the wealthiest tradesmen in the borough. True, there are a few misguided Socialists, but their minority is hopeless. Now these tradesmen are banded together in what is called the local Board of Commerce, so what it amounts to is that the whole municipal life of the borough is conducted by the Board of Commerce disguised under the name of the Town Council. You will see that their position is well-nigh impregnable. Everything is in their hands. They can make what they like and break whom they like."

" You amaze me," said Julian. " Graft? Corruption? In a place of this size?"

" The place stinks of it," said Bellairs, gripping the end of his nose firmly between the thumb and forefinger of his right hand. " I tell you New York gets off where we begin. I could prove to you—but it would take too long and the brandy awaits us—that there is not a job given in this town, not a business deal transacted, not a charity administered without a simultaneous pulling of strings, oiling of palms and, even, a downright holding of the pistol to the head."

" I can scarcely believe it," said Julian.

" Then let me give you one or two examples," urged Bellairs.

" Not more than two, please," begged Mrs. Meredith.

Bellairs ignored the interruption : " Consider the tallow factory. Situated in the middle of the borough it makes life intolerable to the neighbourhood in the summer by reason of the abominable niff, the excruciating odour it emits. But can anything be done about it? Have repeated signed petitions from the inhabitants on the grounds of health and decency done anything to abate the nuisance? They have not. The tallow factory continues and will continue to render the mere act of drawing breath well-nigh insupportable to one-third of the local burgesses between May and

September.   And why ? Because the tallow factory
belongs to the senior Alderman in the borough,
Alderman Fred Twidale.

"Then consider our new lunatic asylum—the
juiciest scandal that even this town has ever staged.
A year ago the Council decided to build a new lunatic
asylum.   Estimates are invited and the job is given
to the one builder in the town who happens to be on
the Council, Councillor Alfred Dogby, last year's
mayor.   This in spite of the fact that Councillor
Dogby's estimate is a clear thousand above the rest
and that he is the most notorious jerry-builder in the
county."

"But this is scandalous," cried Julian, "something
ought to be done.   This state of affairs ought to be
exposed."

"And how ? " asked Bellairs.

"Surely the Press should do something.   The local
journal, the *Chronicle and Gazetteer*, why is that public
organ silent ? "

Bellairs smiled indulgently : "You fail to realise
two things.   First, that Alderman Fred Twidale owns
three-quarters of the *Chronicle and Gazetteer ;* second
that Councillor Cammack, the sales-manager, is
Chairman of the Board of Commerce.   The *Gazetteer*
is simply the subsidised organ of the Board of Commerce
in general and Alderman Twidale in particular.   You
have to get used to these things."

Julian turned to Mr. Phont : "And so this is why
you are founding your newspaper ? You intend to
expose all these shameful goings-on and generally to
set the municipal house in order ? "

Mr. Phont held his port up to the light and examined

it critically : " Precisely, my dear Julian, precisely. At least, if we do not set the town in order we shall certainly set it by the ears.

" After due consideration I have arrived at the conclusion that the best, indeed the only way of doing this, is to found a weekly newspaper—a rival to the *Chronicle and Gazetteer*—an independent journal run upon progressive, nay, offensive lines ; a journal which is calculated to tell the truth, the whole truth, and a great deal more than the truth. Bellairs, I am glad to say, has done us the honour of accepting the position of editor, of becoming, as I believe it is so happily termed in commercial enterprises, the man at the helm."

" Yes," said Bellairs, as steadily as the fumes of the Napoleon brandy permitted, " the second incarnation is at hand. Behold ! the redeemer cometh—and in the guise of a weekly newspaper. The book of the Revelation is about to be published. In these troublous times of trial and tribulation, in these days of fiscal and moral stringency, I intend to shine forth as a light amongst men, a guide, comforter and friend, a lantern, indeed, unto the feet. I conceive it my duty, my sole and sacred vocation to regenerate mankind. My whole existence is to be devoted to the rooting out of all that is false and hypocritical and to the championing of truth, justice and moral rectitude."

" And to damning the bourgeoisie," suggested Julian helpfully.

Again the demoniacal gleam suffused Bellairs' eye : " Zwounds ! the unspeakable bourgeois. The bourgeois sickens me, he turns my gorge, he positively makes me retch. Observe him, as I observed him this afternoon, pullulating in High Street. Observe him, I say, climbing into his mass-produced saloon to bowl home to his unspeakable family, to his fantastically named semi-detached house, to his incredibly vulgar high-tea.

" Imagine him," urged Bellairs further, " spending his evening. After 'igh-tea, he revoltingly gambols in the ' best-room ' for half-an-hour with his already money-minded offspring. Perhaps, with satisfaction, he rattles their little money-boxes, and notes with pleasure that the ' young idea ' already knows the ' value of money '. The children out of the way, he recounts to ' the wife ', to his stringy or bosomy spouse, the triumphs of the day's trade, his sordid transactions in trousers, groceries, art. silk knickers, or ironmongery. The day's triumphs told, he indulges in a little sickly lubricity with the wife. A husbandly peck on the cheek, a proprietorial arm about the haunches. But love yields to trade. He climbs once more into the mass-produced saloon and drives to the club. There, over a game of bowls or billiards, he plans further commercial enterprises and, perhaps, gets a little tipsy if someone else is standing the drinks. A little tipsy, mark you. The bourgeois never gets gloriously, roaringly, paralytically drunk. He hasn't the guts. He just gets contemptibly tipsy."

" Most impressive," said Julian, who was genuinely moved by the oratory. " Most impressive. But I must say, you seem a little severe. Admittedly I am not familiar with the type you so picturesquely, so cinematographically describe, but you seem to lay it on a bit thick."

" I haven't touched the edge yet," answered Bellairs,

the formidable gleam returning to his eye. " I tell you, when you've met the small-town bourgeois in his own sty, you begin to see the point of the little matter of the Gadarene swine. ' Stewed in corruption, honeying and making love over the nasty sty ' as the Bard so aptly puts it."

" But surely," objected Julian, " a man is entitled to live his life as he likes. Surely even the small-town bourgeois can be allowed to make his money, marry what wife he likes, live in what house he likes and conduct his private life as he likes."

" He is entitled to, unfortunately," said the young man, " but he shouldn't be. The small-town bourgeois is not a man, he is not a human, he is a public nuisance, and as such, should be suppressed. Let a man make money, by all means, but not, as he does, money for money's sake. To make money for any other reason than for what money can buy, is low, brutish and immoral. And I don't object to his life so much, as his satisfaction with it, his unspeakable complacency. Complacency, to any decent human being, is the worst of the deadly sins. It is the mysterious sin against the Holy Ghost, for of complacency are bred stagnation, repression and, worst of all, intolerance. Let the bourgeois, if you like, make his thousands out of socks or bananas, or lard or skins ; let him, if you must, marry a common wife and breed a common family ; let him, if you can do no other, find Heaven on earth in bowls, billiards and tipsiness, but for Heaven's sake don't admit that he is justified in being satisfied with it all."

" Almost thou persuadest me," said Julian.

" And furthermore," said the young man, " I have

a few words to say on the mentality of your small-town bourgeois."

" Beneath contempt, I should imagine."

" Without the bounds of possible consideration, rather. He, in his own phrase, ' knows what he likes '. And what does he like ? I will tell you. He likes the London daily with the two million circulation. He likes pictures of fishing-smacks at eventide. He likes cinema organs with plenty of *vox humana* stop. He thinks a poet a fool because poetry is materially profitless, he thinks Picasso incompetent because he doesn't paint like a photograph, and he calls Sibelius' symphonies ' high-brow bunkum ' because he can't whistle them as he can whistle ' Rock of Ages ' when he is digging up worms in his back garden on Sunday afternoons. He sends his son to a public school to prostitute Greek and Latin, whilst he sits at home reading *Poppy's Monthly*."

Strolling in the rose-scented moonlight, Bellairs began to elaborate his plans :

" Ours must be a strong forward polity. We must press on with courage and confidence into the new year, allowing ourselves to be deterred neither by promise, favour nor threat. Sensationalism must be our key-word. We must shock, stagger and above all, expose. And, by God, what and how we shall expose ! Ideas teem in my brain."

" And how much money can you afford to lose ? " enquired Julian.

" The point is immaterial," said Mr. Phont, " so long as we succeed in rousing the borough."

" At first, at any rate," explained Bellairs, " we shall keep the paper down to some half-dozen pages.

The chief feature each week—written by me, I need hardly add—will be a lengthy and staggering article dealing with some particular borough scandal. It will be this weekly article, of course, that will chiefly sell the paper. This main feature will be supported by a slight but sensational news service. Sport will be dealt with thoroughly, but such routine matters as police courts, meetings and so on will be dealt with purely on their sensational merits. In addition we shall have a column of social notes. Notes full of scandal and innuendo and nasty inferences which will be a counter blast to Twyte's ' Spotlights From Many Angles ' in the *Gazetteer*. Ansell can write up these notes on information supplied by me."

" Thanks," said Julian, " I shall enjoy it."

" If we work along these lines," continued Bellairs, " we shall not only lay the foundations of an astonishing circulation, but we shall also keep down expenses. Besides myself we shall only need two men on the literary staff. Of course, as business extends, we shall have to incorporate a trade section to deal with the advertisements and so on . . ."

" Advertisements ? " enquired Julian. " Surely you are a little sanguine ? "

" Not at all. Of course the main tradesmen in the borough won't advertise with us, at first that is ; they will do their best to bust us. But there are many small tradesmen in the town, not to mention the local branches of the big national combines, who will only be too eager to advertise with us. You see we look to make no profit, indeed we are prepared to lose money, so we can offer them nominal rates. In that way we should knock the *Gazetteer* badly."

Mr. Phont rubbed his hands together and pirouetted a few steps on the damp grass : " Really, I must confess I'm beginning to feel quite exalted by the approaching fray. I can see we are engaged on a most notable enterprise. Bellairs, accept my felicitations. I can see that your faculties are, at least, all that you claim for them."

Bellairs bowed silently with dignity and elaboration, then, throwing back his head and lifting his face to the stars, he smote his breast in an imperial gesture.

" This policy of exposure is all very well," said Julian, " but what about libel actions ? So far as I can see the legal profession will make a fortune out of us."

Bellairs swept the objection aside : " Libel actions ? There's no fear of that. You overlook this very important point. Whilst we have all to gain and nothing to lose, precisely the opposite applies to our victims. They daren't face the long-drawn publicity of a libel action even if they were sure of winning. You must realise that the god of the small-town bourgeois is respectability, and to preserve his respectability he will do almost anything. Frankly, I confidently expect that we could, if we wanted, amply cover our expenses by the hush-money thrust upon us by our victims. Have no fear of troubles of that sort. Your small-town bourgeois is essentially a bully and, like all bullies, crumples up like tissue paper when bullied in turn."

" And when do you publish ? " enquired Julian.

" A fortnight on Friday," said Bellairs. " We are going to start off with a great bang. Our first number is going to be devoted entirely to the pillorying of the theatricals in aid of the new lunatic asylum. What vistas of scarifying scandal open before my eyes, what infinities of insidious and infamous innuendo against the highest in the land."

" Yes," said Mr. Phont heartily, " our first issue will be an epic. We are going to get the Rev. Jasper Skillington to write us a special article on the corrupt state of the modern drama. The priest i'faith can turn a swingeing phrase."

Throwing back his head, Bellairs burst into a fit of raucous, baying laughter.

They returned to the house and at Mr. Phont's request, Mrs. Meredith rang for champagne.

" The founding of a newspaper," began Mr. Phont pontifically, " is a task not lightly to be entered upon. It is an undertaking of a serious and even a sacred nature. Therefore we will celebrate it with the true, the blushful Hippocrene."

Julian, Bellairs and Mr. Meredith rose to their feet. Solemnly the glasses were clinked.

" To the naked truth," toasted Mr. Phont, " to scandal, innuendo and sensationalism, to the downfall of hypocrisy, graft and civic intrigue, to the success of the child of my old age, to the honour and glory of . . . of the *Weekly Probe!* Bottoms up ! "

The bottoms were upped.

5

A Formidable Priest

THE REV. JASPER SKILLINGTON, known throughout the diocese as " Root and Branch Skillington," sat in his study with a bottle of whisky, meditating in a broad and general manner upon God.

He was an exceedingly energetic man, troubled with incipient facial eczema and a bouncing lock of pale straw-coloured hair. By persuasion he was low, being of the type known in Anglican circles as a " strong man " ; had his lot been cast amongst the free-churchmen, he would have been accounted eminently " acceptable." In the words of Achilles Bolitho, his bishop, he was " one of my most formidable incumbents, occupied, perhaps, with things temporal rather than spiritual, but gifted with a remarkable nose for sin."

Sin was, indeed, and very properly, the chief preoccupation of the Rev. Jasper Skillington. And sin was for him a very simple matter, for it was precisely synonymous and co-significant with another three-letter word, namely sex.

Under the slogan " Sin is Sex and Sex is Sin," modified by the refrain " Have at it Root and Branch," he had stormed two deaneries and appointed himself rural dean of each. Meanwhile he could never understand why the bishop withheld a canonry. Privately he put it down to Achilles Bolitho's not being

" sound," for if the Rev. Jasper Skillington had a nose for anything beyond sin it was for Popish practices. In his opinion it was at the present time but a step, and a pretty short one at that, from the palace to the Vatican. But as for himself, at his hands, the " spike " might expect, and certainly received, no quarter. In his two deaneries no banner waved, no incense wafted, vestments were vetoed. " No Popery, no wooden shoes," he would genially exhort his curates, but under the superficial geniality none but a crass fool could fail to discern the veiled threat.

The early part of the afternoon had been passed in the act of literary parturition. On the table, between the typewriter and the whisky bottle, lay the bulky manuscript of the next day's sermon, and a swingeing document it was too. The last passage was heavily pencilled :

" The wolf of Sex is gnawing at the vitals of modern society. It is our duty, as practising Christians, to have at it root and branch. In this our ancient borough, at our very thresholds, it stalks abroad seeking whom it may devour. Even at this very moment it is preparing to fall tooth and nail upon a flock of twenty thousand innocent souls, namely the inhabitants of this ancient borough of ours. I refer, of course, to a certain stage play which, as you are all well aware, is shortly to be presented at our theatre for the alleged purpose of raising funds for the new lunatic asylum.

" I have seen the text of this play, the *Well of Passions*. I have read it carefully, and I can only conclude that it would have been more justly entitled ' The Sink of Iniquity.' Towards the most solemn and holy facts of life it displays a levity, a depravity, a loss of moral sense beyond my powers to describe. In it there occur orgiastic scenes of unspeakable lewdity rivalled only, in their loathely concupiscence, by the pagan and filthy ceremonies of ancient Rome.

" That such corrupt debauchery, such monstrous profligacy should be paraded before the public on the pretext of helping the unfortunate mentally deranged, seems to me to be callous, cynical and hypocritical beyond words, and indicative of the greatest moral turpitude. Furthermore, that this degrading performance should not only be promoted, but actually enacted, by members of our local aristocracy, boasting some of the noblest names in the land, indisputably indicates the total and final collapse of morality and decency which I have for so long prophesied.

" To the nobility for centuries past we have looked for a lead in morality, dignity and spirituality, but our trust is grossly misplaced. The great, it appears, far from offering an example of the Christian life, betray us into the hands of Beelzebub and lead us headlong to the bottomless pit.

" Therefore we must look to our own salvation. Placing our trust in Jehovah and our own moral conscience we must, as practising Christians, set our faces sternly against this shameless exhibition of lewdity which is shortly to sully the fair reputation of our noble and ancient borough. We must make superhuman efforts to prevent the presentation of the *Well of Passions*, and, should we fail in this, we must exert our every power to prevent our brother burgesses from rushing headlong to poison themselves at this contaminated source. Aided by the indwelling power of the Holy Spirit, we shall sweep, cleanse, destroy . . ."

But at this point the heat of the July afternoon combined with the fumes of the malted barley had given even the Rev. Jasper Skillington pause. But, always energetic, he had merely exchanged one field of action for another, and was even now speculating on the nature of the Deity.

He was not at all satisfied with the views of the generality of the clergy on this very important matter. From the popular conception of God as a benevolent, if somewhat supercilious, father, he withheld his suffrage. Of God as the great all-originating, all-organising mind he could readily conceive. To God as a kind of super scientist-artist he readily subscribed. After all, when faced with the Milky Way, Brahms' fourth symphony and the miraculous functioning of the human kidneys, why bother to deny God the superman ? But God the father ? No, very definitely, no. That was beyond the leap of even the most agile imagination. There, for the Rev. Jasper Skillington, was all too frequently the rub. What about Japanese earthquakes ? And Chinese floods ? And, for that matter, Indian famines ? Hardly fatherly. If they ask for bread give them a stone. No, God the arch-castigator was more like it and more, indeed to the Skillingtonian taste. God with a whip of scorpions, God as the ultimate flail, God as just retribution, God as DEATH. Yet Jesus said : " I am the resurrection and the life ; he that believeth on me . . ."

The Rev. Jasper Skillington stirred uneasily in his chair as he tried to truncate the straying line of his thoughts. Surely he was not going to have one of his

periodic attacks of the Doubts? There was clink of
glass upon glass. Presently the fumes of the malted
barley had blotted out the Doubts in a roseate mist.
Death, decay, dust, the quenchless fire, the brimstone
pit. The sins of the fathers shall be visited upon the
children unto the third and fourth generation . . .

Juicily the question of the *Well of Passions* was
resumed. In the words of the verger, the next
morning's congregation was to be " dangled o'er the
pit."

An hour later the Rev. Jasper Skillington ceased his
attack upon the typewriter. He sat back flushed and
appreciative. This, he felt, was the stuff. Powerful,
impassioned, bellicose, even. And meaty, too. It
was, he felt, in a direct line with Savanarola, Bossuet
and Wesley. Under his breath, seated below the
apostles who partook of a never-ending last supper
over the mantelpiece, he voluptuously mouthed the
swingeing prose.

There was a tap on the door. The maid announced
Mr. Ulric Phont and Mr. Gilbert Bellairs.

6

A Pub-Crawl

THE TAP-ROOM AT THE
Red Lion on High Street was waxing hearty. The
air was full of the subdued hum of conversation,
tobacco smoke of the ranker kind, and the smacking
of lips. Occasionally there was a prolonged swishing
noise as some veteran ale-supper swept the suspended
drops from his drooping whiskers.

In the centre of the floor stood Mr. Ulric Phont,
that dark and elegant bachelor, splendidly attired in
full evening dress. With him was a considerable party.
In the corner Julian and Bellairs were drinking
Worthington and desultorily playing dart-cricket.
Mrs. Meredith was sitting at a table by herself gloomily
poring over a glass of grocer's sherry.

Mr. Phont, who was waving an inordinately long
cigar in his slender fingers, was speaking :

" Fellow citizens, or more strictly, fellow burgesses,
why should you buy my paper, the *Weekly Probe* ? "

" Why, indeed ? " came from a dolorous looking man
behind a port-and-lemon.

" Ah," said Mr. Phont, " I perceive we have a wit
amongst our number. But, to proceed. You should
buy the *Weekly Probe* because the *Probe* is pithy, pungent
and penetrating. It is all that the *Chronicle and
Gazetteer* is not. It is honest. It is fearless. It is,
in brief . . ."

"A literary cataclysm," put in Bellairs dispassionately as he took Julian's last wicket with a neatly placed bull.

"I thank our friend," said Mr. Phont. "The *Probe* is, in point of actual fact, a journalistic tornado, or will be when it is published. But before I proceed to tell you more . . ."

Mr. Phont waved a long white finger towards the barman and then included the assembled company in a lordly gesture. There were signs of general approval.

"It has been brought to my attention," went on Mr. Phont, "that this noble borough of yours, of ours, is not all that it might be. To put it mildly, I should place it in the category of rotten boroughs. Graft is rampant. Strings are pulled. Wheels, I learn, exist within wheels. There are certain crying scandals that need rectifying. One at least, to my certain knowledge, stinks to high heaven. I refer, of course, to the local tallow-works."

At this point there were grunts of approval. Glasses were, in several instances, set down. Eyes, in many cases, became less fish-like. Mr. Phont had his audience in the palm of his hand. They were swayed.

"Furthermore, there is the little matter of the river drainage rate. In my opinion, a most unfair imposition, and one that, as a newspaper proprietor, I intend to combat unremittingly, without ruth. . . ."

"Without whom?" asked Mrs. Meredith expiringly.

"Ruthlessly, if you like," explained Mr. Phont a little testily. "There are other points I could mention, but those will do for another time. In brief, I place myself and my resources at the command of the local burgesses. It is my aim to clean up our noble town, and make it, if I may say so without undue exaggeration, a place fit for honest men to drink in. I have gathered about me an excellent staff. Mr. Gilbert Bellairs, doubtless known to you all as one who copiously sups his ale and copiously makes love, will be my editor. We have a small, but lively, contingent of reporters who may be trusted to ferret out what they feel too languid to make up. I, personally, shall be business manager. Not, of course, that I know anything about business, but, as I think you will agree with me, I have every right to see how much money I am losing. And now I will introduce to you, if any introduction be needed, which I very much doubt, my editor, Mr. Gilbert Bellairs." Mr. Phont subsided gracefully against the bar and daintily sipped a tankard of mild ale.

Bellairs' immediate response to Mr. Phont's invitation was, to say the least of it, a little disconcerting. Darting out sinuously into the middle of the floor, he threw himself into a wild and exotic dance. The virtuosity of his performance was undeniable. His technique was a commingling of tap-dancing and ballet with an admixture of the sinuous movements of pagan religious dances. Whilst his feet beat a rapid tattoo upon the floor, the upper part of his body and his arms writhed in a series of elaborate and fantastic arabesques. His face bore a look of almost demoniacal ecstasy. The dance whirled faster and faster. His long dark hair floated about his head. His red tie fluttered gaily in the gusts of his own making. Finally, with a terrifying whoop, he pirouetted to a standstill. The surprised silence of the tap-room was punctuated by the dying voice of Mrs. Meredith : " Dear me, what an alarming young man ; too sweet for words."

Bellairs paused and threw back his drooping locks with a magnificent gesture. Then he suddenly gathered himself together, tense and taut. He flung out an accusatory arm and with stealthy steps began to advance upon a harmless little grocer who was quietly sipping milk-stout in the corner. The little man blinked fearfully, plainly terrified by the bizarre creature bearing down so balefully upon him.

" What," hissed Bellairs between his teeth, " can the *Weekly Probe* do for you ? What ? " he cried, suddenly spinning round on his heels and embracing in a single gesture the whole of the crowded room, " can the *Weekly Probe* do for you ? " The silence was absolute.

" It can save your souls alive."

Leaning negligently against the bar, Bellairs began to speak : " Yes, comrades, the *Weekly Probe* can save you from high rates, thin beer and corruption in high places. It can save you from graft, stinks and civic shame. As comrade Phont has indicated, there is something rotten in this ancient borough. What is it ? I will tell you. It is the Town Council. Your Town Council. Our Town Council. Believe me, in yonder council chamber are hatched all the municipal itches that irritate us daily. It is my intention, with the help of my colleagues on the *Weekly Probe*, to expose that council, to show you in all their stinking corruption the men and women whom you have voted into office. To put it briefly, I intend to blow the roof off that council chamber. Watch me, comrades, watch me and lend me your support. That is all I ask you. Watch me and buy the *Weekly Probe*.   Forsake that perjured rag, the *Chronicle and Gazetteer*.   Help me to smash it, that inspired organ of the Board of Commerce.   The millennium is upon you if you have but the eyes to see, ears to hear and mouths to sup the ale of truth. With your support I can raise you from the mire where ye so native crawl.   Utopia is provided for you on an easy pay-way plan.   Twopence a week cash payment brings the Kingdom of Heaven to your back door.   Is twopence a week an exorbitant rental for a desirable residence beyond the Golden Gates ?   No. Then get to it chaps, get to it.   Pin your shirts to paradise by Bellairs out of *Probe*.   And now, perhaps, the company will join with me in singing that grand old shanty, " A beautiful Sinner like Me."

Led by Mr. Phont who pirouetted, a little uncertainly, be it admitted, on a table, the company joined in.   Tankards pounded, ale-ripe voices tuned up, gusts of song floated out into High Street.

As Mr. Phont and his party walked away, distantly, borne upon the frolicsome evening breezes, came gustily detached phrases of song, punctuated by the hollow boomings of ' Praise God ', ' Amen ', ' Stretch IT ', from Bellairs who had delayed to dip his head in a horse trough.

Drinking coffee at Mrs. Meredith's, Mr. Phont said : " Dear me, I must confess I find my first excursion into trade surprisingly agreeable.   Sordid gain has, I can see, undeniable attractions.   The stimulation of the combat, the appeal to the primitive power-urge in a man and so on.   Titillating, I insist, titillating.   And what progress we make.   Last night the George Tap, to-night the Red Lion, if we canvass the Five Bells on Saturday, we shall have firmly established ourselves amongst the *hoi polloi* I feel sure."

"For myself," breathed Mrs. Meredith, "I find the pub-crawling a little depressing. Beer seems to me to produce a remarkable dulling of the faculties. Frankly, I think it all a little coarse."

"Come, come," protested Bellairs, who had followed somewhat erratically on a purloined bicycle, "you are unjust. I hold a brief for all ale-suppers. In the first place, ale does not dull the faculties. True, it induces a peace, a paradisaical placidity, which, at first glance, might be mistaken for dullness. But actually ale is a great organiser of the faculties. To the febrile and overheated fancies it acts as a cooling balm. Personally, I find that a nice tankard of mild improves my intellectual functions to a marked degree. It quells the fruitless fevered coruscations of the mental energies, and directs one's thoughts along organised and profitable channels. Take English literature."

"Thank you," murmured Mrs. Meredith, "you are too kind."

"Take it," insisted Bellairs, "and consider it. Consider the real writers, the men of the grand manner, the hard thinkers and rotund versifiers. Consider the Bard and his minor satellites. Consider Kit Marlowe who was ' stabt in the back in a tavern and died cursing '. Ale-suppers, all, and men of literary genius. But, on the other hand, take Keats and Shelley and the Romantics, the wine-drinkers. Pretty, admittedly, but nothing more. Neat, if you like, natty even, not to mention elegant, but vain in the long run and futile.

'Fluttering their ineffectual wings in the luminous void in vain' as Matthew Arnold once remarked, approximately, that is. No, so far as the intellect is concerned, the ales have it." Bellairs disappeared suddenly into the hall.

"Nevertheless," insisted Mrs. Meredith, "I would sooner make love with a man who was drunk on Tokay than with a man who was drunk on beer."

"For me," began Mr. Phont pontifically, "it is not so much what is drunk in the tavern that pleases me as the general moral implications of the tavern itself. There is something about a nice niffy pub that sums up for the philosopher the whole of life, death and the hereafter. Permit me to elaborate. . . ."

"I should never dream of attempting to stop you," said Mrs. Meredith.

No wit abashed, Mr. Phont elaborated : "One's entry into a tavern is like one's entry into life. One moment one is not there. The next moment one is. Arrived, one bides one's little stay. Vaguely the scene enacts itself, finely unaware of the entry of a new soul. Pointlessly one carries out certain functions, little knowing why, caring less. Then at the end one passes out unnoticed into the dark. There is nothing like a tavern, I insist, for reminding one that one is, undeniably, native where one treads. For the philosopher the tavern is an unrivalled purge to false pride. If the tavern has performed no other function, it has at least proved beyond doubt that man is of the earth earthy and, not to put too fine a point upon it, of the beast beastly."

"I protest," said Mrs. Meredith. "Emphatically I protest. Speak for yourself if you like, but ' of the beast

beastly', no. As a child, I remember, I always shut my
mouth tight in Church when Hymns A. and M.
demanded of me that I should chattily inform Jehovah
that I was an earthworm."

" Blessed be the earthworm," boomed a hollow voice
from the hall, " for of such is the Kingdom of Heaven."
Unsteadily clutching a half-empty tankard, Bellairs
re-entered delicately across the threshold. Water
dripped from his long locks down onto his shoulders.
His nostrils were dilated and his eyes were slightly
glazed.

" Dear me," said Mrs. Meredith, " here is that
alarming young man again. I do wish he wouldn't
keep popping in and out in this surprising manner.
Most persistent. And I hope he won't be sick all over
the Aubusson carpet . . . And he's got some more
beer from somewhere. . . ."

" Beer ? Ale ? " cried Bellairs. " Beer the balm for
the kidneys. Ale the best purgative. Flushes the
lights and enlivens the liver. Promotes smooth and
regular functions. In all cases of stone, gravel and
internal congestion fly to the malted hop."

" Quite," said Mr. Phont, " quite, my dear boy, but
not too medical I beg of you."

" We may be a liberal establishment, in the words of
the seaside boarding houses," protested Mrs. Meredith,
" but we are not a chemist's dispensary."

" But what," asked Bellairs, " is one to talk about if
not one's guts ? One's philosophy is too dull, one's
loves too obscene. Guts for snappy back-chat every
time."

" Too true, too true," mused Mr. Phont. " It is a
lamentable fact, when one comes to reflect upon it, that

what little conversational talent exists to-day is directed almost solely along medical lines. We are all cheerful hypochondriacs. Religion, philosophy, science, literature, music and the fine arts yield to the Home Doctor. We are all Harley Street specialists. We are far more familiar with our own internals than with our own souls. Across the most *recherché* dinner tables in Mayfair, wherever that ultimate paradise may be, the epigram has ceased to wing its barbed flight. The tossing of the conversational ball has yielded to the probing of the surgical scalpel. Over a glass of sweet sauterne one can learn more of a débutante's major bowel in five minutes than one can learn of her religious learnings in five hours."

"Quite likely I should think," said Julian, "because whilst most young women have a major bowel, few, I imagine, possess a New Testament."

"And the detail," protested Mr. Phont, "the astonishing, the overwhelming detail. The things I have had to listen to over roast pheasant. At a single dinner-party, I have followed from the anæsthetist to the convalescent chair an appendix, a duodenal ulcer, a set of tonsils and a birth of triplets. Even a tracheotomy, I am told, is followed with lively and expert interest at the dinner tables of the younger set."

Mrs. Meredith put some records on the radiogram and set the machine in motion. Mellowly and boomingly the negroid jazz filled the room. The piano, guitars and plucked string-bass built up a heavy, insistent background upon which the sweet saxophones and an astringent trumpet wove extravagant designs of melody.

"I fear," said Mrs. Meredith to Mr. Phont, "that

this may offend you a little. Your tastes are, one supposes, more Mozartian than Ellingtonian."

"Not at all, dear lady, not at all. I am a great admirer of the negroid compositions provided they are admitted to be what they are. It is an elementary fallacy to judge jazz by academic musical standards. It is, in fact, a mistake of the first order to judge jazz as music at all. Jazz is not music ; it is the best aphrodisiac. Its appeal is purely physical. It makes no appeal to the intellect as do the classical compositions. Its appeal, I repeat, is purely physical, like a cocktail. Its function is to elate the nervous system and to whip up the baser passions, particularly the sexual passion. Not, perhaps, a very laudable function, but when a thing performs its function adequately, whatever that function may be, one must accord it some degree of respect. And of course the virtuosity of the exponents is amazing. The feats of Armstrong, of Ellington, of Fletcher Henderson may not be of much ultimate moral worth, but at least they are feats which no one else can perform, and the expert is worthy of his hire."

"Negroid jazz," said Bellairs, rolling off the sofa, "is the perfect expression of the inexpressible. It is the voice of the stars of the morning singing together, it is the psalms for Modern Life."

"A little difficult to follow," said Mr. Phont deferentially, "but I have no doubt there is a great deal in what you say."

"I am the prophet of the Lord," remarked Bellairs with satisfaction, and thereupon fell asleep.

"Dear me," said Mrs. Meredith, "that surprising young man. I'm sure he's an unfrocked congregationalist. But talking about jazz, I must say that it is the utter pointlessness of it all that appeals to me. So much like the exquisite fatuity of one's own existence, don't you think ? One blows, one plucks, one booms, one bangs, figuratively speaking of course, and it all amounts to nothing, precisely to glorious nothing, elegant nil."

" I think," said Julian, " we are getting far too philosophic, too maudlinly Sunday-schoolish. Let's dance."

He placed an arm about the fragile Mrs. Meredith and they stepped. For a while Mr. Phont watched them as they swayed and turned and glided in precise yet efflorescent arabesques across the carpet.

" Dancing," he lamented, " is not what it was. Modern dancing is, at its worst, just a disorganised prowling ; at its best nothing more than a fine art. But in the old days it was a strenuous field sport. Ah, those were the days. Strauss and champagne, bosoms and dundrearies. Ballrooms in those days were not so much ballrooms as battlefields. What bumping and boring, what spinning and sweating, what prodigious changings of collars and fannings of busts. And the charming hypocrisy of it all. Consciously or un-consciously, under a veneer of elaborate conventions, the Victorian virgin whirled away her evenings in an ecstasy of calculated sensuality. Consider the thorough-ness of the aphrodisiac. Intoxicating waltz-time, sweet champagne, heady perfumes, voluptuous curves, gilt chairs and red-plush bottoms, chair bottoms I mean, of course. Life, I insist, was in those days indubitably livable. And so simple, too. Values were definite, gambits recognizable. Why, even in my young days, one could reliably assess a woman's accessibility by the cut of her corsage."

The dancers came to rest.   Mrs. Meredith sank into a chair.

" A charming vision, but strenuous.   Personally I prefer disorganisedly to prowl to abandonedly whirling. And I don't know about the clarity of values.   I believe, in those days, if one danced three times during an evening with one man, one was his fiancée, and after four times one was his mistress.   Disconcerting, I call it."

" Not disconcerting, diverting," said Mr. Phont.

" Oh mistress mine," roared Bellairs, suddenly sitting up, " where art thou roaming ?   Oh, stay and hear thy true love's coming that doth sing both sharp and flat. . . ."

" Dear me," said Mrs. Meredith, " I'm positive he's going to be sick, and I've only just had the carpet cleaned. . . ."

" By God, woman, you're right," cried Bellairs.   He disappeared into the night.

7

The Grand Theatrical Scandal

THE ROTTEN BOROUGH WAS agog, for not only was it the night of the Distinguished Amateur theatricals in aid of the new lunatic asylum, but it was also the eve of the publication of the first issue of the *Weekly Probe*.

The public had got wind of the fact that the two events were in some way mysteriously linked, and the burgesses felt great events were impending.

Mr. Phont and Julian were dining with Mrs. Meredith before going on to the show. Bellairs had been invited but had failed to turn up.

In Mrs. Meredith's gold and old rose drawing-room the post-dinner liqueurs were circulating.

Mr. Phont rolled his cointreau round his tongue : " I think we should do well to arrive in good time, Barbara. I am particularly anxious for Julian to enjoy to the full the spectacle of the local aristocracy showing off in front of the common people."

Mr. Phont turned towards Julian who was idly playing the compositions of Gershwin on the long, white Bluthner.

" It is an interesting fact that the two extremes in the social scale, the aristocracy and the working class, should have so much in common. They behave almost identically. Perhaps it is because they are equally unintelligent and uneducated. Both are completely governed by the mob instinct. Both find the summit of bliss in going about in droves to the same old places to do the same old things. Above all, both detest individualism and original thought ; in fact, the duke and the navvy are heartily at one in refusing to think at all."

Mr. Phont finished his cointreau and warmed to his subject. "The only difference between Lord Wycherley and my gardener is the difference of environment. Wycherley's life consists of the hunting field, the moors, Lords, Ascot, Cowes, Deauville, claret and the *Times*. My gardener's existence centres round the football field, the 'Five Bells', darts, Blackpool, beer and the *Daily Express*. There is, you see, no real difference at all. And, as I say, both are heartily in agreement in making it damned hot for anyone who presumes to break away from the herd and act or think for himself."

Mr. Phont lighted a cigar and continued : " Furthermore I have discovered that there are strong resemblances in social behaviour. With both the aristocracy and the working class, getting drunk and mild adultery are considered the two best parlour games. At one end you get gin and co-respondents, and at the other beer and that elusive personality known as ' the lodger '.

"I was talking on this matter yesterday to my housekeeper—a very interesting woman, I may add ; the mother of ten children all with septic tonsils. Really, I am beginning to take an almost fatherly interest in the tonsils of Mrs. Beeton's offspring. From her I learn that the social lives of the exalted and the lowly are marked by the same petty squabbles and insidious back-bitings ; the same subtle snobberies and, above all, the same conversational talents. Sport with the men, diseases with the women. In fact I recently had a conversation with Mrs. Beeton upon what she so revoltingly calls her ' bad legs ' that resembled in every way a recent lecture I attended by Mrs. Congreve on the irregularities of her kidneys."

" It's all due to inbreeding," said Mrs. Meredith. " At one end you get blue blood, at the other the red flag."

Julian, who was now studying a programme of the forthcoming entertainment, interrupted the discussion :

" Can these people act ? I refer to Lady Wycherley and her cast of Distinguished Amateurs."

" They don't act. They merely behave," said Mrs. Meredith succinctly. " However, nobody minds. The Distinguished Amateurs have an excuse for buying lots of new clothes and the satisfaction of getting their photographs all over the illustrated weeklies. On the other hand the burgesses are only too willing to pay their money to gape at the local aristocracy at close quarters."

At this point the telephone bell rang and Mrs. Meredith answered it. A prolonged and involved conversation seemed to be going forward. At length Mrs. Meredith returned.

" That was Bellairs. He couldn't come to dinner as he's been helping Gripps to bill the town. Who is Gripps ? "

" A marvellous man," said Mr. Phont. " He's our publisher. He's reduced publicity to a fine art. Besides he'll be a very useful man to have about the office when deputations of indignant burgesses begin laying siege."

"And Bellairs said," continued Mrs. Meredith, insinuating herself snakily into a flame coloured cloak, "that he's just thought of a marvellous idea. He wouldn't say what it was, but he guarantees uproar before the evening is out."

Mr. Phont joyfully rubbed his hands : "What a lad ! What a treasure the boy is ! Trust him to do something epic."

Mrs. Meredith was reluctant to get her own car out, so, it was agreed that all three should pack into ' Bloody Mary '. Mrs. Meredith sat with Julian in the cockpit, and Mr. Phont perched himself perilously on the tail with his legs hanging down inside. With his hat crushed down over one ear, and his black, scarlet lined cloak flowing in the breeze, he presented the appearance of a beneficent and middle-aged Mephistopheles.

Dusk was falling as they roared down into the borough. The pavements were thronged with burgesses all making for the theatre, and Mr. Phont's progress partook of the nature of a triumph. As he flashed by on his insecure perch he saluted all and sundry with view-halloos and sweeping gestures of his opera hat. Indeed, so uproariously genial did Mr. Phont become when they were rounding the corner by the post office, that he was only saved from being precipitated into the road by Mrs. Meredith who made a timely grab and caught him about the legs.

As they entered the more central parts of the town,

it was at once apparent that Bellairs and Gripps had
not been wasting their time. Every conceivable point
flared with red and yellow posters advertising the
imminent birth of the *Weekly Probe*.

Newsagents' placards, hoardings, blank walls, all
shrieked forth their message. And then, on St. John's
Green, they saw the culminating splash. Gripps, by
a mixture of cajolery and intimidation, had overcome
the Parks, Fairs and Lighting committee, with the
result that the whole of the front of the Town Hall was
plastered with bills. Posters fluttered gaily from every
tree on the green and, as a crowning touch of ironic
impudence, bills were attached to the railings outside
the offices of the *Chronicle and Gazetteer*. And every bill
bore the same device, ' The *Weekly Probe* for the
Naked Truth'. The words ' Probe ' and ' Naked '
were in extra large type and fairly assaulted the eye.

Julian slowed down the car and motored round the
green, the better to admire the display.

" Magnificent," said Mr. Phont, " positively
superb."

" Yes," said Julian, " and note the subtle emphasis
on the words ' Probe ' and ' Naked '. You see how
neatly they've secured the double appeal of mystery
and sex, two of the fundamentals of advertising. They
only need the medical note to make it complete. As
it is it's very good indeed. Think of the mental
associations. ' Probe ' immediately suggests murder,
financial scandals, corruption in official circles, dope
smuggling, white slaving, scandalous living in high
places and Heaven knows what else. Whilst the single
word ' Naked ' conjures up goodness knows what
visions of scandalous cabaret turns, brides in baths,

orgies in New York business men's flats and goings-on
of the worst kind on continental bathing beaches."

"Gad!" cried Mr. Phont ecstatically, "look at
that."

Julian and Mrs. Meredith followed the gesture and
gasped. From the top of the sky-piercing tower and
spire of the parish church an enormous red and yellow
pennant flapped idly in the evening breeze. "The
Weekly Probe for the Naked Truth."

"Jasper Skillington's work, I'll be bound," cried
Mr. Phont. "The man's a hero. I wonder what
the Bishop will have to say to that, not to mention
Salome and Gertrude Warbler. Really, I fear he may
have gone a little too far."

"You seem to forget," said Mrs. Meredith acidly,
"that you not only gave him ten guineas for his
article on the loony-bin theatricals, but you also
promised him a commission on sales."

"You have a nasty, subtle mind," said Mr. Phont,
a little dashed.

When they turned into the narrow street where the
theatre was situated they were faced with an almost-
solid phalanx of burgesses through the middle of which
the police had managed to clear a narrow passage.
Representatives of every class in the borough besieged
the box-offices in close-packed, milling queues, and
numbers of town toughs and idlers helped to swell the
congestion.

The sight of Mr. Phont, perched on the tail of
'Bloody Mary', produced an uproar of whistles,
cat-calls, jeers, and cheers. Slowly the car nosed
through the crowd, and all the while Mr. Phont, still
in the rôle of a Roman General acknowledging a

triumph, bowed from side to side and lifted his hat in
noble gestures.

At length Julian managed to manœuvre the car to
the edge of the pavement, and they alighted. When
they did so, part of the cause of the sensation they were
creating became apparent. On either side of the
pointed tail of ' Bloody Mary ' was pasted a flaming
Weekly Probe bill. Bellairs had indeed been busy.

Mr. Phont took in the situation in a single glance,
and as rapidly turned it to advantage. Standing
up in the driving seat, and flinging back his scarlet
lined cloak with a superb gesture, he began to harangue
the crowd :

" Brother burgesses, behold the writing on the
wall ! The moving finger writes, and having writ,
it is for you to take its words to heart. Act upon its
advice. Buy the *Weekly Probe*. Don't fail to secure
your copy of the first epoch-making edition at once.
Don't delay, and so avoid disappointment. Lodge
an immediate order with your newsagent to-night.
Whatever you do, don't miss to-morrow's issue of the
Probe. It contains extraordinary stories, staggering
disclosures, astounding revelations. The *Probe* stands
for the naked truth. Buy the *Probe* and learn the
scandalous secrets of your local civic life. Get the
inside dope on municipal intrigue and the shameful
secrets of the private lives of your borough worthies.
For sport and scandal buy the *Probe*, I have said."

Amidst cheers and uproar Mr. Phont descended
with dignity from his pulpit and ushered his companions into the theatre. But there was yet one more
gesture to make.

Turning in the doorway, Mr. Phont, with the air

of a Lorenzo de Medici, scattered a handful of small change amongst the clamouring loafers.   Then he was lost to sight.

The entry of Mr. Phont, Julian and Mrs. Meredith into their box caused a considerable stir in the building. In the pit and circle there was much twisting in seats and craning of necks, whilst in the stalls opera-glasses were levelled and a buzz of comment arose.

Julian took the opportunity of surveying the theatre which was already packed to overflowing though the curtain was not due to rise for another quarter of an hour.

It was quite a large building, decorated in an alarming shade of pale green, with elaborate gilt decorations and panel-paintings of Italian pastoral scenes on the walls.   Busts of the Muses stared down superciliously upon the audience at various points. There was one balcony.

Julian next directed his gaze upon the audience. In the first few rows of stalls sat the hunting people who had turned out in force to support Lady Wycherley and her cast of Distinguished Amateurs.

Julian was particularly fascinated by the older specimens. Tall, bony old boys with grizzled moustaches, weather-beaten skins, hooked noses and glazed eyes sat beside their even bonier and hard-bitten wives whose complexions resembled masks of dried orange peel.   Periodically they roared some remark at one another whereupon the whole covey burst into peals of baying laughter.

The younger ones Julian found far more pre-possessing.   The young men were all cast in exactly the same mould—tall, lean, broad-shouldered, cavalrymoustached, slightly bow-legged. The girls were exquisitely trim, and their delicate, rose-petal complexions and fragile looking arms made it hard to believe that they spent four days a week in the saddle. This fact, however, was amply attested on closer examination, by the marked widening of their hips, amounting in some instances almost to a deformity.

The comeliness of the young men and women alike was spoilt, however, by the complete and utter vacancy of their expressions. They seemed sunk in an abysmal swamp of boredom, the surface of which was only occasionally stirred by a few bubbles of forced and mirthless laughter, or an interchange of shouted conversation consisting largely of remarks about horses and ' what.'

Mr. Phont observed Julian's absorption and joined him at the front of the box. Levelling his glasses on the people beneath, he offered a few remarks :

" A fascinating crowd, my dear Julian. And have you noticed how they respond to environment ? The fox-hunting life breeds the fox-hunting appearance. Those fearsome old women down there, for instance, after forty or fifty years of following the hounds begin to look exactly like hounds themselves. Note the heavy jowls and drooping eyes. Why, they're exact replicas of the Vale bitch pack. And consider the old boys down there with whiskers and heads of pure bone. Don't they remind you irresistibly of a lot of cunning old dog-foxes ? It's most remarkable. A most interesting scientific paper could be written on it. Wait until you see Captain Polo. He's the very image of a slinky young vixen."

" I rather like the look of the young ones, though," said Julian.

" Yes," agreed Mr. Phont. " They're certainly a well-bred clean-looking lot. Quite charming, too, in their way. As individuals, that is. As a crowd they're beyond words. They have the irresistible charm of utter uselessness. How they must have delighted Oscar Wilde. Let me see, what was his inimitable *mot* on the fox-hunter ? ' The unspeakable in pursuit of the uneatable ', wasn't it ? A little cruel, perhaps, but very apt."

" Yes," mused Mrs. Meredith, joining them at the front of the box and deeply inhaling a long cigarette, " the charm of utter uselessness and the beauty of utter brainlessness."

" You're very bitter to-night, Barbara," remonstrated Mr. Phont. " I must say I'm very much attached to these young Dianas. Of course one deplores the flat bosoms and widened hips, but there is something about their exquisitely bred appearance, their fastidious cleanliness, their look of cold virginity and their utter unawareness of the world at large that I find infinitely tantalising. Indeed I can fully sympathise with an old friend of mine who once confessed that the sight of a bevy of young hunting beauties turned him into a nymphomaniac on the spot."

But Mr. Phont had now tired of the aristocracy, and was directing Julian's attention to other parts of the theatre.

Under his expert guidance Julian examined the professional class who were ensconced in the stalls immediately behind the aristocracy.

" Observe them," urged Mr. Phont. " Note the

agonised attempts they make to appear at ease and unaware of their exalted neighbours. Look at Doctor and Mrs. Ventricle down there with Colonel Barley and young Gavelkind, the solicitor, and his wife. Observe the fixed smiles, the gallant efforts at casual conversation and the determined attempts to appear unimpressed by the Farquhar crowd next door. If only they permitted themselves to follow their inclinations they would allow their jaws to drop and their ears to wag. As it is they go through agonies of pretence in their attempts to seem at home in Zion."

" Now the bourgeoisie up there in the circle," went on Mr. Phont, " behave more sensibly."

Borrowing the glasses, Julian scanned the ranks of shopkeepers and borough officials ranged in rotund and bosomy tiers in the circle. For these people, for the bourgeoisie, the spectacle of the aristocracy at close quarters was obviously like a draught of sweet champagne. The men, seeming somewhat congested in creaking boiled shirts and very new looking dinner coats puffed a little defiantly at their cigars. Their stringy or bosomy spouses, in satins and sequins, chattered eagerly amongst themselves staring frankly, and, indeed, even permitting themselves an occasional lady-like gesture towards the blue-blood in the orchestra stalls, their faces meanwhile wreathed in smug and slightly fatuous smiles.

" Can't you imagine the conversation up there ? " suggested Mr. Phont. " The ladies (always ladies, by the way, not women) estimating the cost of the dresses, whilst their worthy husbands exchange risqué remarks about the private lives of the local big-wigs, and comfortably reflect that pass-book for pass-book they are quite as good men as Lord Wycherley or Major Cockerell, the M.F.H."

"Give me the common people in the pit every time," said Mrs. Meredith.

"You may have them most certainly," said Mr. Phont, "but undoubtedly their behaviour seems the most reasonable."

Scanning the pit, Julian felt the conclusion was just. The working class was plainly not impressed, but merely curious. They had paid for an evening's entertainment and were manifestly going to have it. The women chattered amongst themselves, commenting upon all that went forward and clucking with well-assumed disapproval when they were deliciously scandalised by some particularly glaring make-up or unusually low cut dress. Their companions, retaining one and all their cloth caps and battered trilbies, stolidly chewed sweets, stoically sucked their woodbines or buried themselves apathetically in the racing pages of the evening papers. Theirs was a strictly business-like attitude. They had come to see a play and they waited for it to begin. Occasionally there was a burst of hoarse laughter supplemented by cat-calls and whistles from the more frolicsome youths who had observed the admirable precaution of taking a few pints on board to speed the evening along. Mr. Phont, meanwhile, as the stalls filled up, was picking out some of the celebrities. "We've got a very pretty little company here to-night. One might describe it as the borough and district in miniature. There's old Cockerell the M.F.H., and his wife with the Farquhars. And I see Captain Polo below us with the Rev. Percy Bedrock of Little Pittle. Really Bedrock will suffer from a rush of aristocracy to the head if he isn't careful. So bad for the arteries, these aristocratic parishes."

" Yes, they're all here," said Mrs. Meredith. " I can see the Warblers in lace and corsets with the Barleys and the young Gavelkinds. Now they've been joined by the old Gavelkinds. Really the old man begins to look more and more like a welching bookie every day. And there are the Ventricles, dear Enid looking more earnest and inhibited than ever."

" And the doctor looking more like an absconding bank manager than ever," supplemented Mr. Phont. " But stay, what's Mrs. Congreve up to ? "

Julian saw a considerable uproar going forward in the stalls. Gradually it became apparent that Mrs. Congreve was trying to climb over a row of seats to join the Farquhars behind her.

Mrs. Congreve was disclosed as a rather blowsy matron of ponderous and all too uncorseted build, with peroxide locks and a flushed and sagging countenance. Climbing perilously over the seats, she poised herself for one breathless moment on the plush and iron. Then she alighted with a thud in the aisle, remarking loudly to the now silent and entranced theatre, the single word ' God '.

" The silly old woman," said Mrs. Meredith with feeling, " she ought to know better at her age."

" They never know better, my dear," said Mr. Phont patiently. " They must attract attention at any price. It's the vice of life to them. But note the superb skill of her performance. Observe how she held it until she had all eyes and all ears fixed upon her. Very fine indeed."

" Well," said Mrs. Meredith, " it's a pity she can't do

it in some other way than imitating a jelly all over the place. Besides it's most unwise to go in for acrobatics on a diet of gin and cocaine."

" Who are the programme sellers ? " enquired Julian who had his eye fixed on four comely young women assiduously parading up and down the central aisle. As they paraded, they chatted animatedly together, apparently superbly unaware of the presence of anyone else in the universe, but taking obvious pains none-the-less that they and their toilettes should be well viewed by all and sundry. Occasionally, when they felt equal to it, they bestowed a programme upon some timorous purchaser with an air of weary condescension, and inevitably showed themselves becomingly incompetent at giving the correct change.

" The two fluffy little blondes," explained Mrs. Meredith, " are the Bott twins. Soap. They've just made the grade, I believe. Dined with the Wycherleys last week. Hence the air of general well-being."

" I rather like the two brunettes," said Julian. " Particularly the tall, tortured looking one with the least on."

" Ah ! " said Mr. Phont, " you mean Myra Malcolm. The best undressed girl in the neighbourhood I always say. I think she's too fascinatingly Dostoievskian for words. A tangled skein of perversions and inhibitions. The saucy little thing with her is Puggy Congreve. Beautifully bastioned, isn't she ? And she has a charmingly commercial turn of mind. Makes a positive fortune out of posing for Cuplift brassière advertisements. She's trying to get on the films. Like so many of the aristocracy nowadays . . . beating about Shepherds Bush."

" And now," said Mrs. Meredith expiringly, " we really are complete. Here's the local Member of Parliament and his spouse."

Julian saw a huge, purple-faced man bearing down the aisle, accompanied by a tall, much be-lipsticked woman with an unusually elongated neck and quantities of diamonds. They were greeted by a polite round of applause.

" All hail to politics," cried Mr. Phont, leaning out of the box and clapping heartily. " Sir Bertram and Lady Buckle, forsooth. Whiffs of Westminster. I wonder how much that complexion costs him in port. Or is it brandy, I wonder ? "

" Lady Buckle's neck," remarked Mrs. Meredith faintly, " is described in the gossip columns as swan-like. Personally, I think she looks more like a hen about to lay an egg. However, she has enterprise. She nearly lost her husband his seat at the last election through allowing her photograph to appear in the local papers advertising a bathroom disinfectant."

" Even the mighty are human in bathrooms," protested Mr. Phont genially.

By this time the hour for the spectacle was close at hand. The orchestra, in which the strings and brass seemed somewhat at variance rhythmically, was working away industriously at the all too inevitable William Tell overture. The stalls had ceased to bay and were intently turning over the pages of pro-grammes. Up in the circle the bourgeoisie were comfortably opening boxes of chocolates and preparing to be deliciously shocked. In the pit the atmosphere thickened and intensified.

Mr. Phont swept the house for the last time with

his glasses. " We seem to be practically packed out
to-night. There are still three vacant seats in the
front row of the stalls, though. I wonder who they
are for. And do you notice the aisle seats in the pit
are all reserved ? Something funny about that."

The mystery of the reserved pit seats was almost
immediately solved. There was uproar at the doors,
and Bellairs entered, followed by a mass of urchins,
clamouring and creating a disturbance of the first
order.

" Good Heavens," said Mrs. Meredith, " what's
Bellairs up to ? Has he brought his family along ? "

Bellairs, attired in a yellow polo sweater and ancient
grey flannels, was engaged in sorting out his infants
and installing them in the aisle seats in the pit. With
the air of a commander-in-chief disposing his forces
for battle, he strode hither and thither, exhorting,
protesting and waving his arms about with florid
gestures. At intervals he shouted and waved to various
disreputable acquaintances.

" What a remarkable range of acquaintances Bellairs
has," mused Mrs. Meredith. " I walked down the
High Street with him the other day. It was like a
royal progress. Every few yards we stopped to talk
to everyone from Major Cockerell to the landlady of
the Railway Tavern. And now, look, he's dispensing
largesse."

This was indeed the case. Having at length settled
his urchins in their seats, Bellairs was distributing
oranges from an enormous brown paper bag. This
completed, he bestowed a final word of advice upon the
lads, tossed a careless quip at Puggy Congreve and
then made his way towards Mr. Phont's box.

Panting slightly from his exertions, Bellairs burst into the box : " Sink me ! I've been labouring all day in the vineyard of the Lord. Sorry I couldn't get in to dinner, Barbara, but I had a brilliant idea at the last minute and was fain to prosecute it. Jerusalem is a trenched city. It is digged about with a pit."

Snatching up the glasses, Bellairs, swept the circle : " Yes, they're all up there, I see. The devil's triplets, the Mayor, Alderman Twidale and Councillor Nurture. There they are, supported I see by Councillor Cammack, not to mention the whole Board of Commerce and the Town Advertisement Committee. Figures of canonised ineptitude, portraits of beatified senility. The children of darkness are wiser in their generation than the children of light, sink me if they aren't. But we'll rouse them to-night, by Gad. We'll have at them and at the seed of their loins from one generation to another."

" Come, come, not too biological please, Gilbert," protested Mr. Phont.

Bellairs replied by whipping a brandy flask from his hip pocket and taking a lengthy pull.

" What are all the little boys for ? " enquired Mrs. Meredith. " We're so fascinated."

Bellairs assumed a mysterious expression : " Ah ! That's a secret. Wait and see. It's my great idea. We'll have some fun before the evening's out."

" We're going to have some now," said Mr. Phont. " Here are Esmond and his football professional."

Such, indeed, was the case. Slowly sauntering down the aisle, gazing beneficently from side to side, came Esmond Duncan, attired in exquisite evening dress and

an enormous teddy bear coat.   Shambling beside him,
like a tame and bewildered gorilla, came the red-haired
football professional.

Smiling genially, nodding first here and then there,
languidly flicking a long white hand first in this
direction, now in that, Esmond pursued his leisurely
course amidst a crossfire of amazed and indignant
comment.   At length he reached the front row of the
stalls and, after depositing the footballer in one of the
three reserved seats, slowly began to remove his
overcoat.

Whilst doing this, he turned his back on the orchestra
and surveyed the house from roof to floor for several
moments.   Suddenly he caught sight of Mrs. Meredith
and, at the same moment, the orchestra came to a
halt.

In the interval of complete silence Esmond's voice
floated up with a weary and languid distinctness :

"A lot of people here to-night, of one sort or
another."

Then, very elegantly, Esmond shot his cuffs and
delicately lowered himself into his seat.   But his
performance was not yet complete.   Finding his coat
a nuisance, he arose once more, and, with the coat
suspended from one forefinger, he swayed again up
the aisle to the cloakroom, acknowledging with a
courtly bow the cries of ' sit down ', and ' cissy-boy ',
and ' pansy ' from the toughs in the pit.

"Marvellous," said Mr. Phont.   "Magnificent
performance. Such   grace,   such   geniality,   such
benevolent contempt for the assembled burgesses."

When Esmond had at last settled himself, there
remained but one seat unoccupied in the whole

theatre, and that on the centre aisle on the front row of stalls.

" I wonder who that seat is for," said Mr. Phont excitedly.

Almost at once his wish was gratified. There was a sound of heavy footsteps, and pounding down the aisle came the Rev. Jasper Skillington. It was plain his blood was up. His lock of hair bounced militantly up and down, his eczemic face was flushed, and from beneath his beetling brows he shot forth glances of vitriolic wrath. He wore an incredibly ancient clerical dress suit of a rough, hairy material, and its greenness was apparent even in the subdued light.

" Hail to the prophet of the Lord ! " cried Bellairs delightedly. " Vials of wrath, bags of brimstone, sacks of sulphur. The Lord will deliver his own. Hell, death and damnation ! The day of Judgment is at hand."

Upon reaching his seat, the Rev. Jasper Skillington paused and swept the house with his terrible glance. His hands clasped and unclasped convulsively. His mouth worked as if he were about to give tongue and call down fire and brimstone, not to mention a legion or two of avenging angels, upon the populace. He directed his flashing gaze from plucked eyebrows to carmined lips ; from tinted finger-nails to plump young bosoms, from naked backs to port-winey countenances. And one and all winced and flushed beneath his horrific condemnation. Then, flinging himself into his seat, he pressed his hands to his face and assumed an attitude of prayer.

" Too thrilling, isn't he ? " said Mrs. Meredith. " To divinely patriarchal for words. And the silent prayer ! What a sense of the dramatic. Quite the Old Testament prophet surrounded by packs of tempting Jezebels."

" I have an idea," said Mr. Phont, " that friend Skillington is going to do something pretty desperate to-night. There's a promising look in his eye. A declaration of faith, perhaps, to the discomfiture of the heathen, or even a good round cursing of the citizens of the Plain."

At this point the orchestra worked up to the finale. The footlights flicked on. The fire curtain rose. All eyes were fixed upon the stage. The silence was complete. But there was yet one more sensation to come. Slowly Esmond Duncan rose in his seat and turned towards Mr. Phont's box.

" When," he asked in his penetrating if adenoidal voice, " is a loose woman not ? "

" What not what ? " cried Mrs. Meredith, leaning perilously out of the box. " Speak up. I can't hear."

" When is a loose woman not ? " repeated Esmond, delicately adjusting his white tie.

" I've no idea," cried Mrs. Meredith.

" When she's tight," said Esmond, and carefully resumed his seat.

Amidst the ensuing disturbance the curtain went up.

The " Well of Passions " rapidly showed itself to be a drama of a very melo kind. It concerned the unfortunate position of a lady of liberal views (Lady Wycherley) who, having made good and married into the peerage, is suddenly confronted with her past life in the shape of an Italian tenor of even more liberal outlook. However, the first act gave Lady Wycherley an opportunity of appearing in various natty costumes ranging from a swimming suit to a bridal gown, so that everyone was very well satisfied.

She was a tall, handsome brunette built on sumptuous lines, and spent most of the act pacing feverishly about the stage registering Mental Agony. In this she was ably supported by Mrs. Caddy, an incredibly thin ash-blonde, and by Mr. Raymond Bouncer, a nice looking, chestnut-haired boy, who went about registering Gentlemanliness.

"I rather like this modern style of acting," said Mr. Phont, "this taking the first two rows of the stalls into one's confidence and letting the rest of the house go hang. The modern play is so much more enjoyable without the text. And what economy it can lead to ! Why, if best came to best, one could just have the actors and no play at all."

"I wish," said Mrs. Meredith, "that Lady Wycherley's swimming suit wasn't so obviously elastic. If she wobbles much more bits will begin to drop off."

"I must say I like it," said Mr. Phont. "I may be old fashioned, but I like the pneumatic touch. One wonders when it's going to go off bang. I wonder if she blows herself up with a bicycle pump. A fascinating idea."

The act at length came to an end with Lady Wycherley and Mr. Bouncer locked in a passionate embrace. Unfortunately, owing to the evident good-will of Lady Wycherley, and the fact that she was at least three stone heavier than Mr. Bouncer, the embrace partook largely of the nature of an all-in wrestling bout.

The curtain descended amidst a storm of clapping,

whistles, cat-calls, and exclamations of shocked surprise.

When Mr. Phont and his party reached the bar it was packed so tight that one could scarcely move. The hunting crowd, collected about Major Cockerell and the purple faced mass of Sir Bertram Buckle, were becoming slightly uproarious under the influence of gin and whisky. Mrs. Congreve was taking cocaine out of a snuff box.

The representatives of the professional class were still making desperate conversation over dry Martinis, whilst the few male members of the bourgeoisie who had been bold enough to enter the bar, slapped one another on the back, poured back port and lemon, and periodically burst into hoarse peals of laughter to keep their courage up.

Mr. Phont conducted his party to the bar and equipped them all with tankards of mild ale. Julian observed with pleasure the incongruous sight of the exquisite Mrs. Meredith quaffing whole-heartedly from a pint pot and looking magnificently bored.

Bellairs wiped his mouth with the back of his hand and turned to Mr. Phont. "Lend me a quid, Ulric. I'm going to fill the Rev. Jasper with whisky. His resolution needs hardening."

Mr. Phont obliged and Bellairs promptly cornered the formidable priest, who was standing alone, scowling, in the middle of the press.

Suddenly, out of the congestion, the willowy figure of Esmond appeared, followed by the bewildered football professional. Esmond put him in a corner by himself with a glass of absinthe in each hand, and surveyed the throng :

" Most amusing evening, what ? My footballer

nearly went mad when Lady Wycherley appeared in the bathing suit. Most unfair on these full-blooded he-men, don't you think ? Too aphrodisiac for words. Really, I thought the lad was going to leap on to the stage and do her a mischief forthwith. And how attractively she quivered ! Too alarmingly jelly-fish for anything."

Esmond paused, and then indicated a small red-haired man sitting on a high stool beside the bar. His head was sunk in his hands, and he miserably contemplated a bottle of brandy that he was methodically emptying. It was obvious that he had been there for a very long time.

" Look," exhorted Esmond, " at the unfortunate Wycherley. I understand he spends the whole evening in the bar on these occasions. Positively can't bear to see his wife being mauled about by young Bouncer. Indeed I hear that during the rehearsals he was so delightfully old-world as to challenge Bouncer to a duel. Called him out in the grand manner on the ground that his stage kisses were altogether too illegitimate."

" And did they run one another through ? " asked Mr. Phont. " Did they spit one another like capons and gallic cocks and what not ? "

" No, my dear, far from it. She sent him to bed and forbade the servants to send up any dinner. However, I believe he climbed down the drain pipe and took refuge with the Rev. Percy Bedrock."

" Well I must say I sympathise with Lady Wycherley," said Mrs. Meredith. " These uxorious spouses. Too trying by half."

" Well you can't grumble so long as they try, can you ? " said Mr. Phont.

" Just look at Bellairs and the priest," said Mrs. Meredith. " There's something on foot, I swear."

Indeed it looked like it. Bellairs was orating and stabbing at the Rev. Jasper with a prodding forefinger, whilst the priest was tossing back whiskies, becoming redder and redder in the face, nodding in fierce agreement, and pounding the bar with clenched fists.

Mr. Phont finished his beer and took Julian by the arm : " Come along, my boy. We'll make a little tour and be as rude to everyone as we can."

" Never turn your back on a Greek," counselled Esmond by way of a parting shot.

The first person Mr. Phont and Julian encountered was the Rev. Percy Bedrock, a tall, thin man with a permanent grin, a facetious wit and markedly bowed legs.

" Ha ! Bedrock," said Mr. Phont, " I want you to meet my nephew, Ansell. The playwright, you know."

Julian bowed and the Rev. Bedrock grasped him warmly by the hand : " Welcome, welcome, my boy. I am always delighted to meet a brother literary man. Comrades in adversity is it not as it were. Ha ! ha ! Truly the literary calling is an arduous one. All kicks and no halfpence, as the saying goes. But in spite of the contumely and scorn of this world, we artists will receive our reward in the next. I am sure of it."

Julian raised questioning eyebrows at Mr. Phont. " Yes," explained Mr. Phont, " Bedrock here is a poet. But I must confess that much of his work is beyond me. I find it difficult to scan and often meaningless, but doubtless that is due to my own stupidity."

The Rev. Bedrock smiled benignly : " Come, come, Phont, you flatter me. I hardly aspire to the title poet ; a humble rhymester, a juggler with the magic of words, perhaps. But still, I do flatter myself that I succeed to some small extent, at any rate, in furthering the cause of Art in this Philistine world."

The parson turned to Julian : " Of course Phont here has not kept up with the modern movement. He still expects poetry to scan. He forgets that free verse is the modern poets' medium ; and naturally the compressed idiom and subtle implication I go in for do seem at first glance a little obscure. Of course communication without comprehension is what I aim at."

Julian nodded understandingly : " Yes, we artists are cruelly misjudged. And you have published much ? "

" Yes, indeed, I cover a wide field," said the Rev. Bedrock. " Perhaps you have seen my weekly verse commentary on the affairs of the town in the *Chronicle and Gazetteer*. I struck off a rather apt little ode last week on the bowls championship final. Then, of course, I write a monthly sonnet for the parochial magazine, whilst the Diocesan Budget is always eager for some trifle from my pen. Of course, I permit no major religious festival to pass without due commemoration."

" Yes," said Mr. Phont, " I always admired particularly your last ; ' Lyric for Lammastide ' wasn't it ? A work of some length," explained Mr.

Phont to Julian, "full of subtle conceits and purple patches. I particularly liked the pagan bits with all the wassailing and festive boards and what not. Dramatic, powerful stuff, and moral, too."

"Well, well," said the Rev. Bedrock, "I must just go and have a word with Captain Polo, a most interesting man, though perhaps not altogether spiritual."

"You must dine with us some time soon," said Mr. Phont.

"Delighted, I'm sure," said the Rev. Bedrock, fixing the unsuspecting Captain Polo with a beady eye, "but not this month, I fear. As you know, Mrs. Polo is expecting a happy event, and really I feel I must be on the spot. Parochial responsibilities, don't you know? In *loco parentis*, as it were."

At this point Mr. Phont and Julian were swept apart by the throng, and Julian found himself pressed against Puggy Congreve. She smiled at him very welcomingly as she half-heartedly tried to retrieve a slipping shoulder strap.

"Permit me," said Julian, and assisted in the readjustment. "I see you believe in putting both the goods in the shop window," he said.

"Well they're rather nice goods, don't you think?" asked Puggy, who was more than a little drunk. "And, I say, aren't you Ansell, the playwright? 'Worm i' the Root' and all that?"

"Yes," said Julian gallantly, "'Worm i' the Root, and now arrow in the heart. Would it surprise you very much if I told you I was passionately in love with you?"

"Not much," said Peggy. "You see I'm pretty

generally considered to be a very desirable freehold property."

Julian smiled mysteriously : " Or, perhaps, a fertile smallholding, chiefly plough-land suitable for oats."

Puggy gurgled deliciously : " Darling, you're too sweet. So smart and witty. Just like your play. Really we must see a lot of one another."

" I'm seeing a good deal of you already," said Julian, " but I must say I shouldn't mind seeing some more."

" Sobriety is the vice of life," said Puggy, eagerly grasping another gin-sling. " But seriously, we must fix something up. What about to-morrow morning ? Do you ride ? "

" It all depends on the time. Never after breakfast," said Julian.

Puggy at this was so consumed with mirth that she had to lean all over him.

" Come, young woman," said Julian, " you're drunk. What's more you're dribbling."

" You should take Horlicks," gasped Puggy. " That would put you right. And now here comes Myra Malcolm. Prepare to be harrowed."

" The three stages of man," murmured Julian. " The plough, the harrow and the rake."

Myra Malcolm surrounded them in a cloud of chypre, fixing Julian with a passionate eye, and speaking on four notes : " Ansell, my dear, I've been looking for you everywhere. That marvellous play of yours. Of course I can see through it all. I can see the bitter agony under the epigrams. And the Russian influence ; too bowel-piercing for anything. Tell me, who was it who wrecked your life ? Was it

a man or a woman ? But of course, don't tell me,
it was some beautiful golden haired boy. Your world
was changed because he was made of ivory and bronze,
the curves of his lips re-wrote your history."

Julian, who was by now considerably the better
for drink, leant over Myra and whispered huskily into
her ear. She recoiled : " You don't mean it ? Lovely
hands, of course. But rather old, surely ? "

" Never too late to bend," said Julian cheerfully.

Another movement of the throng swept Myra and
Puggy away from Julian, but he didn't mind.

Meanwhile Mr. Phont was making a little private
tour on his own. Presently he fetched up before the
Mayor who was talking to Councillors Nurture and
Cammack.

" Well, well," cried Mr. Phont, " three pillars of
local government, though it would be difficult to say
whether you are pillars within or buttresses without
or merely financial drains. Nurture, I trust you
haven't forgotten my timely warning about those
floodlights. And you, Mr. Mayor, that chain of office
looks rather shoddy to me. Are you sure you haven't
pawned the real one ? I notice you've got a very nice
new car. And I have heard the mayoral chain
described as the chain from which all blessings flow,
ha ! ha ! "

Mr. Phont turned finally to Councillor Cammack,
chairman of the Board of Commerce and business
manager of the *Chronicle and Gazetteer* :

" Ah ! and here's my business rival, Councillor
Cammack. Well, Cammack, I hope you're ready
for the fray. How do you like our publicity campaign ?
A tough fight and a dirty one, eh ? And may the

most unscrupulous side win. Well, well, take care
the Board of Commerce doesn't turn into the Board
of Guardians."

Mr. Phont stepped briskly on in search of further
prey.

Mrs. Meredith, meanwhile, was contending with
Major Cockerell :

" Well, Mrs. Meredith, we don't see much of you
nowadays. Perhaps we county people are too dull
for you ? "

Major Cockerell flexed his out-turned knees and
snorted comfortably down his Wellingtonian nose.

" To be perfectly candid," breathed Mrs. Meredith,
" you are."

Major Cockerell smiled indulgently. Indeed, when
faced with Mrs. Meredith's fragile loveliness, he found
it only all too easy to be indulgent. Self indulgent,
in fact.

" Well, dear lady, we may be dull, but at least
we're decent. I don't want to appear personal, but
people are talking."

" How clever of them," said Mrs. Meredith. " I
thought they only ejaculated round here."

" They are talking," resumed Major Cockerell,
upon whom subtle distinctions were lost, " about
your association with this feller Phont. Frankly, my
girl, I don't think your husband would like it . . ."

Major Cockerell sank his voice : " I know he's
got a pedigree a mile long and pots of money and all
that sort of thing, but I understand, between you and
me, that he entertains communist ideas. That young
devil Bellairs is hand in glove with him. Candidly I
think you would be well-advised to cut loose from

that crowd. And now I hear he's embarking on some wild cat scheme of a newspaper. If you're not careful, young woman, you'll be involved in some scandal or other."

Mrs. Meredith's eyelids drooped : " Really, Major, I assure you there's no need to whisper. It looks as if you were making indecent proposals or something. However, I assure you I'm in perfectly good company. It's very kind of the county to offer to take me under its wing, but frankly I would rather be bright and bad than dull and decent. And really what my husband's opinion has to do with you, I don't know. It has little enough to do with me in all conscience."

Major Cockerell reddened, and changed the subject : " Well, well, forgive me if I've rushed in, but I meant it all for the best. Now what I really wanted to do was to persuade you to hunt this season. Meet all the best people, you know. Besides, in these times, with these communist fellers all over the place, we people ought to stick together. Thank God, as long as fox-hunting lasts the Empire is safe. It's typical of all that's best in us. So long as the youngsters ride straight and hard we're all right. But what with these damned cocktails and night clubs and intellectual Socialist johnnies all over the place, you never know what may happen."

" Thanks for the invitation," said Mrs. Meredith, " but I'm frightened to death of horses. Besides, they smell."

Major Cockerell snorted : " Rubbish. And riding is a magnificent exercise. Capital for the kidneys."

" Possibly. But I always feel that the most perfectly functioning kidneys could never compensate for hips

like a flat-bottomed boat. And now, Major, you'd
better run along. I can see your wife's got her eye
on you, and you've already as good as told me I'm a
loose woman."

Thus summarily dismissed, the Major coughed,
flexed his knees once more, and padded away.

" And by the way," Mrs. Meredith cried after him,
" if you want to abuse me to your wife, please call me
a wanton hussy. I've always wondered what it felt
like to be one."

Julian was looking round for his party when he felt
himself seized by the arm and found himself confronted
by Miss Salome Warbler. She was drinking lemonade,
and her stays creaked.

She tuned up forthwith : " You're young Ansell,
aren't you ? "

" Yes, indeed," said Julian, hastily backing away
from Miss Warbler's impending bosom. " That's me.
Young in years but old in vice."

Miss Warbler shook him slightly : " You're drunk,
I fear. Your breath has a smell."

" Then I can't be well," returned Julian smartly.
" I must take Californian syrup of figs."

" I am determined to tell you," said Miss Warbler,
" how very much I disapprove of your play. There
are far too many of you smart, dirty-minded young
men about to-day. Your play I consider uncommonly
obscene."

" Thank you," said Julian suavely. " I take that
as no mean compliment. It is extremely difficult to
to be obscene uncommonly. The words are so
overworked."

" Every play, every work of art should point a noral," said Miss Warbler severely, fixing Julian with her basilisk look.

" Well, mine most certainly does," he protested.

" And what moral, I should like to know ? "

" Aha ! " answered Julian roguishly " the moral of immorality. And now, if you will excuse me, I will go and finish getting drunk. The second act will be starting at any moment, and I am still at least three whiskies away from Heaven."

With the second act the " Well of Passions " began to simmer and showed every promise of rapidly coming to the boil. The Italian tenor demonstrated himself an expert in vice-control and began to expose Lady Wycherley's past in a series of alarming cadenzas.

Lady Wycherley appeared successively in hunting-kit, dining pyjamas and a winter-sports outfit, whilst Mr. Bouncer went about looking harrowed.

As the act drew to its close, Bellairs, in Mr. Phont's box, began to show signs of suppressed excitement. Periodically he leant over the edge of the box and peered down anxiously into the stalls.

" I wonder," he muttered, " if I gave the old boy enough. A pity I didn't round those whiskies off with a dash of brandy. But still, I think he should be screwed to the sticking point."

" What on earth are you talking about ? " asked Mrs. Meredith. " I wish you wouldn't be so mysterious. So bad for the blood pressure."

But Bellairs was too deeply occupied in scanning the front stalls to reply.

The act finally worked to a climax with Lady

Wycherley forging a cheque in her husband's name
to close the mouth of the Italian tenor. The audience,
however, had the thrilling suspicion that, even if his
mouth were successfully closed, he would still talk
through his nose.

As Lady Wycherley flung her pen down with a
dramatic gesture, the act came to a close. The curtain
ran down and was immediately raised again as the
first stutters of applause began to break.

Lady Wycherley and Mr. Bouncer, together with
the Italian tenor, began to advance towards the
footlights.

Then, at the critical moment just before the clapping
broke into full spate, there was a hoarse roar from the
stalls and the Rev. Jasper Skillington leapt into the
central aisle and pointed a trembling finger at Lady
Wycherley.

His hair flapped vigorously about his ears, his eyes
flashed f..th sparks of fire, and in a thunderous voice
(rendered somewhat erratic by half-a-dozen whiskies)
he began to declaim :

" Out upon thee, thou painted Jezebel, thou wanton
baggage, thou canonised figure of profligacy ! The
hand of the Lord shall be stretched out against thee ;
he shall compass thee about with pitfall and with gin.
What then shall avail thee the painted face, the tired
head and the looking out at the window ! Verily thy
hour is at hand. Gird thy loins in sackcloth and ashes
and heap dung upon thy head ! For thou hast done
a shameful thing. Thou hast exposed thy body upon
the legitimate stage and thy nakedness to the man in
the street. With debauchery thou temptest the
innocent, with lewd words thou seducest the children

of the Lord from the paths of righteousness. Behold I, I Jasper Skillington, clerk in Holy Orders and twice a rural dean, shall call down upon thee flaming coals of fire. A murrain shall descend upon thee and thine. Boils and blains shall afflict thee. Thy marble baths shall run with blood and in thy most secret chambers shall frogs abound . . ."

By this time uproar had broken loose in the theatre. The audience was standing on the seats, clamouring in the aisles, and giving vent to a storm of cheers, hisses and exhortations.

Major Cockerell, supported by Colonel Barley and a mob of attendants, made a concerted rush at the Rev. Jasper Skillington and bore him, still shouting, to the ground. The rest of the stalls joined in, and a wild struggle ensued in the course of which the priest, aided by the power of the barley spirit, broke free and leapt into the orchestra pit, leaving his coat tails behind him in the grasp of Sir Bertram Buckle

Having thus won for himself a brief respite, the Rev. Jasper leapt on to the conductor's rostrum and fulminated once more :

" Woe unto thee thou devil's brood ! Thou hast laid hands upon the prophet of the Lord. Thou hast rent the seam of his garment. Thou hast kissed the lip of lechery and bathed in the sink of iniquity. But the wrath of the Lord is kindled against thee. The blasphemous mouths of thy menkind shall be stopped, and a whip of scorpions shall be laid unto the naked backs of thy womenkind. The brimstone pit . . ."

But here the formidable priest was fetched a shrewd blow over the pate with a saxophone, and he was lost to sight in a sea of heaving humanity.

All was jubilation in Mr. Phont's box as the uproar slowly subsided.

" Magnificent," said Mr. Phont, " what grip, manner and approach. What rotundity of style, what thundering periods. By Gad ! I've never heard anything like it. Talk about Hell and Gehenna ! "

" I hope," said Mrs. Meredith, " that clap over the ear wasn't too serious. Martyrdom would be taking it a bit too far."

Bellairs arose and bowed : " Alone I did it. At least with a bottle of whisky. Some story it'll make to-morrow morning. Thank Heaven it all went according to schedule."

" You cold-blooded monster," said Mrs. Meredith. Bellairs drained his hip flask and prepared to leave the box : " You mark my words, we haven't begun yet. Skillington's performance was only a curtain raiser. But, bless my soul, I must go and see my urchins. By the way, a word of warning. Whatever you do, don't leave this box during the last act."

Mr. Phont looked suspiciously after the departing Bellairs : " Now I wonder what that lad's up to. Surely he's not got something else up his sleeve."

" After this nothing can surprise me," said Mrs. Meredith. " By the way how charming it must be to have one's path set about with gins."

By this time the turmoil had largely subsided. After a delay of ten minutes, occasioned by a fit of hysterics on the part of Lady Wycherley, the curtain rose on the last act of the " Well of Passions."

As the situation became increasingly tense, the audience began to forget the episode of the Rev. Jasper

Skillington. The play slowly but surely began to re-establish its grip on the burgesses.

Eventually the dénouement arrived with Lady Wycherley confronted by an outraged Mr. Bouncer, a Mephistophelian Italian tenor and an inadequately forged cheque.

Suddenly Julian pointed down into the pit :

" Something's going to happen.   Look at Bellairs."

Down in the central aisle in the pit Bellairs stood surrounded by his urchins.   Then he raised his hand. With one accord his ragged satellites took aim and threw.

In the dim light Mr. Phont and his party saw what looked like innumerable little glass vials sailing through the air to fall with a faint tinkling amongst the packed audience.

For a moment nothing happened.   Then, slowly at first, but gaining in strength second by second, a most appalling stench, a most incredible niff, began to flood the theatre.

" By Gad ! " cried Mr. Phont, " stink bombs . . ."

Within a quarter of a minute the whole theatre was in a state of pandemonium.   Strong men, their handkerchiefs pressed to their faces, stampeded madly for the exits.   Women screamed, pushed helplessly hither and thither by the seething mob.   Noisome liquid trickled down collars and spread in sickening pools on starched shirt fronts and powdered backs. Seats were uprooted, coats parted company with shoulders and flimsy dresses were ripped to shreds.

Colonel Barley, heroic officer that he was, leapt on to the stage, crying in stentorian tones for order.   But his pleas fell on deaf ears.   The burgesses, who conceivably might have faced fire and water, were utterly demoralised by sulphuretted hydrogen.

Then Colonel Barley received a malodorous gift of his very own in the right ear. At the same moment the lights went out.

Some time later Mr. Phont and his party emerged staggering from the theatre.

In the street outside there was indescribable turmoil. Cars bucked and roared impotently in the heaving mass of burgesses. Several free fights had started, and police whistles filled the night with melody. To complete the confusion, a wild clanging of bells announced the arrival of the fire brigade.

Mr. Phont and Julian, with Mrs. Meredith sandwiched between them, fought their way to an isolated corner and pulled up for a breather.

Suddenly, out of the press, Bellairs appeared. His eyes flashed, his locks floated on the breeze, his jaw jutted :

" Well, and how did you like it ? You noticed how neatly I potted Barley from the wings ? Now we really have got a story. I've just nipped round to the office to get the machines going. We shall be on the streets by eight o'clock. Gad ! we shall absolutely clean up the borough. I'm running off five thousand to start with. By the way, Ulric, will you go and bail the priest out ? You won't have much trouble. He's putting the wind up the police with his cursing. And while you're at it, give me a fiver. I had to bribe a chocolate girl to show me where the light switches were." Bellairs was gone.

At three o'clock in the morning Mr. Phont, Julian

and Mrs. Meredith were fortifying themselves with black coffee and sandwiches at the Priory.

Mr. Phont gestured towards the recumbent figure of the Rev. Jasper Skillington. He lay, stertorously breathing through the fumes of the whisky, with a beef-steak bound upon a burgeoning lump upon his pate.

" And a happy time was had by all," remarked Mr. Phont.

8

Beans for the Burgesses

AT THE OFFICES OF THE
Weekly Probe the work, as Mr. Phont so aptly phrased
it in the Virgilian, glowed.

In the publisher's room Augustus Gripps, that
unrivalled director of affairs, sat grimly ensconced
behind a ponderous desk. He was attired in a flowing
overall, pencils protruded from his ears, and from
time to time he took up the telephone and issued
clipped monosyllabic commands. A perky young
office boy dashed in and out, whilst the red and yellow
Probe delivery van repeatedly skidded to a standstill
outside the door and dashed away again loaded with
fresh supplies of fodder for the sensation starved
appetites of the burgesses.

At ten o'clock work was still at fever-pitch. The
first five thousand copies were well-nigh exhausted
but continuously the telephone on the publisher's
desk trilled, bearing urgent demands from frenzied
newsagents for further supplies of the *Weekly Probe*.

At ten-thirty Augustus drained the last bottle of
beer from his private cellar behind the gas stove,
picked up the telephone and established contact with
the machine room. Presently a thudding and pulsing
shook the building ; another two thousand copies
were under way.

In the editorial department upstairs there was an

atmosphere of sober triumph. Mr. Phont and his followers were established in various attitudes in the reporters' room. Mr. Phont himself, wearing a flowered brocade dressing-gown over his evening clothes, stepped briskly about the floor, rubbing his hands and addressing words of encouragement to all and sundry.

"Never," he remarked as he splashed the soda into his brandy, "never have I felt myself so stimulated. Never have I apprehended such a glow about the vitals, such a sense, as the poet so nicely puts it, of something far more deeply interfused. Doubtless it is the spiritual exaltation consequent upon the successful undertaking of some great moral task. The soul is at one with the cosmos ; one acknowledges the universe. The borough," concluded Mr. Phont, " is roused, the burgesses are set by the ears, a notable commercial enterprise is launched. What more could one ask ? "

" Nothing except a Seidlitz powder," breathed Mrs. Meredith in a more than usually expiring voice, " and a steaming bath. I've got a head like a bucket and a throat like a doormat."

Mrs. Meredith, who was gloomily crouching over a primus stove in one corner making coffee, spoke not without reason. None of Mr. Phont's party had been to bed the previous night. After a hurried snack and a brief readjustment of clothing they had taken home the Rev. Jasper Skillington, put him to bed under Julian's care and had then proceeded straight to the office of the *Weekly Probe* where they had remained continuously, assisting at and applauding the birth of that precocious literary infant.

In the opposite corner to Mrs. Meredith, Bellairs, stripped to the waist, was trying to shave in front of a small cracked piece of mirror. With one hand he wielded the razor, in the other he held a large currant bun and in his less occupied moments he sang hymns or recited appropriate Biblical texts.

" Hair," he remarked as he tenderly negotiated the angle of his chin, " resembles the wicked man. It flourisheth like the green bay tree. On the other hand it resembles charity inasmuch as it flourisheth in the most unexpected places. Most inconsiderate I call it."

Turning towards the rest of the company Bellairs warmed to his subject. His eyes gleamed and glittered through swathes of soap and he gestured dangerously with his open cut-throat : " Consider, for instance, if you will be so kind, my manly chest. Manly ? Yes. Hirsute ? No. And yet by all the rules of the game, by all the affidavits of the female novelists, the manly trunk should carry a concomitant fungus. It is, I maintain, singularly exasperating. The broad, level surfaces, the rolling pampas of the human terrain remain uncropped, whereas the jutty cliffs, the hidden . . ."

" The coffee," interrupted Mrs. Meredith firmly, " is ready. And for Heaven's sake, Bellairs, put on your vest and stop looking like Father Christmas."

Bellairs compromised by draping a towel about his neck and assuming the general attitude of a high priest.

As they addressed themselves to the coffee and sandwiches, a thudding and trembling announced the restarting of the machines. Mr. Phont picked up the 'phone and conducted a rapid conversation :

"That you, Augustus? Two thousand more, indeed? Most gratifying. Capital, capital. The country agents clamouring for more, you say? Good, very good. And we've cleaned up the borough, you think? Excellent. What's that? Print ten thousand next week? Oh, rather! Twenty thousand if you like. Our message must reach every home. Our Mission Field is a wide one. Bread upon the waters, you know. He who reaps must sow, if you take me. The borough seething, you say? Ha! Ha! No more than I had expected. We've put the yeast into the unleavened bread so to speak. Well, good-bye, my lad. If you want a drink just send the boy up."

Mr. Phont turned to his companions: "An inestimable fellow, our Augustus, but stern. No fooling on the job. Destined I'm sure to become head of a correspondence school for young men intent on getting to the top, though precisely to the top of what I always hesitate to enquire. Augustus, I feel, has very definitely got that ' let me be your father ' personality."

"Rather a rash kind of personality I always think," murmured Mrs. Meredith. "After all there are so many opportunities."

"Augustus doesn't like you," said Bellairs suddenly, pointing a half-chewed banana sandwich at Mrs. Meredith. "You don't accord with his stern ideas of what the British Mother should be."

"But I'm not a mother," protested Mrs. Meredith. "At least not in so far as I am aware. I mean I never noticed it."

"That's the point," said Bellairs, nodding so vigorously that the drying soap fell in downy clouds from his face. " And furthermore he doesn't approve of the way you dress. He says," and here Bellairs indicated Mrs. Meredith's closely fitting sweater, " that you show your shapes too much. . . ."

Mrs. Meredith was overcome : " My dear, how marvellous ! At last the divine, the ultimate phrase. I show my shapes, I exhibit my shapes, I even demonstrate my shapes. . . ."

" Or more simply," suggested Mr. Phont, " you have your shapes."

" The gift of shapes," breathed Mrs. Meredith. " The gift of tongues, the gift of grace, the gift of faith, the gift of the Spirit. . . ." She leaned back in her chair, yawned, stretched luxuriously.

" Not to mention the free, or ocular gift, viewable at all times without obligation to purchase," said a voice from the doorway.

Julian, still in tails and looking haggard, stepped into the room.

Mr. Phont hastened to greet him : " Welcome, my boy. You're just in time for family prayers. And how is the man of God this morning ? His pate, more particularly ? The lump ; does it still continue to burgeon ? "

" The priest," said Julian sipping his coffee, " is rampant. All efforts to get him to sleep failed. In fact the housekeeper had to assist me to tie him to the bed with a clothes line. Apparently alcohol has a delayed action with him and that combined with the crack on the head has made him pretty savage."

" What," asked Mrs. Meredith peering closely at Julian's shirt front, " are those lewd designs on your chest ? Have you been to a reunion dinner or something ? "

Julian glanced down deprecatingly at some roughly executed designs on his front : " Well, to tell you the truth, I couldn't calm Jasper until I agreed to play noughts and crosses with him all over my shirt. I may say he cheated consistently."

" Of course if you say it's noughts and crosses," breathed Mrs. Meredith, " I won't argue with you."

" Well, if you insist," said Julian irritably, " I will confess that it isn't noughts and crosses. If you really want to know, it's a series of illustrations for the Song of Solomon."

Bellairs now applied himself to a scrutiny of Julian's shirt front : " And very fine, too. What strength and economy of line. What passionate directness of feeling. What a grand confession of the smothered libido of a parish priest."

" And, I may add," said Julian, " that he filled in the odd moments by solemnly excommunicating the Bishop."

" Up Skillington, down Bolitho," cried Mr. Phont. " If we don't get Jasper a bishopric by the time we've finished I shall consider our duty unfulfilled."

Julian drained his cup : " And by the way, it's about time we began to put ourselves in a state of siege. Unless I'm very much mistaken we shall shortly be called upon to endure the ordeal by burgess. I made a rapid tour of the borough before coming on here from the vicarage and there seems to be a good deal on foot."

" Aha ! " said Mr. Phont, " the hosts of Midian. They begin to prowl and prowl around."

" They do," agreed Julian. " I saw the Vestry Virgins sallying forth complete with hob-nails and ash-plants. Deacon, Twidale and Nurture were in conference with Cammack outside the Gazetteer, and unless I'm much mistaken Barley is at this very moment champing on the threshold."

Bellairs leapt to his feet and began to wave his arms about : " Alarums without ! Barricade the bastions, man the machicolations ! Despatch pursuivants to the wapentakes, heralds to the hundreds, sound the sackbuts in the sokes. Up with the drawbridge, down with the portcullis. A sortie, a retreat. A Bellairs, a Bellairs." He rushed violently from the room.

Mr. Phont calmly lighted a cigar : " So we've roused them, have we ? No more than I thought. Well, well. My only regret is that I wasn't present in the spirit to see the burgesses get their beans."

" A pill for every palate " was the editorial motto of the *Weekly Probe*. The first issue definitely corroborated the slogan.

At the Grange the Misses Warbler were in the process of being armed for the assault. The Warbler blood was up. The spirit that had urged earlier Warblers to wrest iron from the reluctant earth was kindled afresh in the ample bosoms of the last scions of that formidable brood. On the upper floor of the Grange, in their contiguous bedrooms, Salome and Gertrude were showing of what stuff they were made, in more senses than one. The oaken floors, the massive furniture, the ponderous crockery, the voluminous hangings quivered to the heavy tread of feet that demanded to be, and indeed were, shod in nothing under tens.

Salome, in the Tudor room, was being buckled into her corsets. As she tramped the floor her maid trailed hopelessly behind, panting and dragging desperately at the intricate contrivance of strings and whalebones that was designed to compress the form of her mistress into something approaching human shape. Altogether they resembled two overgrown school children playing a particularly violent game of ' horses '.

" Blast ye, Vetch," cried Salome as she glared short-sightedly at her copy of the *Probe*, " stop playin' with those damned laces. If they won't meet, let 'em hang. Gertrude ! " and her raised voice made the toilet ware ring. " Gertrude ! d'you see what that little cur Phont's got here ? Nosey Parker."

But Salome received no immediate reply, for in the next room even greater uproar prevailed. Here, in the Stuart bedroom, Gertrude was undergoing the matutinal torture of being inserted into her buttoned boots. She was a martyr to ' bad feet ', and what with corns, bunions, callouses and in-growing toe-nails she was having a pretty poor time of it. Her maid, crouched like a trembling votary at the feet of some Egyptian deity, plied the button-hook and endured obloquy.

" Damn your eyes, Campion," cried Miss Gertrude Warbler as the heel of the left boot smartly touched up a particularly tender spot, " how many times am I to tell you to use the small ebony shoe-horn for the left foot ? And if you touch that again," she indicated an unusually rotund bunion, " I'll sack you. Salome ! Salome ! " And the canopy over the enormous four-poster quivered until the dust flew, " d'you see this ? Do you see what that little cad Phont's got here ? Meddlesome Matties. . . ."

The feature of the *Probe* that was touching the Misses

Warbler so closely was a last minute inspiration of Mr.
Phont's. It was a back page column under the brief
heading ' WHO ? '   In Mr. Phont's own words :
" The *Probe* must not be too unrelievedly serious.
Whilst maintaining always its solid moral character,
it must, at the same time, be touched up here and there
by a more blithe and frolicsome note. With this aim
in view I have conceived the idea of an amusing weekly
column entitled ' WHO ? ' Something delicately
insulting, elegantly gross, a rude social frolic so to
speak. The idea is to have three or four paragraphs,
written in the style of fables, each referring to some
particular borough worthy. Our readers will have a
lot of quiet fun trying to identify the victims."

The Misses Warbler were now having a lot of quiet
fun in identifying themselves. Snorting and stamping,
quivering and grinding their all too mobile dentures
they read in unison the fable of the ' Parish Priest and
the Nosey Parkers '. It ran thus : " Once upon a
Time there was a Worthy Parish Priest who spent his
Energies in cultivating the Garden of the Lord and
weeding out Sin. Now this Gardener of the Lord
was a very Busy Man because his Allotment was a
very wicked one and there were a lot of Weeds to be
pulled up and consigned to the Fire that is never
Quenched. He was, moreover, a Low Churchman and
would have nothing to do with High Church Practices.
For a time his Allotment prospered, and his Crops
grew and he kept the Weeds down. But soon he began
to be pestered by two Nosey Parkers or Meddlesome
Matties. They were up to all kinds of Naughty
Pranks and made his life well-nigh Intolerable. They
changed the Flowers on the Altar and interfered all

round and were always at him to go in for Popish
Practices. They were all for Incense and Processions
and Cribs at Christmas, but the Priest was a Stern Man
and was firm with them and said he was not going in
for Gas Attacks or Route Marches in his Church, nor
was he going to play at Dolls' Houses. But the two
Nosey Parkers kept pestering him until he went into a
Decline and Died. And the two Meddlesome Matties
were pleased because they felt sure they had made
certain of Eternal Life and would be on the Credit side
of the Ledger at the Last Audit. Now in the Fullness
of Time they also Died and Everyone said ' Thank
God ', as it was generally agreed that their Time had
been altogether too Full. They presented themselves
confidently at the Golden Gates when the Time came,
and they knocked and St. Peter answered the Door.
And they said let us In for we are Two Good Anglo-
Catholics. But St. Peter said Bad Luck ; my Master
is a Noncomformist. MORAL : Nosey Parkers Please
Turn Back."

So the two Misses Warbler gathered up their ash-
plants and went to call on Mr. Phont. And they were
in a Very Bad Temper.

Colonel Barley came down to breakfast feeling like
death warmed up. He had passed a restless night speculating and conjecturing upon his favourite subject, the
British Empire and its future. He anticipated the worst.
Balefully he champed his grilled runions and glowered
across the table at his wife. He got little sympathy.

Leila Barley was what Major Cockerell called ' a
fine figure of a woman ', by which he meant that she
was pleasantly pneumatic and eminently worth a second
glance when caught stooping in evening dress.

When in one of his not infrequent amorous moods the Colonel found her an ideal helpmeet, but in his more serious moments he found her regrettably inadequate. The British Empire left her, to put it bluntly, frigid and once even in a fit of pique, she had owned to a passing passion for a young Communist. However, it appeared that she had been fascinated more by the aphrodisiac qualities of his long black beard than by his political creed. So while Colonel Barley golloped his runions and dwelt upon the disgraceful scenes of the previous evening, Leila dabbled half-heartedly in her grapefruit and pondered the autumn fashion lists.

At length the Colonel could contain himself no longer. He thrust his cup of half cold coffee from him and opened up : " Disgraceful. Positively disgusting. Never have I witnessed such imbecile behaviour, such a disreputable exhibition of mob hooliganism. If last night's fiasco is the sort of thing the British public will tolerate I can only anticipate the worst. We may as well throw up the sponge at once ; abandon India, put Canada and Australia up for auction . . . "

" Darling," protested Leila closing her eyes and pressing a crimson-tipped hand to her forehead, " not so violent, please, you know I can't stand the Empire at breakfast, especially when it's my . . . "

The Colonel interrupted with an air of injured dignity : " I am sorry, my dear, if I bore you. I should have thought, however, that even to you the welfare of our far-flung possessions, the future of our great heritage, the well-being of our sacred trust would have been of at least a passing interest."

Leila remembered that her dress-allowance for the

quarter was already exhausted and that she wanted some new lingerie. She adopted a more pacific attitude : " I'm sorry, darling. Of course I think the Empire is really a very good thing and all that. And I should simply hate us to lose it or start giving bits away to Huns and Dagoes and what not, but I tell you I don't feel awfully bouncey this morning. And anyhow I think you're far too pessimistic. I really thought it was all rather amusing last night, especially the Vicar."

" I'm glad you find that sort of thing humorous," said the Colonel with ponderous sarcasm. " Personally I can only regard it as an indication of the hopeless decadence of the British People. How, I should like to know, is the dignity of Church and State to be maintained when men like Skillington go about getting as drunk as lords and making shameless exhibitions of themselves in public places."

" But, darling, he was saving souls," protested Leila, finally abandoning her grapefruit. " And anyhow I don't think he was really terribly drunk. More zeal than gin if you ask me. Exaltation of the spirit and all that kind of thing. Besides, isn't there something in religious circles about the end justifying the means or something ? "

" Bah ! " remarked the Colonel. " Popish doctrines. Roman tarradiddle, Jesuitical jugglery. It all began with that fellow Newman. No wonder we let Ital play hokey-pokey all over Africa when half the upper classes are steeped in Catholic balderdash. However," and the Colonel's eye glittered. " I settled Skillington's hash last night. He won't forget that clip on the ear I gave him in a hurry."

" Too uncouth," protested Leila. " I hate to hear

you talk like that, darling. It always makes me think of corduroy trousers and woollen pants and things."

" There you go again," said the Colonel. " I should like to know what's wrong with woollen pants. I've always worn them myself and I always shall. And none of your shorts either. Pants to the ankles for me, and long-sleeved vests as well. I shall always maintain that when a nation takes to silk underwear it is well on the way to rapid dissolution. What does it lead to ? Nothing but a race of decadent young puppies like that Esmond Duncan. And I am convinced, Leila, that your own health would improve out of all recognition if you followed my advice and wore wool next to the skin. These skimpy silk falderals lead inevitably to a lowering of the vitality and a consequent weakening of the nation's stock."

" I ask you," breathed Leila, " to imagine me in long sleeved pants and vests to the ankles. Positively, I should scratch myself to shreds. And anyhow I don't see why you should object to Esmond Duncan. He's really amazingly amusing and he does marvellous imitations of Douglas Byng. By the way I've asked him to dinner next Monday."

The Colonel arose from the table and pushed back his chair : " Leila, I forbid it."

" Indeed ? And may I ask why ? " said Leila with dangerous calm.

The Colonel cleared his throat : " In the first place I consider him a bumptious, ill-mannered young. . . ."

" Puppy," supplied Leila viciously.

" And further," went on the Colonel, " if you must know, though I hesitate to level such an indictment against any man, I understand that he is a self-confessed . . . ah . . . a blatant . . . er . . ."

" Oh, I know all about that," answered Leila wearily. " But don't you think that makes him all the more amusing ? At least he's something out of the ordinary."

" I can see you are determined to be wilfully aggravating, Leila. However, I shall not lose my temper, as that is a sign of weakness. I will only say this, that if young Duncan comes into this house I go out. I will not stay under the same roof with him."

Leila eyed her outraged spouse coldly over the coffee-pot : " For the last time, Lionel, I won't be bullied. I will stand a good deal, but I will not endure the British Empire at breakfast as well as at luncheon, tea and dinner. Furthermore I will not have pants-to-the-ankles and long-sleeved vests pushed down my throat, nor will I have you dictating to me who I shall or shall not entertain to dinner. Don't forget what I told you the last time this sort of thing occurred. If there's any more argument you know what to expect, or rather what not to expect. And anyway, if what you say is correct, I should be quite safe with Esmond Duncan. Besides he does the sweetest tricks with dinner-plates. Spins them up into the air and catches them behind his ears and things. So let's have no more nonsense. Finish your kidneys and run along to the office at once."

Colonel Barley, who valued his domestic comforts even higher than the integrity of India or the wearing of woollen underclothing, was quelled. Gloweringly he got on with his meal.

Presently the strained silence was broken by a knock at the door. The butler entered, bearing upon a salver a copy of the *Weekly Probe* : " I have taken the liberty, sir, of bringing this . . . ah . . . this publication to your notice. It contains matter which, I think, you should see. . . ."

The Colonel snatched up the paper and waved it threateningly at his wife : " More tomfoolery unless I'm very much mistaken, more unbridled hooliganism. Cockerell tells me that fellow Phont is behind all this, Phont and that young Communist devil Bellairs. A calculated campaign of subversive propaganda. I've an idea they were behind that disgraceful exhibition at the theatre last night. I don't trust that Phont an inch, too much money and nothing to do. He was abominably rude to me the other day about the Territorials. What the country is coming to when men in his position go about openly expressing Socialist sentiments and perverting the youth of the nation I don't know. If I had my way I'd take a leaf out of that feller Hitler's book and have men of Phont's kidney put straight into a concentration camp. And a stiff term in a labour corps would do that young cad Bellairs all the good in the world. As for publications of this sort," and here the Colonel tapped the *Probe* with a militant forefinger, " I'd have them suppressed. In fact I'd bring the whole press of the country under a rigid censorship. . . ."

" Quite," agreed Leila, wearily reaching over for the *Probe*, " but in the meantime let's have a look at this rag. There may be something about us in it." Idly she turned the pages of subversive propaganda.

Meanwhile the Colonel warmed to his work : " If last night's business can be brought home to them, and I intend to exert myself to the utmost to see that it is, those fellers will find themselves in a pretty tight corner. Breach of the peace is a serious charge, and if I'm on the bench, as I thoroughly intend to be, I promise you I'll make it mighty hot for them. A heavy fine or a stiff term of imprisonment is the least they deserve."

" There certainly was a pretty lively panic," said Leila, lighting her cigarette. " By the way, darling, that chiffon of mine was ripped from stem to stern. I shall really have to have a new. . . ."

" It was only by the grace of God," continued Colonel Barley, " that there were no serious casualties. I have rarely seen such a display of mob hysteria. However," and here the Colonel bridled a little. " I do flatter myself that I did my best in the circumstances. You noticed how I. . . ."

" Yes, Lionel, I thought it awfully heroic of you to go leaping about like that, crying for law and order and what not. Quite like Gordon or Florence Nightingale or somebody."

" Well, we Army men have our code, my dear. It was the least I could do as an officer and . . . ah . . . a gentleman. That's what the Army teaches a man, a cool head in a tight corner."

" Pity it didn't work as well as it might have done," mused Leila who could never resist a timely dig. " I mean they didn't seem to take a great deal of notice, did they ? "

" That was not my fault," said the Colonel sharply. " Another shocking instance of the deplorable state the country has got into. If the upper classes can be reduced to the condition of hysterical animals by a bad smell, what, I should like to know, will they do in the face of mustard gas, thermite and. . . ."

" I should imagine," breathed Leila, " that they will die. Quickly and rather messily, too. By the way, darling, I think this is what Eccleston meant you to see. I don't know whether it will interest you. . . ." Leila leaned back comfortably in her chair and began to blow smoke-rings in happy anticipation of the wrath to come.

Colonel Barley, for he was more than a little short-sighted, pressed his face close to the middle page of the *Weekly Probe* and exploded.

Bellairs had done himself proud. Under a double-head, in the largest type the *Probe* possessed, entitled " The shadow of the Swastika : a solemn Warning to Local Youth," he had let himself go. For two columns, with copiously blacked paragraphs, the rumbling prose boomed forth its message. Flowing period was piled upon flowing period, crashing metaphor flowered into exotic simile, staccato ejaculation commingled with polysyllabic elaboration. " I haven't the faintest idea what it means," had been Bellairs' dictum, " but it reads well. Figuratively speaking I have unbuttoned myself."

Broken snatches of phrase flashed cinematographically across the Colonel's glazed eye : " A deeply rooted militarist conspiracy aimed at coercing the youth of the borough into a relentless organisation designed to further the aims of High Finance and Universal Carnage . . . Behind this many-tentacled monster lurks a man of mystery, a ruthless war-monger . . . Fair promises leading inevitably to shattered bodies and ruined homes . . . A personality exhibiting all the dreadful stigmata of the military mind, unbridled megalomania, insensate folly, raging blood-lust, crass stupidity . . . The Fascist axe hangs by a trembling hair above our necks, the shadow of the Swastika darkens our thresholds . . . It will be the sacred duty of the *Weekly Probe* to combat unremittingly, without ruth, the dark and hidden forces of Military Despotism. The *Probe* will not rest until it has penetrated the veil of mystery surrounding these deadly forces which bid fair to shatter the public-weal and disrupt the placid calm of this noble and ancient borough. In the face of no matter what persecution by vested interest, no matter what insidious attacks by unprincipled despots, the *Probe* will regard it as a solemn trust to root out this monstrous evil and to expose in all its staggering moral turpitude-the dread figure that lurks in the shadows."

Colonel Barley uttered a strangled grunt and flung the paper to the other side of the room : " Monstrous. Intolerable. Libellous balderdash. By God, I'll break their backs. That little snipe Phont, I'll twist his neck for him. The military mind . . . what is it he's got there ? By heaven, I'll . . ." The Colonel dashed across the room to retrieve the paper.

" Something about insensate folly and crass stupidity, wasn't it ? " murmured Leila who was enjoying herself heartily. She leaned over her husband's shoulder and indicated with a pointed carmine talon the precise passage. " Oh, yes, and unbridled megalomania and raging blood-lust."

Suddenly she wrinkled up her nose and pointed an accusing finger at her husband : " Darling, what on earth have you been doing ? You smell, distinctly, of bad eggs."

The Colonel emitted an epileptic squeak : " Smell ?

What do you mean smell ? What the devil do you mean by telling me I smell ? Haven't I got enough to worry about with all this infamous vapouring without your going about telling me I smell."

"But, darling, you do. Positively you reek. Absolutely malodorous. Really I can't think . . . It's your hair."

Savagely the Colonel ran his fingers through his thinning locks. From behind his right ear he produced a lump of sticky, reeking paste. Bellairs' little gift was still with him.

Roaring, Colonel Barley galloped out of the room. The house trembled to the impact of the front door and Leila caught a glimpse of her husband passing down the road at a fine round pace. In one hand he brandished a rhinoceros hide whip. Leila shrugged her magnificent Jean Harlow shoulders and picked up the telephone. "That you, Esmond, my love ? "

Meanwhile at the all too depressingly bijou 'Llandudno' in St. James Road, the residence of Alderman Deacon, the Mayor, a tense situation prevailed. The *Weekly Probe*, that happy harbinger, had arrived at the moment when the Mayor was just setting out to sit upon the bench at the local court of summary jurisdiction. And now the judicial calm of Alderman Deacon's somewhat vacant countenance was dissipated. Rage, chagrin and bewilderment passed in rapid succession across the face that at the best of times bore a remarkable resemblance to an old English sheep dog. The Mayoral whiskers trembled, the mobile lines of the chest, so aptly designed for the couching of the chain of office, contracted and expanded alarmingly. The passing of the civic boots across the mock-Turkey carpet made to tremble the congested ornamentation of the ' best room '. Upon the mantelshelf the two china fruit-baskets, won at a coconut shy in his reckless youth, rocked perilously as the Mayor navigated a hazardous course from the bulbous couch by the door to the bamboo plant-stand in the bay window. The photographs perched upon lace doyleys on the piano slithered alarmingly back and forth. Indeed, an astonishing work showing Alderman Deacon and his wife—their expressions surprisingly glazed—upon their honeymoon at Llandudno fell violently to the ground, was irreparably smashed, and was ground to pieces under the agitated Mayoral heels. Mrs. Lucy Deacon, accompanying her husband as nimbly as her considerable and uncorseted bulk would permit, supplied an obligato of outraged comment.

The matter that came so closely at Alderman and Mrs. Deacon was a bright, chatty half-column written by Julian at the instigation of Bellairs. The latter had hit upon the happy scheme of running a series of biographical sketches under the title " the Chosen People : Borough Worthies Week by Week." This week he dealt with the Mayor ; and, indeed, how. Julian, working upon information supplied by Bellairs, had adopted a naïve, an almost child-like style, the candour of which left little or nothing to be desired. There was that which brought a flush of shame to Alderman Deacon's flaccid cheeks, an oath to his prim nonconformist lips, a sinking feeling to the pit of his comfortable guts.

" Plain Deacon as our Mayor delights to call himself with such disarming honesty, presents the impressive, indeed one might say the overwhelming spectacle of the authentic self-made man. Not too artistically made, perhaps, somewhat rough-hewn even, but solid right through ; solid, indeed, from top to bottom. Born of hard labouring, if undistinguished stock, and a month before his due time, he received his early education at one of the local board schools. Plain Deacon, as we might expect and, in fact, as we are all well aware, never had much time for the three R's and soon abandoned the enervating study of English grammar and the fine arts for the more practical sphere of affairs. His genius for organisation was rapidly exhibited when, at the age of eleven years, he founded a holiday outing fund amongst his school fellows. Unfortunately, simultaneously with the publication of the first balance sheet of this undertaking his scholastic career was cut short by an untimely expulsion, so that we have no opportunity of studying the methods and development of this his earliest enterprise.

" Upon leaving school he entered the local ironstone quarries where for many years he was exclusively occupied in wheeling barrows up formidable slopes, thus proving beyond dispute that the hand that wheels the barrow rules the borough. Here, too, our Mayor undoubtedly learned much about the desirability of rapidly Getting To The Top.

" Alderman Deacon speedily gained the complete confidence of his colleagues and employers, and, on being promoted foreman, was swept into the maelstrom of local politics. He successfully contested the St. James' ward as a Socialist and rapidly won for himself the title of the Strong Man of the Council.

" Gradually, with ripening years and maturing

judgment, Alderman Deacon's political colour-scheme began to modulate from the scarlet of the left through the pale pinks and greens of the centre to the solid and more restful indigo of the right. Since then he has passed through the Mayoral chair no less than four times, he has extended his activities in every direction and has gained a well deserved popularity amongst all sections of the burgesses except, perhaps, the extremists of the left.

"Indeed, of late years his public life has been, perhaps, more social than political, and in the new sphere our Mayor has not failed to exhibit that originality of mind that has distinguished his actions at all times. Many delightfully whimsical stories are told of him, such as his amusing gesture at his first dinner party with Lord Wycherley when, after the dessert, he was observed to remove his false teeth and place them in his finger-bowl. Again, one is reminded of his charming old-world candour at last year's Hospital Ball when, after fox-trotting with Lady Buckle, he was heard to remark that he, at any rate, was 'all of a muck-sweat.' One recalls, too, the irresistible frolics he was observed to be enjoying with Miss Puggy Congreve at a recent Licensed Victuallers' Dinner when he passed a happy hour flicking out his dicky into Miss Congreve's face, she meanwhile, with all the good humour in the world, doing her best to catch it in her mouth. . . ."

"Of all the bloody impudence," said Councillor Sam Nurture. "Of all the bloody sauce," he elaborated, forcibly if repetitively.

"It's actionable, that's what it is, Sam," said Mrs. Beryl Nurture, hissing slightly through her new dentures and jangling the innumerable bangles upon her skinny arms.

" Actionable ? " said Councillor Nurture, " I should blasted well think so. I shall take steps, you see if I don't, and bloody quick too. This feller Phont's getting above himself. Him and that young Bellairs and that Mrs. Meredith, they're behind all this, and it's got to stop. Libellous, that's what it is. Slanderous, if I'm not very much mistaken."

" That Mrs. Meredith's no better than what she ought to be," remarked Mrs. Nurture nastily. " They say as the goings-on up there is something scandalous . . . And the dress she 'ad on last night."

" Ah," agreed the Councillor, " very like. And there's going to be some more goings-on before I've finished. Goings-on as'll make some of 'em think twice afore they publish any more of this sort of thing. I'm off to see young Gavelkind now, and then we'll see what Twidale can do. It's scandalous, it's nothing but a shameless and unprincipled attack upon them as guides the affairs of the borough. It's a bloody . . ." But by this time Mrs. Beryl Nurture had placed a bowler hat upon her spouse's head, pressed an umbrella into his hand, and dispatched him on his way to consult Nathaniel Gavelkind and Son, solicitors and Commissioners for Oaths, as to the possibilities of having a stab at Mr. Phont.

As she resumed her seat at the breakfast table in the kitchen (for the Nurtures, in spite of having lunched at the high table with Lord Wycherley and Sir Bertram Buckle at the last Agricultural Show, had not yet completely rid themselves of certain lower-class habits) she reflected for a moment upon her husband's vocabulary. It was time, she decided, now that Sam had a tail-coat as well as a dinner-jacket, that he stopped using the word ' bloody'. Also, she reflected, that as Chairman of the Borough Advertisement Committee, it was high time he became more careful of his grammar. She had often noticed that when excited he had a lamentable tendency to use such words as ' afore ', and such fanciful constructions as ' them as '. In the meantime, however, there were sterner matters afoot. Grimly she took up the *Weekly Probe* and once more directed her gaze (more than a little cross-eyed, be it admitted) upon the fable of " The Naughty Councillor and the Gas Lamp."

" Once upon a Time there was a Naughty Town Councillor who thought less of the Welfare of the Borough than of Lining his own Pocket. Now this Naughty Councillor was a Member of the Parks, Fairs and Lighting Committee, so that when it was Resolved to put five new Flood Lights in the High Street he saw to it that they were Gas Lamps and not—as is the General Practice—Electric Lamps. This was because the Naughty Councillor had a Lot of Shares in the local Gas Company, and naturally he liked to see his Dividends Going Up, whilst on the Other Hand he hadn't any shares at all in the Electricity Company which was Bad Luck, and he often blamed himself for being a Blasted Fool for not getting in on the Electricity Company in a Big Way as he felt it was the Coming Thing.

" However, the Flood Lamps were put up and the Naughty Councillor was very smart and got one erected smack outside his own Shop on the Ground that it was situate at a very Dangerous Corner and would save a lot of Lives, but really he thought it would sell a Lot of Hams, for He was a Grocer in a Big Way of Business. Now for a Long Time the Naughty Councillor flourished exceedingly because the Burgesses were attracted by the Big Light outside his Shop Window and gathered in Crowds to look at the Sausages and Polonies and Brawns, and it was not until they had bought them and got them Home that they found they were nearly all Bread and Gristle. But one Evening in the Early Autumn a Tragedy occurred.

" The Naughty Councillor was in his Shop and it was nearly Dark and it was Closing Time. So as it was Dark and he had had a Good Day he thought he would have a Bit of Fun with one of the Young Ladies who Served behind the counter. So after he had Locked Up he induced the young lady to serve behind the Counter in a rather Unusual Way, and she Served readily because otherwise she feared she might Lose her Job and then her Widowed Mother who was dying of Consumption might Starve ! But unfortunately for the Councillor he was so Frolicsome and in such a Hurry that he forgot to draw the Shop Blind, and whilst the Unusual Business was going on behind the Counter the Gas Lamp outside was suddenly Turned On and several House-Wives of the Lower Classes, whose faces were pressed against the Window coveting the Pork Pies they could not afford to Buy, saw Everything. So the Naughty Councillor was in more Senses than one Undone and he had to resign from the Town Council and go out of Business and finally he Hanged Himself with a pair of Woolworth's braces in a Public Convenience. MORAL : People who live in Glass Houses should never forget to Draw the Blinds.

Alderman Fred Twidale, ex-Mayor, was, in a mild way, a financial genius. His father ' Nosey ' Twidale, originator of the local tallow works, had left him a small fortune of several thousand pounds. Fred, being of an urgent and ingenious temper, had, by the time he was fifty, turned this sum into something not far short of half-a-million.

In appearance he was rather deplorable, being long in the body and correspondingly short in the legs. Further, he boasted a plenitude of chins and a remarkably cold eye.

By nature he was at once sanctimonious and ruthless. Carping to a degree over such innocent diversions as mixed bathing and extended licensing hours, he would not, nevertheless, think twice before smashing with cold-blooded ferocity any business rival who stood in his path.

By these means he had established himself in such a position that there scarcely existed a single urban pie in which he had not a finger. He owned a three-quarter controlling share in *The Chronicle and Gazetteer*. Local businesses of every sort and kind, properties of every variety, public offices of every description, all, directly or indirectly, came under the influence of Alderman Fred Twidale. Indeed, it was freely bruited in certain circles that Alderman Deacon, the present Mayor, was nothing but a puppet in the pay of Alderman Twidale, a convenient tool by which the latter might extend still further his already comprehensive grip upon the local body politic.

Now in spite of his many objectionable qualities,

there was one very engaging feature about Alderman Fred Twidale and that was his social self-sufficiency, his faculty for ' keeping himself to himself '.

Unlike his brother business-chiefs, Fred never tried to muscle in on the social racket ; nor, indeed, did his wife, his daughter and his numerous sons. Money-making, buying fur-coats and sexual frolics were respectively their out-of-hours diversions and with those they were perfectly content. Lord Wycherley and his circle had no attraction for Alderman Fred Twidale and his family. Sir Bertram Buckle left them cold, whilst it was rumoured that on one occasion Alderman Fred had advised Major Cockerell to go to Hell and stay there.

In his rigid mode of life Alderman Fred Twidale permitted himself but two sentimental foibles, and they again were of a disarmingly ingenuous kind. Firstly, in spite of his half-million, he resolutely refused to move from the modest villa of his father in Tollemache Terrace. Secondly, and again in spite of his half-million, he resolutely persisted in maintaining the family tallow-works in the middle of the town although it was by now quite the most insignificant of his enterprises and more of a liability than an asset to him.

Now, the local tallow-works, if amusing to Alderman Fred, were, as Mr. Phont had often pointed out, a most damnable nuisance to the burgesses. Odorous at all times, the establishment bid fair in the hot summer months to render existence intolerable to a great part of the populace. But Alderman Twidale was resolute, immovable in the face of petition and threat. The tallow-works were there and there they stayed. And

Alderman Twidale, being who he was, they stayed. His motives were obscure. Partly, perhaps, his pride was titillated at being able to play hokey-pokey with the nasal organs of a fair-sized borough. Partly, perhaps, in some obscure way, he regarded the tallow-works as a kind of family totem, a kind of permanent an unignorable monument to the Twidale clan.

Conceive, therefore, of Alderman Twidale's posture when, opening his copy of the *Weekly Probe*, he found no less than two columns of swingeing prose, under a streamer and a double head, solely devoted to giving his precious tallow-works what for and how :

" Civic Stinks Mean Civic Shame," he read. " Unspeakable Urban Odours : Typhoid Menace Stalks Borough."

With ominous calm Alderman Fred Twidale adjusted his spectacles and pursued the text :

" An offence that stinks to high Heaven . . . an intolerable state of affairs . . . a grotesquely ludicrous position . . . The public health, the social amenities, the common weal of the fairest borough in the land at the mercy of a foul effluvium, an unspeakable exhalation . . . the new plague of Egypt . . . the menace of typhoid . . . impending decimation of a helpless populace . . . innocent little children with their grimy handkerchiefs pressed to their little noses . . . strong men staggering under the malodorous breath of a fell stench . . . women stretched upon beds . . . the rights of the people flouted by a single individual . . . a cynical disregard for the common dictates of humanity . . . an enquiry shall be set on foot . . . steps shall be taken . . . The *Weekly Probe* will not rest until this abominable niff, this smelling scandal, this appalling threat to the health and happiness, nay the very life-blood of the borough is tracked to its putrescent source, purged, and blotted out for ever." Mr. Phont had been in his best style.

Alderman Fred Twidale's reactions to this attack upon the child of his heart were at once interesting and typical. Rage there was not, nor appeal to his family. Only did he settle his pince-nez more firmly, arrange his chins, call to his bull-terrier and set out upon his matutinal course to his office.

The *Weekly Probe* had made a very dangerous enemy.

It was an inspired stroke on Bellairs' part when he decided to solicit the close collaboration of the Rev. Jasper Skillington in the production of the front page story for the *Probe*. Alone, each was uncommonly formidable ; conjointly they were irresistible.

In conference with Mr. Phont, Bellairs had expressed himself with the utmost certainty : " In my fixed opinion we should take the strong moral line over this Grand Theatrical Scandal story. In my view we can't do better than muscle in for all we're worth on the religious racket. Unless I'm much mistaken it's the coming thing. Moral fervour is what we want ; outraged principle ; the innocent populace being led astray by an immoral and decadent aristocracy. Now the man to put that sort of dope across is indubitably the Rev. Jasper Skillington. I intend to give him a free hand."

Thus it came about that Bellairs and the formidable priest conjointly led the paper.

The results were entirely satisfactory. " Divine Wrath Strikes Local Burgesses," ran the front page streamer. " Heavenly Judgment on Lewd Spectacle.

Modern Sodom Smitten," echoed the strident double-head. Then there followed close upon three columns of rumbling, reverberating prose, the literary unbuttoning of ruthless youth and outraged age.

Bellairs led off with a column of his best descriptive stuff dealing with the extraordinary scenes in the theatre on the previous evening. Having dealt in a saucily provocative manner with the social side of the affair he proceeded to a spirited account of the martyrdom of the Rev. Jasper Skillington in the orchestra pit. By the time he had done with the priest's performance the latter was elevated to the status of a St. Sebastian and Bellairs hinted darkly that the local burgesses might expect to hear more from the Almighty touching upon the shameful treatment they had meted out to their vicar and rural dean.

From this Bellairs passed to a vivid presentation of the final scenes of uproar consequent upon the throwing of the stink-bombs. He did not hesitate to assert that here was a concrete manifestation of divine wrath, and that the irresponsible hooligans who had precipitated the pandemonium were the agents, albeit unwittingly, of an outraged divinity.

At this point the Rev. Jasper took over and for well-nigh two columns. After an initial passage of turbulent if somewhat turgid moral exhortation, he passed on to a skilfully drawn analogy between the Rotten Borough and Sybaris, Babylon, Carthage and other antique sinks of iniquity. Thence he proceeded to a well-judged attack upon the local aristocracy on the grounds of criminal irresponsibility, moral decadence, and, in particular, sexual debauchery. He pursued with a detailed condemnation on moral and artistic principles of the " Well of Passions," and rounded off with an impassioned warning on the shape of things to come.

Bellairs took over for the last lap, and in a half column of the most swingeing dramatic criticism proved beyond the faintest shadow of doubt that it would be an affront to the British Drama and a studied insult to the intelligence of the British People if Lady Wycherley or any of her cast of Distinguished Amateurs were ever permitted to set foot upon the stage again.

Altogether it was a very happy performance.

An atmosphere of extreme tension brooded over Brackenbury Hall, the residence of Lord and Lady Wycherley. There had been very little sleeping the previous night. Hysterical outbursts had been more popular, *crises de nerfs* commingled with threats and objurgations directed at the mysterious perpetrators of the theatrical débâcle.

The only person who seemed at all satisfied with the posture of events was Lord Wycherley himself who incurred everyone's extreme displeasure by maintaining a grim air of brandified complacency. ' I told you so,' he was heard to remark on more than one occasion, and prior to rolling into bed he had told his valet, in all confidence, that if he could discover the protagonists of the uproar he would give them a five-pound note apiece, damned if he wouldn't. For unless he was very much mistaken this spelled the last appearance of his wife upon a public stage for some considerable time to come.

Lady Veronica Wycherley herself, though it was now

almost eleven o'clock in the morning, had only just arisen from her bed. She had only managed a couple of hours of restless slumber, and that under the influence of a soporific. Breakfast, even in the shape of a dose of grapefruit, she could not for a moment contemplate. However, in spite of all, she still contrived to look attractive enough in a suit of apricot silk pyjamas as she paced restlessly about the room in the manner of an irritable Juno.

At least the faithful Mr. Raymond Bouncer thought so as he sat glumly on the foot of the bed smoking his post-breakfast cigarette. He was not feeling too sure of himself at the moment because when the butler had arrested him with the request that he should immediately present himself in his hostess' bedroom, he was just contemplating a speedy retreat to the sanctuary of his bachelor apartment in Half Moon Street. Life, he felt, in the provinces was apt to be altogether too exhilarating. At length Lady Wycherley ceased her pacing and came to a halt before the disconsolate Mr. Bouncer :

" Well, Raymond, what are we going to do about it ? "

" Do about what whrup ? " asked Mr. Bouncer hiccoughing, for he had bolted his kipper.

Lady Wycherley shuddered : " Darling, don't tell me you've been eating kipper. How could you after all we went through last night ? Positively I couldn't eat a thing. And I had to take veronal before I could get off to sleep at all and then I didn't get a wink. Not a wink. And there you sit bolting kippers and hiccoughing all over my bedroom and not being a bit helpful. Really, Raymond, I think you're being awfully callous." Lady Wycherley showed signs of losing her always rather uncertain temper.

Mr. Bouncer pulled himself together. His hostess was, as he knew all too well, of an extremely passional turn of mind. She was easily roused, a laudable virtue enough in amorous exchanges, but alarming in altercation :

" It's difficult," he remarked judicially, " to know quite what one can do. It's not as if we knew who was really responsible. Of course, we might tackle that damned parson, but I don't see that doing us much good. He's obviously raving mad."

" But the cads who threw those stink-bombs. They ought to be prosecuted or something," said Lady Wycherley peevishly. " It's absolutely disgraceful. Why don't the police do something ? And think what fools we've all been made to look. It'll be all over the county by now. I don't know how I'm ever going to look anyone in the face again. What swine people are," went on Lady Wycherley warming to her work, " what unspeakable, unutterable cads and beasts and bastards."

Mr. Bouncer who, for all his youthful years was a gentleman of the old school, winced to hear that last word on the tongue of a lady, especially a lady who had accorded him the domestic comforts. However, he was beginning to feel on firmer ground : " I agree. Most unsportsmanlike. Not at all British. Of course the trouble is these people have never been to a decent school. It makes all the difference. Now at my school . . ."

" Damn your school," said Lady Wycherley testily.

" Don't be more of a fool than you can help, Raymond. Do provincial urchins usually go to public schools ? Have a bit of sense for a change."

Mr. Bouncer floundered once more. It was, he reflected, extremely difficult to think coherently when an undeniably handsome woman insulted you with her voice and mesmerised you with her shapes at one and the same time. Determinedly he averted his eyes from his hostess' mobile bosom and replied : " In my opinion, Veronica, much as it may go against the grain, the best thing we can do is to keep as quiet as possible over the whole affair. We shall gain absolutely nothing by kicking up a fuss. We'd far better ignore the whole thing and let people forget about it as soon as possible. As I say we've no idea who's responsible, so how can we start prosecuting people ? "

" All the same," said Lady Wycherley, looking sinister, " I believe I know who really is behind it all. It's that little cad, Phont, and that bitch, Barbara Meredith. That woman exasperates me. She hasn't the morals of a cat."

In view of certain favours he had received at Lady Wycherley's hands, for want of a better word, Mr. Bouncer could not help reflecting that she was scarcely in a position to cast the first stone. However, he refrained from pointing out any such discrepancies. Instead he rallied round as best he could :

" Oh ! I agree. That Meredith woman's capable of anything. A pretty low type if you ask me. But I can't think Ulric Phont would sponsor such hooliganism. After all he's Eton and Balliol you know. That ought to see him all right. He belongs to the

Bath and Bucks too. No, I can't think Phont would behave so badly.

"I wouldn't trust the little swab an inch," said Lady Wycherley savagely applying the wrong shade of lipstick. "And then there's this paper he's supposed to be bringing out, the *Weekly Probe* or something. A dirty, yellow scandal-rag from what I can make out. Heaven knows what there'll be about last night in it."

Mr. Bouncer was by way of being sceptical : "Oh ! that's all talk if you ask me. I doubt if Phont and his crowd could ever rise to the pitch of getting a paper out at all, and if they did I should think it would be a pretty average amateur effort. I shouldn't worry about that . . ."

"I should, by God," cried a hoarse voice from the door. "I should worry like Hell, I should."

Lady Wycherley and Mr. Raymond Bouncer looked round sharply to find themselves confronted by a dishevelled and savage looking Lord Wycherley.

He cut a peculiar figure. He was attired in red and white striped pyjamas that were several inches too long for him in the leg. His shabby green dressing-gown, however, barely reached his knees. His pale red hair stood up in a tangled knot upon his crown whilst his slightly myopic, fish-blue eyes popped and goggled alarmingly. In one hand he grasped a tooth-brush and with the other he brandished a copy of the *Weekly Probe*.

"Worry like Hell, I should," repeated Lord Wycherley somewhat monotonously. "Just take a look at that," he went on, viciously thrusting his copy of the *Weekly Probe* under his wife's nose, "just take a dekko at that. You should worry."

But Lady Wycherley did not immediately apply herself to the proffered publication. Instead she surveyed her husband with a remarkably cold eye as he hiccoughed resonantly from time to time and bounced about the bedroom. His behaviour, she reflected, was of a most unaccustomed kind. There was not that deference, that diffidence even, in his general port and mien that she had come to expect in her dealings with him. Her voice rasped :

" Charles ! Will you kindly leave the room at once. I can't imagine what you think you're doing bouncing into my room like this, belching and shouting about all over the place. Kindly go and have your bath. When I want you I'll send for you."

But Lord Wycherley was a new man this morning. In the first place he had an appallingly thick head and a devilish temper from the previous night's brandy. In the second place he had been immensely stimulated, elevated in fact several stages above himself, by the *Probe's* swingeing attack upon his wife, his wife's friends and their theatricals. Now he no longer stood alone. Formidable allies had espoused his cause. His fibres were toughened. He was not to be browbeaten by anyone.

" You shut your trap," he remarked succinctly and pushed Lady Wycherley sharply in the stomach so that she fell back breathless upon the bed. Then he turned his attention to Mr. Raymond Bouncer who was dodging about near the door.

" And as for you, Bouncer, I should like to know what the devil you're up to in my wife's bedroom. No good I'll be bound. Some underhand hokey-pokey business unless I'm much mistaken. It's a nice state

of affairs, I must say," continued the outraged peer,
" when I have to sleep at the bottom of the corridor
whilst my wife plays rough and tumble in her pyjamas
with every Tom, Dick and Harry.   Come, sir, come,"
cried Lord Wycherley, making threatening passes at
Mr. Bouncer with the toothbrush, " an explanation
if you please."

" I assure you," began Mr. Bouncer with dignity,
" that you are under a complete misapprehension.
Your wife requested me to attend upon her purely in
an advisory capacity with regard to last night's
deplorable affair . . ."

" Ho ! " said Lord Wycherley vulgarly, " so that's
what you call your fun and games, is it ?   An advisory
capacity, my eye.   I may say, Bouncer," and here
Lord Wycherley's port became distinctly menacing so
that Mr. Bouncer backed hurriedly against the dressing
table and sat down on a powder puff, " that I've had
enough of your damned impertinence.   For the last
fortnight I've watched you mauling my wife about like
an all-in wrestling match.   I've had enough of it.
Enough of it, I say, and if you don't make yourself
scarce within the next twenty minutes I'll make it
uncommonly hot for you.   Now get out."   Lord
Wycherley's voice cracked under the emotional strain
on a high falsetto ; the effect, however, was none the
less impressive, none the less grandiose.

Mr. Bouncer paused dramatically at the door : " I
consider your behaviour, Lord Wycherley, that of a
cad and a boor.   Were you not my host, my senior in
years, and obviously half-drunk I should find myself
obliged to administer a severe chastisement.   I can
only repeat that I consider your behaviour a disgrace

to yourself and the peerage. In sterner times men were called out for less . . ."

" And in modern times they are kicked out for less," cried Lord Wycherley, taking a running swing at Mr. Bouncer's posterior. But that young man was already half-way downstairs.

" Number one," remarked Lord Wycherley grimly re-entering the room.

Meanwhile Lady Veronica Wycherley, having partially recovered from her husband's rough handling, sat up on the bed and caught sight of the *Weekly Probe* that lay open beside her. With a tense expression she began to peruse the front page and, as she did so, her eyes began to dilate, her throat worked, her splendid bosom strained at the apricot silk of her jacket, her scarlet tipped fingers quivered. Suddenly she emitted a piercing scream, flung the paper to the floor and, exasperated beyond the pitch of endurance, picked up a black rose bowl and hove it smartly through the window.

" Ha ! " said Lord Wycherley as the glass and china tinkled musically upon the gravel below, " so it rouses you, does it ? It comes pretty close, what ? Well it was no more than you all deserved, going about making exhibitions of yourselves in public like that. I warned you that it would bring you no good. And now look at you," emphasised Lord Wycherley with grim satisfaction, " what are you all ? Nothing but a jibe in the mouth of the mob, nothing but a public laughing stock. Regular figures of fun. It'll take some living down, I can tell you."

" What," said Lady Wycherley with ominous calm, " are you going to do about it, Charles ? "

"Nothing," rejoined her husband with smug complacency, "absolutely nothing. I warned you but you chose to ignore me. Now you've got yourself into this jam you can jolly well get yourself out of it. Personally I don't blame Phont and his crowd in the slightest. You presented him with a grand chance for making hay and he's made it."

"You think Phont was responsible, then?" enquired Lady Wycherley dangerously.

"I'm sure of it," replied her husband, studying the *Probe* front page with every sign of satisfaction, "but you needn't bank on that. There's no real proof that he had anything to do with it. In my opinion he'll get clean away with the whole thing, and personally I wish him the best of luck. This neighbourhood has needed a jolly good purge for a long time, and unless I'm much mistaken Phont's the dose of salts. By the way, do you see what they've got here about yourself?"

Lady Wycherley scanned Bellairs' half column of dramatic criticism. "Lady Wycherley," she read, "at least produced a wardrobe that did something to alleviate one of the dullest plays it has ever been our misfortune to witness. As a mannequin, therefore, we are inclined to hand her the currant bun. But as an actress she has a good deal to learn. However, when she has overcome her complete vocal inaudibility and awkwardness of gesture, when she has developed a sense of dialogue and timing, when she has learnt to talk to the audience instead of to herself, then she may develop into quite a competent mummer."

With a sobbing scream Lady Wycherley tore off her pyjamas and grabbed her stockings : "The unspeakable lout," she cried. "The miserable, unutterable little cad. I'm going straight round to the Priory to wring his beastly little neck. I'll . . ."

Lord Wycherley watched his wife with a cynical sneer : " And I've no doubt you'll be made very welcome. By the way, you'll need this, I'm sure." He courteously handed her a suspender belt. " Very welcome, I'm whrup . . ."

But Lord Wycherley's sarcasm had proved his undoing, for his wife had let him have it on the ear with a Sheffield plate candlestick.

" Such fun, such fun I never did see," mused Pycroft, the butler, as things began to warm up above stairs.

Meanwhile a state of considerable liveliness existed at the *Weekly Probe* office. Bellairs having organised the position, the garrison was now manning the defences.

The outworks, in the shape of the publisher's room, were held by the redoubtable Augustus who had instructions to deal with anyone below the status of a Town Councillor. The more important burgesses were to be passed aloft to Mr. Phont and his squad in the reporters' room.

Here preparations were actively proceeding. The middle of the floor was occupied by a ladder that projected through a trap door on to the roof. Upon this Bellairs had posted himself as a look-out. His legs were visible to those below, and in a hoarse voice which, he explained, was of a nautical character, he kept those in the room underneath informed of the tactical position without.

Mrs. Meredith was on the telephone to Augustus in the publisher's room : " Yes, that's what I said.

Quantities of printers' ink and a paint brush. Yes, the blackest and stickiest you've got. Send a boy up with it."

Julian was busy at a small wall safe full of neatly ranged and tabulated portfolios, whilst Mr. Phont was busy after his own frolicsome fashion.

" All are welcome," he remarked blithely as he adjusted a contrivance of elastic attached to a watery sponge across the doorway. " The first rule for all social entrepreneurs—be prepared. Dear me, this little scheme, so effective in all its crude simplicity, takes me back to my prep. school days. Lackaday ! *Nous n'irons plus aux bois . . .*"

Mr. Phont stepped back and surveyed his handiwork appreciatively, his head on one side : " Really, I think I should have made a rather good military tactician, though like Cynara's lover, after my own fashion. Something in the Napoleonic line don't you know, something a little Lawrentian. I shall always maintain that it needs a really great imaginative artist to conduct a war in a really amusing and instructive fashion. The idea is fascinating ; Waterloo after Wagner, Theomopylæ after Titian, Passchendaele after Picasso."

" Avast there ! " suddenly bellowed Bellairs from the roof. " Belay there ! Furl the mains'ls, let go the royal t'gallants ! Abaft, abeam, a grappling iron ! Grape-shot, grape-fruit, and keep your powder dry ! The burgesses are upon us. Barley on the port bow, the Vestry Virgins to stabud, a wet sheet and a flowing sea and St. George for Merry England." He pricipitated himself violently down the ladder and began to pace the floor with what he imagined was a nautical roll. " Kiss me, Hardy," he cried and smote himself heavily upon the bosom.

" Steady the Buffs ! " cried Mrs. Meredith busy with her printers' ink, " my need is greater than thine."

Mr. Phont snatched up the telephone : " Augustus ! Augustus ! Stand to ! The hosts of Midian prowl and prowl around ! Hold the Misses Warbler and let Barley through. Yes, I said let Barley through. No, don't break his run. Let him come. I've got welcome written on the door."

For several moments Mr. Phont and his squad waited in tense silence. Then, from the room below, from the wooden staircase came the noise of rapid and ponderous footsteps. The Colonel had stormed the outworks without opposition.

" I am coming, I am coming," breathed Mr. Phont rapturously. " Knock and it shall be opened . . ."

There was a fearful crack as Colonel Barley's boot took the lower panel out of the door. Then things began to liven up. The door was flung back upon its hinges, for a split second a crimson, heavy jowled countenance glowered into the room, and then the water-laden sponge took the man of war smartly in the left ear. Cursing and stamping fit to split, the Colonel dashed the water from his eyes and essayed to stem the stream that was trickling down his collar.

" And what," asked Mr. Phont, drawing himself up with dignity, " is the meaning of this unwarrantable intrusion ? "

For several seconds Colonel Barley glared speechlessly about him.

" If you had looked you would have seen a notice on the door to the effect that visitors are requested to knock," pointed out Mrs. Meredith kindly. "That's what comes of being impatient."

Meanwhile Colonel Barley had found his tongue : "Intrusion ! What the devil do you mean intrusion ? This damned hooliganism is intolerable. I'll have no more of it," and the military fist made the mahogany desk tremble, "no more of it, I tell you. I'll have the whole lot of you prosecuted. I'll gaol every man-jack of you . . ."

"Not to mention every woman-jill of us," murmured Mrs. Meredith wittily.

"And as for this blasted paper of yours, I'll . . ."

"Manners," interposed Julian coyly from the background, "manners. Don't forget there's a lady present, Colonel, or a female at any rate."

"A wanton baggage for preference," breathed Mrs. Meredith.

"And as for you," cried the Colonel advancing menacingly towards Bellairs who was lolling back in a swivel armchair, "as for you, you slanderous young puppy, I've half a mind to break your impudent neck."

"He's got half a mind, anyway," said Mrs. Meredith triumphantly, "fifty per cent. more than I ever expected, I must say."

". . . Nothing but a hot-bed of Communism," trumpeted Colonel Barley. "I give you fair warning the town won't stand for this sort of unlicensed rowdyism. If you lot are under the impression that you can come into this town and turn everything upside down with your libellous rag of a newspaper you're very much mistaken."

"Nevertheless we seem to have made a pretty promising beginning. I mean we're rather on the

right path as it were, don't you sort of feel ? " Mr.
Phont smiled coyly and shot his cuffs. " Definitely
the budding plant, I somehow fancy."

But the Colonel was still at it : " You'll close this
office at once and get out of the town immediately.
You'll hand me a written apology . . ."

Bellairs, who had been wearily lighting a cigarette,
suddenly straightened up. His chin stuck out and
that formidable gleam came into his eye. Mr. Phont
retired happily from the fray. This, he felt, was very
definitely Bellairs' party. Just his stoup of sack
in fact.

Slowly Bellairs looked the outraged Colonel up and
down. Then he remarked laconically : " Pills to
you."

" Pills ? " spluttered Colonel Barley.

" Yes, pills. And not liver pills, either," said
Bellairs. " And when you've quite finished spitting
all over my desk and dribbling all over the floor
perhaps you'll explain the meaning of this extraordinary
behaviour. This military tomboy stuff may impress
the local Territorials but it doesn't impress the *Weekly
Probe*. I would have you know, sir, that there is such
a thing as the liberty of the subject, the sacred rights of
the individual. Perhaps you would care to see my
views upon the matter in a little article in this week's
Probe. ' The Shadow of the Swastika.' I recommend
it to your notice. It contains some admirable sentiments couched in my usual florid yet pungént style . . ."

But here the Colonel once more came to the boil :
" You unprincipled young cad ! You'll retract every
word of it. It's a scandalous libel and you'll answer
for every word of it in a court of law. And what's

more," proceeded the Colonel, getting into top gear, " you'll have to answer for that business at the theatre last night. A breach of the peace, nothing less, endangering the lives of the audience. I'll have the whole scandalous affair brought home to you and you'll pay for it dearly, believe me . . ."

" And so," said Bellairs suavely, " you imagine the *Weekly Probe* was behind last night's skirmishing ? Well, well, who knows ? But before we go further into that, permit me to read you an excerpt from my tersely written account of the evening's frolics."

Bellairs picked up a copy of the *Probe* and cleared his throat : " At the height of the pandemonium," he read, " just before the scene was plunged into utter darkness, our special correspondent who was present, distinctly noticed a tall, dark, heavily-built man standing on the stage, shouting and waving his arms about. Though the identity of those responsible for the outrage is still a mystery, it seems more than likely that this man had something to do with it. Fortunately a *Weekly Probe* photographer who was on the spot secured a flash-light picture of this mysterious individual. This photograph, though too late for insertion in this week's issue, is available for inspection at our offices and will be published next week. So seriously do we regard this outrage, so foul a blot do we feel it to be upon the fair escutcheon of the borough that we offer a reward of ten pounds to anyone who can identify the subject. And now, Ansell," concluded Bellairs, calmly turning to Julian, " will you be so kind as to hand me portfolio B. B for Barley."

For a moment Bellairs lolled back in his chair and surveyed Colonel Barley slowly from head to foot.

Then he flipped open the portfolio and pushed it across the desk : " Rather entertaining, don't you think, Colonel ? "

Colonel Barley passed from red to mauve, from mauve to mottled purple and thence to chlorine green as he goggled down at a snapshot of himself, caught in mid-gesture above a seething mass of burgesses, upon the stage of the theatre.

At that moment a boy poked his head round the door : " Please, Mr. Bellairs, there's a lot of folks downstairs come to look at that there photo."

With a dramatic gesture Bellairs picked up Colonel Barley's rhinoceros-hide whip and gave it a resounding crack : " The whip-hand, Colonel Barley, the whip-hand. Good morning."

" Superb," crooned Mr. Phont as the sounds of Colonel Barley's retreat died away, " colossal. What omniprescience, what incomparable flair."

" So so," said Bellairs, magnificently casual, " but elementary."

In the background Julian and Mrs. Meredith solemnly executed a hornpipe.

Then the telephone trilled. Mr. Phont snatched it up : " Augustus ? Yes, yes ? The Vestry Virgins ? You fended them off ? Good. Ah ! yes, yes, you took a strong line, that's the stuff. A subtle line, you say ? A what ? A walking advertisement ? Strewth ! "

With one accord Mr. Phont and his companions dashed to the window and looked out into the street.

" Heaven help us," cried Bellairs ecstatically, " pressed down and flowing over."

Pounding down the street, baying, stamping hob-nailed shoes, gesturing with upraised ash-plants went the Misses Warbler, and, attached to the back of each, gaily fluttering in the breeze of their own making, was a glaring red and yellow *Weekly Probe* contents bill. Already they were followed by the makings of fair-sized and highly appreciative crowd.

Mr. Phont was just making play with the brandy bottle when further sounds of turmoil arose from the room beneath.

" More guests, I fancy," said Bellairs poking his head round the door, " more deputations of blistered burgesses."

Suddenly he nipped back into the room : " Alderman Deacon and Councillor Sam Nurture.   Pity we haven't got time to fix that sponge up again."

" Perhaps," said Mrs. Meredith, " I could wipe their eyes with this syphon."

" No," said Bellairs, settling himself at the desk. " I rather fancy subtlety is what's wanted here.   Force yields to finesse and not before time."

At that moment there was a smart tattoo upon the door and the Mayor and Councillor Nurture pressed themselves into the room.   They breathed heavily ; their glances were indicative of mental perturbation.

" To what," began Mr. Phont suavely, " do we owe this altogether unexpected pleasure ? "

Meanwhile Mrs. Meredith was busily pushing forward two chairs into which Mr. Phont made haste to press the two protesting visitors : " The Mayoral feet must be weary, the consular calves must be more than a little fatigued so hot is the day.   And now perhaps a little dash of brandy might not come amiss."

" Now look 'ere," said Councillor Nurture, managing at last to get a word in edgeways, " me and 'is worship 'aven't come 'ere to waste our valuable time chattin' and boozin'. Let's get down to business."

" Ah," concurred the Mayor. " And I'm goin' to speak my mind."

" Fancy," breathed Mrs. Meredith, " the Mayor's got a mind, too ; at least I suppose he must have if he's going to speak it. Really the borough is getting too depressingly intellectual by a long way."

" Just sentiments," agreed Mr. Phont pleasantly. " Let us get down to business by all means. I may say I am urgently in need of my luncheon, whilst you, Mr. Mayor, and you, Councillor Nurture, doubtless have pressing engagements with quantities of ironstone and pork pies respectively. But a little brandy surely wouldn't come amiss."

" I don't take no alco'ol," said Alderman Deacon sternly. " As a Congregationalist of many years' standing I takes a firm line against spirituous liquors of all kinds. They do a man 'arm. They saps 'is energy."

" Dear me," said Mrs. Meredith, " I thought that was quite another sport."

" What do they know of Heaven who only soft drinks sup ? " quoted Mr. Phont sadly. " However, perhaps precept and example may succeed where the spoken exhortation so lamentably fails." He emptied his tumbler.

At this point Bellairs, who had been champing up and down in the background with ill-concealed impatience, took command. He approached the two burgesses and wagged a finger at them :

" Shoot," he said laconically, and spat into the waste-paper basket.

Alderman Deacon, who prided himself upon his cold blood and general mental equilibrium, cleared his throat and opened up : " We 'ave come, Nurture and me 'as come, to demand an explanation and an apology."

" That we 'ave," burst in Councillor Nurture, " and I may tell you I've just been to see young Gavelkind 'oo informs me 'as 'ow I've got grounds for proceedings agen yer."

" Apologies ? " asked Mr. Phont. " Proceedings ? Explanations ?   What talk is this ?   Kindly explain."

" Now don't you go trying to brazen it out," advised Alderman Deacon.   " You all knows well enough what I mean.   What about this 'ere paper you're publishing ? "

" It's doing very well, thank you," said Mr. Phont. " As a matter of fact I'll tell you in all confidence that we've cleared eight thousand copies.   If you would care to invest any money I can assure you it's a going concern . . ."

" And it'll damn soon be gone altogether if I know anything about it," said Alderman Deacon smartly. " I warn you," and here the Mayoral whiskers billowed and shook, " I gives you fair warnin' that all this 'ere 'as got to stop.   What about all that stuff you put in about me ?   What about that I'd like to know ? "

" Ah," agreed Councillor Nurture forcibly, " and that there tarradiddle about the Naughty Councillor. It's libellous, that's what it is, it's slanderous and you'll 'ave to answer for it in a court of law."

" I come 'ere," resumed Alderman Deacon, getting once more into his stride, " as the chosen representative of this 'ere borough, and what I says now goes for the 'ole Town Council as well. And what I says is this, that we 'oo guides the destinies of this town is not going to stand for this sort of unlicensed 'ooliganism. If you, Mr. Phont and Mr. Bellairs, if you two think as 'ow you can come into this town and start turnin' everything upside down you've got 'old of the wrong end of the stick. If you think as 'ow you can start flingin' scandalous libels at the 'eads of them 'as runs this borough you're mightily mistaken and that's flat."

" And what do you propose to do ? " asked Bellairs sharply.

" Do ? " shouted Alderman Deacon. " You'll know soon enough what we intends to do. We'll make it so damned 'ot for you that you'll close down this 'ere scandalous paper and get out of this 'ere borough a sight quicker than what you came in. And furthermore," and here the Mayor dribbled slightly in his whiskers through excitement, " I may say you'll be very lucky if you avoids a prosecution for breach of the peace. I've just been with the Chief Constable 'oo informs me that in 'is opinion it's you lot wot was be'ind last night's disgraceful proceedin's at the theatre. So what 'ave you got to say to that ? "

Bellairs lit a cigarette and inhaled deeply. Slowly he blew out the smoke and eyed Alderman Deacon between narrowed eyelids.

Suddenly he sat up with a jerk : " What have I got to say ? Why, I've got a hell of a lot to say, Alderman Deacon. In the first place, allow me to tell you a few home truths. My comrades and I on the staff of the *Weekly Probe* have taken a strong dislike to this town. In our opinion it is nothing but a hotbed of graft,

hypocrisy and complacent smuggery.   It is our avowed
intention to turn it upside down and inside out.   We
intend to shake it to the core, set it by the ears and
purge it to the very bowels.   As you may have noticed
we have made a very promising start, but only a start.
We shall go on.   In the face of no matter what opposition, no matter what threats, bribes or favours held out
to us, we shall go on.   For a very long time, Alderman
Deacon, for more years than I care to recollect, you
and men of your ilk have been playing hokey-pokey
with the affairs of this borough.   But the day of
reckoning has come.   To put it bluntly, you, Alderman
Deacon, and the rest of your confederates are for it.
Your number is up.   If you think you can bluff the
Weekly Probe as you have bluffed the innocent burgesses
you are very much mistaken.   You speak of prosecu-
tions, of libel actions, of drastic measures of suppression.
Well, Alderman Deacon," and here Bellairs' voice
rasped, " just allow me to tell you this ; if you and
your confederates haven't seen the inside of a gaol
before this day twelve month I shall be very much
surprised."

" And now," continued Bellairs, turning to Julian,
" to save further argument kindly hand me files D
and N.   D for Deacon ; N for Nurture."

Slowly Bellairs weighed file D in his hand whilst
he contemplated the Mayor with grim satisfaction :

" Now, Alderman Deacon," he began chattily, " I
have here a very interesting little portfolio and, strange
as it may seem, the contents are all about you.   You
appear surprised ; but not nearly so surprised as I was
when I began to dig into your past career, Alderman
Deacon.   Really, I had no idea of all the fun and games

you had been up to. However, I won't bore you by going through it all. I will call your attention to one matter only." Here Bellairs peered more closely into the file. " The little matter I have in mind is a balance sheet. It is a very old balance sheet—almost twenty years old—so that perhaps is why it looks so odd. It seems to appertain to an ironstone workers' sick and dividing club."

With a strangled shout the Mayor made a dive for the file, but he was too late. Bellairs had slipped it into a drawer.

" Come, come, Alderman Deacon," he remarked coyly. " Manners, manners."

Alderman Deacon, who had gone grey-green in complexion, slumped back in his chair, goggling.

" And now," said Bellairs, taking up file N, " we come to the hideous past of Councillor Sam Nurture. I see something about an affiliation order in his early youth, but that, I fancy, is hardly worth our notice. After all, boys will be fathers. But here I see," and again Bellairs' gaze concentrated, " we have a singularly interesting little note written by a man named Tompkins. Poor Tompkins, it appears, hanged himself in a public convenience, but not before he had committed to paper some rather startling accusations about one Samuel Nurture. A pity," concluded Bellairs, looking meditatively at the ceiling, " that the coroner never saw this note. I fancy he might have been amused."

For several moments there was complete silence punctuated only by the stertorous breathing of Messrs. Deacon and Nurture.

At length the latter leaned forward. A sickly smile

appeared upon his countenance : " Now surely, Mr. Bellairs, there's no reason for us to lose our tempers over a little matter of this sort.   No doubt we can come to some amicable arrangement.   Now shall we say a hundred pounds ?   Or I might make it guineas."

Bellairs smiled acidly : " So that's the game, is it, Councillor Sam Nurture ?   Bribery and corruption. Come, come, sir.   Go to, go to . . .   That sort of thing may get past in the local council chamber, but not here."

" Perhaps I was a little hasty," began Alderman Deacon.   " I have the welfare of the borough so closely at heart that I am afraid my zeal sometimes causes my tongue to run away with me.   Now I'm thinking of selling out my holdings in the gas company . . ."

" Stop, stop," cried Bellairs clapping his hands to his ears.   " Really this is too immoral, too scabrous by half.   No, my lads," and again the nasty rasp crept into his voice, " I've caught you on the hop this time and on the hop you stay.   These," and here Bellairs tapped the two portfolios, " I shall retain as guarantees of your good behaviour.   And now, perhaps, you will be wanting to get along to report to your committees, not to mention your legal advisers.   Good day."

" What," asked Mr. Phont as they watched from the window the two burgesses making all speed down the street, " is that curious black ring on the Mayoral bottom ?   And on Nurture's, too, I see the same monogram.   Very curious.   Rather indecent, I somehow feel."

Following Mr. Phont's gaze the others saw that the seats of the two burgesses' light summer flannels bore a clearly marked black circle.

"It looks to me as if they had sat down on something," hazarded Julian.

"Or just come away from somewhere," said Bellairs. "Very rude I call it."

"I must have my own childish pleasures," breathed Mrs. Meredith, and she indicated the two chairs so recently occupied by the Mayor and the Chairman of the Town Advertisement Committee. Upon the seat of each was a neatly drawn circle of printer's ink.

"A woman of parts," breathed Mr. Phont rapturously as he capered about the room.

"There's only one thing that worries me," said Bellairs over the post-luncheon coffee at the Priory. "I wonder if we were well-advised in letting go at Twidale's tallow-works as we did. He may kick up trouble, and with his money and influence he could make things deucedly awkward for us. I'm rather afraid we over-egged the pudding a little there. In view of his three-quarter share in the *Gazetteer*, he won't exactly love the *Probe* in any event."

"Mr. Bellairs wanted on the 'phone, please," said the housemaid. "Alderman Twidale. He says it's urgent."

"I thought as much," said Bellairs getting up grimly. "I fear we're in a tough spot."

He left the room, and snatches of his conversation floated in from the hall : "Alderman Twidale? Yes, this is Bellairs of the *Probe* speaking. What's that ? "

There followed a long pause and then Bellairs tuned up again : "Retract all I've said ? Pills to you, Alderman Twidale, I say pills to you. An apology and damages ? Have a banana. Yes, I said have a banana and you know what to do with it, too. You'll bust us, will you ? Well, just you try." The receiver was slammed down and Bellairs re-entered looking distinctly grim.

"Just what I feared. He's going to cut up rough. We're in a jam, chaps."

"But surely," protested Mr. Phont, " he can't do much."

"He can do enough to put us down the sink if he really gets vindictive," said Bellairs. " I was a fool to publish that stinks article."

"But what about the files ? " enquired Julian. " Can't we put him on the spot like Deacon and Nurture ? "

"That's just the point," said Bellairs. " We've got nothing on him. Alderman Fred Twidale has led a depressingly moral life, and furthermore he has always kept on the right side of the law, if only just."

"Shall we have to try and come to an arrangement with him, then ? " asked Mr. Phont. " I hardly like truckling to men of Twidale's kidney."

Suddenly Bellairs' jaw jutted : " No, stab me, we'll have no truckling. We'll beat him at his own game. We've got nothing on him yet, but, by Heaven, we'll put something on him. We'll frame him good and proper. Just leave it to me." Slamming the door behind him Bellairs went out.

"Where's he gone ? " asked Mrs. Meredith. " To get tight ? "

"Really, my dear," remonstrated Mr. Phont, " you shouldn't ask tactless questions. I can only tell you that in Bellairs' opinion there is more stern thinking done in the privy than in the study. I can only conclude that he practices what he preaches. You see, he'll be back soon with some marvellous scheme, not to mention half a dozen epigrams and a brace of cosmic comments."

The housemaid appeared again : " Lady Wycherley, sir. She seems in a hurry."

Mrs. Meredith arose purposively : " This is my cup of tea. I've been waiting for this for a long time. Leave her to me."

Mr. Phont contemplated Julian ruefully across the table : " Well, my boy, such is the peaceful life of the provinces. However, troubles are like bubbles, they're born to fade away. At least I sincerely trust so. By the way, I feel rather sorry for Lady Wycherley. Barbara's so passional when roused."

But Julian, overcome by the stress of life, had fallen sound asleep where he sat.

9

Burgess Frolics

SEVERAL DAYS HAD PASSED since the soul-stirring publication of the first issue of the *Weekly Probe*, and the borough was beginning to settle back into its pristine coma. At the Priory, however, a pleasant state of suppressed excitement was to be apprehended.

Since Alderman Fred Twidale's ultimatum nothing had been seen of Bellairs who was keeping to his rooms with a stock of Mr. Phont's brandy to aid his cerebral motions. The Rev. Jasper Skillington was still nursing his battered pate, Mrs. Meredith was having a few days in bed, whilst Mr. Phont and Julian recouped themselves with a little mild gardening. The *Probe*, meanwhile, was left in the care of the invaluable Augustus and Bellairs' new assistant, Sidney Stipend, a Stavroginesque young man with a remarkable flair for scandal and a mind tortured and soured by a young woman who would never ' come to the point '. Whether he referred to the amorous or the dialectic point was not clear.

It was the last morning of July when Julian struggled down to breakfast at half-past ten to find Mr. Phont walking briskly about the hall and rubbing his hands gleefully.

" I have just been on the 'phone with the incomparable Bellairs," began Mr. Phont. " He is very drunk, but assures me he has hit upon an infallible

174

scheme for putting Fred Twidale on the spot. At present he is polishing up the details. All I know is that he wants me to take him up to London to-day to make contact with a certain young medical student named Pogo Tuddenham. He, I gather, is an essential part of the scheme for Twidale's undoing. Meanwhile," concluded Mr. Phont, " Bellairs suggests that you spend the afternoon with the Rev. Percy Bedrock at the Little Pittle Annual Fête and Gala to be held at the Rectory in aid of the new Church Heating System and Choirboys' Outing Fund."

" I shall enjoy that," said Julian busy at the sideboard. " If there's one thing I like more than another it is a nice Annual Fête and Gala. Besides, I feel we are in literary duty bound to lend our support to the Rev. Percy Bedrock."

" True," agreed Mr. Phont, " and don't forget the Grand Historical Pageant, written and designed by the Rev. Percy himself. He, I understand, impersonates the Venerable Bede, whilst Salome Warbler is to take the part of Queen Elizabeth in another scene."

" There should be some quiet fun to be got out of that," mused Julian, thoughtfully, champing his kedgeree.

" Yes, hot it up if you can," urged Mr. Phont. " Bellairs badly needs a back-page story before Friday. And now I must be getting along to the Metropolis. I rather think I shall call on Jenny Flower. Shall I give her your love ? " he concluded roguishly.

" Jenny Flower," mused Julian. " Really I had almost forgotten about her. No," he concluded with energy, " you can warm her pants for her and tell her from me that her methods are at once too expensive and too complicated. Tell her that since coming down here I have been completely converted to the agricultural as opposed to the urban types. More passion and less palaver. By the way, what's Puggy Congreve's telephone number."

Mr. Phont twinkled genially : " Ah ! youth, youth ; the pertinacity and resiliency of youth, flitting lightly like a butterfly from Flower to Congreve. In the torrid twenties rebuffs serve but as apéritifs to the amorous feast, alimonies as liqueurs. When the blood pulses strongly, when the muscles are taut, no matter how exacting the lady of our affections we can always make a stand. But how soon the rot sets in. From the triumphant thirties how rapidly we pass through the frenzied forties to the lamentable, the frigid fifties. And then," concluded Mr. Phont, his voice taking on a tone of the acutest melancholy, of the most profound pathos, " and then if we would make a stand, how often, alas, must we do so with our backs to the wall."

" By the way," said Julian as Mr. Phont was leaving, " talking about telephoning, if you really are going to see Jenny Flower you might try pressing button B to see if you can get some of my money back."

After a nice little luncheon of salmon mayonnaise and iced hock, Julian proceeded to attire himself as a lily of the field. He adopted his musical comedy outfit of white scarf, double-breasted dark blue jacket, white flannel trousers and pussy shoes. Then he climbed into Bloody Mary and set out for Little Pittle Rectory.

The Little Pittle Fête, under the energetic guidance of the Rev. Percy Bedrock, had gradually pushed itself into a position of considerable local importance. It was now one of the principal annual burgess frolics.

As Julian spanked Bloody Mary along at a good brisk pace he overtook, with a benedictory whiff of burnt Castrol R, bevies of smug burgesses in their mass-produced family limousines, and streams of sweating cyclists and pedestrians, all heading for Little Pittle.

The Little Pittle benefice was what is known in clerical circles as a ' plum '. The Rectory was large, the grounds extensive, the living some twelve hundred gross (nine-fifty nett approx.), whilst the duties demanded of the incumbent were merely the curing of some two hundred and fifty souls. At the moment of Julian's arrival the opening ceremony was just taking place on the wide gravel sweep before the front door. He was about to navigate the gateway when he was held up by an ancient churchwarden with a clotted beaver and a thick gold Albert. Impatiently Julian tapped his accelerator pedal with consequent roarings, bangings and cracklings whilst the gate-keeper extricated himself from the region of Bloody Mary's radiator and approached :

" It'll cost yer a bob," he remarked tersely.

" It'll cost me nothing," replied Julian, who was feeling rather rampant. " Press," he added laconically.

" Press ? " asked the old man sceptically. " You bain't from the *Chronicle and Gazetteer ?* "

" No, don't be rude," replied Julian haughtily. " I bain't from no *Chronicle* and no *Gazetteer*. I be from the *Weekly Probe* I be, and furthermore my good man I bain't agoin' to pay. Not so much as a 'apenny, I ain't."

At the mention of the *Weekly Probe* the churchwarden jumped as if stung. A mixture of awe and suspicion overcast his countenance :

" I don't rightly think as 'ow I ought to let yer through," he mused doubtfully. " Not for nowt."

" Don't think," advised Julian letting in the clutch, " it doesn't suit your kind of face."

Thereupon Bloody Mary leapt forward, throwing a spurt of smoke and gravel into the faces of an interested crowd of yokels who had gathered round to assist at the argument. Having thus successfully passed the portals, Julian circled the drive with a lot of unnecessary banging and growling, drew up with a lavish skid and dismounted. Staring haughtily about him, he languidly made his way towards a seat on the front row, produced a notebook and pencil from his pocket and sternly surveyed the assembled company.

His appearance, he noticed with satisfaction, was not passing unnoticed. Whilst his immediate neighbours showed a tendency to shrink away from his vicinity as if he were plague-stricken, those at more distant points made no bones about rising from their seats to have a look at him. Furtive glances were directed at him from all sides, whilst in many quarters there was much leaning together for the exchange of knowing and disapproving comment. Heads were deprecatingly nodded ; eyebrows significantly raised.

Two rows to his rear he was conscious of the presence of Mrs. Sam Nurture and Mrs. Deacon, both of them sweating profusely in striped silk dresses and gold bangles. Their zeal, unfortunately for them, outran their discretion. Broken snatches of chat came clearly to Julian's ears. " 'E's a one if you like . . . 'e writ that shockin' dirty play that's on in London . . . always 'angin' about up at that Mrs. Meredith's . . . 'e's on the *Weekly Probe*."

Slowly Julian arose and turned about. For a moment he surveyed the two discomfited matrons with a withering glare. Then he spoke in clear, ringing tones audible to the assembled company : " Mesdames Nurture and Deacon, whilst your undoubted interest in my humble person flatters me exceedingly, I must regretfully ask you to refrain from discussing my private life in public. If I can be of any service to you in a private capacity, however, you have only to call upon me at my home address between the hours of eleven p.m. and nine a.m. when your slightest wish shall be my command upon a cash payment of the usual fee."

As Julian resumed his seat the horrified silence was broken by the timely outbreak of the National Anthem.

In the front rows the upper classes stood rigidly to attention with that slightly defiant look upon their faces such as is inevitably conjured up by that inspiring lyric. Those who held, or who had held at one time, commissions in His Majesty's Services produced the authentic pose—chins up and out, chests (or, as in some cases, stomachs) up and out, thumbs to seams of trousers, feet at an angle of forty-five degrees. Those who had no connection with His Majesty's Services did their best somewhat sheepishly to follow suit. The women, all too well aware how lamentably unbecoming to a woman is the attention position, hung their heads slightly as if in prayer and endeavoured to avoid dropping their handbags. All succeeded in looking supremely ridiculous. It was a pity, too, that the Rev. Percy Bedrock, who fancied himself as an accomplished vocalist, had pitched the whole business several tones too high.

At the conclusion of this trying ordeal there was a grateful resumption of seats and the preliminary passes were opened by Major Cockerell. The Major, in an ancient greenish tweed coat, an M.C.C. tie and yellowish shoes turned up at the toes, presented the appearances of a rather frowsy parrot. He cleared his throat, flexed his knees and broke out : " It gives me great pleasure, ladies and gentlemen, to come here this afternoon to open these . . . ah . . . these proceedings. But, deeply conscious as I am of the honour conferred upon me, I have no intention of boring you good people with any poor remarks of mine. . . ."

" Good," remarked Julian resonantly.

" The cause, as you are all well aware," resumed the Major, " is a most worthy one. I refer, of course, to the choirboys and the church stove. It is high time that something was done for the choirboys. The lads have always displayed a remarkable sense of sportsmanship and esprit de corps. They are deeply imbued with the team spirit. They have consistently played the game and, though springing from . . . ah . . . from humble surroundings, they have never failed to conduct themselves in the true public-school tradition. In a word they play cricket." (Applause.)

The Major warmed to his work : " As one who solemnly believes that the integrity of the British Nation and our far flung Empire can only be maintained upon a solid basis of unity between Church and State, I recommend you to support our worthy cause this afternoon whole-heartedly." Here the Major paused to catch an approving nod from Sir Bertram Buckle in the front row. " I remember once at Jubbalpore when I was officer commanding. . . ."

" Keep to the point," urged Julian so distinctly that several of his neighbours turned round and stared at him. However, they were met by such a ferocious scowl that they very rapidly looked away again.

Five minutes later the Major was still remembering. Most of India had been traversed. A short tour of the Union of South Africa had been undertaken, and now the Major was expatiating upon the beauties of the harbour of Rio de Janeiro at sunset.

" Sunrise," corrected Julian truculently as the iced hock began to take a firmer grip, " not sunset."

Even in the front rows boredom was now beginning to become apparent. Sir Bertram Buckle was plainly looking at his watch, whilst Captain Polo was crossing and uncrossing his legs, impatiently jingling his small change and tugging feverishly at his moustache.

" We do not want to go to war," the Major averred. " God forbid ! Those of us who have seen active service, those of us who fought for King and country in the last great holocaust, those of us who saw Ladysmith and Mafeking piously hope we may never live to see another war. But," and here the Major adopted a crouching attitude and wagged a menacing forefinger, " war may yet be forced upon us. The Hun is still the Hun. A single spark may at any moment send the Mediterranean up in flames. There is the Yellow Peril. There is the Red Menace. Consider, too, our solemn responsibilities towards our great Empire, the Great Commonwealth of Nations. Under the shadow of the Union Jack lie vast tracts of territory inhabited by savage tribes. These must be policed, the Pax Britannica must be maintained, and to carry out these obligations we must be prepared." Here the Major put on pressure but, unfortunately, his voice cracked on a falsetto, giving more than ever the impression of an indignant parrot. " In view of these contingencies the O.T.C's should lie close to the hearts of all of us. They should be our deep concern. The O.T.C's are not militarist organisations ; they turn a boy into a clean, manly fellow, ready to take hard knocks and, if need be, by God, to give 'em. The O.T.C. teaches a boy self-reliance, the ability to command. In these dark days when our frontier is the Nile. . . ."

But at this point relief came from an unexpected quarter. The Rev. Percy Bedrock who, too, was determined to have his say, was seen to lean forward in his seat and smartly twitch the Major's coat-tails. Testily the Major turned and exchanged a few whispered remarks with the Rector. He was seen to shrug irritably and colour hotly. Then he turned once more to the audience :

" Well, my friends," he remarked pointedly. " The Rector informs me that my time is up. Doubtless he has some words of wisdom for you himself," here the Major permitted a note of sarcasm to creep into his voice. " In the meantime I recommend you to go and make hay while . . . ah . . . the sun shines. It is your duty as good Churchmen and true blue Con-servatives," concluded the Major, becoming exquisitely waggish, " to go home with empty purses. Throw your money away," he exhorted, getting carried away on the flood of his own eloquence, " spend it like water. And don't forget," and here the Major looked singularly arch, "that the money that you burn to-day will warm you in church next winter."

Amid polite, if forced, mirth and clapping the Major

sat down. His good humour was quite restored now that he had got in his little quip so satisfactorily. After all, he had been working at it for the past ten days.

After the Rector had made a few disjointed remarks in the course of which he misquoted extensively from Wordsworth and accurately and even more extensively from his own work *Lyric for Lammastide*, the gathering dispersed to be robbed of its hard-earned monies.

Julian was drifting about vaguely when he heard himself addressed as ' young man'. He turned round to find himself faced by Major Cockerell.

" Well, young man," asked the Major genially, " I saw you taking notes of my little speech. Anything that wasn't quite clear ? " The Major, who dearly loved to see his lucubrations in print, was always affable to reporters.

Julian felt the bile in him rising as he contemplated the Major rocking complacently back and forth on his heels. He immediately determined to be insulting. " Anything not quite clear ? My dear sir, it was all perfectly clear—clear as mud. Never have I heard a more pitiable display of complacent balderdash, of wandering, disconnected drivel in all my life. As a confirmed pacifist and anti-militarist, I take the strongest possible exception to all that blurb about Empire and O.T.C's. The Great Commonwealth of Nations, forsooth ! I can see nothing to be proud of in our having wrested one third of the globe from its rightful owners by a series of acts of unprincipled banditry. You seem to forget, my dear sir, that Mussolini has but repeated in Abyssinia to-day what we began in India a hundred years ago. And, further-more, permit me to inform you that if the British left

India to-morrow, all that they would leave behind them would be a W.C. and a bottle of Eno's Fruit Salts. And as for that alleged joke of yours about the church stove, why it's the weakest crack I've ever heard outside a B.B.C. variety programme. And now you silly old smug, complacent, bone-headed, hypocritical humbug, good afternoon."

Having vented his spleen, Julian felt much better until he met the Rev. Percy Bedrock who was carrying round a large china doll, asking people to guess its name. He buttonholed Julian who at once decided to be fatuous.

" Rahab," he said smartly as he handed over his twopence.

" Come, come," said the Rector smiling archly to show that even if he was a parson he was well up to an indelicate allusion, " Jezebel, perhaps, or even Aholibah, but not Rahab."

" Naughty, naughty," replied Julian roguishly. Then his gaze concentrated and he eyed the cleric sternly : " Go to, go to, Rector. I'm surprised at you. I can guess what games you were up to as a young rip about Oxford."

" Taking notes, I see," remarked the Rev. Percy turning the discussion rapidly. He indicated Julian's book and pencil. " Taking notes, ah yes," he repeated.

" Taking notice," said Julian mysteriously.

" You write shorthand, I see. An invaluable accomplishment. A great advantage in no matter what walk of life one may pursue. An admirable training for mental alertness. A convenient preservative for those profound and golden thoughts that flash like lightning into the mind."

" And flash like greased lightning out of it if you don't MAKE A NOTE OF IT," supplemented Julian. " Motto for every young man desirous of getting to the top of the ladder," he continued. " Make a note of it. There's plenty of room at the top. Go to night-school. Don't be content with your present post. I was once in your position but look at me now. I had ambition. I stuck in hard at it. I studied at home." Julian was getting really worked up and waved his hands about elegantly. Occasionally he stabbed with his pencil, causing the Rector to give back hastily, and he fixed the priest with a basilisk stare in the manner of the Pelman prospectus.

" Quite," said the Rev. Percy Bedrock, avoiding Julian's flapping notebook by a neat side-step, " quite. By the way I trust you're staying on to see my Potted Pageants. Profound and mellifluous, I flatter myself. Comprehensive yet terse. Like Mr. Noel Coward I do the whole thing, you know ; music, settings and text. You will notice a distinct Picasso influence in the settings, whilst much of the music derives from Bartok. The text, of course, is in pure iambics. I pique myself that I have caught not a little of the rotundity, the rolling reverberation of the Bard. But it's strenuous," concluded the Rector sadly, " terribly exhausting this versatility. How I sympathise with Leonardo da Vinci ! I often wish I could limit the scope of my talents but the artistic spirit permits of no idling. Besides, there is one's duty to the public. If one has the stuff in one," and here he significantly tapped his forehead, " if the impulse is there is one justified in thwarting it ? Is one justified in depriving the world of one's maximum output ? I think not."

" And you are taking all the parts yourself ? " asked Julian chattily.

" No, I fear not. I haven't the time. I have restricted myself to the Venerable Bede and John Wilkes."

There was a pause. Suddenly Julian said :

" Not so you'd notice."

" Notice what ? " asked the Rev. Bedrock, pulling down the doll's skirts and preparing to move on.

" I don't write shorthand not so you'd notice," said Julian vaguely and ungrammatically.

" Then I was mistaken ? " asked the Rector, indicating some mysterious meanderings on Julian's notebook. " Those are not shorthand symbols ? "

" I don't know what they are," said Julian confidentially. " I just do it for fun. I think it looks rather business-like and professional. Those marks just sort of come when I waggle my pencil about. Good afternoon."

" That young Ansell," said the Rector to Major Cockerell a little later, " is either drunk or insane." The Major agreed, specifically and at length.

In the meantime Julian was attracted by the sound of tennis balls and went to investigate.

On arriving at the front of the Rectory he found a tennis tournament going forward on the Rev. Percy Bedrock's two excellent courts. Tea-tables were set out under the trees, and on the side lawns were distributed the various stalls and side-shows.

At the Little Pittle Annual Fête and Gala the tennis-tournament was taken very seriously, and Julian made his way to the number one court where a considerable crowd of spectators were ranged upon benches watching

a violent mixed doubles contest. Julian immediately
spotted Puggy Congreve who was partnered by a portly
man of middle age attired in a straw donkey and a
remarkable belt of large proportions that encircled his
loins like a horse's girths.

It was at once evident that Puggy and old Joe Calcraft
were out for blood. In no mean fashion they were
putting it across an equine looking girl partnered by a
dashing young Air Force cadet. Joe Calcraft's methods
were full of guile. Every stroke was strictly unorthodox
in its execution but, at the same time, subtly malign in
intention and craftily effective in result. It was plain,
however, that his mobility was strictly limited ; indeed
he manifestly considered it both unhealthy and un-
dignified to run a foot if it could possibly be avoided.
The result was that Puggy was kept busy capering
backwards and forwards picking up those shots (and
they were not many) that escaped the frying pan swing
of her partner.

And a very pretty sight she made too, Julian decided
as he watched the game for a while before making his
presence felt.

She was wearing a dark blue shirt and a pair of wide-
legged white shorts. She danced about the court as
lightly as a ballerina, and produced her strokes with a
delicious flowing, rippling grace. Her shirt was
plastered to her elegant torso, and Julian felt that whatever the ' Cuplift ' people paid her it was no more than
she deserved. Back and forth she sped, now clouting
the cover off the ball with all her strength, now
executing the most delicate of drop-shots, now cursing
roundly and vigorously the poaching proclivities of her
portly partner.

Just as Puggy finished off a particularly long rally with a brilliant smash from an impossible angle, Julian emerged from the background, draped himself elegantly over a bench beside one net-post and clapped heartily.

Immediately Puggy saw him. She waved her arms in the air, flung down her racket and, totally regardless of her partner and opponents, skipped off the court towards Julian : " Hi ! Ansell ! Hi ! "

" Darling, you," crooned Julian and stepped onto the court to meet her.

" Well, this is a nice surprise," said Puggy sweetly, smiling bewitchingly and tossing back a tumbling lock of hair. " What are you doing here ? "

" Looking at the sweetest thing this side of Heaven," said Julian bowing elegantly. " And I say," he added candidly as he caught the mixed scents of her perfume and her warm young body, " you don't half smell nice."

" Yes, these vital animal odours, don't you know," mused Puggy, hitching up her shorts, " so tantalising to the male. At least they say so in the magazine stories. By the way, don't you like my gear ? " She indicated the shirt and shorts.

" Too divine for words," asserted Julian, " and," he added subtly, " I like the window dressing. Perky yet discreet ; delicate yet bold."

Puggy stretched slowly, offering him her shapes and enveloping him in another cloud of warm scents : " Yes, rather effective don't you think ? A special new sports type they sent down on approval this morning. I'm trying it out. It has a rather amazing counter poise device giving a reverse diagonal uplift. Forgive me if I become technical. . . ." With all the enthusiasm of the well-paid expert Puggy ran through a variety of illustrative poses.

" I'm intensely interested," asserted Julian. " Could we not manage to work in a little practical demonstration ? Afterwards in the shrubbery, perhaps ? "

" Will you please be kind enough to resume your game," said a stern voice from the other side of the court. " You are holding up the whole proceedings. Others are waiting to use the court."

Julian and Puggy looked round indignantly to find themselves being apostrophised by Nathaniel Gavelkind, Solicitor and Commissioner for Oaths, who was perched aloft in the umpire's chair at the other end of the net. He eyed them sternly, and impatiently rapped his score card with a large red pencil.

" Who is that fellow ? " inquired Julian loudly.

" Darling, he's the referee man," explained Puggy equally distinctly. " Old Gavelkind, the solicitor. Heaven knows why they've put him on this job. He knows damn all about it, and he's as astigmatic as a coot. He's been making the most absurd blunders all the afternoon. He gave three of my last service aces out when they were obviously well inside."

" Ha," said Julian sternly, " more underhand work, I perceive."

" But I serve overhand, darling. What do you take me for ? " corrected Puggy testily, picking up her racket.

" I speak purely metaphoric," stated Julian. " More hocus-pocus, more borough racketeering. Nothing, I apprehend, is free from corruption, not even the noble and ancient sport of lawn tennis. Shocking ! The *Probe* will look into this matter."

" Will you kindly get off the court, sir," shouted Mr.

Nathaniel Gavelkind, preparing to dismount from his perch. "You can conclude your interesting conversation elsewhere."

"Presently, my good man," said Julian soothingly, "presently." He surveyed the irate umpire coldly and then turned to Puggy who was sauntering back on to the court : "I can quite believe you're being twisted. I don't like the look of this fellow at all. He looks exactly as if he had just stolen something. . . ."

"He has," said Puggy with emphasis. "Three of my service aces."

"Then," said Julian sternly, draping himself over the net post opposite to old Gavelkind, "I shall remain to keep a personal eye on the proceedings. Any further hole and corner business will be nipped in the bud forthwith ; you have my word for it. The *Probe* will see fair play."

The respite afforded them by the little conversational interlude had put new spirit into the equine girl and the cadet, with the result that the set began to drag. The points were closely contested and the game developed a tedious habit of running to several deuces. In the meantime Julian was rapidly losing patience. Puggy looked so entirely the whole shooting match that he was overwhelmed by an urgent desire to kiss her. Eventually, on Puggy's service, the score reached five-four and vantage striker. Julian with a sigh of relief felt that the end was in sight. Viciously Puggy swung her racket and netted her first serve. Violently she bashed in the second and Julian saw it pitch six inches inside the side lines.

"Fault," cried Mr. Gavelkind. "Double fault. Deuce."

But this was too much for Julian. Violently he began to jump about, running into the middle of the court and waving his arms in the air excitedly :

" In, in," he cried. " What's all this ? Fault be dashed. In, in. A foot inside. Play the white man, Gavelkind. Dash it all, man, where's your sportsmanship ? Deliberate falsification of the score. I shall report it to the committee. I'll have you struck off, struck off I will, not 'arf."

With joyous whoops the spectators clamoured on to the court to join in the argument. Mr. Gavelkind lowered himself from his chair and padded balefully across the court :

" And who the devil are you, sir ? Mind your own confounded business and get off this court. I'm umpiring this game and when I want advice from you or anyone else I'll ask for it."

" Six and eightpence to you," retorted Julian. " You go and buy yourself four pennyworth of tort. Get back, you silly old man, to your hereditaments and messuages. You're not fit to umpire a game of skittles. It strikes me you don't see at all half the time, and when you do you see crooked."

Nathaniel Gavelkind approached closer to Julian and breathed hotly in the region of his chest : " Confound your damned insolence, sir ! You must be drunk, sir, or insane. Clear off this lawn at once or I won't answer for the consequences. As a member of the legal profession I warn you . . ."

" Powers of attorney to you," scoffed Julian, " and likewise affiliation orders ! You had better," and here Julian adopted a markedly sinister aspect, " you had better moderate your tone, sir. Perhaps you are not aware that you are addressing the sports editor of the *Weekly Probe*. Have at you, sir ! The *Probe* for fair play ! The eye of the *Probe* is directed upon this tournament. You had better watch your step, Mr. Nathaniel Gavelkind, you had better return quietly to your commissioning of oaths or you may be pushed off the bus and that without any ejectment order."

An interruption occurred at this point in the shape of the Rev. Percy Bedrock who ran across the lawn wringing his hands and yelping shrilly :

" What is this unseemly wrangling, dear me, yes, yes ? Peace, peace. Permit the Church to intervene. Let us approach the matter in a true Christian spirit. Let us not speak in wrath. Let us seek guidance from above!"

" Guidance from above be blowed," said Mr. Gavelkind savagely. " This young whipper-snapper here, this impudent young puppy . . . " He glared nastily around, but fruitlessly. Julian and Puggy Congreve were no longer of the company. They had folded their tents and stolen away.

" Perhaps," said the Rector resignedly, " it is just as well. The young man is, I fear, unhinged."

" Dashed unhinging, those hinges," commented Julian as he relaxed into the back seat of the Rector's ancient Humber.

Puggy had led the way to the cool retreat of the old coach-house at the back of the Rectory. The Rectorial hearse seemed an admirable love-nest. She climbed in after Julian.

He received her and they opened the office. After a time Puggy squirmed erect and pinched Julian's nose whereupon he emitted a noise like an electric hooter.

" Darling you," cried Puggy delightedly and poked

him in the stomach whereupon he neighed like a goat.
For several minutes they played this game with all the
goodwill in the world. A bit later on Puggy said :
" Tell me, sweetness, why do you hiccough when you
kiss me ? I call it rather vulgar."

" We are wonderfully and fearfully made," remarked
Julian sententiously after a long pause, a dreamy look
in his eyes.

" Let not your left hand know . . ." supplemented
Puggy. " At last I know what it feels like to be on the
horns of a dilemma."

" An itch in time feels fine," said Julian. " By the
way, my love, what is the most attractive part of a man
to the average woman ? "

" Now I wonder," mused Puggy, trying to push her
legs over the back of the front seat and squeeze the
ancient bulb horn between her feet. " Now I wonder.
The hands I think. Yes, definitely ; the hands. And
the way they're used," she added appreciatively.

The ancient bulb horn suddenly gave tongue. They
broke away.

When they got back to the tennis court they found a
brisk search going on for Puggy. She and Joe Calcraft
were scheduled to do battle with a nonconformist pastor
and an elementary school-mistress. They noticed that
the referee had been changed. Mr. Nathaniel Gavelkind had been supplanted by Sir Bertram Buckle who
was doing the benevolent despot from the high chair.

" Come along, young woman," he cried breezily, yet
briskly, to Puggy. " Can't wait all day, you know.
Others are waiting to use this court."

" All right, Bertie. Keep your hat on," replied Puggy
cheerfully. " Old Bert's all right," she added, turning

to Julian. " He'll do the decent thing by me. I'm glad you shifted old Gavelkind."

" The power of the *Probe*," said Julian clearly, beating himself upon the chest. " If you have any trouble with this Buckle fellow just notify me. We'll have no nonsense."

" 'Urry up, young Congreve," grunted Joe impatiently. " And I should button your blouse up if I were you. Even if you have been down the orchard there's no need to go advertising it all over the place."

" I'm hot," explained Puggy, squinting down at herself and flushing slightly.

" Very likely," said Joe, glowering over the net at his opponents, " but this is not the place for showing it."

Julian dallied long enough to see Joe and Puggy take the first game, and then he sauntered off to disport himself until tea-time.

After wasting sixpence on the hoop-la, he expended twopence on a dip in the bran-tub but only succeeded in getting bran up to his armpits and a satin pin-cushion with a view of Lincoln Cathedral on it for his pains.

Then his notice was attracted by a mysterious looking red and white striped tent standing under the cedar tree. He drew up and read the notice : " Let Zenobia read your hand. Your fortune for half-a-crown. See what the future holds."

Julian resolutely pushed aside the tent flap and went in. Sitting at a small table furnished with a crystal and a pack of cards sat a female disguised in flowing oriental robes. A thin veil covered her face. The interior of the tent was stifling and gloomy.

" Rat it," remarked Julian testily as he bashed his nose against the tent pole. He sat down sharply.

" Ah ! you come," remarked the veiled female huskily.

" It seems like it," said Julian.   " Blast that pole."

" It is good you come."

" I'm so glad you're glad to see me.   We always endeavour to oblige.   In fact I'm often described as the little ray of moonshine."

" You were fated to come.   It is written in the stars. You see ? "

" I see stars, if that's what you mean," said Julian bitterly, rubbing his bashed nose.

" We were fated to meet," continued the veiled houri oracularly.   " Our paths were fated to cross.   It is fate."

" A garden fête in fact," said Julian wittily. Suddenly he began to find the heat very oppressive, and the conversation seemed to have reached something of an impasse.   " Well," he urged briskly, " shall we get on. I understand one can be fortunate for half-a-crown.   A reasonable charge I must admit."   He pushed his half-crown across and held out his hand.

" You prefer I use ze crystal or ze cards or ze hand ? " enquired his interlocutor.

" Yes," said Julian comprehensively.

" Ze hand, I sink.   It ees more pairsonal."

" By all means," agreed Julian heartily.   " I'm all for the personal, ze pairsonal, touch.   Hands across the sea and all that sort of thing."   He surrendered his hand into the purple-nailed grasp of the veiled lady.   In the meantime he closely scanned the veiled features.   What he could see of them seemed vaguely familiar.

" You 'ave ze artistic tem'erament," she began. " You are ze literary type."

" Too true, too true," agreed Julian.   " I wield ze

facile pen.   Mr. Ansell's delicate, yet pungent, wit,"
he quoted.   " His inimitable flair for the just word.
His unfailing sense of theatre.   His sensitive feeling for
situation.   This delightful, airy, pungent trifle will be
assured of a long run.   Or, on the other hand," he
continued, running into his best form, " this flimsy,
threadbare conglomeration of stale obscenities and
borrowed epigrams.   This loosely constructed frippery,
forced in its situations, unbelievable in its characterisa-
tion, reminiscent of a rude and unoriginal fifth form
school-boy in its alleged humour."

During this outburst the houri continued to pore over
his hand.   For a moment Julian had an uneasy feeling
that his shirt-cuff wasn't too clean but, he reflected, it
was too dark to see, anyway.

Suddenly his companion thrust her face so close to his
own that he recoiled briskly : " You are ze grand
amorous type.   You make love.   You break ze many
hearts."

" 'Earts," corrected Julian.   " Ze many 'earts."

" You 'ave ze many affaires."

" Well, well," replied Julian airily, " I don't deny
I've had my little peccadilloes.   Mere casanoves-
queries, though, mere tumblings on sofas.   Nothing to
signify."

" But you vill be brought to book," prophesied his
antagonist in sinister tones.   " Zere is a great tragedy
before you.   It vill break you de 'eart."

" Good," said Julian, " now we're coming to it.
We've been dwelling too much in the past.   Let's have
a dip at the future.   After all that's what I paid my
half-crown for.   Proceed, woman."

" You vill fall in love wiz a beautiful golden-haired

boy. He vill break you ze 'eart. You vill know ze agonies of ze frustrated libido. . . ."

The mention of the golden-haired boy touched a chord in Julian's memory. Dimly before his mind's eye floated a vision from the previous week, a vision of the theatre saloon bar with a tense young woman breathing down his collar and making suggestions.

" Well," cried Julian delightedly, " if it isn't Myra Malcolm. By all ze gods, ze so irresistible Myra."

" Julian ! " cried Myra vibrantly as she raised her veil. " Julian ! This is fate." She looked at him meltingly with her incredibly long black eyelashes.

" I'm going to kiss you," said Julian, nipping round the table in a business-like manner. " You arouse the worst in me."

" The worst ? The best ? Who knows ? " demanded Myra cryptically as she came to grips. The best, decidedly the best, she decided as the minutes flew past and Julian's technique displayed itself in a series of mesmerising cadenzas.

" And all for half-a-crown," mused Julian ten minutes later as he pushed back his hair. " Dashed reasonable I call it."

Julian pondered for a few moments and then turned to Myra : " I say, would you mind if I swapped places with you for a time ? I should rather like to have a dip at this fortune-telling business. I imagine I could whack out some rare old stories."

Myra appeared to hesitate. Professional zeal and a sense of duty struggled against a realisation of favours received.

Julian nipped into the breach : " Of course, my dear, I don't see any reason why we shouldn't have a week-end in town together some time. I've really got a most amusing little flat."

" Well," said Myra, " of course if you really want to I don't see any reason why you shouldn't."

" Capital, capital. Hand over the robes of office," cried Julian. " The ultimate mysteries are about to be revealed. The final, the ineffable phrase is shortly to be uttered."

Myra slipped out of the tent and Julian sat down behind the crystal and the pack of cards and carefully draped the veil over his features. He experienced a distinct sense of elation. He hadn't long to wait for his first customer. A rubicund young country woman in flowered silk insinuated herself shyly into the tent and sat down at the table. She pushed her half-crown across and proffered a moist pink fist.

" No," said Julian, using an odd falsetto, " no, my dear young lady, for you the crystal. There be mysteries that only the crystal may reveal." He applied himself to the crystal whilst the young woman trembled in delicious expectation.

" I see," said Julian noncommittally, " much that is good and much that is ill. Through great tribulation you will win through at last to the haven where you fain would be. Love will cross your path, and hate, and jealousy. Sorrow and joy will not be absent, nor will laughter, tears and most of the seven deadly sins."

" Ah," said the young woman breathing heavily, " go on."

Julian drew in the breath between his teeth shudderingly and whispered : " But here the crystal is cracked. I seem to see as if in a glass darkly. The shapes whirl in a black mist of hate and death. The furies scream at the cross-roads. In the forest the dancers dance the dance of death. Ah ! " concluded Julian working himself up to a fine pitch of frenzy, " I cannot look. The vision is too terrible for human eyes. Terrible, unspeakable, hellish apparitions." His voice quivered and he pressed his hands to his eyes. There was a considerable pause.

" Is that all," asked the young woman at length. " Not much for two and a kick, I don't think."

" Not much ! " repeated Julian nettled. " More than enough, I should have thought. However, we'll have just one more dip." Again he grovelled over the crystal, and permitted a series of strange grunting noises to escape his lips.

" Ah ! " he cried excitedly, " the mists begin to clear. They thin. They get thinner. Less dense. Not so thick. I see amongst the mists a face, yes, a dark handsome face, a male face, the face as of an Etruscan god."

" Ar. That'll be Bert," remarked the young woman dispassionately. " 'As 'e got a Clarke Gable moustache ? "

" 'Ar, 'e 'as that," agreed Julian, falling into the vernacular, " and a long black beard. And I see a woman in his arms, a fair-haired, apple-cheeked woman with the figure of a Demeter ; a ripe, mature woman, strong, fertile, vital. They embrace. Their lips are sealed in a long, swooning kiss. The man is drawing the life out of the woman. He is sucking out her soul at her lips. Closer, closer they press. They are locked in a mad, ecstatic embrace. Now he is. . . ." Here Julian stopped suddenly.

" Goo on," cried the young woman excitedly, " goo on."

Julian again pressed his face to the crystal.   Then he looked up : " I cannot goo on.   The mists thicken again.   They swirl.   The vapours descend, and not before time in my opinion."   He sat back and signified that the meeting was at an end.

The young woman looked at him closely : " You aren't 'arf a one, you ain't."

Julian recoiled suspiciously :   " Well, my good girl, perhaps you'd better be getting along.   Others wait without.   Indeed at any moment they may begin to let them down through the roof.   My time is limited, my talents exhausting.   The crystal has gone blank.   It will tell us no more."

" Not 'arf a one, you ain't," repeated the young woman.   " Give us a kiss," she added unexpectedly, and leaning across the table, she tweaked up Julian's veil.

With a strangled bleat he recoiled : " You young cow, you impertinent young hussy," he managed at last to ejaculate as he kicked back his chair and tried to nip round the table to the exit.

The young woman neatly interposed her considerable bulk and cut him off : " Now then, ducky," she admonished roguishly, " it's no good trying to run off.   I knew 'oo you was as soon as I saw you.   You're young Mr. Ansell what's on the *Weekly Probe*.   You ain't 'arf a party, you ain't."   Again she pressed herself in Julian's direction : " Now come on, there's a good boy.   Give us a kiss."

" And if I don't," gasped Julian, backing away from her perspiring bulk.

" Why, I'll scream out," explained the young woman genially, " and then they'll all come in and see 'oo you are and I shall say," she concluded in a matter of fact tone, " as 'ow you was trying to interfere. . . ."

" Heaven help me," cried Julian pathetically.

" It won't, not now. Not unless you kiss me," said the young woman happily. " My name's Rosy," she added somewhat inconsequentially. " Rosy Parnham, it is."

" Well, Miss Parnham," said Julian sternly, " I consider you an immoral, lascivious and unprincipled young cat. Take that." He imprinted a fleeting dab upon her moist forehead.

" That's not 'arf a kiss," cried Rosy sharply. " Come on, give us a proper one."

The next thing that Julian knew was that Rosy had clipped him in an almighty buss, was pressing him backwards against the tent pole and was raining a multitude of wet, salty kisses upon his countenance. Violently he struggled, kicking, and lashing out with his hands, but he was hopelessly entangled by his flowing garments. Furthermore he was hopelessly outweighted. He decided to yield, and strangely enough, having once yielded he began to find it rather pleasant. With a kind of masochistic pleasure he gave up the struggle. Mighty muscular arms grasped him in a marathon embrace, crushing the wind from his lungs. A warm, moist, cushiony pneumaticism enveloped him like a feather bed. Stinging, smacking kisses closed his eyes and smothered his gasping mouth. This, he supposed, was the real rural frolic, the authentic agricultural amorous exchange. What strength, what passion, what an overwhelming emotional cataclysm. How different from the delicate and fastidious exercises on white satin sofas which had so far been his lot. In this brief moment he witnessed the complete upheaval of his conceptions of the amorous technique.   Previously he had but experienced the earth tremor.   This was the genuine, the all enveloping earthquake.

At length he felt himself pushed back into his chair. Rosy paused in the doorway : " You don't know much yet, but you'll learn," she said comfortingly.   Then she was gone.

Shaken, exhausted, outraged yet undeniably exalted, Julian scrambled out of his robes and escaped from the tent.   Idly he began a tour of the Rectory gardens, having ascertained that Puggy was still disporting herself violently on the tennis court.   Leaving the stalls, the predatory females and screaming children behind him, he wandered on until he found himself in the scented calm of the rose garden.   He lowered himself thankfully on to a stone seat and lighted a cigarette.   He permitted his mind to become completely vacant.

Presently he heard a sound of hurried footsteps on the stone path and looked up to find himself confronted by a delicious and sumptuous blonde in a natty little hat and a skilfully cut linen dress.   The vision glanced irritably about her and pulled at a cigarette   Julian immediately recognised Mrs. Leila Barley.   He arose and bowed :

" Forgive me, madam, but you appear to be at a loss. Perhaps you lost something ?   Permit me to offer my poor services."

Leila looked up sharply and considered him : " You're Julian Ansell, aren't you ? "

" Yes, indeed.   Foot loose and fancy free," replied Julian, quickly summing up the type he had to deal with.

" I'm looking for Esmond Duncan," said Leila Barley plaintively.   " He promised positively to meet me here for tea. He's ten minutes late now." She fluttered incredibly long lashes in Julian's direction.

"Unmannerly young cad," said Julian sternly. "However," and here he directed a gaze full of subtle innuendo at Mrs. Barley, "however, I shouldn't wait any longer if I were you. I saw him a few minutes ago near the tennis courts with a red-headed young gladiator. . . ." Julian was a ready liar when necessary.

Leila stamped and succeeded in looking incredibly fetching : " Really he's too bad. He's always running after that footballer, and he swore across his heart to take me to tea." She bit her full underlip.

"Well, then," said Julian, shaping up to her, " I see no good and valid reason why I should not step into the breach. Perhaps you will give me the pleasure of taking you to tea." He turned on his equivocal smile that was intended to convey subtlety, villainy and romantic devilry of every description. It did.

"Well," said Leila, " that's very kind of you. But I don't want to take advantage of you."

" I hope you will," said Julian fervently. " I most certainly hope you will."

Leila enveloped him in an expensive perfume and an expansive smile and they moved off.

Julian led the way to the tea enclosure under the trees but rapidly decided that the amenities were inadequate. Determined mothers bounced howling babies on their knees. Perambulators up-ended the unwary. The heat of the sun had curled the bread and butter into the most unlikely shapes, and the cakes were beginning to run off the plates onto the tablecloths. Wasps and other pests rendered mastication exceedingly hazardous

and, above all, there was no privacy.　This, Julian felt
very definitely, was the time for privacy.

" Most uninviting," he proclaimed loudly.　" Very
badly organised and, doubtless, scandalously dear.
We will seek fresh beds and sofas new."　He took Mrs.
Barley by the elbow and guided her into the Rectory.

" This, I take it, is the drawing-room ; and very nice,
too," said Julian.　" There's something very delightful
about these old-fashioned drawing-rooms I always
think, particularly on a hot day."　He surveyed the
faded wall-paper, the comfortable old chairs, the bowls
of roses, the old satin-wood piano.　The blinds were
drawn and the room was cool, dim and perfumed.

Leila sank elegantly into a low armchair and peeled
off her gloves : " What are you going to do to me
here ? "

" Give you tea," said Julian ringing the bell and
helping himself to one of the Rev. Percy Bedrock's best
cigarettes.

After a considerable pause an angular housemaid
appeared.

" We should like tea as soon as possible," said Julian
loftily.　" The Rector mentioned some strawberries and
cream.　Perhaps you will see into the matter."

The maid gaped uncertainly for a few moments and
then paddled off.　Julian drew up close to Mrs. Barley
and smiled flashingly.

" Really, you're rather wonderful," she breathed.

" I know," said Julian abstractedly.

When she had finished her strawberries Leila got up
and, meditatively sucking a polished finger nail, began
to willow about the room :

" You know you upset Lionel very much with that article about the Territorials. He's been quite off his feed ever since. I must say it's taken some of the steam out of him."

Julian arranged himself artistically on the sofa : " Ah yes ! The outraged spouse and so on. He started misbehaving all over our office, you know, and we had to take him severely to task."

" Poor Lionel," mused Leila, " he's so earnest. He gets things into his head and they stick indefinitely. All last week it was woollen underwear ; long sleeved vests and pants to the ankles and all that kind of thing."

" Marriage is always a mistake for high-spirited types such as you and me," said Julian. " We are too sensitive, too intolerant, we have not sufficiently the give and take temperament. We are, I feel, designed for the fleeting passion. Our love affairs should be numerous and brief."

" I suppose you have been in love with heaps of women," suggested Leila somewhat naïvely.

" Well," said Julian airily, " I keep pretty well to my quota, but between ourselves I'm beginning to find that love is rather like an artesian well, the deeper one goes the profounder the bore. Besides," he continued, warming to his work, " I resent the demands that a love affair makes upon one. Beginning as a harmless pastime it degenerates all too rapidly into downright hard work. Consider the emotional stress and strain, the demands that are made upon one's time, not to mention one's purse. I doubt if it's worth it. But still one persists, one is always ready for just one more amorous excursion in the hope that it may prove more entertaining than the last. And, of course, it never does prove more entertaining. In love more than in any-thing else man is a creature of bad habit ; he never learns by experience. With a ridiculous optimism he pushes on from horizon to horizon in the vain hope that at last he will reach the promised land, the land of tumbling, irreproachable houris. It is really all rather pitiable. Or heroic. It depends which way you look at it. ' We are the pilgrims, master ; we shall go always a little further.' But I have always had an uneasy feeling that pilgrims of any kind, particularly the amorous pilgrim, are more than a little ridiculous."

Leila, who felt that the discussion was getting rather too philosophic, took steps to bring the conversation down to earth : " The trouble I find," she remarked intensely, " is that I can't find the perfect man."

" Aha ! " said Julian, " an idealist, I perceive. Apollo or nothing for you. Well, well, I must confess that I used to think somewhat along those lines once myself. If I couldn't have the Venus de Milo I'd have no one. But I soon found it didn't pay. One must make do with the hand-maidens. The goddess reserves herself for the gods."

" The trouble is," said Leila, determined to keep to hard facts, " that I never seem to be able to find a man who combines passion with polish."

" Proceed," begged Julian. " This promises of interest."

" What I mean is," explained Leila intensely, " that a man who is profoundly passionate, deeply desirous, always lets one down by having dirty finger nails, or by sweating or by using his hands clumsily. I once knew a divine rowing-hearty," she mused ecstatically. " He was the most passional man I ever knew, but he spoilt it all by his fumbling and his whiskers. He never bothered to shave properly."

" I sympathise," said Julian earnestly, " I sympathise profoundly. Fumbling is the unforgivable amorous gaucherie. I suppose that's why concert pianists are such successful lovers. And whiskers, too, I realise must be unendurable. In fact one of the main reasons for my never having married is that I feel no woman can reasonably be expected to look upon her husband in the morning with his overnight growth burgeoning upon his countenance."

" And the other type," pursued Leila, " have no guts. Now take Esmond Duncan. . . ."

" Quite," said Julian understandingly. " Perfectly turned out—hair like clotted honey, hands like gardenia blossoms, a voice like the cooing of the turtle dove. But passion ? No. Amorous avidity nil."

" Precisely," agreed Leila peevishly. " The man's dumb. Do you know I asked him to dine alone with me the other night and do you know what he said ? "

" I've no idea," said Julian, patting the cushions on the sofa.

" He said he was learning to play billiards." Leila Barley's bosom heaved with suppressed indignation.

Julian meditatively tapped a cigarette on his pointed and polished thumb nail : " Passion and patine," he mused. " A big order ; however, one can but do the gentlemanly thing."

He arose and took Mrs. Barley's hands. Mysteriously he drooped his eyelids and smiled. Dewily, expectantly she smiled back at him through the clouds of scented smoke.

" You beautiful thing," whispered Julian, pulling her

down on to the sofa. " Would it surprise you very much to know that I was passionately in love with you ? "

Apparently Mrs. Barley had suspected it for some time.

After some minutes had passed Leila said : " Really, darling, you managed that rather cleverly."

" Never," replied Julian complacently, " shall it be said that Julian Ansell is a fumbler."

Presently an agitated step was heard outside in the hall. Julian and Leila had only just time to disentangle themselves before the Rev. Percy Bedrock came panting into the room. He was plainly much disturbed :

" Ah ! Ansell, my boy, I have been looking for you all over. Making yourselves comfortable I see, ah yes," he added, catching sight of Mrs. Barley who was rapidly readjusting herself.

" Very comfortable, thank you," agreed Julian.

The Rector began to pace about in a markedly agitated manner : " I wonder, my boy, if you could see your way to doing me a favour, a great favour. It's about Bishop Oglethorpe. He has, I regret to say, got exceedingly drunk, so drunk in fact that he cannot possibly appear."

" Bishop Oglethorpe ? " enquired Julian, mystified. " Are you having a Confirmation or something ? Or a pastoral visitation, perhaps ? The bishop drunk ! Shameful ! Disgraceful ! I shall personally refer the matter to the Church Assembly, not to mention the Ecclesiastical Commissioners. And I shouldn't be surprised if Queen Anne's Bounty hadn't something to say about it."

The Rev. Percy, who was only too well aware of Julian's spate once he got started, held up his hands protestingly : " My dear boy, you misunderstand me. You are labouring under a complete misapprehension. We are at sixes and sevens."

" I'm relieved to hear it," said Julian sternly. " But still, drunkenness in episcopal circles should not be blinked. It must be faced. . . ."

" The Bishop Oglethorpe I refer to," nipped in the Rector opportunely as Julian momentarily paused to draw breath, " is an historical character."

" Ah," said Julian sentimentally, " he has passed over. He has passed beyond the veil. No doubt all the tankards pounded for him on the other side. But not before time I must say. However, de mortuis. . . ." Julian assumed an' air of sanctimonious gloom.

" I refer to the last scene of my historical pageant," insisted the Rector, " the crowning of Queen Elizabeth by Bishop Oglethorpe. As you know Miss Salome Warbler is taking the part of the . . . ah . . . the Virgin Queen. Young Percy Todd, my organ-blower, was to have taken the part of Bishop Oglethorpe but, as I say, the wretched boy has become hopelessly inebriated at the critical moment. He shall answer for it, I vow. I intend to challenge him with it. But he is more sinned against than sinning. I fear he is being led astray. He has got in with a group of loose companions. But," and here the Rector looked imploringly at Julian, " this regrettable business puts me in a very awkward position. Unless I can find a substitute for Oglethorpe the whole of the last scene will fall through. Miss Warbler will be furious and I shall be very deeply grieved."

" Grieve not," cried Julian, thumping himself on the chest. " Be of good cheer. I, even I, will be Bishop

Oglethorpe. I, Bedrock, am your man. The pageant shall proceed."

" My dear boy," cried the Rector, " this is indeed providential. You are indeed a very present help in trouble. Come, we will run you through your part. It is comparatively simple, and fortunately you and Percy Todd are much of a muchness."

The Rev. Percy Bedrock dragged Julian from the room. Mrs. Barley followed at a more leisurely pace, a look of dreamy reminiscence in her eyes. At last a young man with perfect hands. The ultimate, the apocalyptic lover. The final, the unbelievable combination of polish and passion.

Meanwhile Puggy Congreve and Joe Calcraft were walking disconsolately about the garden. They had won the tennis tournament and now they were thoroughly fed up with one another.

" I don't know why that damn parson can't give us our prizes now," grumbled Joe, " instead of keeping us hanging about for this theatrical tomfoolery. I'd got a lovely bit of tripe for supper."

Puggy did not reply. She was busy wondering where Julian might be. Presently they found themselves on a side lawn faced by serried ranks of Sunday school children about to give a hymn recital. The children, who were in charge of an inhibited looking woman with protruding teeth and a fixed grin, were obviously only slightly less depressed than the audience. Their shrill, treble voices piped and wobbled in the evening air with a fine disregard alike for tune, rhythm and intelligibility. All the children wore remarkably glazed expressions due to a recent and enormous strawberry tea. They fidgeted from foot to foot, pulled at their clothes and some abstractedly picked their noses. Meanwhile the lady with the grin pounded away at a piano, marking the time by vigorous nods of the head.

" Poor little devils," said Puggy, " it's a shame. Half of them want to go somewhere. They'd be rather sweet if they didn't look so swollen with food."

" Poor little devils be hanged," said Joe Calcraft. " It's my fixed opinion that there are far too many people in this world already." He mounted one of his favourite hobby horses and warmed up : " Now look at these miserable little wretches here. Most of them are mentally deficient and those that aren't are tubercular or suffer from rickets or boils or Heaven knows what. The doctors ought to be ashamed of themselves keeping stock like this alive. What will these kids do when they grow up ? You mark my words, they'll each go and have twenty little degenerates worse than themselves. There are far too many people in this country," concluded Joe Calcraft vehemently. " If I had my way I'd gas all this lot. Gas the lot, I would." He surveyed the children with an air of profound gloom.

" Let's go," said Puggy glumly. " It's sights of this sort that drive one either to chastity or contraception. Besides I positively can't bear to watch that child on the left of the front row any longer. I swear it'll be guilty of an indiscretion in the next few seconds."

" Gas the lot of them, I would," said Joe Calcraft turning away. " Wipe 'em all out, that's my idea."

Suddenly from the rear of the Rectory appeared a motley trio consisting of Julian, Esmond Duncan, and the red-headed footballer. Between them they carried a sack that oscillated violently and emitted shrill squeaks and grunts.

" Darling you," cried Julian, shaping up to Puggy.
" We've got a most almighty jape on foot."

" Swine," said Puggy aggrievedly. " Where've you
been all the time? And what have you got in that sack."

" I've been kissing women and succouring the
Rector," said Julian handsomely. " And as for the
sack, there's a pig in it."

" Yes, positively, my angel," said Esmond ecstatically.
" The authentic pig in a poke. A greasy one, too. A
dear little greasy-weasy piggy-wiggy. Ernest caught
it," continued Esmond, indicating the footballer.

" Ar, I caught un," said the red-haired youth. " I
catched un oreight."

Esmond clasped his hands and surveyed the hearty
with a worshipping gaze : " Positively, my dears, you've
no idea. Ernest was marvellous ; simply angelic. He
positively tore round the field after the pig like anything,
knocking the yokels all over the place, and finally he
fell on it. Positively overlaid it so to speak. It was
masterly."

" Ar. I dropped on un oreight," soliloquised the
young footballer, " I dropped reight atop of un, the
little b——"

" And what are you going to do with it now ? "
enquired Puggy with growing interest.

Esmond simpered ecstatically : "We're going to
release it in Miss Warbler's missionary stall. My dears,
it'll be epic, quite Homeric in fact. Conceive of the
position—pigs among the petticoats and what not.
Positively paradise."

" Yes," explained Julian, " you see you and I go to the
front of the stall and engage the Vestry Virgins in
missionary back-chat whilst Esmond and Ernest slip the

porker in under the rear flap. Then for the rough and tumble."

" Darlings, all of you," cried Puggy, scampering on ahead.

The Misses Warbler, with typical Warbler bounce, had set up their stall of missionary literature next to the front gate of the Rectory so that all who patronised the fête and gala in what capacity soever were held up and made the subjects of religious brigandage.

When Puggy and Julian drew up the Misses Warbler were just congratulating themselves upon having cleared out a particularly sticky line in fireside tracts and bedside mottoes. They were elated with missionary zeal. Julian and Puggy they eyed with acute suspicion.

" Good evening," began Julian genially, " the Mission Field is a wide one. Ah yes, indeed."

" We are deeply interested in the work of the Church Overseas," said Puggy smiling brightly. " Mr. Ansell here is seriously considering devoting himself to the propagation of the gospel in foreign parts—aren't you, you idle devil ? " she concluded, prodding Julian in the stomach.

" Mind what you're doing with my tripes, blast you," said Julian savagely. Then he beamed once more at the Misses Warbler : " Truly the vineyard is a large one and the labourers few. Thousands there be, nay millions," he cried, warming to his work and waving his arms about violently, " millions there be awaiting the word. There they are, black, coffee-coloured, yellow, pink, red, white and blue, there they are, I say, wallowing in sin and outer darkness, awaiting one and all the word. The word go. Is it right ? Is it just ? No, indeed. It is a scandalous shame, a standing

reproach to all practising Christians.   It is up to us all
to devote ourselves mind, body, soul and bank balance
to the cause of the Church Overseas.   It must con-
stantly occupy the forefront of our minds, we must
mention it regularly in our prayers.   The untold
millions in China, India and darkest Africa, the
incalculable myriads wallowing in paganism and
heathen debauchery cry out upon us.   They wait, a
harvest ripe for the reaper.   Their cry goes out, how
long ?   Can we ignore that cry ?   Can we shut our
ears and blind our eyes to the posture of our brethren
overseas ?   We cannot.   I say we shall not . . ."

" Yes," said Puggy meditatively as Julian gulped for
breath, " the soil is fertile, it requires only the seed.   I
am reminded of the case of my great-uncle Hezekiah.
Hounded out of London by duns and maintenance
orders, he betook himself to the reaches of the Upper
Congo.   There amongst the savage negroes, the be-
nighted blackamoors, he set his barrow down.   From
the fastnesses of the jungle, from the malarial swamps,
the naked savages flocked to his tent."

" And now," said Julian, " upon the site where once
were enacted blood-sacrifices, unspeakable sexual
orgies and all the unmentionable abracadabra of voo-
dooism, stands a handsome Anglican cathedral.   Built
by the bands of pious blackamoors, it stands a perpetual
monument, a permanent beacon to the triumph of right
over blight.   There it is, a work of love, a shining
example of Christian endeavour.   True, it is only of
mud and wattle and leaks something cruel on the choirboys' heads, but a cathedral nevertheless it is.   Puggy's
great-uncle may justly be said to have slipped one over
in the short rib.   Now when the single bell sends forth

its dulcet call over the fetid jungle of a Sunday morning, crowds of black worshippers may be seen slowly wending their way in twos and threes to the sacred edifice. The smile of brotherly love illumines those faces so recently contorted by the grin of hate. The discreet smock now veils those forms so recently flaunting a diabolic nudity. . . ."

" But," said Puggy, " the work cannot go on without funds. And funds are the rub."

" The rub ? " enquired Julian sceptically, annoyed because Puggy had stopped his flow. " What do you mean, the rub ? "

" Shakespeare, you illiterate oaf," she explained, and then proceeded : " In many parts missionary endeavour is perforce having to draw in its horns ; and just when it should be poking them out. Why ? The answer is simple—lack of funds."

" And that," cried Julian, slipping in again neatly, " is where we, as practising Christians, come in. This is our responsibility. Must we stand by and watch the ground so hardly won slipping back into its pristine state of filth and squalor ? We must not. We cannot. But how, you ask, can we help ? What part can we play in this great human drama? The answer is simple. All of us, even the most humble, can do our bit."

" Not 'arf we can't," interposed Puggy, " and this is how. Let each of us take home to-night a missionary box and place it in some prominent place in the home. Then let us make a firm resolution, and keep to it, to set aside a small sum each week for the box. Some of us, of course, cannot afford so much as others, but no sum, however slight, is to be scorned. It is the regular sacrifice that counts, the small weekly offering regularly

set aside. It is surprising how these little amounts add
up at the end of the year."

"It is an' all," agreed Julian heartily. "And is the
sacrifice too great to make? Surely not. A packet of
cigarettes less per week, fewer attendances at the local
cinema, a slight cutting down on gin and lipstick, are
not these small hardships worth the redemption of a
human soul?"

"And how," agreed Puggy. "But before we go any
further, just allow me to tell you that my great-uncle
Hezekiah wasn't peddling Bibles. It was illicit
whisky."

"Can I show you young people anything," enquired
Salome Warbler threateningly.

"I've no doubt you could," said Julian agreeably,
"but I shouldn't look."

"I should like to know," said Puggy earnestly, "the
precise number of modesty vests issued to the women of
the Upper Congo cannibal tribes during the year
ending March 31st, 1935."

At this point Esmond released the pig.

When it was all over they toured over to the village
pub for a pint.

"Upon my tripes," cried Julian, "I never saw anything like it. I would never have believed that a single
small porker could have wrought such havoc. Old
Gerty trod on it first, didn't she?"

"Yes," crooned Esmond, "and then it bolted clean
up Salome's skirts."

"But that was after it had got the cross-stitch book-
markers stuck all over it," cried Puggy, "and then Gert
sat down in the paste pot. She blinded something
'orrible, she did."

" But when did Salome get that pile of hymn books on her belly ? " enquired Julian earnestly. " Was that before or after the roof fell in ? "

" Oh ! after," said Puggy. " Definitely after, because it wasn't until she got a crack on the ear with the tent peg that she began to wave her legs about."

" Shocking, wasn't it ? " said Esmond. " Flannelette they were, I swear ; red flannelette, secured below the knee with elastic."

" But how did the whole damn thing collapse ? " demanded Julian. " That's what I want to know. It seemed to turn turtle in mid-air and engulf the populace."

" I lifted un," said the red-haired youth gloomily. " I up-ended un good and proper I did."

For the past few moments a glazed look, always indicative of profound thought, had been spreading on Julian's countenance. Suddenly his brow cleared : " I've got an idea. Positively the only idea I've ever had. Bishop Oglethorpe rings the bell. Puggy, Esmond, gather round."

They went into committee.

The Rev. Percy Bedrock's Potted Pageants were being presented in the Village Hall, just across the street from the Rectory. The Rector had made certain of a good house by providing a free fish and chip supper on the Rectory lawn for all ticket holders at the close of the day.

When Julian and Esmond and Puggy reached the Hall, they found that the last scene but one was just drawing to a close. The Rev. Percy, attired in monkish robes, was busy doing his stuff as the Venerable Bede. In point of actual fact he had just died, harrow-

ingly and protractedly, all over the stage.   Now he was
being carried off by a bevy of choirboys dressed up as
novices.   The scene was a solemn one.   The village
orchestra was scraping away at what was termed on the
programme a ' solemn musick '.   Meanwhile, to the
accompaniment of much creaking and grunting, the
inert Bedrock was slowly being carried out.   Puggy and
Julian watched breathlessly from the back row.

" They'll drop him, I swear they'll drop him," cried
Puggy, jumping from one foot to the other.

" Take the strain !   Pull ! " cried Julian, crouching
down and assuming the attitude of a tug-of-war coach.

" They're pulling him to bits," protested Esmond.
" Literally the poor old boy's stretching yards.   They'll
tear him limb from limb and his innards'll drop out all
over the floor."

" I wonder if he's got bowels of compassion," mused
Puggy.

Meanwhile the perspiring choirboys had almost
completed their task.   After many tense moments and
ticklish situations they had at last managed to get the
Rector's head and shoulders off the stage and into the
wings.   True, he had received one or two nasty clips on
the ear, and a few shrewd jabs on the hinder parts as the
stage furniture was negotiated, but the general effect
was impressive, was grandiose.   Throughout the whole
ordeal the Rector had maintained himself in a rigid
attitude with his head lolling back and a splendidly
vacant expression upon his features.

Then, just as the cortège was about to pass from view,
Julian, who was lying on his stomach at the back of the
Hall, cried forth : ' Drop it.'

The effect upon the panting and nervous choirboys

was revolutionary. With one accord they dropped it. At least those responsible for the Rector's bows dropped it. Those responsible for the back end, however, maintained their convulsive grasp upon his heels. The result was that the Rev. Percy's head hit the boards with a resounding whack, whilst his feet remained aloft. At the same moment, owing to his tip-tilted posture, the skirts of his cassock ran back about his waist, revealing the whole of the clerical nether parts clothed only in a pair of voluminous white pants.

" Shocking," declared Julian as they tumbled ecstatically out of the Hall. " Upon my soul I don't know what Anglican circles are coming to. Inebriate organ blowers and trouserless parsons. Disgraceful ! "

" I had no idea old Bedrock was so interesting," cooed Esmond.

At this point the village schoolmaster, who was stage managing, came bounding up.

" Mr. Ansell, sir, kindly come this way at once. We have been seeking you all over. The Rector and Miss Warbler are most anxious. The penultimate scene is now concluded. You will have to hurry with your dressing if you are to be in time."

Julian lifted his hand : " Enough ! Bishop Oglethorpe is not unaware of the responsibilities of his sacred trust. The Queen shall be well and truly crowned. And as for you, Puggy," he concluded, wagging an admonitory forefinger at her, " you must play your part. Skip along now to the Rectory with Esmond as fast as you can. You'll be sure to find one somewhere. Bring it along to me, back-stage, as quick as you can." Then he turned upon his heel with dignity and followed the gesticulating pedagogue.

" I trust Bedrock is breeched again by now," he remarked sternly. " If not, you may depend upon it Bishop Oglethorpe will have something to say in the matter. Pshaw."

Five minutes later Puggy and Esmond, the latter carrying a sack over his shoulder, insinuated themselves through a side door in the Village Hall and discovered Julian who was putting on his vestments and make-up in the furnace room.

He was a surprising sight. A cardboard mitre reclined waggishly over one ear, a cope was hitched negligently over one shoulder whilst a stupendous growth of false whisker burgeoned from his jaws, flowered voluptuously over his chin and hung in a matted thicket to his waist. His pastoral staff, which he wagged menacingly at Esmond, consisted of an elongated ash-plant wrapped in tin-foil.

" Have a care there, have a care there," he cried as Puggy and Esmond burst in. " Put off thy shoes from off thy feet for the ground whereon thou standest is coaly."

" Will no one rid me of this priest ? " cried Puggy.

Esmond gave the whiskers a playful tug : " You shoot over the covers, milord Oglethorpe ? "

" Bulls to you," cried Julian, rescuing his beaver. " Papal ones. And, by the way, you can consider yourself excommunicated."

" We've got one," said Puggy triumphantly, producing the sack. " A beauty."

" Darling you," said Julian, spitting slightly through the whiskers. " I promote you henceforth chamber-maid extraordinary with Letters Patent to the Palace of Oglethorpe. And as for you, Esmond Duncan, I ordain

you Plenipotentiary without portfolio and Comptroller
General to the Annual Choirboys' Outing."

There was a scuffling in the passage without, and the
Rev. Percy Bedrock appeared. He carried a gilt
cardboard crown and waggled it feverishly in Julian's
direction : "The crown, my dear boy, the crown. I nearly
forgot it. That would indeed have been unfortunate."

" Milord to you," said Julian loftily. " More
respect, Bedrock, more reverence if you please, or you
may find yourself inhibited. Have a care, have a care.
The episcopal wrath is dire when roused. And now,"
he concluded, " you may all go. Oglethorpe would
fain spend a few moments in peaceful meditation before
performing his solemn offices upon the person of the
Virgin Queen."

Puggy and Esmond settled themselves down in the
front row with the Rector. The curtain was down at
the moment and the village orchestra was having at
" Shepherds Hay ". The Rector looked about him
complacently. The Hall, he noticed with satisfaction,
was full, and further, many of the more distinguished of
local residents had stayed on to see the Potted Pageants.
He nodded familiarly to Sir Bertram and Lady Buckle
on his left, whilst behind him he caught a glimpse of
Captain Polo with Mrs. Farquhar. Further back was
a solid phalanx of substantial burgesses. Major
Cockerell was parading up and down the gangway,
smoking a cheroot and quelling the more uproarious
yokels at the back.

" Most encouraging this interest in the drama,"
remarked the Rector to Esmond. " The arts still have
their place. Philistia's triumph is not yet complete.
A most satisfactory enterprise, I flatter myself. There

is still a public, you see, for works of high seriousness."

" Yes," agreed Esmond chattily. " I understand they still get remarkable attendances at the Cochran shows. But personally my taste is more for the ballet. Spectre de la Rose and L'Après Midi, don't you know. So interesting."

" Pity those boys dropped you on the floor like that," said Puggy tactlessly. " Still, you're not as light as you were, are you ? "

The Rector frowned irritably. " Yes, yes. Most annoying, sheer carelessness. Those lads have no sense of responsibility. I shall bring the matter home to them sharply. Unless they show a proper contrition I shall certainly deprive them of their summer outing."

At this point the orchestra struggled to a close and the curtain went up.

The scene was a remarkable one. In the middle of the stage sat Miss Salome Warbler attired in a robe of somewhat moth-eaten red velvet and a large white ruff which threatened at any moment to throw her into an apoplexy. Her face was heavily powdered and upon her head she wore a red wig at a distinctly rakish angle. Quantities of rings entangled her fingers, whilst coils of unlikely looking pearls were festooned above her neck and bosom. She sat perfectly rigid and directed a baleful and threatening gaze upon the audience. On all sides she was surrounded by a heterogeneous herd of villagers attired in the Rev. Percy Bedrock's conception of Elizabethan costume. Doublets and hose, cross-garters, stomachers and ruffs were mingled with a fine disregard in a bewildering yet undeniably colourful kaleidoscope. An outburst of applause greeted this overwhelming spectacle.

Suddenly, from the wings, a single cornet gave out a wavering and dissolute croak, whereupon the orchestra launched out into the National Anthem and the audience scrambled to its feet. When this surprising interlude was over there was a dramatic pause, and then the cornet again broke forth, this time more powerfully if at the same time juicily. As the note died away, a heavy step sounded in the wings and Julian complete with staff, whiskers, and mitre strode ponderously onto the stage. Immediately Puggy and Esmond led an outburst of clapping.

" Now for it," whispered Puggy as the applause died.

Shouldering his way across the congested stage with leisurely dignity, Julian at length drew up behind Miss Warbler who still sat rigidly and balefully in the midst. For the last time the cornet sounded. Then Julian was seen to fumble for a moment in his robes. Slowly he raised his hands aloft, paused for a second and then lowered them swiftly to Miss Warbler's waiting head. A round, white object threw back the glare of the foot-lights. There was a deathly hush and then the audience blew up.

Out in the road Puggy and Esmond discussed the technicalities :

" I always did like the white enamelled variety," mused Esmond.

" Yes," agreed Puggy. " Especially with a blue rim."

10

Framing the Burgess

LEAVING THE TURBULENCE of the Village Hall behind them, Julian and Puggy scampered across to the Rectory and tumbled into Bloody Mary. Puggy insisted upon driving, and after several false starts they embarked upon an entertaining, if somewhat erratic, course through the village.

" The old bus has got her guts about her, anyway," cried Puggy, changing down neatly and broadsiding out on to the main road. " She seems sound enough in the privy parts."

Breathlessly Julian agreed. He could not restrain a kind of strangled squawk as they cut sharply across the bows of an oncoming hearse.

Puggy was sitting bolt upright at the wheel, her saucy profile lifted eagerly to the breeze and her equally saucy shapes quivering attractively as the hard-sprung Bugatti bounced and trembled. The straps of Julian's white racing-helmet flickered about her ears and she had adorned herself with his goggles.

" Where are we going ? " shouted Puggy, her words coming disjointedly through the slip-stream. " I can't ask you to dine with us. Mother's run out of cocaine and she's screaming the roof off."

" You'd better trough with us for Heaven's sake mind that Daimler," gasped Julian in one mouthful as he cringed down into the cockpit.

" It's old Cockerell," cried Puggy joyfully. " Watch me bore him off the road."

The Bugatti leapt forward, the speedometer needle flickering up to sixty-five. In one rush they were running beside the Daimler, Puggy meanwhile conducting a fan-fare upon the hooter. The two cars coursed along together for a couple of hundred yards. Then Puggy began to edge in by degrees, pressing Major Cockerell nearer and nearer to the grass. Julian was conscious of feverish gesticulations and bellowed threats. Suddenly he felt the back of the seat hit him in the neck as Puggy put her foot down and cut savagely across the Major's track. After a while Puggy looked back : " He's just getting back onto the road," she remarked chattily. " Cockerell lacks decision, that's his trouble. He lacks thrust."

By the time they reached the Priory their bag was a weasel and two boiling fowls. Whooping uproariously they tumbled into the house. Shepherding Puggy before him with urgent little smacks upon the well-filled seat of her shorts, Julian pressed forward to the drawing-room. Through the door came the murmur of voices and the sound of someone declaiming, of someone in full oratorical spate.

"Good. We've got a party," said Julian, "and Bellairs is back on the warpath unless I'm very much mistaken."

They shouldered in. They were just in time for the pre-dinner sherry.

Mr. Phont fluttered forward and pressed glasses into their hands : " Well, well, well. The prodigals return. Such goings-on I never did hear. Disgraceful frolics at local parsonage. What's all this I'm told ? Tumblings in tents and fumblings in Rectorial parlours."

"Not to mention episcopal pleasantries and privy conspiracies," cried Bellairs. The rear flap of his cerise sports-shirt was hanging down outside his dark blue flannel trousers.

"We roused them, I fancy," said Julian modestly. "You appear to have heard all about it?"

"Indubitably," said Mr. Phont. "The inestimable Mrs. Beeton was there and kept a stern eye on the proceedings throughout. We have heard all, and a very jolly afternoon you seem to have had, too."

"I quite agree about the back seats of Humbers," said a husky voice from the french windows.

Mrs. Meredith looking divine in smoke-blue chiffon with a large yellow flower at her bosom, drifted haphazardly into the room. "Youth will be served," she added cryptically.

"And so will dinner, I hope," remarked a stertorous voice from the sofa.

Here reclined at full length an enormous young man in brown plus-fours and heavily nailed shoes. His large indeterminate face was wreathed in a bland if at the same time rather vacant, grin. Upon his tremendous chest he balanced the sherry decanter, and periodically he tipped it perilously towards his mouth, permitting a stream of the liquid to flow uninterruptedly down his gullet.

"Pogo Tuddenham," announced Mr. Phont. "Tuddenham of Thomas's to give him his name about town. A connoisseur of the inward parts."

"That's it," said Pogo, suddenly levering himself upright. "We digs and we delves and some very surprising things we finds, too."

"He's just been telling us the most divine story,"

cooed Mrs. Meredith, " about when he opened old
Granny Maypole, the novelist.   It seems that when the
works had been removed somebody mislaid them, and
Pogo had to fill the old boy up with yards and yards of
bicycle tube."

" Yes," said Pogo, rising to his full height and
stretching enormously.   " We fixed him up with
Dunlop tripes.   Of course, there's only one draw-back.
When he gets an attack of the wind he expands in a
rather surprising manner."

" I want a bath," interrupted Puggy plaintively.
" I'm as sticky as a fly-paper."

" A bath," cried Mr. Phont, striking a posture.   " A
bath, by all means.   I'm rather proud of my new bathroom.   Black marble and stainless steel fittings.   Lead
on, young woman, I will attend to the matter personally."

" Perhaps I too can be of some assistance," suggested
Julian suavely.

" I hardly think so," mused Mrs. Meredith.   " If I
remember, there is no key-hole."

" Ha ! " cried Bellairs.   " A soft answer turneth
away wrath."

" And a soft towel keepeth away chaps," rejoined
Puggy smartly.

With the Burgundy Mr. Phont rapped smartly upon
the table with his fork.   He raised his glass :

" To the success of to-night's enterprise.   Let us
quaff."

" To-night's enterprise ? " gaped Julian, setting down
his glass.   " Don't tell me there's another frolic on foot
to-night ? "

" There is, indeed," said Mr. Phont, " and one of no
inconsiderable moment.   To-night we do the dirt on

Twidale. To-night we frame a burgess. Proceed, Bellairs."

Bellairs, who had been unwontedly subdued all the evening, refilled his glass and slipped into top-gear :

" The prevailing situation, as you are all well aware, is a tense one ; past, present and future. It is not too much to say that the fate of the *Weekly Probe* hangs in the balance. It sways in the scales. To be brief, if we don't bust Twidale, he'll bust us, which would be a pity."

" Unthinkable," said Julian sternly. " Expand."

" For the past few days," proceeded Bellairs, " as you are doubtless well aware, I have been in retirement. I have given myself up entirely to meditation and an excellent old Cognac. Sleep that knits up the ravelled sleeve of care has been absent from my couch these many nights."

" That in any event would do something to relieve the overcrowding problem," suggested Mrs. Meredith.

Bellairs ignored the interruption : " As a result I have fructified. I have borne fruit. I have a plan. A plan, if I may say so, at once Machiavellian in its subtlety and Napoleonic in its simplicity."

" And breath-taking in its audacity," said Mr. Phont doubtfully. " I must admit that in spite of my un-bounded confidence in the incomparable Bellairs, I feel a distinct qualm, an undoubted twinge."

" Audacious it is," agreed Bellairs, " and not without its element of risk. Should we fail I admit we are for it. But, on the other hand, if we fail to take prompt and drastic action we are equally for it. Desperate situations demand desperate remedies. As I say, it's us or Twidale. Personally, I prefer it should be Twidale."

" Carried," said Julian. " And your scheme ? "

Bellairs rose to his feet : " To-night we kidnap old Twidale."

" Strewth," exclaimed Puggy through her savoury.

" We ? " enquired Julian. " What do I have to do ? Crown him one or something ? "

Bellairs winced : " My dear Ansell, how can you ? Effective I may be but never, I contend, crude. Neat but not gaudy. Those are my methods. Twidale is to be chloroformed. All you have to do is to drive Ulric's Bentley."

" And then ? " enquired Julian. " If there is any and then."

" Compromised," snapped Bellairs, " utterly and completely compromised. So well and truly framed in fact that henceforth he will be just there." He made a minatory gesture with his down-turned thumb.

Pogo Tuddenham sat back and twiddled his thumb : " Of course we shall probably kill the old bird. Chloroform's queer stuff. Remember I don't know anything of the condition of the patient's heart."

" Hard," said Mrs. Meredith, " hard as a sub-deb's. But I like the term patient."

" Of course," mused Pogo, playing with his dessert knife, " there's no reason why I shouldn't do a job on him if we get him under all right. I mean we might have an odd gland or two out."

" I should imagine," suggested Mr. Phont judicially, " that an aldermanic thyroid would offer many points of interest to a physiologist."

" Meanwhile," exhorted Bellairs, " kindly pass me the grapes. Never forget the Napoleonic maxim that an army marches upon its stomach."

" As is only all to lamentably evident when one regards Colonel Barley's boys on a route march," agreed Mr. Phont.

At a quarter to ten Julian, Bellairs and Pogo Tuddenham loaded themselves into Mr. Phont's big black Bentley saloon. There was an air of do or die about the party. Bellairs for once was tolerably mute. Pogo had his shoulders up to his ears and his jaw stuck out in a very aggressive manner. Julian, behind the wheel, fingered his moustache lovingly, always a sign of high nervous tension.

Bellairs glanced at his watch : " Well, we may as well be off. Expect us back within the hour, chaps."

Julian let in the clutch and the car moved forward.

" Don't forget to write," urged Mr. Phont. " We shall be thinking of you at home. Drop us a picture postcard, preferably of the lewder type."

As the car nosed down the drive, Bellairs was seen to be hanging out from one of the rear windows :

" We few, we happy few," he announced, " we band of brothers. . . ."

Mr. Phont shepherded his remaining guests back into the house : " God's arm strike with us ; 'tis a fearful odds."

Under Bellairs' direction, Julian steered an intricate course through the meaner streets of the borough until they emerged at length on to Tollemache Avenue, a long, ill-lighted, tree-lined road leading from the centre of the town to a ridge of high ground on the outskirts where dwelt a considerable burgess coterie under the imperial sway of Alderman Fred. Twidale. Half-way along Tollemache Avenue, at a point where the houses became fewer and were set back behind discreet stone

walls, was the property of Major Cockerell. A
cavernous, yew-lined drive led up to the house. Into
the mouth of this gloomy tunnel Julian gingerly backed
the Bentley and turned off the side-lights. In the
rapidly thickening darkness the car was almost invisible.

Bellairs glanced at his watch and threw a few
muttered words of explanation to Julian : " Old Fred
comes padding along here every night at about ten
o'clock from his club. The idea is to pop out of the
gateway here, give him the works and bundle him into
the car. Then we drive like blazes."

" Brief, bright and brotherly," opined Pogo
Tuddenham, flexing his formidable biceps. " The old
gentleman had better not get tough," he added grimly,
" Pogo feels in form to-night."

" That's the talk," said Bellairs appreciatively,
" that's the attitude. Meanwhile I'll just nip down the
road a bit and see what's what."

Bellairs slipped out of the drive and moved away in
the shadows. Pogo and Julian, meanwhile, surrep-
titiously puffed at cigarettes in the back compartment
of the Bentley.

The minutes slipped by. A quarter past ten sounded
from the parish church. The twilight throbbed and
died out.

" I wish things would begin to happen," grunted
Pogo. " This sort of thing gets on one's nerves. It's
as bad as one's first operation. I remember. . . ."

" Sink me," hissed Bellairs, suddenly materialising
out of the shadows, " there are complications."

" What ? You mean the old boy's not going to turn
up after all ? " enquired Pogo regretfully.

" He's going to turn up all right," hissed Bellairs, " in

fact he's just coming up the road now.   The point is he's got Charley Quilt, the chief constable, with him."

"Well that scuppers us," said Julian feeling for the starting switch, "we'd better get while the going's good."

"Not on your kidneys," growled Pogo.   "One or two, what's the odds?   We'll take them both.   I never have liked police officials as a class.   Let them all come. Why spoil the mortuary for a ha'porth of corpse?"

Bellairs' eyes glittered.   Suddenly he began to heave with suppressed and Gargantuan mirth :

"Zwounds, Tuddenham, you're right.   We'll take the brace.   Quick! the bag.   They'll be here any minute now."

Pogo Tuddenham plunged into the back of the car and emerged with a small black bag.   A sickly sweet smell hovered in the night air.

"Here," quoted Bellairs aptly, "where all trouble seems dead winds' and dead waves' riot in doubtful dreams of dreams."

"Doubtful dreams be dashed," declared Pogo. "One sniff of this and it'll be good-bye to all that for Messrs. Twidale and Quilt."

Approaching along the pavement came the thud of heavy, aldermanic footsteps.   The shrill pipings of the Chief Constable's voice mingled with the stertorous grunts of his companion.   It was plain that they were engaged in indignant discussion.

"I'll take Twidale, you take Charley Quilt," snapped Bellairs as he and Pogo took up their positions behind Major Cockerell's gate posts.

Julian sitting tensed behind the Bentley's steering wheel, felt a curious heaving sensation in the pit of his

stomach.   Nervously he ran over the switches to see
that all was in preparation for a discreet departure.

Suddenly, framed in the lighter shadows of the gateway, appeared the figures of the two burgesses.   The
stiff incline of Tollemache Avenue was telling on their
stamina and, all too completely unaware of the danger
lurking in the drive-way, they paused for a moment to
regain their breath.

" It's got to be put a stop to," Alderman Twidale was
saying weightily.   " I'm not going to stand for a crowd
of unprincipled rapscallions coming into this town and
turning my private affairs upside down.   If they'd kept
their fingers out of my pie I shouldn't have objected, but
if they think they're going to put anything across Fred
Twidale they're barking up the wrong stick ; they've
got hold of the wrong end of the tree.   I shall expect you
to take action immediately.   You can be assured of my
support in any measure you may see fit to take.   And
measures, Quilt," went on the Alderman threateningly,
" I shall expect you to take, and them forthwith.   I
won't stand for it, Quilt, I warn you.   I won't stand for
it a day longer.   Phont and that *Weekly Probe* crowd has
got to be cleared out of this town double quick, and
what I says in this town goes."

" You may rest assured, Mr. Alderman," fluted the
Chief Constable anxiously, " that measures shall be
took and that forthwith.   I shall do all that lies within
my power to see your wishes carried out."

" Well," grunted the Alderman, preparing to move
off again, " that's that and flat.   You know where you
stand now, Quilt.   But mind, I want to see things
happening, and happening quick. . . ."

It fell to Julian, crouching in the driving seat of the

Bentley, to see Alderman Fred Twidale's wish gratified, and that in double quick time.

From the shadows of the gateway two figures launched themselves into the midst of the two burgesses. The scene rapidly developed into a formal design of whirling limbs. There was the pleasant thudding sound of a few shrewd blows. There was a strong sickly-sweet whiff of chloroform. Then the party finished as rapidly as it had begun.

" Get going," rasped Bellairs, " and keep going." He appeared beside the car dragging Alderman Twidale negligently by the heels.

" A pair of bags and a trunk, porter," grunted Pogo Tuddenham as he heaved the Chief Constable into the back.

The doors slammed, the motor growled into life and the Bentley shot out onto Tollemache Avenue.

" Neat but not gaudy ; those are my methods," Bellairs complacently announced from the back seat.

Meanwhile Pogo was busy with his patients. " Pulse satisfactory," he remarked at length. " They've both gone under very nicely. Strong birds these burgesses. Tough as young fighting-cocks."

" A devil's brood," agreed Bellairs.

" Straight home ? " enquired Julian as they reached the end of Tollemache Avenue.

" Go to, go to, my boy," said Bellairs. " Strategy is the word. Tact for tics so to speak."

Under Bellairs' guidance, Julian drove off the road and turned into a narrow and murderously bumpy cart-track. They lurched and bounced along this for a couple of miles with the lights off. At length, after a severe shaking, they emerged onto a country road.

" Now you know where we are," said Bellairs. " We're out on the Little Pittle road just beyond Bedrock's place. Pull in here. This is where we swap cars."

" What a tactician, what a strategist," said Julian reverently, as he nosed the Bentley into a forlorn looking farmyard.

" Now then, Pogo," ordered Bellairs, " help me to shift the clients into your car. Careful with Twidale, his trousers appear to be coming off."

Between them they carried the inert forms of the two burgesses to an ancient Morris Cowley saloon that was nestling in a cart-shed.

" A poor thing but mine own," announced Pogo. " She boils from the word go, but she exhibits a remarkable turn of knottage."

" And now," directed Bellairs, " we shall drive straight back to the Priory with our two clients." Here he prodded the Alderman familiarly in the stomach. " You, Julian, had better take the Bentley out to the Manford roadhouse. Have a drink there, if you can get one. If not, a glass of milk. Then come straight in on the main road. After which," he concluded, " I fancy we shall have covered our tracks pretty adequately."

The Morris quivered into life and trundled off in a surprisingly business-like manner. Julian sighed and gave the Bentley its head.

" What ! two of them ? " said Mrs. Meredith incredulously as Pogo and Bellairs laid out their two victims in the hall, " what an embarras de burgess ! "

" Upon my soul," exclaimed Mr. Phont, " they do

look a pair of beauties.   Regular figures of fun. Positive
laughing-stocks and no mistake."

"Like so much chilled beef," mused Puggy,
meditatively kicking Alderman Twidale in the loins.

Bellairs bustled in from the drawing-room :

"To business," he remarked briskly. "Let us
proceed with the task in hand."

Under his direction Alderman Fred. Twidale and
Chief Constable Quilt were carried into the drawing-
room and dumped on the sofa.   Bellairs then produced
a large suit-case :

"The props," he remarked as he emptied the contents
out on to the floor.   "A trick to frame a burgess. And
now, perhaps, the ladies had better withdraw for a few
moments. . . ."

When Puggy and Mrs. Meredith re-entered the
drawing-room they encountered a remarkable vision.
The Chief Constable and the Chairman of the Watch
Committee were arranged upon the sofa in attitudes of
shameless debauchery.   Their clothes had been
removed and they were clad in brilliantly striped
pyjamas. Their locks were libidinously ruffled and
they wore paper hats at rakish angles. They were
surrounded on all sides by empty champagne bottles,
cigar-nubs, and illustrated papers of the ruder sort.
The effect was surprisingly depraved.

"And now," announced Bellairs, "it but remains
for the ladies to do their stuff."

He advanced upon Mrs. Meredith and enveloped her
in a dazzling silk dressing-gown. Protestingly she
submitted to a lavish application of lipstick and a
methodical disordering of the hair.

"Capital," exclaimed Mr. Phont as he flicked a tress

over Mrs. Meredith's right eye, " capital. Really, my dear Barbara, you begin to resemble Chrysothemis after a particularly tough night at the Golden House."

" Low, that's what I feel," complained Mrs. Meredith, as she arranged herself artistically on Alderman Twidale's lap. " Low and loose."

" A bit more leg I think," said Bellairs as he twitched the skirts of the dressing-gown apart.

Obediently Mrs. Meredith extended the gleaming serpents of her elegant legs. Then she lighted a cigarette, picked up a champagne glass, and placed an arm about the Alderman's neck :

" At last," she exclaimed expiringly, " I achieve my apotheosis. At last, I apprehend, I am become the authentic wanton baggage."

" And if there are any other ambitions of a like kind that you desire to consummate, I shall only be too glad to assist," remarked Bellairs as he busily helped Puggy Congreve to pull off her blue sports-shirt.

Puggy, a ravishing sight in her pleated white shorts and the latest ' Cup-lift ' model, kicked up her heels and ran through a few tap-steps. Then she collapsed joyously upon the Chief Constable's midriff.

" Have a care," warned Pogo Tuddenham. " Steady with the constabulary tripes. You'll completely deflate the old boy if you're not careful."

" Something smacking slightly of the acrobatic, I fancy," mused Bellairs. " Something suggestive, albeit mildly, of sweat and swing."

" A picture from Port Said," agreed Mr. Phont as Puggy arranged her legs under the Chief Constable's chin and permitted her fascinating torso to droop backwards over one end of the sofa.

Bellairs stood off and surveyed his handiwork appreciatively : " What a fine swirling composition," he remarked. " What a powerful sense of anatomical form. What a superb flair for counterpoised grouping."

" Shameless voluptuaries," agreed Mr. Phont, clucking disapprovingly. " Deplorable debauchees. It now only remains to record these abominable antics in permanent form for the benefit of posterity."

" Yes," said Bellairs, diving into the suit-case and emerging with a camera and flashlight apparatus, " The *Weekly Probe* for the Naked Truth. The *Weekly Probe* for the nude, if not the eternal, verities."

" Nudity is truth, truth nudity," quoted Pogo Tuddenham surprisingly.

" Now then, you girls," exhorted Bellairs. " Turn your faces to the wall. There's no need to compromise the house-party. We may have to publish these photographs before we bring the Alderman to heel. Figures speak louder than faces."

The flashlight fizzed thrice.

"A notable addition to journalistic and artistic enterprise," remarked Bellairs as he put away the camera.

" My boy friend's waking up," said Puggy suddenly. A series of stifled grunts from Chief Constable Quilt corroborated. His limbs began to twitch, whilst a distinct shudder passed through the Aldermanic frame of Fred Twidale.

" They're still alive, then," remarked Pogo Tuddenham with interest. " Well, that's a relief, anyway. I hate to lose a patient."

" The sacks," cried Bellairs. " The pokes for the pigs." He hurried out into the hall and returned with two large sacks.

Whilst Puggy and Mr. Phont pushed the now half-conscious burgesses into their trousers, Bellairs and Pogo Tuddenham slipped the two capacious sacks over their upper ends and secured them at the waist with quantities of rope.

"The original stuffed capon," said Bellairs, prodding Alderman Twidale in the nethers. "Thou trunk of humours," he quoted, getting into full spate. "Thou bolting-hutch of beastliness ; thou swollen parcel of dropsies ; thou huge bombard of sack ; thou stuffed cloak-bag of guts ; thou roasted Manningtree ox with the pudding in's belly. . . ."

"Thou reverend vice," took up Mr. Phont, addressing the Chief Constable. "Thou grey iniquity, thou father ruffian, thou old white-bearded Satan."

A growling and burbling in the drive announced the return of Julian. A moment later, looking pleasantly dissipated, he appeared in the doorway :

"Am I too late for the nudies ? How are the mighty fallen ! "

Mr. Phont indicated Puggy who seemed in no hurry to get dressed : "The stars in their corsets fought against Sisera," he remarked.

"Come along," cried Bellairs vigorously. "Lay to there. We must get rid of these bodies. The dogs must be returned to their vomit."

"Let us begin and carry up this corpse, singing together," chanted Mr. Phont as they pushed the bodies into the Bentley.

"Along High-street and stop outside the Town Hall," commanded Bellairs as they loaded up.

"But surely," protested Mr. Phont, "this is all a little gratuitous. Surely there is a grave danger of our being apprehended in so public a spot.   After all, with the original bodies in the bag we are hardly in a position to argue nice points of law with an interested constabulary."

" My dear sir," said Bellairs aggrievedly, " you surely don't think that I have neglected to ascertain the beats of the local constables ?   If you had bowled home with three sheets in the wind as often as I have the timetable of the nocturnal ramblings of the local police force would be graven ineradicably upon your heart. The St. John's Green beat is entrusted to Constable Coot to-night, and unless I am very much mistaken he is at present knocking back a pint with the landlady of the ' Goat and Compasses '."

The Bentley swerved to a halt in front of the Town Hall steps.   Pogo Tuddenham descended and bundled Alderman Twidale and Chief Constable Quilt out on to the pavement.

" Prop them up against the pillars," advised Bellairs. " And let us not neglect to garnish the dish."

He surrounded the recumbent burgesses with a formal design of the champagne bottles and rude magazines.

" Quite a picture," mused Pogo Tuddenham.   " A post-card from Marseilles. Dear Mother, We are having a wonderful time.   Getting drunk and sleeping out every night.   Love from Fred and Charley."

" A dreadful warning," said Mr. Phont, " to the youth of the borough. A signal admonition to all adolescents."

Back at the Priory, Pogo Tuddenham lifted his face for a moment out of his tankard :

" One of the nicest Sunday-school outings I ever assisted at.   Well organised.   That's what appeals to

me—org . . . organis . . . shorganisation," he completed triumphantly.

"Quite," agreed Mr. Phont. "The *Probe* touch.
The Bellairs flair. There are, to employ a vulgarity,
no flies on Bellairs."

"How very inconvenient for him," sighed Mrs.
Meredith.

11

The Shape of Things to Come

IT WAS A DAY TOWARDS
the end of September. In Bellairs' room at the *Weekly
Probe* offices an important conference was going forward.
Bellairs was lying on his neck with his stockinged-feet
on the desk. Julian and Mrs. Meredith were playing
noughts and crosses. Augustus Gripps was brooding
over his sales statements. Mr. Phont was walking
briskly up and down, stylishly handling the cocktail
shaker.

Fortified by the dry Martinis, the company at length
proceeded to business.

" After prayers and the reading of the minutes of the
last meeting, the proceedings were opened by our
esteemed editor," suggested Mr. Phont.

Bellairs rose and bent a stern glance upon all concerned : " We are assembled this morning," he began,
" upon business of the first importance, I may say of the
utmost moment. We have reached a forking of the
ways. We have arrived at a vital stage in the life of the
Weekly Probe, a psychological moment in the development of our campaign to rouse this Rotten Borough.
But before I elaborate, I call upon our proprietor, Mr.
Ulric Phont, to outline our progress and achievements
hitherto."

Mr. Phont coughed coyly and started in :

" Our progress has been," he intoned, " little short

of phenomenal.   That, I think, we may claim without
the slightest fear of successful challenge.   In the short
space of only a little over two months we have succeeded
in shaking this Rotten Borough to the core.   Burgesses
of every class and calling have been set by the ears,
jolted in the short ribs and kicked in the seat of their
complacent pants.   By a combination of high resolve
and low cunning we have achieved some remarkable
results.   Permit me to offer a few well-chosen examples.
By means of our Grand Theatrical Scandal we have
revealed the hideous corruption of the local aristocracy
and made a notable stand on behalf of artistic integrity
and moral rectitude.   By a series of vivacious and
ruthless journalistic thrusts we have abolished an unjust
river-drainage rate and set on foot a comprehensive
scheme of slum clearance.   With equal success we have
interfered in the religious sphere.   In securing the
resignation of the Misses Warbler from the Parochial
Church Council it is not too much to say that we have
launched an unparalleled blow on behalf of the
Anglican Church and dealt a singular stab to Popery.
And last, but not least," concluded Mr. Phont impressively, " we have secured the total abolition of civic
stinks.   By a stroke, the simplicity of which was rivalled
only by its audacity, we have secured the closing down
of the local tallow-works.   Now, for the first time for
fifty years, the burgesses breathe the pure, uncon-
taminated airs of Heaven.   In my earnest submission,"
said Mr. Phont, resuming his seat, " such achievements
as these are deserving of a title nothing less than
Homeric."

    " Have a gimlet after all that," suggested Mrs.
Meredith hospitably.

" And now," said Bellairs, " I call upon our publisher, the inestimable Augustus, to give me a few remarks upon the financial situation."

Augustus slowly levered himself out of his chair and applied himself to an involved sheet of figures. He began to read in a pessimistic and toneless voice : " Circulation, nett circulation that is, ten thousand per week and still rising. Advertisement revenue improving nicely. A stiff canvassing campaign would double it in a month. The expansion of the paper from six to ten pages, including a picture page, has increased sales, nett sales that is, by two thousand per week. In two months' time, if the present rate of progress is maintained, the enterprise should be yielding a clear profit."

Mr. Phont leapt joyfully to his feet : " At last, at last I am the authentic press-baron, I suspect. I own a newspaper, and not only a newspaper but, as our friend Augustus so aptly puts it, an enterprise. A business undertaking, a financial venture and, what's more, one that is going to show a profit. Remarkable ! Upon my soul, an extraordinary thing ! I can scarcely believe it of myself. Really I am not certain whether to be uncommonly delighted or profoundly shocked."

When Mr. Phont had come off the boil, Bellairs once more arose and beat upon the desk to command attention.

" Now for it," remarked Julian, triumphantly drawing a line through his three noughts to the discomfiture of his opponent.

" Cunning swine," said Mrs. Meredith and, inhaling deeply she leant back and considered Bellairs.

" I love Bellairs," she mused dispassionately. " He's of such an urgent and forceful temper. A pity he sublimates his libido so completely in the practicalities. Do you know, he's never once so much as made a suggestion to me."

" Stop wrangling, you two," commanded Mr. Phont. " You're as bad as a couple of lawyers ; always at sixes and eights."

" As I was saying," began Bellairs patiently for the third time, " we have arrived at a crucial point in the life of the *Weekly Probe*. In every campaign," he continued, getting down to it nicely, " in every campaign, of no matter what sort or kind, there arrives, sooner or later, a psychological moment. A moment when the wise general, the leader equipped with flair, verve, and élan, gathers the whole of his forces and launches them in a single terrific and decisive onslaught. If he avails himself properly of this moment he is rewarded by complete and instantaneous victory. If he allows it to escape him the enemy is enabled to rally and recoup, and the struggle may drag on interminably and indeterminately."

" The gift of tongues," breathed Julian reverently.

" This moment has arrived in our campaign," shouted Bellairs, and he brought his clenched fist down with a crash upon the desk. " By a series of well timed thrusts we have got our enemies on the wrong foot. They are completely unnerved. For the moment we are psychologically on top. We must not permit the moment to escape us. Now, I am convinced, is the time ; the time to deliver our final, overwhelming and shattering thrust. The preliminary moves have been well and truly executed. It remains but to deliver the coup de grâce." He paused impressively.

" You have," said Mr. Phont, " indubitably our ears.

Proceed. Elaborate. Expand. Upon what front, may I ask, is this final assault to be delivered ? "

" Upon the new borough lunatic asylum," said Bellairs quietly. He sat back with an air of quiet triumph.

" My God," whispered Mr. Phont reverentially, " I had completely forgotten about that little racket."

" I, on the contrary," said Bellairs, " have not. I have always entertained the liveliest interest in the new borough lunatic asylum. It has been my constant concern. And," he added, assuming a markedly ferocious expression, " I have been making a few pointed enquiries during these last weeks. I have dropped a hint here, I have asked an ingenuous question there. In a word, I have probed. And some very interesting discoveries I have made, too ; discoveries which, if properly handled, will spell the complete and utter disruption of local politics in general and the Town Council in particular."

" Sink me," breathed Mr. Phont through the tense silence. " Explain."

" Explain I will," said Bellairs grandiosely. " And that by the Socratic method. Augustus," he commanded, " kindly show in Mr. Herbert Andrews."

There was a subdued shuffling in the passage, and Augustus re-entered, shepherding before him a depressed looking little man with a watery eye and an unparalleled growth of whisker. He was clad in a purplish suiting, yellow boots and a red tie. His expression was one of mingled bounce and bashfulness.

" What whiskering," whispered Mrs. Meredith. " What a boskage. Talk about the tiger country ! "

" Ah ! " said Bellairs pleasantly, " Mr. Andrews.

How are you, my dear sir ? Take a seat. Have a drink. Make yourself at home. We're all friends here," he added, gesturing at the remainder of the conference.

Mr. Phont, turning on frank charm as only Mr. Phont could, pressed a tumbler of whisky into the little man's hand and urged him into a chair. Very soon the atmosphere became one of cosy geniality.

" And now, Mr. Andrews," began Bellairs, " perhaps you would be good enough to answer a few questions for the benefit of my colleagues here. Although we personally are well enough acquainted with one another's ah . . . aims, Mr. Andrews, my friends are still somewhat in the dark. I look to you to help me in clearing up the situation." Bellairs permitted himself a sly wink.

Mr. Andrews signified his willingness and Bellairs got to work.

" Name ? "

" 'Erbert Handrews, sir."

" Profession ? Walk in life ? "

" Builder's foreman. Now outer work."

" Now, Mr. Andrews," said Bellairs, tapping his teeth with his pencil, " I believe that up to a short time ago you were employed by Councillor Alfred Dogby as foreman in charge of his building operations in the new borough lunatic asylum ? "

" I was that."

" And for reasons with which we are not at present concerned, you were dismissed ? "

" Ar ! Just afore we got the roof on and I missed me bloody bonus, I did an' all." Mr. Andrews showed signs of acute indignation.

" Quite," interrupted Bellairs hurriedly. " Most unfortunate. A crying scandal. But to proceed. Unless I am much mistaken the construction of this asylum is being administered by a special committee of the Town Council ? "

" Ar. That's right."

" And this committee consists of the Mayor, Alderman Tom Deacon, together with Councillor Sam Nurture, chairman of the Town Advertisement Committee, and Councillor Alfred Dogby, our esteemed local jerry-builder ? "

" You said it."

" Now we are getting at the root of the matter," murmured Bellairs, rapidly making notes. " We approach the guts of the job."

Fixing the little man with a piercing gaze, he proceeded :

" Now, Mr. Andrews, I believe that this asylum is being constructed of reinforced concrete ? "

" Reinforced muck, if you ask me."

" Quite. But first things first. In work of this kind I understand that you employ, or should employ, one part of cement to six parts of sand and gravel."

" That's the size of it," agreed Mr. Andrews. " Them's the proportions."

" Shortly before your unfortunate dismissal you began, I believe, to smell a rat ? You began to apprehend, I believe, that there was something rotten in the state of Denmark ? "

" I thought all along as 'ow there was some okey-pokey business on 'and, if that's what you mean."

" You have holed out in one," said Bellairs. " And further, Mr. Andrews, upon the occasion of your dismissal, your unjust and untimely dismissal as I still maintain, you conceived it your duty as a true and loyal burgess to bring me this ? "

Bellairs opened a drawer in his desk and produced a large chunk of concrete.

" Ar. I did an' all. I says to myself I says, Bert, there's summat queer agoin' on 'ere, summat 'as needs lookin' into. And Bert, I says, if there's anyone 'as ought to 'ear about all this 'ere it's them at the *Weekly Probe*. . . ."

" And, by Heaven, Bert Andrews, you were right," cried Mr. Phont. " The *Probe* for the Naked Truth. Bring your scandal to the *Probe* and the *Probe* will see it through."

" In brief," went on Bellairs, " it was your fixed opinion, Mr. Andrews, that there was some monkey business going forward over the quantities for the concrete."

" That's wot I thought, mister ; and I still thinks so."

" And you are right, Mr. Andrews. With your unfailing perspicacity you have again drawn the cork."

Slowly Bellairs raised the lump of concrete in his hands and fixed his audience with a basilisk eye :

" Permit me to inform the meeting that I have had a lump of this stuff analysed. And what do I find ? I find," hissed Bellairs, sinking his voice to a conspiratorial whisper, " that whereas the proportion of sand and gravel to cement should be six to one, it is, in point of actual fact, ten to one. In other words, the amount of cement used in the construction of the new lunatic asylum is about half what it should be."

" Which means," prompted Julian.

" Which means," said Bellairs, " that by the time

everything has been settled up, Alderman Deacon,
Councillor Nurture and Councillor Dogby will have
pocketed between them a rake-off amounting to something not far short of a thousand pounds."

" In other words," mused Mr. Phont, " the Devil's
Triplets are pocketing a thousand pounds of the local
ratepayers' money."

" Precisely," said Bellairs, spitting with extraordinary
accuracy into the wastepaper basket.

When Mr. Herbert Andrews had departed in
company with two five pound-notes, Mr. Phont again
plied the cocktail shaker.

" What I can't understand," he complained, " is how
this business has been kept dark.   What, for instance,
has the architect been up to ? "

" My dear Ulric," protested Bellairs, " your child-
like innocence drives me to despair.   Surely you don't
suppose that for one moment Dogby would countenance
an architect ?   The thing has been designed by Toby
Taplow, the Borough Surveyor."

" Old Toping Toby," mused Mrs. Meredith.   " No
wonder everyone mistakes the place for the Vale Hunt
Kennels."

" Which fact," proceeded Bellairs, " brings me to
another juicy ramification.   Take a look at that."

He handed over a sheet of notepaper.

Mr. Phont at length uttered a low whistle :

" How on earth did you get hold of that ? "

" It wouldn't interest you," said Bellairs airily.   " But
I may say it cost the *Weekly Probe* fifty pounds."

" And cheap at the price," said Mr. Phont.   " Really
I'm completely unhinged.   Utterly flummoxed.   Can
such things, I ask myself, be."

" What's it all about ? " demanded Mrs. Meredith.
" I wish you two would stop behaving like a pair of
cinquecento toughs."

" It is merely," said Bellairs, " the rough draft of a
note from Toping Toby to Messrs. Titley & Snooks, a
firm who trade in building materials. He states that
he cannot possibly consider advising the acceptance of
their estimate until they are prepared to raise his
honorarium (delightful euphemism) by a further
twenty-five quid. A smart lad, old Taplow. He gets
a double rake-off. One from his boy-friends in the
building trade and another from Dogby and company
to keep his mouth shut."

" Well," said Mr. Phont ruminatively, " we seem to
be in possession of all the ingredients for a very singular
pill ; a regular surprise packet I might say. The only
question now is, when are we going to post it. The
staging of an epic scandal of this kind calls for a certain
amount of pondering. It calls for cogitation."

" The stage is already set for us," said Bellairs.
" These burgesses have a most remarkable capacity for
decorating their necks with nooses. Just wag your ears
at this for a moment." He waved an official looking
document at the meeting. " This is an interesting
little notification I received yesterday morning from
Messrs. Deacon, Dogby and Nurture."

" I warn you I shall stop my ears," protested Mrs.
Meredith. " I'm sure it must be extremely indecent."

" Come," reproved Julian, " a filthy mind is a
perpetual feast."

" Dear Sir or Madam," read Bellairs. " As you are
doubtless aware, our splendid new Borough Lunatic
Asylum is now nearing completion. An enterprise

unique at once in its modernity of design, its spacious-
ness of accommodation and its comprehensiveness of
equipment, it is fully in accord with the present
progressive policy of this our ancient municipality. . . ."

" Laboured in construction," opined Mr. Phont.
" But weighty.   Futile yet florid."

" As may readily be anticipated," read on Bellairs,
" the expenses involved in an undertaking of these
proportions do not end with the completion of the
edifice.   The institution has to be maintained.   Now
it is the desire of the local burgesses that our Asylum,
like our splendid hospital, should be conducted upon a
voluntary basis and, with this end in view, the under-
signed, the responsible committee, are setting on foot a
fund to be known as the ' Asylum Foundation and
Maintenance Fund ' . . ."

" With which is incorporated," suggested Julian,
" the Town Council Graft and Rake-off Deposit."

" And now," continued Bellairs, " we get to our bit,
the bit that affects the *Weekly Probe*."

He once more addressed himself to the communication : " With this in view, it has been decided that the
official opening of the Asylum on the thirtieth inst.
(make a note of the date) shall be marked by a Grand
Charity Gala.   (For details see enclosed poster.) Such
a scheme will, we feel sure, serve the dual purpose of
fittingly celebrating an epoch-making step forward in
the development of our borough and of establishing on
a firm and solid basis the Asylum Foundation and
Maintenance Fund.   In conclusion, dear sir or madam,
we look to you, as director of one of our principal local
enterprises, to co-operate and play your part whole-
heartedly in the forwarding of this highly deserving and

charitable cause.   Yours very sincerely, Alfred Dogby, Samuel Nurture, Tom Deacon (Mayor)."

Bellairs put down the epistle and looked about him triumphantly : " We shall co-operate, I fancy.   And whole-heartedly too."

" Meanwhile," suggested Julian, " let's have a look at the programme."

" Eve of the Gala Ball," read Mrs. Meredith.   " A Grand Fancy Dress Ball to be held in the Town Hall from nine p.m. to three a.m.   Music by Jerry Bottome and his Boy Friends.   Spot Waltz Competition. Handsome Prizes.   Refreshments at Moderate Prices. Sir Bertram and Lady Buckle have graciously consented to attend . . . you must take us all to this, Ulric," demanded Mrs. Meredith with something approaching a display of enthusiasm.   " We must have a nice party for the Grand Eve of the Gala Fancy Dress Ball."

" You shall, too," agreed Mr. Phont kindly. " What shall we all wear, I wonder ?   What fun we shall have rigging ourselves out."

" And now let us see what the Gala itself offers for enterprising citizens such as we," said Bellairs. " Collectors in fancy dress will parade the streets from six a.m. . . .   Crowning of the Borough Beauty Queen upon St. John's Green at eleven a.m., followed by a Display of Country Dancing by Miss Bogworthy's pupils . . .   In the afternoon a Grand Trade Procession Representative of Local Industry . . . Local Artists' Eisteddfod and Exhibition at the Museum . . . Major Cockerell's Tea for Poor Children on the Cricket Field at four p.m. . . . And at six p.m." concluded Bellairs significantly, " we get to the business part of the matter.   At six p.m." he continued, reading with great emphasis, " Sir Bertram Buckle will preside over the Opening of the New Borough Lunatic Asylum, the Ceremony to be performed by Bishop Achilles Bolitho."

" And that, I take it," suggested Mr. Phont, " is where we muscle in."

" Precisely," agreed Bellairs summoning all his editorial dignity. " It is at that point that the *Probe*, to speak figuratively yet forcefully, will enter the omnibus. And, I may say, you can look forward to some very interesting results."

" And the plan of campaign ? " hazarded Mr. Phont delicately.

" That," replied Bellairs, dramatically clasping his brow, " is as yet unborn. But mental coition has taken place. Cerebral conception has occurred. Gestation progresses. Mentally I am gravid, far gone. Presently I shall bring forth. My fructification is imminent. I am sure of it."

" Then," suggested Mr. Phont, " I have no doubt we may now go home for luncheon."

" Give me where I may sit," said Bellairs, " and I will move the world."

12

The Lunatics' Ball

"ALLURINGLY ECCLESIASTICAL ; teasingly celibate." Mr. Phont addressed Julian who was mincing about the drawing-room at the Priory attired in a long brown dressing-gown and sandals.

"Abelard, that's me," explained Julian. "Abelard the amorous anchorite. How do you like the bare legs ? A little extravagant, I fear."

"Not at all, my dear boy. I'm all for the Baden-Powell motif. Or, at least, I should be if I possessed such neatly turned ankles as yours, and such fascinatingly prehensile toes."

"I like your get-up," said Julian generously. "There is something impressively Augustan about the winding-sheet and the evergreen peruke."

Mr. Phont, who was striking attitudes in front of a long mirror, seemed mildly irritated :

"I presume you refer to my toga and my chaplet of bays. Hardly Augustan. Neronian, rather. I aim at a smack of decadence."

"Heliogabalus, perhaps ? " suggested Julian.

Mr. Phont winced : " My boy, go to, go to ! Now I ask you, who should I represent but Petronius ? Petronius Elegantiarum. Arbiter of the elegances, director of taste, patron of the arts. . . ."

Mr. Phont drew himself up haughtily and, crossing his arms upon his bosom, advanced a foot in the manner of one about to leave an escalator.

" Not to mention singer of episcopal beavers."

" Come," twinkled Mr. Phont, completely mollified by this discreet reference to his riotous past, " come. We can wait for Bellairs no longer.   We must go and pick up Barbara."

" Barbara the paradisaical pick-up," mused Julian as he disentangled the Bentley's hand-brake from the skirts of his dressing-gown.   " You know, Ulric, it surprises me that I have not yet fallen violently in love with her."

" Not half so much as it surprises her," advised Mr. Phont.   " If I were you, my boy, I should not hesitate to prosecute a few amorous passes with her.   Barbara is a singular woman inasmuch as she makes love with her head as well as her heart."

" Both rather irrelevant, surely," suggested Julian.

When they arrived, Mrs. Meredith was engaged in a long distance telephone altercation.   Mr. Phont sat down at the piano and embarked upon suite Bergamasque.   Presently he began to rhapsodise :

" Barbara, in the words of Pater, has that delicate sweetness which belongs to a refined and comely decadence.   Hers is the charm of late September roses, of pale blue early autumn afternoons, of the strained white harmonies of Clair de Lune. . . ."

" In other words, more than a little spent," breathed a husky voice from the doorway.

Mrs. Meredith, accompanied by her usual ghosts of gardenias, advanced and let fall her black and silver cloak.   She revealed herself in a shell-pink dress of Grecian design.   Fragile sandals were bound upon her long white feet, and her toe-nails were burnished gold. There were white flowers in her hair.

Mr. Phont bowed low as he kissed her hand :

" Lesbia as ever was," he remarked appreciatively.

" You like me ? " enquired Mrs. Meredith. " I draw the cork ? " She turned with a voluptuous grace, the folds of her dress clinging about her gracile limbs.

" Divine," said Mr. Phont solemnly. " Indescribably exquisite. White rose of the rose-white water, a silver splendour, a flame."

" Positively the whole shooting-match," agreed Julian generously. " The feet of my love as she walks in the garden are like lilies set upon lilies."

" Dear me," sighed Mrs. Meredith, " such a harrowing ten minutes. A call from Hamburg from my husband. Really Lancelot is becoming too depressingly Galahad for words. He makes such extravagant demands of one. Do you know that within five minutes he told me to smoke less, drink less and . . . "

" Love less," suggested Julian archly.

" That, of course," said Mrs. Meredith through several smoke rings, " is not altogether my own affair."

" True," agreed Mr. Phont. " It takes two to make a cradle."

" And three to make a divorce," sighed Mrs. Meredith. " Really housekeeping is becoming an overwhelming problem with this scarcity of co-respondents."

" The domestic servant problem," said Julian lugubriously.

" The outlook is indeed a gloomy one," agreed Mr. Phont. " This paucity of play-boys strikes at the very root of divorce law and maintenance order. Before long, I suspect, we shall all be compelled to take the straight and narrow path. Caps over the windmills will replace nighties over the bed-rails. Having made our bed, there will be nothing to do but die on it."

"It all boils down to the old question of supply exceeding demand," said Julian profoundly. "There have been too many hands making night work."

"Well, we can't wait any longer for Bellairs," said Mr. Phont. "I expect he's up to some of his parlour pranks again."

"Petronius, Abelard and Lesbia," mused Mrs. Meredith. "Lust, chastity and perversion. We could write a veritable symphony for the eternal triangle."

"We will leave the car," announced Mr. Phont, "upon the borough car-park, the envy of the civilised world from American Memphis to Muscovite Tomsk."

As they approached the Town Hall it became evident that there was something of unusual interest going forward at the entrance. A mixed crowd composed of dancers in fancy dress, and professional borough idlers was milling about the rococo façade and gazing up into the heavens. As cars drew up in rapid succession and disgorged their occupants, the crowd progressively swelled until it extended across the road.

Mr. Phont quickened the pace : " What's going on here ? " he asked. "A sign from Heaven unless I'm much mistaken. The breaking of the seventh seal I shouldn't be at all surprised."

They drew up and pressed through the outskirts of the throng. As they worked their way through, a large saloon stopped and ejected Lord and Lady Wycherley. Simultaneously, out of the darkness above, boomed forth a tremendous and sepulchral voice. Resonantly, pregnant with infinite menace, it rolled out upon the still night air. It was the voice of Nemesis, the voice of the Final Auditor :

" Lady Veronica Wycherley, otherwise known as the Husband's Handful. Owes five hundred pounds to her dressmaker and a week-end at Brighton to her book-maker . . . Lord Wycherley, the Great Cham of Cuckoldry. Can drink more brandies at a standing than any other peer. Is well known in all the best houses ; licensed houses . . . Sir Bertram Buckle or the Westminster Wambler. Suffers from water on the brain and housemaids on the knee. A great worker in the cause of the Expanding Naval Programme . . . Lady Buckle. Does it offend ? Do your guests notice ? . . ."

The voice stopped. In the street a satisfactory uproar was developing. A blur of white faces was raised towards the roof of the Town Hall. Cars were hopelessly bogged in a heaving crowd of burgesses. Charley Quilt, the Chief Constable, was directing two officers who were trying to bring a ladder to bear on the building. Arms were raised in gesticulation, and the air was shattered by a buzz of supposition.

Suddenly the voice, the disembodied booming, broke forth again : " Mrs. Congreve last looked out on the feast of Stephen, when the snow lay roundabout deep and crisp and even . . . Reverend Percy Bedrock, from verse to worse . . . Colonel Barley, the Mussolini of the maltings, the Hitler of hops . . . Reverend Jasper Skillington, the paragon priest, the criterion of clerics, the urban purge. Much fancied for the episcopal stakes. . . ."

Panic-stricken, the occupants of the accumulating motors began to make frenzied dashes for the shelter of the Town Hall, but without avail. The omniscient presence above, the empyrean janitor, picked them out inexorably, announced them and supplied a ceaseless flow of brisk biographical remarks.

" Major Cockerell, the Conservative cowboy. Rides straighter for his gates than any man in the hunt. Ask him why his wife can't keep a cook . . . Miss Puggy Congreve, always in her cups. Attributes the majority of accidents to getting on the wrong sides of curves . . . Miss Myra Malcolm, the girl who would but couldn't, the Freudian Handbook. Keenly devoted to Siamese cats. . . ."

The voice suddenly ceased as the two constables scrambled up on to the roof. There was an outbreak of hoarse shouts and threats and a scraping of constabulary boots. For a second a dark figure appeared out of the shadows of the clock-tower, and then a large megaphone came tumbling down onto the pavement. There was a scream of diabolical laughter. After ten minutes the two policemen descended. Slowly the crowd dispersed.

" Well, a good pull is half the bedclothes," said Mr. Phont. " This party has set a remarkably high standard from the word go. Bellairs, of course."

" I suppose you're right," sighed Mrs. Meredith. " And I'm disappointed. I really thought that for the first time I was going to meet my Maker on level terms."

" You shock me," said Julian. " I should never have thought that you had any terms."

It was plain that the inhabitants of the Rotten Borough intended the Lunatics' Ball to be a roaring success. The foyer was crammed with burgesses attired in a dazzling array of costumes. A crowd six deep was wedged against a long American bar, whilst the staircase leading up to the ballroom was well nigh impassable. Only by a militant use of the elbows and shoulders could any progress be made. A running buzz of conversation beat insistently upon the ears. The prevailing topic was the roof episode so recently concluded. There was an unmistakable stir when Mr. Phont, Julian and Mrs. Meredith entered.

" You see," said Mr. Phont triumphantly, "what a thing is bubble reputation. As soon as anything untoward occurs it is immediately taken for granted that the *Probe* has been at work."

" Have a care there, have a care," cried Julian sternly to a butcher who was about to step backwards all over Mrs. Meredith. He supplemented his warning by putting a protective arm about Mrs Meredith's waist. He was gratified to note that she leant warmly against him for a moment and brushed him with her cool, remote glance.

" Faint heart never won landlady," she murmured.

Mr. Phont bustled up, shepherding a waiter with a tray of drinks. It was typical of Mr. Phont's social virtuosity that he should have secured the only available waiter in the first two minutes.

" Don't you think I'm rather fetching ? " fluted a voice behind them. " Rather ravishing, don't you feel ? "

They turned and were faced by Esmond Duncan. He wore a kind of green tunic and carried a silver-backed hand-mirror. He gazed about himself somewhat short-sightedly, having removed his spectacles.

" Well, this is an eyeful," said Mr. Phont. "Narcissus, of course."

" Sweet of you to guess," crooned Esmond. " By the way, have you been up to the ballroom yet ? "

" No," said Mrs. Meredith. " We don't feel equal to facing the stinking populace."

Esmond clasped his hands ecstatically. " But, my dears, you must. You must go up and see Jerry Bottome. He's incredibly divine. A great big, burly, muscular oaf. And what a sense of rhythm, what abandonment ! "

" Jerry Bottome and all his little joy-boys," mused Mrs. Meredith. " What a bolting-hutch of beastliness."

" Marvellously depraved types," expatiated Esmond. " They've got a string-bass player who fairly plucks the guts out of you. And then the pianist's positively Regent's Park. Thatches of hair all over him like a gorilla."

Suddenly the crowd in their vicinity began to whirl and eddy and break apart. A heavy step shook the floor, and, cleaving a passage through the press, an enormous figure advanced towards them. It was Bellairs. He wore a suit of brown buckram, stupendously bolstered out with pillows, and he twinkled genially at them through a phenomenal growth of whisker. Swaying somewhat on account of his false paunch, he advanced upon them waving a tankard of mild ale :

" How now, mad wags ! 'Sblood, I am as melancholy as a gib-cat or a lugg'd bear."

" Falstaff as ever rolled," cried Mr. Phont delightedly. " Straight from the Boar's Head, Eastcheap. How would thy belly fall about thy knees ? " he concluded, poking Bellairs in the florid curves.

" We enjoyed the gossip column from the housetops," said Julian. " Pithy yet pictorial."

" A decided coup, I flatter myself," agreed Bellairs,

" but merely an apéritif. We shall work methodically through all the courses. And now, how about a little tour? We mustn't forget our social obligations, nor, of course," he concluded, complacently arranging his stomach, " our visceral responsibilities."

They moved off. The first person they met was the Rev. Jasper Skillington. He was dressed up in an old cassock and in his hand he carried a lengthy trident. His hair was disordered, his complexion rubicund, and he gazed about in a distracted manner.

" I've guessed," breathed Mrs. Meredith. " Solomon Eagle. Do I get a prize? "

" How hardly," began the Vicar, " shall a rich man pass through the eye of a camel. A wanton ministering," he proceeded, working himself up, " to the animal instincts. A shameless orgy of lascivious lewdity. I look about me, and what, I ask you, do I see? "

" A regular eyeful, I shouldn't wonder," said Bellairs.

" I see spirituous liquors in every hand, I see un-principled baggages, hussies lost to all grace, flaunting their triumphant nudity before the concupiscent eyes of drunkards and debauchees. But they will pay for it. The bill will have to be footed. At the final trump each will have to present an account. Then will come the great reckoning, then the last winnowing. Then shall the pits of Hell gape open, then shall the fires that are never quenched blaze up anew. Then shall these dyed in the wool profligates, these case-hardened voluptuaries, be required to face the music . . ."

" Sackbut, psaltery and shawm," said Mrs. Meredith. " But I don't like all this talk of accountancy. I once knew a girl who was engaged to a chartered accountant. Poor thing; he would try and instruct her in the mysteries of double entry and all that sort of funny business. She broke it off in the end."

" Look," cried the Rev. Jasper Skillington suddenly. He pointed a trembling forefinger. " Is is possible? Is it credible? "

" Well, really, now you come to mention it, I hardly think it is," said Mr. Phont.

Advancing towards them was Puggy Congreve. As she approached, the throng melted away on either side of her. A stunned silence descended upon the whole company. She became the focal point of two hundred fascinated eyeballs. For Miss Puggy Congreve was, apparently, completely naked. It seemed, at first glance, that all she had on was that benign and slightly vacuous smile that accompanies the sixth cocktail. She drew alongside and propped herself up against the stairway, surveying Mr. Phont and his party with a saucy eye.

" Stripped to the buff unless my eyesight fails me," remarked Bellairs judicially. " Well, this is a pick-me-up and no mistake."

" Not quite," corrected Mrs. Meredith. " Not quite to the buff. If you look long enough you'll see a bathing suit, though perhaps that rather overstates the facts."

Puggy tittered coyly : " Caught you all, you dirty old men. The new Cuplift Invisible and Soluble Swim Suit. The latest whim of the continental plages. . . ."

" The work of an artist, of a supreme virtuoso," Mr. Phont congratulated her. " An artist, moreover, who manifestly conforms to the dictum of the great Matthew Arnold ; an artist who composes with his eye on the object."

" Well, I've looked long enough," complained Julian irritably, " in all conscience, but I'm dashed if I can see anything."

" Then, my boy, you must either be totally blind or unspeakably blasé," reprimanded Mr. Phont, " for there is a devil of a lot to see. A veritable Cook's tour including all the points of principal interest."

" Three guesses," said Puggy going off at a tangent. " And it's not Lady Godiva."

" The three graces with two missing," said Julian weakly.

" Poor Julian," breathed Mrs. Meredith, " he's lost his grip. Really, I never suspected he was so passional."

" We buy it," said Bellairs. " Or, more strictly, we buy you."

" Unnecessary, I should suggest," said Mrs. Meredith cuttingly. " Personally I should imagine she's given away with a packet of something."

" I have it," cried Mr. Phont. " The Naked Lady. Ah, beautiful, passionate body that never has ached with a heart, and all that sort of thing. Not to mention thine amorous girdle full of thee and fair."

Suddenly they heard a hoarse croak behind them. The Rev. Jasper Skillington, his face contorted with demoniacal wrath, was levelling a soda syphon at Puggy.

" The fires of lust," he remarked, " shall be quenched." He depressed the valve. " The heat of the lascivious woman shall be slaked."

" I told you," gasped Puggy in paroxysms of mirth, " that it was soluble."

In due course Mr. Phont and his party fought their way up to the ballroom. Some two hundred dancers were packed together in gyrating and undulating heaps.

Bellairs addressed himself to Mrs. Meredith :
" Vacant or engaged ? "

" The train is still in the station," she replied,
demonstrating acquiescence, " though how I'm going
to get near you with that paunch, I can't imagine."

" You must balance on it," directed Bellairs.

" Doubtless we shall meet later," said Mr. Phont to
Julian. " At the moment I have designs upon the
barmaid from the Granby, the little tease." He sped
away.

Julian was just permitting himself an anticipatory
frisson as he surveyed a charming bevy of hairdresser's
assistants, when he felt someone breathing hotly upon
the back of his neck. He turned about and met Myra
Malcolm. She was swathed in white from throat to
ankles and appeared more than usually haggard.

" I'm Chastity," she announced. She pronounced it
chustutuh.

" Well, we can soon remedy that," said Julian kindly,
as he guided her into the mêlée. " I thought at first
you were a dental surgeon."

Myra, Julian rapidly discovered, had a curious
method of dancing. Raising her shoulders to the
neighbourhood of her ears, she thrust the upper part of
her body fiercely against him. Her lower parts, on the
other hand, strayed about in every direction, whilst
she undulated continuously from head to foot. The
result was that she appeared to be a flying buttress
supporting the tottering wall of her partner. Actually,
as Julian soon discovered, it was the tottering wall that
supported the flying buttress. He therefore abandoned
dancing, and they shuffled round talking about love.

" If only," Myra was saying, " love could be entirely

spiritual, a pure union of soul with soul. If only we
could burst the fetters of the flesh. The body revolts
me. I cannot contemplate the physical acts of love
without suffering a terrible revulsion. And so you see,
I'm thrown back upon my Siamese cats. I suppose it
all dates back to when I was a child and discovered the
cook and the gardener in the hot-house. Really,
you've no idea. . . ."

" I bet I haven't," agreed Julian heartily. " But
really, my dear, you should take steps. Have yourself
psycho-analysed. I mean you can't go on like this
indefinitely, falling back on cats and so on. After all
it's so grossly unfair on the cats. Besides, you're living
a hopelessly unbalanced life. Think of that. In
denying the physical, you're only half alive. You must
accept the existence of the physical. You must live
actively and fully with both body and spirit. Otherwise
you are in a state of semi-paralysis, and I can only fear
the worst. Besides, cats ! I ask you ! Why, they're
always . . ."

" They're not," denied Myra indignantly. " Mine
never do."

" I was merely going to remark that cats are always
spawning in one's bed and so on. I've frequently
heard my great-aunt Thyrza assert that . . ."

" My cats never kitten," said Myra abruptly. " I
should never permit it."

" Then your cats only half exist. They are not
living fully with both mind and body. Have them
psycho-analysed."

" You're rather frightening, you know," said Myra
at length. " I suppose I really ought to make an
effort."

" You ought," agreed Julian warmly, " if you don't want to be strangled by hanks of inhibitions."

" You would help me ?   You would be my guide ? "

" That has long been my fixed intention," said Julian agreeably.

" You seem to know your way about this warren," he remarked irritably as they stumbled down a dark passage.

" Of course she does.   It's Mrs. Warren's profession," fluted a lisping voice from the darkness.   " Have a spot of sofa."

Julian struck a match and caught a glimpse of Esmond sitting resignedly upon the lap of Mrs. Barley who was clasping him determinedly about the waist.

" Damn," said Julian as he and Myra collapsed in a heap on the sofa, " that was my last match."

" So much the better, my dear," crooned Esmond. " The children of darkness are wiser in their degeneration than the children of light."

" A regular mixed thrill," grumbled Julian, removing an elbow from his mouth.

Gradually they sorted themselves out and settled down to a little serious loving.

Eventually Julian found his petrol lighter and illuminated the scene with a fitful flame.

" Well I'm dashed," he remarked indignantly. " You ? " Esmond was sitting on his knees, smiling seraphically.

" But of course, my dear.   We changed ends at half time."

Julian precipitated him violently to the floor. Meanwhile, Mrs. Barley and Myra Malcolm unknotted themselves with chagrin.

In the ballroom Mrs. Meredith and Bellairs, with Mr. Phont, were inspecting Jerry Bottome and his boys who were jumping into Tiger Rag with great gusto.

" There can be no doubt," said Mr. Phont, " that jazz is the royal road to paradise, the short cut to the fields of Asphodel. Just look at these fellows. Consider that chap slapping away at four chords on the string bass. Knee deep in beatitudes unless I'm much mistaken, drowning in a sea of other-worldly bliss. I'm perfectly convinced that the Heavenly choir will turn out to be a quartet of negro skat singers."

" Knocking back jazz cocktails at the golden bar of Heaven," suggested Mrs. Meredith.

" Yes," went on Mr. Phont, heartily applauding the final execution of the tiger, " I shouldn't be a bit surprised if all the philosophers have been barking up the wrong tree. I think, therefore I am, forsooth ! I slap, therefore I am, more likely. I pluck, I twiddle, therefore I am. Who knows but what the ultimate bliss is to be found in slapping out interminable combinations of four chords on a string bass ? "

" The ultimate bliss," said Bellairs, " is to be found in unbuttonings on benches after supper. In running after wenches in flame-coloured taffeta. In rumblings and wamblings in the belly . . ."

" In all the grossest corporeal exercises," said Mrs. Meredith. " I rather think you're right. I rather fancy Bellairs is barking up the right tree."

" Whatever I may do with trees," said Bellairs with dignity, " I don't bark up them."

There was an agitated fluttering behind them, and they were accosted by the Rev. Percy Bedrock. He was attired in a kind of vest and kilt of sack-cloth and carried a ukulele.

"Poets," said Mr. Phont handsomely, "are the trumpets that sing to battle ; poets are the unacknowledged legislators of our time."

"I'm Homer," explained the parson, permitting himself a quick smirk. Then he turned to Mr. Phont with extreme urgency. His expression was harrowed.

"Lend me," he hissed, "a penny. Quickly."

"To take a pill and then come out with nothing but paper money is the classic example of penny wise pound foolish," announced Mr. Phont.

Meanwhile Julian and Mrs. Barley were fighting their way down the stairs to the bar.

"But who do you represent ? " asked Julian earnestly. "Who are you dressed up as ? "

"Guess. And mind your great feet. You're stampeding all over my skirt."

"Sorry. Lucrezia Borgia, Laïs, Thaïs and a dozen more."

"Will you mind your feet ! You're trampling me under foot again. I might be a doormat. You'll tear every shred of clothing off my back."

"More likely a bath-mat. And if you will keep pulling up without due warning, and if you will keep dashing your nethers into my stomach, I shan't have the slightest compunction in tearing every shred of clothing off your back. There's little enough on the front as it is. Strewth ! Talk about measure pressed down and flowing over ! . . ."

"Coarse beast." Mrs. Barley glared at him ferociously.

"And now we're really getting down to the gutter,

coarse beast yourself, and low hound into the bargain."

Quarrelling enjoyably, they at length reached the bar.

" One American bar is worth all the symphonies of Beethoven," said Julian.

They were butted from the rear and made way for Bellairs' paunch.

" Ha," he remarked, giving Mrs. Barley's outfit a comprehensive glance, " getting down to brassière tacks, I see. Most reprehensible." He clucked volubly. " More haste, less aniseed," he admonished the barman who was mixing a " *Probe* Press-Up " to Bellairs' original recipe.

They were joined by the Rev. Percy Bedrock who was now looking easier. He sipped a glass of hot milk.

" A capital binder," he remarked explanatorily.

" The immorality of the present age is distressing to those of a devout mind," complained Bellairs. " Just look at Bedrock here, running into debt all over the place and drinking milk. A sad example of the prevailing laxity of modern standards of living."

" Would you say," fluted Esmond, willowing up, " that I was terribly drunk ? "

" It is an extraordinary thing," the Rev. Bedrock was saying to Julian, " that one can sail the seven seas without suffering so much as twinge of the nausea ; but the Channel will undo one."

" Will it really ? But how immodest," said Julian.

" Yes, indeed. I remember last year I was returning from the continent with the Dean. All was well until we reached Dover. The Dean erupted first. Like myself, of course, artificial fittings. All was lost, all was lost."

" Including the copies of Ulysses and Lady Chatterley

The Boys Brigade classes would suffer, I fear," said Julian sympathetically. " I, too, have frequently desired to travel," he continued. " I, too, am haunted by the far horizons. For still my purpose holds to sail beyond the sunset, and the baths of all the Western stars until I die. I long to travel cabin to the Mexique Bay. I long to bowl my hoop far on the ringing plains of windy Troy. Damascus, Ispahan and Samarkand, Tyre and Sidon, not to mention Split ! My eyes yearn for a single glimpse of Arthur's Seat ! Willingly would I stand even at the cost of being silent, upon a peak in Darien. I am only too ready to see Naples and try, whilst sunset, I mean sunrise, over Rio Harbour would be nothing short of beer and victuals to me. But," and here Julian lowered his voice impressively, " but, I repeat, these ambitions are as nothing to my primary urge. Lurking in the depths, murking in the lurky profundities of my id, there is one o'erwhelming desire, one irresistible impulse. Shall I tell you what it is ? "

" Do."

" Guess."

" I never gamble."

" Then," said Julian, " I must tell you. It is to pull the Pennine chain."

" Would you," enquired Esmond, " say that I was remarkably boozed up ? "

" You really ought to join the chain library," Mrs. Barley was urging Bellairs. " Really one can discover some awfully curious books."

" The trouble with those chain libraries," said Bellairs crushingly, " is that they don't pull the chain nearly often enough."

" A regular plumbers' conference," cried Mr. Phont,

suddenly popping up amongst the waiters behind the bar and busying himself with the bottles. " All these West Central jokes are too choirboys' outing for words. And by the way," he corrected Mrs. Barley, " one doesn't talk about curious books. Curious volumes is the phrase."

" Would you," demanded Esmond, " say that I was tremendously tight ? "

" I haven't got to the bottom of you yet," said Julian, suddenly turning upon Mrs. Barley. He was now fairly drunk. " Your eyes speak volumes ; curious volumes, what's more."

She seemed taken aback.

" But I intend to ; mark my words. Sooner or later I shall get to the bottom of you. Who are you ? Speak up, woman ! An assumed modesty ill becomes you. Your appearance is provoking, let me tell you. Uncommonly aphrodisiac. Riggish, upon my soul."

" I'm Lady Castlemaine," explained Mrs. Barley, backing hurriedly.

" And to think," said Julian disgustedly, " that I had thought of making an honest woman of you."

" What's this I hear ? " murmured Mrs. Meredith, drifting up, " about making honest women ? "

" It's only Julian going all Salvation Army," explained Mr. Phont kindly. " He always gets deplorably moral on gin. All Boothish if you take me."

" How about carrying out some preliminary moves on me ? " asked Mrs. Meredith, turning Julian upside down with an expiring glance. " There's scope for a man of enterprise and energy."

" I am proud," said Julian magnificently, " to constitute myself *l'esprit d'escalier des dames galantes*."

After supper the Lunatics' Ball really began to bounce. Jerry Bottome and his boys had worked themselves up into a fine frenzy, whilst the younger element were loving one another all over the Town Hall, lying down irresponsibly on the floor, anointing one another with cocktails and vomiting promiscuously.

Mr. Phont assembled his party and addressed a few words of exhortation to them : "This party needs livening up a bit. It needs the *Probe* touch. Bellairs, Julian, I look to you to play your parts."

That Mr. Phont's myrmidons intended to play their parts, and contrapuntally too, was not long in doubt. Down in the gentlemen's cloakroom Julian stood with the skirts of his dressing-gown upraised whilst Bellairs carefully secured to his posterior, by means of tapes, a stout piece of leather studded with tin-tacks. When all was ready, Julian lowered his skirts and ran his hand gingerly over his seat : "That should rouse them," he remarked judicially. "That'll make them skip like young rams unless I'm much mistaken."

"Do you think you're quite drunk enough ? " asked Bellairs solicitously. "It's a grand idea. I should hate to see it spoiled for a haporth of gin."

"Tright as a dum," said Julian, belching profoundly.

"I really ought to be launching Skillington," said Bellairs, "but I'll watch the first round."

When they got back to the ballroom they found that Mr. Phont had displaced Jerry Bottome and was elegantly conducting the orchestra into the Blue Danube.

"Couldn't be better," said Julian. "Now watch. We'll make these fine fat fairies skip like old tups."

Stepping with exaggerated care he advanced upon Mrs. Kindle, the butcher's wife, a stupendous woman with a magenta complexion and a tow-coloured wig. Wordlessly he seized her about the waist and they gyrated irresistibly into the dance. Bellairs watched with interest.

Accelerating rapidly, Julian and his partner circled the room until they caught up with Major Cockerell and Mrs. Congreve who were pump-handling around with the utmost goodwill. As he drew level, Julian worked up to his maximum velocity, executed a neat reverse turn and, hurled irresistibly onward by the enormous mass of his partner, collided rear to rear with Mrs. Congreve. Immediately a wail of intense agony rent the air. Mrs. Congreve, flinging Major Cockerell from her bosom, clapped her hands to her seat and, leaping violently up and down, gave vent to a series of desperate cries.

Julian and Mrs. Kindle, meanwhile, carried on by their accumulating momentum, continued their devastating course through the ballroom. In rapid succession Julian severely rasped Lord Wycherley who was standing inoffensively in a doorway, scarified Lady Buckle who was standing in a corner trying to get off with Jerry Bottome's first trumpet and, coming round for the second time, neatly punctured Major Cockerell discovered bending over Mrs. Congreve who was lying full length on the floor kicking her legs up into the air and laughing harshly.

With a bitter whoop Major Cockerell grasped his affected area and made a pass at Julian who had precipitated Mrs. Kindle into an aspidistra and was now making a discreet withdrawal. Roaring in falsetto, the Major leapt at Julian's retreating figure but failed to allow for the *Probe* touch, for Bellairs, with typical élan, snatched up a saxophone and hooking the Major neatly round the ankle, projected him head foremost through the bass drum.

" It's a good party," mused Mr. Phont happily as he abandoned the orchestra and followed Bellairs from the room.

In the foyer Julian encountered Puggy Congreve who was now dressed again. They whooped joyously and fell into one another's arms.

" Darlings, both of us," said Julian handsomely.

" Look what I've got," said Puggy, producing a large pot of sticking paste. " I've just been home to fetch it. Let's put it on the seats. It's terribly good fun to watch them when they come out."

" If they ever manage to prise themselves off," replied Julian, excitedly leading Puggy down the back passages.

Entrenched behind a potted palm at the foot of the stairs, Mrs. Meredith, Esmond Duncan, and the Rev. Jasper Skillington were drinking champagne out of Sir Bertram Buckle's top hat.

Esmond was tearful : " Jerry Bottome's a most awful cad. He cut me dead when I asked him if we hadn't met somewhere before, and now he's blowing soap bubbles out of a clarinet with Myra Malcolm in the women's cloakroom. I'm heartbroken, positively numbed."

" Never mind, darling," consoled Mrs. Meredith, " you've always got your footballer, though I suppose he's in training now."

" That's all off," wailed Esmond. " He wouldn't let me sing to him. Said he preferred Bing Crosby."

Esmond began to sob quietly upon Mrs. Meredith's lap.

The Rev. Jasper Skillington was glowering through the palm leaves at a bevy of lovelies including Lilias Farquhar, the Bott twins and Primrose Willing, a young woman of parts, most of which were visible.

" It's a crying scandal," he averred, " all these young girls flaunting themselves like so many lights o' love. Naked and unashamed, that's what they are. They don't boast so much as a camisole between them."

" Well," sighed Mrs. Meredith, " I can forgive any girl for not boasting about a camisole. After all, they went out with antimacassars and Ernest Dowson."

" My spleen boils at the sight of them," stated the Vicar. " I suffer dudgeon. Like so many Rahabs, they are."

" Like so many prize cattle, if you ask me," said Mr. Phont, suddenly popping his head through the palm leaves and surveying them roguishly, " like so many pedigree heifers. Consider. The processes are exactly the same. Their parents, like conscientious stock-breeders, nurture them anxiously from their youth up with a view to ultimate and profitable sale. Like prize cattle they are dieted and groomed with untold care and uncounted cost until the great day arrives when they are put on show. The coming-out. The more fortunate ones, those who are presented at court, may be aptly compared to the first-rate animals who achieve the ring at the Royal show. The less fortunate ones have to be content with the Bath and West, the Great Yorkshire, the Lincolnshire and so on."

" He speaks in riddles," said Mrs. Meredith.

" Then," continued Mr. Phont fancifully, " the

buyers appear, the bored and case-hardened experts, the magnificently blasé young men with mantelshelves-full of invitations which they never answer, and who shall blame them ? For their benefit the prize young specimens run through their paces, exhibit their points and proffer their pedigrees. Meanwhile the anxious parents, the conscientious breeders of débutante stock, having staked far more than they can conveniently afford, anxiously pray that their exhibits may catch the judge's eye. Occasionally a sale is triumphantly effected and the contract signed at St. George's, Hanover Square. It is almost gratifying. A magnificently utilitarian, if somewhat degrading, system."

" Tell me where is fancy bred ? " said Mrs. Meredith, " in the heart or in the bed ? "

" It is an allegory," proceeded Mr. Phont, " capable of almost infinite elaboration. One may compare indefinitely, and with great moral profit. Take, for example, the great basic problem of mind versus matter. Any of us who have been sufficiently unfortunate to attend débutantes' coming-out balls are only too well aware that for the successful breeding of débutantes, as with prize beasts, it is essential to see that the mind is left a complete blank. The mind must be left fallow, totally uncultivated. For if there is anything that militates against a gold-medal body, it is a spark of human intelligence. In this age of intense specialisation you can't have it both ways. There isn't time. The physical and mental standards are too high. You've got to concentrate either on the mind or the body alone. You can't do both and hope to reach the top flight. You can't combine success at stud with success in the study."

At this point Miss Primrose Willing rustled past, swaying slightly and laughing happily to herself.

" Shameful ! " cried the Vicar. " Look at the Jezebel ! Listen to the voluptuous rustle of the garments of luxury, the abandoned frou-frou of the skirts of sin."

" A fanciful conceit," conceded Mr. Phont.

" Not skirts, Vicar," corrected Mrs. Meredith. " Stockings. Primrose Willing is painfully knock-kneed. You're listening to the authentic music of the sheers."

" What a conservatory of sensitive plants," cried Bellairs, beating himself heartily on the paunch as he rolled towards them. " What a hot-house of delicate tubers."

He pounced upon the Reverend Jasper Skillington who, with his face securely wedged in the top hat, was gargling with the dregs of the Château Yquem. Protesting volubly, he submitted to Bellairs' blandishments.

" Is he desperate yet ? " asked Bellairs of Mr. Phont. " Would you say he was screwed to the point of derring-doings ? "

Mr. Phont surveyed the priest with an expert eye : " Hardly, I think. If you're thinking of pitch-forking him into some mad-waggery or other, I should recommend a couple of brandies as a preliminary priming. At the moment he's not so much desperate as disorganised."

The party broke up. After rolling Esmond under the sofa, Mr. Phont and Mrs. Meredith made for the ballroom. They had a parting glimpse of Bellairs arranging the vicar against a doorpost and making oratorical passes at him.

On the stairs they were joined by Puggy and Julian.
The former was mildly hysterical.

" Too excruciating ! We've got three of them
utterly stuck. Poor darlings, they can't move without
skinning themselves. Such language ! "

" And, you see, the beautiful part about it is,"
explained Julian laboriously, " they can't get up to
unfasten the doors. They'll have to smash the place
up to get at them. Such a hullaballoo you never did
hear. We left old Ma Nurture drumming away with
her heels like a regular Ravel Bolero."

When they reached the ballroom they found that
things were warming up a bit. Jerry Bottome, with a
saucepan on his head and Myra Malcolm under one
arm, was leading his boys in a spirited version of John
Peel. The young men of the borough, hurtling about
the room, were whooping and cursing in a joyous
rough and tumble, whilst the general mass of dancers
formed into closely linked circles and rotated vigorously, if aimlessly, in the manner of so many football
scrimmages.

" I can't bear to see so much energy being so aimlessly dissipated," said Mr. Phont. " Organisation is
what we want. Method."

In a very short time he had organised a Rugby
football match in the centre of the ballroom, with
Julian, who was hanging by his toes from a chandelier,
acting as referee.

Meanwhile, Bellairs and the Reverend Jasper
Skillington were shinning up the fire escape at the back
of the Town Hall. Bellairs was dragging a length of
hose-pipe behind him and exhorting the Vicar : " It's
all perfectly simple, Vicar. I tell you there's a trap-

door in the roof of the ballroom. I discovered it when I was up here earlier in the evening doing the gossip column stuff. All we've got to do is to yank up the trap and give them the works."

" The fires of lust shall be quenched : the heat of the lascivious shall be slaked," hiccoughed the Reverend Jasper Skillington. He stood up on the coping and waved his trident menacingly over the building.

Bellairs thrust his head over the edge of the roof and looked down into the yard below where Augustus Gripps and Sidney Stipend were trundling the borough fire-engine out of its shed. For several minutes there was a confused clanking of ironmongery. Then Augustus' voice floated up gloomily yet purposively :

" Rightaway, above there ? "

" You're on the hydrant, all right ? " called down Bellairs.

" And how ! "

" Pumps oke ? "

" I'll say so."

" Then wait 'til I say go," ordered Bellairs. Still trailing the hose, he scampered over the roof after the Reverend Jasper Skillington who had located the trap-door and was tugging at it feverishly. With a combined heave they swung the trap up and back and, crouching down on their knees, gazed into the ballroom below.

" The shameless voluptuaries ! " cried the Vicar, shaking his fists at the dissipated throng heaving and swaying all unconsciously some twenty feet below. " The abandoned debauchees ! Spawn of Satan ! Devil's brood ! Beelzebub's litter ! "

" Contact," cried Bellairs at the top of his voice.

" Contact," came up from below.

Bellairs thrust the quivering, spurting hose into the Vicar's arms :

" Give 'em the works, Skillington. Have at them root and branch. Now's your chance to pluck brands from the burning. Put the sinners in soak. Pickle the profligates."

Emitting a strangled bellow, the Reverend Jasper depressed the nozzle of the hose and swept the ballroom with a reaping enfilade.

Bellairs, extended upon his stomach, the hissing jet sizzling past his right ear, gazed down delightedly upon the turmoil. At the end of his first traverse, the Vicar silenced the band. Working back across the room he scored a bull in Colonel Barley's midriff, turning him completely head over heels. A circular sweep anni-hilated a compact bevy including Lord and Lady Wycherley, the Farquhars, Major Cockerell and Sir Bertram Buckle. A concentrated burst directed along one wall accounted for a covey of saucy nubility in the shape of the hairdresser's assistants. Then the stampede began.

" You've got them on the run," exhorted Bellairs enthusiastically. " Take them in the rear, as they go for the exits."

And take them in the rear the Vicar did. Ceaselessly, relentlessly he directed the powerful jet upon the screaming and struggling burgesses as they fought frenziedly towards the doorways. The last out was the Reverend Percy Bedrock, his departure expedited by a well-directed fountain in the seat of his kilt.

In two minutes the ballroom was empty. But up on the roof Bellairs could feel the fabric of the building quivering as the drenched populace fought its way down the stairs, through the foyer and out on the street. The night was filled with dolour.

" Good shooting," said Bellairs handsomely as they made for the fire escape. " I couldn't have done it better myself. The wrist-work was superb."

The Vicar, gesticulating and frothing, sought to give tongue, but to no avail. In the prevailing excitement he had inadvertently shot his uppers through the trap-door and now they lay in a myriad fragments on the ball-room floor.

" Never mind," said Bellairs consolingly. " You can put it down on your expenses sheet for the month."

Gripps was awaiting them with the *Weekly Probe* delivery van. Bellairs bundled the Reverend Jasper Skillington inside and tumbled in after him. They did not linger.

" What," asked Bellairs, sorting himself out, " are all those bottles ? "

" We cleaned up the bar when the fun started," explained Augustus.

At the Priory Bellairs began to hold forth :

" There is no end to what one can accomplish, provided one is equipped with a stern moral purpose. Sink me ! I've mislaid my belly."

13.

The Day of Judgment

8.0 A.M. "A KNIGHT'OOD,"
said Councillor Sam Nurture resonantly. " I 'ad it
from Wycherley 'imself at last night's meeting of the
'ighways committee. Nurture, 'e says, unless I'm much
mistaken, 'e says, there'll be a knight'ood coming your
way before long. And if this 'ere asylum business goes
through O.K. it's a certainty, a dead cert." Councillor
Nurture assumed a Napoleonic stance and smiled
smugly at his substantial image reflected in the wardrobe mirror. " Sir Samuel and Lady Nurture," he
ruminated juicily, " 'ow do you like the sound of that,
Beryl ? 'Ow would that look in print, eh ? Amongst
them present, Sir Samuel and Lady Nurture."

The prospect so dazzlingly held forth by her husband
did something to neutralise even the native acidity of
Mrs. Nurture's sentiments. She contrived a smile :

" And no more than what you deserves, Sam, after
a lifetime of devoted public service." She smoothed
down the morning coat that snugly shrouded her
husband's curves, flicked a speck of dust from the glossy
pillar of his top hat and pressed a neatly rolled umbrella
into his moist palm. " No more'n what's your due,
Sam, after a lifelong service in the cause of the welfare
of the borough. It's what I always says, the ingratitude
of the public's something crool it is, something wicked."

" Ar," replied the Councillor abstractedly, " it's

284

'ard, it's real 'ard. But us as 'as the welfare of the borough at 'eart takes the kicks with the 'apence. We gives of our best and looks for no reward beyond the knowledge of a difficult task, a thankless task, fulfilled to the best of our knowledge and ability. As Wycherley says at the last Prosecution of Felons dinner, the life of a public man is an 'ard one, and 'is reward lies in 'is own conscience."

Councillor Nurture perched himself gingerly on the edge of a chair and continued to survey himself in the mirror. He congratulated himself that no other member of the local authority could come near him for grace and dignity when it came to putting on morning clothes. Indeed, when he was betailed, top-hatted, spatted, and umbrella-ed, he could scarcely recognise himself as the same Sam Nurture who for six days a week dispensed pies, brawns, sausage and polony across a marble-topped counter. Sir Samuel Nurture, he mused vaguely and ecstatically, Sir Samuel Nurture, knight ; for a life of singular devotion to public service . . . At length he pulled himself together, glanced at his watch and prepared to take his departure.

" Must be getting along now, Beryl. Me and Dogby and Deacon's 'aving our photos took at eight-thirty for the *Chronicle*. We've got an 'eavy day before us, we 'ave. A day 'eavy with responsibility."

" Don't forget what I told you about getting next to 'is Lordship at Luncheon," reminded Mrs. Nurture sternly. " You get in early and reserve your seat. You know 'ow Dogby and Deacon pushes."

Councillor Nurture permitted himself a sly wink : " Seeing as 'ow Wycherley received a case of best Scotch from yours truly this morning, I don't look for no trouble in that quarter." He stamped majestically forth.

Mrs. Nurture had just betaken herself upstairs to do the slops, when Mrs. Kindle burst in. She was magenta and blown.

"Why, Flossy," exclaimed Mrs. Nurture, "whatever brings you round at this time? I've only just finished getting Sam off. 'E's got a day 'eavy with responsibility before 'im."

"'Ave you," cried Mrs. Kindle, effectually riding down Mrs. Nurture, "'ave you 'eard about young Ansell and that Mrs. Meredith? Of all the scandalous be'aviour! Of all the shameless 'ussies!" Mrs. Kindle paused to marshal her invective. They settled down happily to a quiet half-hour of smutty gossip.

8.0 a.m. Mrs. Meredith, her hair a dark shadow on the pillows, lay crucified in a mist of silk and lace. The wax-white petals of her eyelids were closed. Her peony-red lips smouldered. She appeared not to breathe. A cup of China tea lay untouched upon a bedside table.

From the adjacent bathroom came the sounds of Rimsky-Korsakov's Chanson Indoue and the scent of gardenias.

"Julian," cried Mrs. Meredith huskily, "Julian. Come forth."

Presently Julian emerged. A bath towel was kilted about his waist. Another was draped around his shoulders. He wandered about the room, brushing his teeth in an abstracted manner and whistling frothily from time to time.

"Don't I smell nice?" he remarked chattily. "I

must say I like the gardenia bath salts. Most exotic.
The toothpaste, on the other hand, is too pepperminty.
Of the general architecture of your bathroom I strongly
approve, whilst your husband's razors are obviously of
the first quality."

"You've got the boskage off?" enquired Mrs.
Meredith earnestly. "I may open my eyes?"

"Smooth as an infant's posterior. The skin you
love to touch, in fact."

"But I don't love to touch infants' . . ."

"My face, I mean. And now I'm wiggling my
toes. Most fascinating. Really, Barbara, I've got the
most engaging toes. Ulric says so. Did you notice
them?"

"Don't be irrelevant, darling. What are you doing
now?"

"Still wiggling my toes. I could go on for days."

"Stop wiggling," sighed Mrs. Meredith, "and listen."

"I am all ears. By the way, I wish my legs were
hairier."

"Too revolting. Now, concentrate." Mrs. Meredith
levered herself up on one elbow and waved a sheet of
notepaper. "This is from my husband. He's decided
to go off to Czecho-Slovakia or Bosnia or Naxos or somewhere. Down there in the bottom right-hand corner,
you know, looking towards the top."

"Very creditable," mused Julian, scanning himself
with interest in the dressing-table mirror. "So
comforting to know that people really do go to those
places. They say we are a decadent race, forsooth!
By the way, my nose is most annoying. It really is a
full quarter-inch too long. A beaver, plainly, is the
only solution. Clotted for preference."

"And he won't be back for six months." Mrs. Meredith relaxed again and gazed intently at the ceiling.

"Uncommonly civilized of him," said Julian.

Silence.

"Well," breathed Mrs. Meredith, "still wiggling?"

"I'm thinking."

Mrs. Meredith winced: "My God! At eight o'clock! Immoral. Positively degrading."

"I've got an idea," said Julian suddenly, swinging round and delicately fingering his moustache. "We must co-habit. Think of it! Here am I under contract to write three scenarios and a funny play during the next few months. Here are you under contract to expire of galloping ennui. The solution is obvious. We must co-habit. We must go into domiciliary partnership. We must co-habit."

"That dreadful word, darling. I know you're frightfully proud of it, but do stop it. It reminds me of Maidenhead and proctors and things."

"Well, what about this co- . . . . this living together?"

"I've heard worse notions," breathed Mrs. Meredith. "And how do we murder the time? What have you to offer?"

"An up-to-date service flat in one of the best quarters. The West-end readily accessible by bus and train. A young man quiet and clean in his habits, a lavish spender on an uncertain income, and equal to all reasonable demands."

"But the time, how do we slaughter it?"

"We pass the morning in getting up. The afternoon is spent in literary composition, the evening in various forms of lewdity . . ."

"And the night," asked Mrs. Meredith, "the night?"

"In matters of mutual interest."

"But of course we must do it," said Mrs. Meredith with something approaching energy and lighting a a cigarette. "The whole thing is manifestly an Act of God. You're too brilliant."

"Good," said Julian. "Then that's that. We'll go up to-morrow. We can but give it a trial. Of course if we get positively nauseated with one another we can go out of business at any time. By the way, I should warn you this is my first enterprise."

"Don't," begged Mrs. Meredith, "perturb yourself. I'm fully familiar with the ropes . . . or should it be sheets? These nautical terms, too trying. Now kiss me."

Julian kissed her mouth without much interest.

"Not there," said Mrs. Meredith. "Where's your originality? Not there . . . not there . . ."

"Ah! I see," said Julian, "you want the Grand Tour. Why didn't you say so at first?"

When it was all over, Mrs. Meredith ran her fingers through Julian's hair and began to work it into a series of little plaits.

"Don't," said Julian testily. "I'm thinking."

"Darling! Not again. You really have a low mind."

"Of love," said Julian, resuming his tramping round the room, "of love. I am pondering upon love."

"Boring. Boring. Excruciatingly tedious."

Julian sat down again at the dressing table and began to attend to his hair with the silver and enamel brushes: "Of love in the grand manner, in the Dantesque mood.

Of love on the philosophic plane, from the psychological viewpoint, from the spiritual angle."

" I am not listening," said Mrs. Meredith resolutely.

" Love," proceeded Julian, " in the real connotation of the word implies, unless I am much mistaken, a spiritual as well as a physical fusion. It implies a complete merging of personalities."

" This tea is stone cold."

" As I see it, love is an eternal compromise, a physical, spiritual and intellectual compromise. Before long you are no more yourself, you are partly someone else."

" I must have a gin and lime."

" Now, for my part, I am determined to keep my personality whole. I am determined to remain myself wholly and completely."

" What," asked Mrs. Meredith, " is all this leading to ? What are you trying to say ? "

" I am trying to warn you as delicately as may be not to expect me to fall in love with you. For one thing I haven't the time. For another thing I can't stand the emotional stress and strain."

" But why should you ? "

" I had always supposed that co-habitation presupposed a love affair. If not, why, as it were ? "

" That's an idea," mused Mrs. Meredith, " definitely an idea. But you needn't worry. I've no use for all this fusion business, this commingling of personalities and what not. I've no use for this deliberate complicating of the issue, this mediæval shrouding of love in a fog of spiritual affinities and soul liaisons. One should see love as it really is."

" And how really is it ? " enquired Julian earnestly.

" A matter of tucking up."

Whilst Mrs. Meredith sipped her gin and lime, Julian walked round the bedroom. With a bare toe he meditatively stirred Mrs. Meredith's stockings that lay in a shimmering pool on the dark blue carpet. He picked up a wisp of lace from a chair and ran it through his fingers : " I don't know why, but there is something infinitely fascinating about a woman's bedroom, especially with a few intimate garments lying about. Without the occupant I mean. One has the impression of being in a holy of holies, of participating, albeit vicariously, in the ritual of a wicked and intriguing religion. The mysterious bottles, the inviting drawers, I speak carpenterially, the mirrors, the elusive perfumes. Not to mention such outstanding architectural features as the bed, the bath and the dressing-table. All hint at exotic passions, beatific visions, occult practices and exquisite vices. Even the dullest and plainest of women becomes an irresistible Circe when viewed, so to speak, through her bedroom door. I could elaborate . . . "

" In our bagnio," said Mrs. Meredith decidedly, " pre-luncheon philosophising will definitely be prohibited."

8.0 a.m. Alderman Tom Deacon paused upon the Mayoral threshold and wagged his neatly rolled umbrella at his wife, at the same time arranging the chain of office more snugly upon his ample chest :

" You mark my words, Emma, a knight'ood. I 'ad it from 'is Lordship's very lips at last night's meeting of the Finance Committee. Deacon, 'e says, unless I'm much mistaken there'll be a knight'ood coming your way before long. And if this Asylum scheme goes through smoothly, it's a certainty, a dead cert."

"And no more'n what's your due, Tom, after four strenuous years at the 'elm of public affairs. Where would this borough be without Tom Deacon, that's what I says. When I thinks, Tom, of the new industries as you've got into the district, when I thinks of our splendid car park and our unique sewage system, I stands appalled at the ingratitude of the public. Appalled."

"The lot of a public man is an 'ard one," replied the Mayor sententiously. "As 'is Lordship says at the last Prosecution of Felons dinner, the reward of a public man lies in 'is own conscience, in the knowledge of a difficult task, of a thankless task, performed to the best of 'is skill and ability. I 'ave never looked for reward, that I can honestly aver. What I've done for the welfare of this borough I've done out of a sense of 'uman kindliness and public responsibility. 'Owever, I don't deny as 'ow a knight'ood would be 'ighly gratifying. And no more, I says it with all due recognition of my failures and shortcomings, no more, I says, than what I richly deserves. Now I must go to 'ave me photo took for the *Chronicle*."

"Don't forget to sit next 'is Lordship at the luncheon," reminded Mrs. Deacon sharply. "Get in early and reserve your seat. You know 'ow Nurture and Dogby pushes."

"Seeing that 'is Lordship 'ad a case of the best Scotch from yours truly this morning," replied the Mayor, permitting himself a sly wink, "I don't anticipate no trouble in that quarter." He rolled forth.

Mrs. Deacon had just betaken herself upstairs to do the slops when Mrs. Quilt burst in :

" Well, I never, Emma, aven't you 'eard ? Not about young Bellairs and that Puggy Congreve ? Of all the disgustin' goings-on ! Of all the shameless 'ussies ! And 'er a Catholic and 'er father Chairman of the County Council ! "

Mrs. Deacon, having put on the tea kettle, removed her teeth, and they settled down happily to half an hour's smutty gossip.

8.0 a.m. In Bellairs' two-room loft over some disused stables in Monks Road, the alarm clock went off like a rocket. Puggy Congreve, looking attractively tousled, yawned, rubbed her eyes and stretched. Presently, with a sudden access of energy, she kicked back the bedclothes and sprang out of bed :

" These alarm clocks," she mused, admiring her pearly pink nakedness in the long, uncertain mirror, " these alarming alarm clocks. Too alarming."

She danced round the bedroom and then, bending over Bellairs, who lay upon his back in suit of crimson silk pyjamas, snoring stertorously, she kissed him on the mouth. At the same moment the alarm clock went off for the second time. With an explosive curse Bellairs sat up in bed, snatched up a shoe and hurled it at the offending clock, effectively silencing it. Pushing his hair out of his eyes, he leant back on the pillows and surveyed Puggy with a dispassionate stare.

" Idle swine," said Puggy. " Comatose hound."

" Lascivious bitch," retorted Bellairs and slapped her smartly on the rotundities.

Puggy descended upon him and for some time they

engaged in a mild rough and tumble on the bed. Eventually they rolled off onto the floor, a tangled knot of arms and legs, after which they did a little loving.

" My mouth's like the vestibule to Gehenna," announced Bellairs.   " Who's for an urge-and-purge ? "

After the gin-and-lime, Puggy lit a cigarette and fell once more to admiring herself in the mirror. Eventually she planted herself in front of Bellairs who was trying to blow smoke rings without much success.

" You know, darling, I really am most desperately comely."

" It's this blasted draught.   Blows one's best rings all sideways.   You see, the idea is to blow a good fat ring, then insert the nose through it and sniff, whereupon one looks like a pig with a ring in its nose.   Vastly entertaining.   Morally significant, what's more."

" Boar, darling. Boar with a ring in its nose.   Not pig."

" Have it your own way. Boar, sow, gilt, farrow, anything you like, but don't quibble. This blasted draught . . ."

" Darling, do stop puking and listen.   I was saying how well set up I am."

Bellairs abandoned his rings and regarded Puggy who was looking distinctly irritable.

" Very nicely marked.   Definitely Crufts."

Mollified, Puggy picked up the girdle of Bellairs' dressing-gown and knotted it about her waist, permitting the tassels to hang down in front.   Then she began to mince around.

" You know, darling, it's awfully queer.   In the utter nude one feels as virtuous as a refrigerator, but a single

garter turns one bang-shoot into a postcard from
Marseilles."

" A profound truth, my love, and one long since
established by the Gauls.   In fact I would go so far as
to say that it is the only Gallic contribution of any
significance to Western civilisation."

" I don't suppose," said Puggy, " that this bordello
boasts a bath."

" But of course I have a bath.   It is one of the
outstanding architectural features of the boite.   This
way to the vomitorium."

In the outer room, behind a wooden partition, was an
ancient hip-bath above which was suspended a large
bucket with a perforated bottom.

" Gents' natty shower," explained Bellairs.   " The
patient stands in the tub whilst the attendant pours in
from aloft.   Result, a revivifying cloudburst that tones
up the tissues and tempers the passions.   Kindly step
in."

" But how thrilling," cried Puggy, leaping up and
down ecstatically in the tub.   " How divinely outpost
of the Empire.   Too tiffin and chota peg.   Ouch ! "
Screaming and gasping she submitted to the icy deluge.

" The soap is in the sink to your right.   Personally I
scrape down with a curry comb.   The towel is
incubating in the gas-oven."

" Charming lobster," remarked Bellairs as Puggy
towelled herself to a glowing pink.   " Disgustingly
healthy you look.   Like a French salon photograph.
You know, the sort of thing they advertise in obscure
corners of the shilling monthlies.   How does it go ?
Real life photos (loathsome word).   A variety of
fascinating poses.   Assorted col's, five-shillings, ten-

shillings. Send for sample packet two-and-six. If under twenty-one, applicant must state age and profession."

" Yes," cried Puggy, " and those thrilling books they advertise in the nudist magazines. Girls' School in Paris and Maria Monk in a Nunnery (good) and all that sort of thing. I'm always immensely stimulated by that ' good ' in brackets. Regular snorters, I'll wager."

" If you had devoted as much time and money as I have to pornographic literature," said Bellairs loftily, " you would realise that it is uniformly dull. A study of thwarted adolescence by a respectable woman novelist is far more entertainingly gross. Furthermore, I observe that you have rendered my one and only towel useless for the next twenty-four hours. Kindly pop it in the gas-oven. I shall have to use the sheets. And now, if you will oblige with the bucket . . . steady, I do not bathe in my pyjamas. They cost me fortynine shillings and elevenpence halfpenny . . . I thank you . . . Another bucket, I think. Very stimulating. Most beneficial. Cold water on the spinal column out-teases the most obscene caresses. Tiberian antics are as nothing to a cold douche."

When it was all over, Puggy applied herself to her exercises. Lying on her back on the floor and waving her legs about in the air, she eyed Bellairs who was performing with the utmost violence on a rowing-machine :

" You know, darling, you really are rather alarmingly hirsute in your buff. Quite simianly shaggy. Old English sheep-dogly. I'm not sure I quite relish it. Couldn't you be singed or something ? Couldn't you organise a five-weeks' deforestation plan or something?"

Bellairs paused in his labours : " Well-wooded I may be, but it seems to me that you yourself are scarcely in a position to cast the first stone. If you don't like the outward and visible signs of an inward and physical vigour, you don't have to look."

Over the coffee and boiled eggs Puggy said: " Don't you think we might get this Mr. and Mrs. Everyman business on an organised basis. After all, now I've got this new contract with the Cup-lifters and you've got this editorship with the *Communist Comrade,* we shall both need to live in London. Why not let's muck-in together ? Set up a communal sty and root in unison ? We could halve out-of-bed expenses."

" You are proposing, I take it, a long term tuck-up ? "

Bellairs rasped the whiskers on his chin and adopted a judicial aspect. " I like the idea," he announced at length. " It has many inviting features. There is just one point that needs clearing up. We shouldn't be expected to go in for love and all that sort of thing ? I mean love in capital letters."

" Not in capital letters, darling."

" Then," said Bellairs conclusively, " I'm all for it. We will open the office forthwith."

The telephone rang and Puggy responded. As she listened she showed every sign of a growing excitement. Eventually she slammed down the receiver and turned, flushed and sparkling to Bellairs who was entangled in his shirt :

" Darling, too winsome ! You can't possibly guess. I'm quite shattered."

" Well, get on with it. Don't stand gibbering at me like a Watteau nymph with the D.T's."

" Mother's died.   Shuffled off last night from an overdose of veronal."

Bellairs' head emerged through the top of his shirt : " Uncommonly obliging of her, I call it. Very creditable.   Do you mind finding the cigarettes ? "

8.0 a.m.   Councillor Alf. Dogby, tough and aggressive, stabbed a grimy forefinger at his wife :

" That's what Wycherley says at last night's 'ealth and 'ousing committee.   Dogby, 'e says, there'll be a knight'ood acoming your way afore long unless I'm much mistaken.   And if this 'ere Asylum business goes through O.K., it's a certainty, a dead cert."

" And no more'n what you deserves, Alf," said Mrs. Dogby.   " No more'n what's your just and rightful dues.   'Ere you are, day in day out working yourself to a shadder to provide decent 'omes and amenities for the poor folk of the borough, and what do you get ?   Not so much   as   a   Thankyou."   Mrs.   Dogby   sniffed emphatically and handed her husband his bowler hat which he pulled down firmly to the ears.

" Ingratitude," said the Councillor, " ingratitude. It's what we public men expects.   As Wycherley says at the last Prosecution of Felons dinner, the lot of a public man is an 'ard one.   'Is reward lies in the knowledge a difficult task, a thankless task, fulfilled to the best of 'is skill and ability.   'Is reward lies in 'is own conscience.   Mind you, Sarah, what I've done, I've done without thought of gaining honours or recompense. What I've done 'as been done out of a sense of 'uman decency and public responsibility.   'Owever, I don't deny as 'ow I didn't expect before this some little recognition of three unique urban 'ousing schemes."

" Ingratitude," corroborated Mrs. Dogby.   " That's
what it is with the workin' class, take all you can lay
'ands on without so much as a Thankyou.   Even if all
them fireplaces did fall out up at Wycherley Crescent, I
don't see as 'ow you was to blame, Alf.   That's Taplow's
look out, that is. . . ."

" Now that'll do, Sarah," said Councillor Dogby,
wincing perceptibly.   " I can't stand chattin' 'ere all
day.   Me and Deacon and Nurture's got to 'ave our
photos took for the *Chronicle*."   He prepared to stump
forth.

" Don't forget," urged Mrs. Dogby sharply, " to get
next 'is lordship at luncheon.   Get in early and book
your seat.   You know 'ow Nurture and Deacon
pushes. . . ."

Alf. Dogby winked ponderously : " Seein' as 'ow 'is
Lordship received a case of the best Scotch from yours
truly this morning, I don't anticipate no trouble in that
quarter.   Ta, ta ;   and don't you forget, Sarah, I wants
a nice bit of tripe for my supper."

Mrs. Dogby was just betaking herself upstairs to do
the slops, when Mrs. Wilkinson, the borough Sanitary
Inspector's wife, rushed in :

" You mean to tell me, Sarah, you 'aven't 'eard ?
Not about Phont and Gladys Bumpstead from the
Granby ? "

" Not 'er as is Beauty Queen ? " asked Mrs. Dogby
incredulously.

They settled down to half an hour's nice, smutty
gossip.

8.0 a.m.   " Love," cried Mr. Phont in accents of the
acutest agony, " love.   That terrible, terrible word,

that wicked word, that word gravid at once with the
profoundest melodrama and the most uproarious
farce. Love ! Oh, my God, Love ! ''

Mr. Phont, attired in his flowered brocade dressing-
gown, paced agitatedly about his delicate and perfumed
bedroom. From time to time he raised his hands in
gestures of despair ; from time to time he paused and
surveyed, with mingled exasperation and sympathy,
the sobbing pneumaticism of Miss Gladys Bumpstead
who lay, a rosy if somewhat blowsy vision, upon his
magnificent cinquecento bed. Miss Bumpstead, who
boasted a depressingly cultured voice and saw life
filmically, raised her flushed yet undeniably attractive
face from the pillows and became reproachful : " But,
Ulric, you told me you loved me. You told me you had
never met anyone like me before . . .''

" True," ejaculated Mr. Phont grimly, " true."

" And now you cast me on one side like an idle
plaything, like a . . . like a sucked orange." Sobs
shook the cinquecento bed.

" Heaven help us ! " burst forth Mr. Phont, no
longer able to control his indignation. " Heaven help
us, pressed down and flowing over ! From the female
conception of love, good Lord deliver us ! ''

Carried away by his own rhetoric, Mr. Phont began
to pace rapidly about the room, soliloquising and
gesticulating : " Love to the intelligent man, is no more
than a form of Swedish drill, a delightfully complicated
game of halma, a game subject to certain recognised
rules and gambits, a game played purely for its own
sake, *pour le sport*. It is a delightful, airy thing, a matter
of epigrams and silk stockings, of carefree tumblings on
white satin sofas. The most acceptable form of

intellectual and physical exercise. Or it should be. But love to the average woman, to you, Miss Bumpstead," continued Mr. Phont, sternly addressing the prone houri, " is nothing of the kind. It becomes a grim routine of vulgar passion and sordid situations. The average woman, in which category I may say I am forced willy-nilly to include you, Miss Bumpstead, possesses a deadly talent for melodramatising life in general and love in particular. She lacks the light touch, the detached attitude. Love, for the average woman, is a matter of eternal passions and ecstatic embraces, of spiritual mergers and soul liaisons, of psychological upheavals and emotional crises. And furthermore," added Mr. Phont, speaking with an air of fastidious disgust, " unless I am much mistaken, it is also a matter of marriage, and hearth-stones and offspring. It is intolerable. It is insupportable." Mr. Phont clucked deprecatingly and raised his hands towards the ceiling in a gesture of despair.

" But you said you loved me," persisted Miss Bumpstead, beginning to show some signs of irritation.

" You could hardly expect me to say that I hated you."

" And now you have had your way with me, you cast me on one side like a . . ."

" Not, I beseech you, like a sucked-out orange," cried Mr. Phont hastily. " Not that. During a crowded and eventful life I may have been guilty of arson, barratry and rapine, but I protest I have never sucked an orange. There are limits, there are bounds to one's indecencies."

Miss Bumpstead suddenly sat upright and burst out : " If you want to know what I think, I think you're a nasty, dirty old man.   And you ought to be ashamed of yourself, you did, luring an innocent young girl into your clutches with false promises and taking advantage of her and then casting of her on one side like a sucked . . ."

Mr. Phont held up one hand in the manner of a policeman arresting a line of traffic : " Come, come. Old, I may be, and nasty into the bargain, but dirty, no. As for yourself, Miss Bumpstead, youth I grant you, but innocence, no."   Mr. Phont noted with relief Miss Bumpstead's loss of temper. With the reproachful paramour his native courtesy and consideration placed him at a disadvantage.   But with an outraged inamorata his native diplomacy usually won the day. He made haste to clear the matter up : " Now, Miss Bumpstead, may I suggest that we face this painful situation in a calm and judicial manner.   By following a cool and reasonable course I anticipate that we shall speedily arrive at a solution satisfactory to both parties. You allege, I believe, that under a smoke-screen of false representations I have, as you so effectively put it, taken . . . ah . . . advantage of you. . . ."

" I do, too.   And you know it."

" We will not argue the point, Miss Bumpstead.   I admit it.   That is, for the purposes of arriving at a speedy settlement I admit it.   I reserve, however, the right to refute it in my own conscience."

" I shouldn't 'ave thought you 'ad any."

" *Touché*," bowed Mr. Phont, " *touché*. A distinct hit.   However, to proceed.   It occurs to me that you, as occupant of the honourable and responsible position of the Gala Beauty Queen, will desire above all things to cut a suitably dazzling dash upon the happy occasion of your coronation which, unless I am much mistaken," Mr. Phont consulted his wrist, " is due to take place within some three hours from now.   I propose, therefore that you repair forthwith to the local beauty parlour and request them to do their damnedest, the damage to be debited to myself.   You will find two five-pound notes," concluded Mr. Phont, visibly wincing at the intro-duction of the commercial note, " in the corner of the bathroom mirror.   Your breakfast shall be sent up. Meanwhile I bid you a very good morning."   Mr. Phont left the room with dignity yet not without a measure of celerity.

10.45 a.m.   At The Gables, Puggy Congreve and Miss Primrose Willing were drinking gin potions and playing Nat Gonella records.

" Marvellous man," mused Puggy, " such guts."

" Alarmingly gutty," agreed Primrose.   " A bit of a do, by the way, your old woman pulling the chain.   Of course it'll ease the domestic motions a bit, won't it ? "

" Rather.   She was a distinct trial at times, you know, a definite teaser.   What I mean is one doesn't mind tippling and so on, but this 'ere doping's another ticket altogether.   Throwing fits regardless, and screaming fit to bring the place down.   Pitched the savoury at the Bishop at dinner the other night and insisted on telling rude stories to the Butler."

" Most diverting to the outsider, but trying in the home," sympathised Primrose.   " I'll thank you for a funeral baked meat."   She indicated the cheese biscuits.

" Of course, you've heard about the Wycherleys,"

said Puggy, shouting above the hot swing. "His Lordship was copped after the dance last night lathering the Tollerton statue on St. John's Green with a shaving brush and scraping away with a cranking-handle. They do say, too, that the Metropolitan police are on him for running an illicit still in a mews in Lancaster Gate."

"But, my dear, it'll be the making of him. He'll get a film contract right off the chuck."

"And Veronica's definitely taken off with young Bouncer. He's resigned his commission and they're going all troglodytic. Going to root in a cave in the Wye Valley. Delve their own plot and weave their own loin-cloths and so on. Too muscular."

"And have you," said Primrose, assaulting the gin-bottle, "heard about Esmond Duncan and the Barley's?"

"Not so much as a puke, sweetest."

"But it's epoch-making, astonishingly Cenci. It seems Micklethwaite was going to sack Esmond for feeding absinthe to the Arts Sixth. Then Leila intervened and told Lionel that he'd got to bring pressure to bear as chairman of the Governors and have Esmond re . . . what do you call it? . . re-instated."

"Don't be literary," said Puggy sharply. "Go on."

"And he's done it, my dear. Under the threat of suspended domesticities, he brow-beat Micklethwaite up hill and down dale. And what's more, Esmond's going to dig at the Barley's. Leila insisted on it."

"A very highly civilised arrangement," said Puggy. "By the way, darling, before you clear off, would you care to have a dekko at the corpse? It's all perfectly seemly, I assure you. Neatly laid out and shrouded and what not."

"I hardly think so, lovey. I do believe in trying everything once, but honestly I'm a shade queasy over corpses. Besides I never got on with it too well, you know. It might cast a spell over me or something, mightn't it? I mean give me cross-eyes or rickets or fling me into a decline or something."

"Just as you like," said Puggy sharply. "Don't think there aren't plenty of people ready and eager to look at it. Only don't say I didn't give you a chance."

"I know, darling. I'm not spurning your corpse. I know you're frightfully proud of it and rightly. Honestly, I envy it like anything. But it's just that I can't stomach it. I've got a death complex or something. A most divine Jew once told me I had at the Chelsea Arts Ball, so it must be true . . . Goodbye, darling. I'm looking forward immensely to the interment."

"Finnicky gin-swiller," mused Puggy savagely.

10.30 a.m. Mrs. Meredith and Julian were comforting Esmond Duncan.

"But, my dears," said Esmond, coyly fingering his always somewhat spotty chin, "it's too souring. I'd got everything worked out. After my resignation from Micklethwaite's Academy I was going to live peacefully in Bromley with Uncle George. He knits, you know. A positive wizard at jumpers and cummerbunds and things. I was going to hold his wool for him and perhaps take up a little mild crocheting and look after the cats and things, and now what do I find? This Barley woman has pitch-forked me back into my job and set me up as a kind of one-man seraglio. Really, I can't cope with it. I'm bruised, positively shattered. Conceive my posture ! My whole life taken by the scruff of the neck by a virile, bouncing Boadicea. I shall succumb, I know I shall. I'm not strong enough to deal with this sort of thing. She'll have her way with me, I swear it, before I can say knife." Esmond sighed deeply and, placing his feet neatly together, sat down gracefully.

" Well, don't say knife," advised Julian.

" I'm sorry for you, Esmond," said Mrs. Meredith. " You always did appeal to my maternal instincts. But you must use guile. What about the red-haired gladiator ? Can't you use him as a . . . as a go-between ? "

" But, my dear, haven't you heard ? He's gone. Lurched me without so much as a single scruple. He was married to Myra Malcolm at eight o'clock this morning. They've gone to take charge of a Salvation Army hostel in Barking Creek or Biggleswade or somewhere."

" This by and large yoking," protested Mrs. Meredith, " positively saps one's foundations."

" And poor Bedrock," Esmond wambled on, " you've heard about him, of course ? "

" Not another ode ? " begged Mrs. Meredith. " I couldn't bear it. Not another covey of sonnets."

" No, my dears. He's resigned his benefice. The Bishop's discovered that he's the editor of *Teasing Topics*."

" You mean that deliciously chatty weekly ? " demanded Julian. " Well, sink me. The man's a gem of purest ray extreme. You've noticed the new feature they're running? Intimate Glimpses."

"But, my dear," explained Esmond, "that was his undoing. One gathers that he published an intimate glimpse of Bolitho's daughter wearing a spaghetti beaver in an Italian restaurant in Soho when she was up for a Girl Guide rally."

11.0 a.m. Mr. Phont, from the attic where he had taken refuge, heaved a profound sigh as he saw Miss Gladys Bumpstead disappear down the drive. He had scarcely regained his library when Bellairs burst in, frothing and foaming.

"I can't stay," said Bellairs, pacing rapidly round the room, "for the machinery of urban affairs demands the attention of my personal monkey-wrench, but have you heard?"

"I have suffered," said Mr. Phont, reverently sinking his voice. "I have endured."

"It's about Twidale," cried Bellairs. "He's bust. He's been trying to corner the Patagonian hat market and the bottom's fallen out."

"Of the hat or the market?" enquired Mr. Phont who was still much shaken.

"Come," said Bellairs, "come. Don't you see the inference? He'll want to realise all he's got. Now's our chance. Twidale owns a three-quarter share in the *Chronicle and Gazetteer*. We buy him out at bargain prices and this Rotten Borough's in our pocket!"

"I always knew you were a genius," said Mr. Phont reverently.

"You were always an intelligent man," said Bellairs handsomely. "Now we mustn't lose a minute. We must get at him right away while he's still rattled. And what's more, you'll have to do it yourself, Ulric. I haven't time to deal with the matter myself. Go in and bounce him, and don't give him a penny over seven thousand. Oh! and before I forget. There are two rumours floating about that sound newsy if you have time to look into them. I hear the Vestry Virgins are getting at Bolitho to inhibit Skillington for flying that *Weekly Probe* advertisement streamer from the church spire ; also I understand Skillington has recently been buying up enormous quantities of petrol and tar and other combustibles. I leave it to you. Hotcha!" Bellairs was gone.

"How infinitely more restful," mused Mr. Phont, "are affairs of commerce than *affaires de coeur.*"

11.0 a.m. St. John's Green was surrounded by a heaving throng of burgesses. In the clear space in the centre Miss Gladys Bumpstead sat enthroned. She was swathed in a kind of surplice and looked about her with a sickly smirk. Amidst polite clapping the Mayor approached and placed a palpably cardboard crown upon the Beauty Queen's head. Then he embraced her thoroughly, to an accompaniment of delighted squawks and whistles from the spectators.

"He's mauling her about, the old cad," said Mrs. Meredith, "and he's going to deliver himself at any moment now. You can let her off any time you like."

She addressed Julian who had his head inside the bonnet of Bloody Mary. No sooner had she uttered than the Bugatti's electric hooter began to emit a continuous, high-pitched scream. Julian slammed down the bonnet and, taking Mrs. Meredith by the arm, guided her into the crowd :

" Well," remarked Julian primly, " if they can manage to stop that trumpeting within five or ten minutes they're cleverer men than I."

By the time Mrs. Meredith and Julian had gained a place of vantage on the Town Hall steps, the crowd about the green had begun to eddy, disintegrate, and form up again in a surging mob round Bloody Mary. Within a few minutes the High-street was completely blocked. Meanwhile traffic in both directions was piling up in a series of fascinating heaps. Impatient motorists, singly at first and then in mass, began to sound their hooters until the air was shattered by an overwhelming symphony of assorted boomings, wailings and squawkings. Miss Gladys Bumpstead and the Mayor were left in bewildered isolation in the midst of the green, the former continuing to stare vacantly into space, the latter opening and shutting his mouth in the manner of a dazed haddock. At length two policemen began to trundle Bloody Mary, still emitting a forlorn and earpiercing bleat, down the street. After them followed some hundreds of interested burgesses offering a variety of advice.

" Hasn't she got a beautiful upper register ? " said Julian proudly, as the trumpeting began to fade into the distance. " I only hope they won't do her larynx an irremediable mischief."

Attention was refocussing itself on the green where the Mayor was embarking upon his remarks for the third time. But he was not destined to have a hearing. Miss Bogworthy, taking advantage in her excitement of the first available silence, struck up on her harmonium, whereupon a crowd of bored looking elementary school-children straggled forth on to the green and began to dance aimlessly in a ring about the now completely hypnotised Miss Bumpstead.

Asthmatically the harmonium wheezed, desperately Miss Bogworthy pounded away, disintegratedly her frowsy looking pack of pupils galloped and galloped about Miss Gladys Bumpstead. Occasionally the spectators raised a half-hearted round of clapping.

But just when the proceedings seemed likely to expire of sheer inanition, a diversion occurred. Whooping and cavorting, Esmond Duncan leapt over the railings of the green and scurried into the midst of the gyrating children. He was clad in his Grecian tunic of the previous evening and carried a basket of rose leaves. His head was thrown back, his eyes were closed. Spinning, leaping, undulating, skipping, he embarked upon an astonishing *pas seul*. The rose leaves fluttered in the air, a pale pink snowstorm.

" Art," said Mrs. Meredith, " art."

11.45 a.m. The customary comatose peace of the *Chronicle and Gazetteer* office was disrupted.

In the editorial sanctum, Mr. Cuthbert Twyte, interrupted at the composition of his weekly column of chatty little notes, glowered paralytically at Mr. Phont who was tripping airily round the room.

" Really, Twyte," said Mr. Phont protestingly, " I must request you to stop gibbering and concentrate. As I have been explaining for the last five minutes with all the patience and courtesy at my command, the *Chronicle and Gazetteer*, as such, no longer exists. I have bought out Twidale's share. Henceforth the *Chronicle and Gazetteer* will exist merely as a subsidiary journal to the *Weekly Probe*, if it continues to exist at all. I have not yet decided upon what course I propose to pursue. As regards your own position, Mr. Twyte, I shall be prepared to retain your services as a reader. That is if you are prepared to wear clean linen and desist from throwing egg and snuff all over your waistcoat. Smartness," concluded Mr. Phont, striking a brisk attitude, " smartness, Twyte ! That is the key-note of Phont Publications Limited. Intellectual and sartorial smartness ! Think it over. Good morning."

In the sales-manager's room Bellairs leant menacingly over the desk and gesticulated threateningly at a blanched Councillor Cammack.

" The day of reckoning, Cammack, that's what it is. The final audit, and long overdue I may say. The *Chronicle and Gazetteer* is swept away, and with it that blood-soaked, tear-stained racket the Board of Commerce. The era of graft, corruption and oppression is at an end. The era of purge begins. The millennium is at hand. As regards your own position, I may decide to retain you as advertisement clerk, or I may not. That depends upon Mr. Phont and the prevailing condition of my kidneys during the next few days. They are not too amenable just now. Think it over, Cammack, think it over, and whatever you think, think twice. Good-day."

2.45 p.m. Mrs. Meredith, Mr. Phont and Julian stood in stricken silence in the art room of the museum. They were contemplating the works of the local artists. They had just been through the Eisteddfod.

" And after the male-voice choir, now these water-colours, these watery water-colours," protested Mrs. Meredith. " Too Barryish, too whimsy-whamsy for words.   Now one realises why Van Gogh was reduced to amputating his ears."

"I must confess I don't share your virile tastes," said Julian.   "I can't cope with those pictures like an interior decorator's pattern manual.   I'm all for a nice foggy water-colour.   It's more restful ;   besides a judicious Scotch mist covers a deal of bad drawing. Give me fishing smacks at eventide and two heifers and a brace of well-disposed partridges."

"They always paint in the flies so cleverly, don't they," said Mrs. Meredith vaguely.

In the meantime Mr. Phont was taking up a series of professional poses in front of a portrait of the Mayor. He rose upon his toes and then sank upon his heels. He cocked his head first this way and then that.   He extended his arm and squinted through his fingers :

"What a grand, swirling composition !" he ejaculated.   "What chiaroscuro, what power and economy of line !   Well seen, finely got, by my halidom !   What a subtle juxtaposition of contrary planes !   What a plangent contiguity of diatonic scales !"

"Yes ?" said Julian, "yes ?"

"But bad portraiture," said Mr. Phont.   "It's like him."

"He's sweating paint," said Julian.

"And look at this," begged Mrs. Meredith.   "This chunk of sculpture, Mother and Child by Gertrude Warbler."

"Did you say and or with ?" enquired Mr. Phont. "A remarkably fine piece of plumbing, however."

Suddenly their meditations were interrupted by a burst of turmoil from the street outside.

" Sink me ! " exclaimed Mr. Phont, " the Grand Trade Procession representative of Local Industry. Let us chivvy forth or we shall miss the commercial cameos."

From the steps of the museum entrance they looked down the High-street. A long line of decorated drays and lorries was wending its way jerkily along the road, and each vehicle bore a tableau representative of some particular urban commercial racket.

Mr. Phont lost no time in constituting himself commentator as the tableaux passed by : " Agriculture, I see, and Iron Founding. Butchery and Drapery. Hairdressing, I take it, is represented by this gaggle of white-clad virgins on the tumbril."

" And Plumbing, look," urged Mrs. Meredith, " here comes Plumbing. Complete down to the last detail. But I don't care for the pitch-pine seat."

" And here comes Pharmacy," cried Julian, " hot upon the heels of Plumbing. But oughtn't they to be reversed ? What a significantly stylish design of fruit salts."

" It's like a poem by Gray or Colley Cibber or someone," said Mrs. Meredith. " You know the sort of thing, Plumbing and Pharmacy come hand in hand whilst Drapery treads a measure in the rear."

" Absolutely," agreed Mr. Phont, " very apt. And here we have jocund Brewing in whose footprints treads grave Stone-Masonry. How pungently moral ! What an object lesson for the town rakes. Let us mingle tankards with headstones, mild ales with mausoleums."

At this point Mr. Phont's philosophising was rudely interrupted by a sudden uproar at the head of the

procession.   The line of vehicles came to an abrupt
halt and began to tie itself in knots.   The burgesses
lining the route began to push and run up the roadway.
Then the air was shattered by a raucous bellowing and
down the street in a headlong rush came a herd of
delirious cattle.   Panic-stricken the crowd broke and
scattered, taking refuge in the nearest shops.   Agriculture
and Iron Founding, bearing the full brunt of the
initial shock, were turned over and trampled under
foot.   Butchery was hurled through a plate-glass
window, whilst Pharmacy, Drapery and Plumbing
were swept bodily down the High-street and into the
market place.

"The Bellairs touch," said Mr. Phont, when it
was safe to venture forth.   "Did you notice that
particularly determined young bullock making hay of
Drapery?   I mean the brindled beast with a pair of
outsize combinations on its horns.   An exquisitely
comic effect."

"Yes," said Mrs. Meredith, "and that uncommonly
bulky cow that overturned Plumbing and got the
pitch-pine seat round its neck."

5.0 p.m.   Bellairs, Mr. Phont, Mrs. Meredith and
Julian stood upon the pavilion steps on the cricket field
and gazed down upon a scene suggestive of the recent
passage of a tornado.   The turf was strewn in all
directions with smashed chairs, overturned tables,
ripped linen, and squelchy bogs of trampled food.
Bellairs, waving his ash-plant like a field-marshal's
baton, explained the major points of interest :

"A Napoleonic coup, I flatter myself, a Machiavellian machination.   I don't know why, but Cockerell's

tea for poor children has always irritated me. A mere vote-catching business if the truth be known. So I decided to employ the *Probe* touch. Simple, too. I merely introduced a half-dozen of my toughest urchins, suggested a few gambits and behold the results."

" Most gratifying," said Mr. Phont. " It reminds me poignantly of extension nights at the old Shinbone in Greek-street."

They picked their way carefully amongst the wreckage, Bellairs demonstrating the course of the upheaval.

" This brown pond indicates the point where my lads pulled the taps out of the tea-urns early on in the proceedings. Mind that puddle of cream buns. Lady Buckle fell full length in it I seem to remember. As I was saying, the shortage of tannin had an adverse effect on the children. My lads had only to cast a few reflections on the legitimacy of the birth of their nearer neighbours, and the whole shooting-match blew up. Cockerell was just tuning up on O.T.C's and Jubbalpore when he fielded a seed-cake in the right ear. Mind the jam-patch. Barley's been up to the chops in that."

6.0 p.m. The great moment was at hand. All the burgesses of any significance whatever in the Rotten Borough were jammed in serried ranks before the stupefying façade of the new Borough Lunatic Asylum, awaiting the enactment of the opening ceremony.

Facing the crowd, with their backs to the main doors, sat the Town Council, the Board of Commerce and the Town Advertisement Committee. In front of them, at a red-plush covered table bearing the key of office, sat the Mayor and his two colleagues on the Asylum

Construction and Maintenance Committee, Councillors Sam Nurture and Alf. Dogby. With them was Mr. Toby Taplow, the Borough Surveyor. They were flanked by Sir Bertram and Lady Buckle, Major Cockerell, Colonel and Mrs. Barley, and Lord Wycherley who looked seriously under the weather. Isolated in lone splendour sat the Bishop, Achilles Bolitho, acutely conscious of the imminence of his approaching peroration.

At length the proceedings got under way. After a somewhat disjointed expression of grandiose sentiments, Sir Bertram Buckle called upon the Mayor to welcome the Bishop and to say a few words upon the construction and aims of the Asylum.

Alderman Tom Deacon rose, hawked portentously and started in : " An 'igh-minded undertaking typical of the 'umane and progressive spirit of this our noble and ancient borough . . . An elegant and spacious edifice combining beauty and dignity with utility and service . . . A perpetual memorial of municipal enterprise and an enduring reminder of man's responsibility to 'is neighbour . . . I shall ever regard it as a singular 'appy circumstance that this unique event should occur during my passage through the Mayoral chair for the last time. I regard it as the crowning glory of a life time of devoted public service . . . It is with sentiments of the profoundest pleasure and pride, therefore, that I 'and over this 'ere key to milord Bishop and call upon 'im to . . ."

But at this point the ceremony came to an abrupt halt. Cleaving a passage through the midst of the throng came Chief Constable Quilt accompanied by four oversized policemen. In a compact squad they elbowed their way forward ; forward until they fetched up face to face with the Mayor, Councillors Nurture and Dogby and Mr. Taplow. Then, across the petrified silence, came the jerky pipings of the Chief Constable's voice :

"Mr. Mayor, Councillors Nurture and Dogby, Mr. Taplow, I arrest you upon a charge of fraudulently converting . . . public monies . . . amounting to one thousand pounds. . . ."

10.0 p.m. Mr. Phont, Mrs. Meredith, Julian, Bellairs and Puggy Congreve were lounging amongst the champagne bottles at the Priory.

"A nice curtain, I flatter myself," said Bellairs. "Very nicely timed. But what's that ? "

A long, low, humming sound pierced the night.

"The fire buzzer," cried Mr. Phont. "By Heaven, what a day ! Let's go,"

They tumbled into the Bentley and swung out of the drive. Down in the centre of the town a leaping pyramid of flame cleft the darkness.

"The Church," cried Bellairs. "The sacred edifice is in flames. A holocaust, an inferno ! "

Charging recklessly through the thronged streets, Mr. Phont drew up at the *Weekly Probe* offices where they left the car and picked up Augustus Gripps.

"It's Skillington," the latter explained. "He's filled the place up with petrol and tar and set it off. They say he's up on the tower and he's got the two Miss Warblers locked up in the crypt."

Bellairs led the way over a series of back-gardens and brick-walls and within a few minutes they gained the church-yard.

Flames poured out of the windows and the tower and spire were a solid pillar of fire.   A dense cloud of black smoke, shot by fountains of sparks, billowed and surged above the building.   The roar of the flames and the crash of falling timbers and masonry were stupefying.

Bellairs, who had been on a tour of investigation, returned panting : " They've got the Vestry Virgins out.   A bit singed, I believe, that's all.   But the priest's still inside somewhere.   They can't get at him now.   It's hopeless.   They'll just have to let the place burn."

Paralysed, Mr. Phont and his party stared up at the blazing tower.   Suddenly a gust of wind swept aside the flames that enveloped the base of the spire.   Simultaneously a black, gesticulating figure appeared on the coping silhouetted by the blinding glare behind.   It was the priest.   Smoking shreds of clothing clung to his gaunt frame.   In his hand he bore a trident, and as the breathless crowd stared upwards, he shook it in a menacing gesture at the town spread out beneath.   At that moment a miraculous silence fell and, distinctly and reverberatingly, the voice of the priest thundered down on the masses cowering below :

" Woe !   I say woe unto thee, thou Rotten Borough ! Verily, verily, I say unto thee it shall be more tolerable for Sodom and Gomorrah on the day of judgement, yea, for the cities of the plain, than for thee in thy latter days. . . ."

There was a terrific spout of flame and a wild scream.

" The Reverend Jasper Skillington !   There went a man."

Mr. Phont bowed his head and turned away.

Envoi.

At the crest of the hill at the southern extremity of the town, Mr. Phont halted the Bentley and invited his companions to alight.

Together they looked down upon the Rotten Borough peacefully spread forth in the early morning sunshine. The only sign of movement was a drifting spire of smoke rising from the blackened ruins of the parish church.

" Behold," cried Mr. Phont, " the New Jerusalem ! Look well, my friends, look well ! Let no detail of the scene escape you, for your eyes dwell upon a miracle. One and all, we have been permitted by a kindly providence to play leading parts in one of the greatest social and moral revolutions of modern times. There below us in the valley lies a community which, but three short months ago, was stained to the core with graft, hypocrisy and corruption. Now, purged and cleansed by our ingenuity and industry and by the blood-sacrifice of a very gallant priest, it shines forth as an example to the world at large, as pure in affairs temporal and spiritual as the heart of a little child."

" And now," resumed Mr. Phont more lightly, turning back to the car, " we go to direct our several plows along fresh furrows. You, Bellairs, will doubtless continue to conduct a career of spiritual redemption from the editorial chair of the *Communist Comrade*. Miss Congreve will further the cause of yet more complicated and alluring underwear. Julian will continue to manufacture rude plays at enormous profit, whilst

Barbara will embark upon a course of acuter and more exquisite ennui. . . ."

"And you," suggested Mrs. Meredith, "and you, Ulric?"

"And I too, my dear Barbara, I too go to take up the new life, the vita nuova. A whisper flutters round the metropolis, growing, as it goes, from a whisper to a clarion call : Ulric Phont is coming back ! In Carlton House Terrace the sleepers turn in their arm-chairs. In Mayfair bedrooms the débutantes turn in their beds. In the environs of Piccadilly Circus the restaurateurs rub their hands and Eros restrings his bow. Ulric Phont is coming back ! In Conduit Street the cutters agitate their shears. In Shaftesbury Avenue and the dear old Square the theatrical managers refurbish their box-offices. In the furthest Soho the Turk and the Infidel contrive yet more strange and curious dishes. Park Lane is stirred and likewise Berkeley Square. The Park itself puts on a more glowing autumnal foliage. Ulric Phont is coming back ! "

"But," breathed Mrs. Meredith, " I thought . . . "

"But me no buttocks," retorted Mr. Phont roguishly. "You thought my retirement was irrevocable ? And so, I must confess, did I until this morning. But, by an exquisite paradox Ulric Phont, dilettante, bon viveur, arbiter of the elegances and patron of the Arts, has achieved salvation through that which he once so deeply scorned. I mean the world of commerce and affairs, the realm of sordid gain. I discovered this morning that my trousers will no longer stay up without the support of braces."

THE END